The Reunion

A Novel

Manda —
My Giants buddy! Hope
you got a preview of
SF and enjoy!
♡ Liz

ELIZABETH ALOE

For Rylee.

ISBN-13: 978-0615647845
(Piper Publishing)

One

The Emmy statues were so gold and shiny.

Standing alone in the conference room, thirty-two year old Charlotte Campbell counted twenty three trophies in the glass case. Trying not to let them intimidate her as she waited for the third interview at one of the top news stations in San Francisco, Charlotte practiced the questions in her head. Why do you want to work here? What are your goals? What do you feel is your best achievement and your biggest failure? It had been a couple years since she interviewed, but she knew these questions inside and out. Interviewing was the easy part—it's what came afterward that was hard.

Although she was seeking a position with the online team, she still felt very much at home in an old fashioned newsroom. Give her a deadline or an eleventh hour panic and she always kept her wits about and it was probably her biggest strength. Somehow the work would get done.

Charlotte was by no means a workaholic. She considered that a strength as well—balancing work and life. Many news organizations, however, frowned upon it especially in a culture like the Bay Area where it seemed everyone lived to work rather than worked to live. It didn't help that she chose a career in an industry that worked every hour of every day. There were no holidays when it came to the news. Fortunately, Charlotte learned early on she didn't have that full blown drive to be the person always in front and ready for action—the one who got to work before dawn and left after midnight. Unless it was an earthquake or terrorist attack, she preferred her evenings and weekends away from the office.

After spending a year out of college in Washington State at a small local television station, she found herself homesick for California. Depressed, she missed wearing flip flops and skirts in January. She also missed her friends and family. As luck would have it, Charlotte's college roommate Ali Baxter offered Charlotte the second bedroom of her San Francisco apartment. After settling in as a city girl, Charlotte quickly found a position with top ranked online media company, CNET, producing technical news. But that luck eventually turned after 9/11 when the tech industry crashed about as hard as a speeding car into a brick wall. She was laid off along with thousands of others and spent the next couple of years working menial jobs for little pay. She was so tired of being broke.

"What do you think?" said a male voice from behind her. Turning around, it took about a millisecond for her brain to register who spoke to her, but another five seconds for her brain to signal her mouth to speak.

"Trevor?"

"Charlotte?" Trevor Sheldon asked completely as surprised as she.

"Hi!" Charlotte said trying to find words that didn't make her sound stupid in front the one person from her past she never expected to run into—ever. Finally, over the loud whoosh of blood in her head and the fast beating of her heart, she made her lips move. "I'm interviewing. The receptionist put me in here to wait," Charlotte explained as she let her college friend hug her. She could feel her hands shaking as his chest pushed into hers so tightly. "Wow. Trevor. It's really good to see you. It's been, what, almost fifteen years!"

Pulling away, she felt almost uncomfortable as he looked hard into her eyes before he did a sweep of her body. Charlotte knew he wasn't checking her out intentionally because he looked just as stunned as she felt. When his eyes lit up and his smile grew wide she knew then he was just really excited to see her. "You haven't changed much. You still look the same, Charlotte—you look great. How is my favorite former trainee?" he asked.

"I'm good. Really good. I've been living in the city for the past few years and share an apartment with Ali—you remember her, right? You look great, too, Trevor. You haven't aged at all." *That's a huge lie. He's aged alright. In such a mature way and he looks even cuter than he did back then.*

Trevor laughed and it brought back the memories of how close they once were in college at Cal Poly in San Luis Obispo—a small town located near the coast halfway between San Francisco and Los Angeles. Nicknamed SLO by the locals, it was the one place Charlotte ever felt truly at home—as if she belonged there. Trevor had been Charlotte's mentor her freshman year when she started as a DJ at the school radio station, KCPR. He was three years older and starting his senior year when they met and Charlotte developed a crush rather quickly. Standing over six feet, his hazel eyes and short sandy brown hair were a handsome match, but it was his voice that drew Charlotte completely in. It had a deep, mellow sound that accentuated each word.

It was as if they were back under the spell of college, alone in the studio talking and getting to know one another for the very first time. Was he married? *No ring*. Does he have a girlfriend? Would they be working together? *How crazy is this?* She couldn't control her thoughts as they fired away like gunshots in her mind.

"I'm the morning producer and usually out the door by two most days since I get here really early, but I had to stay a bit later today and I'm so glad I did. Who are you interviewing with?" he asked before being interrupted by a female voice behind him.

"She's interviewing with me," the woman said winking at Trevor before turning her attention to Charlotte. "You must be Charlotte Campbell. I'm Michelle Reed."

"You have a good one here, Michelle. Hire her," Trevor said putting his arm around Charlotte as if to add meaning to his words. Leave it to Trevor to use his charm on a woman. It worked every time—at least it did for Charlotte and she was now blushing so hard her cheeks felt like they were on fire.

"Okay, Trevor. I'll take that into consideration," she laughed. "Come on Charlotte. I'm very excited to talk to you."

"Charlie, I'll stick around for a bit and we can catch up afterwards," Trevor said using the nickname he'd given her when they first met.

"So how do you know Trevor?" Michelle asked as she led Charlotte through the offices and cubicles.

"We went to college together."

"Cal Poly, right?"

"Yes—wow, how did you know?"

"It's on your resume," Michelle replied with a smirk. "And Trevor mentioned he graduated from there as well."

The energy of the room changed as they entered the newsroom—it was as if the air went from zero to sixty miles per hour in five seconds. Televisions, hung from the ceilings, were tuned into the cable and overseas news stations. The sound of voices mixed with typing caused a din that meant an important deadline was looming. It was the sort of controlled chaos Charlotte thrived in.

Once in Michelle's office, she took the seat closest to the desk while Michelle took her own seat focusing on Charlotte's resume. Feeling a bit overwhelmed, Charlotte tried to knock Trevor out of her mind as the interview started. It took a few seconds before she found her ground and started a good rapport with Michelle who was the associate vice president of the online news department. Even though this is usually the formality portion of the interview process, Charlotte still went at it as if the job was on the line. All thoughts of Trevor dropped away as she concentrated on selling herself.

The interview lasted about fifteen minutes after which Charlotte accepted Michelle's "we'll be in touch" finality. The hard part came now waiting for the phone to ring but Charlotte felt confident. Maybe Trevor would have some pull and would put in a good word.

Following Michelle back through the newsroom to reception, Charlotte wondered where Trevor was now. If she got the job, would she be working near him? Is he really back in her life after all this time?

She and Michelle said goodbye with a handshake and before Charlotte could leave, the receptionist said she had a message from Trevor who asked her to wait for him. Excited and nervous, she didn't know what to do with her time while she waited, so she pulled out her phone to text Ali—the one person in the world who would understand why this was such monumental news.

You'll never guess who I just ran into? Trevor Sheldon!!!OMG!

It took a few seconds before Ali's reply beeped. *Trevor?! No way. Can't wait to get deets.*

So much to tell you! Charlotte continued. *Going out in a few. I'll let you know what happens.*

Good luck and behave! Ali warned bringing smile to Charlotte's face. That was Ali's signature saying whenever Charlotte would go out on a date.

Roommates all through college, Ali turned into the sister Charlotte never had. Their relationship had weathered dates, boyfriends, breakups, gossip and most importantly the major change of growing up after graduation. As a graphic design major, Ali moved to San Francisco right after school to pursue her career with the online startups. Despite the tech crash, Ali still had her job at the Gap where she designed the company's websites. She had been living alone, but when Charlotte decided to move back to California and settle in San Francisco, Ali graciously offered the second bedroom claiming the help with rent would allow her save some money. Moving back in with Ali was like putting on a pair of old comfortable jeans.

After twenty minutes, Trevor appeared startling Charlotte off of her Facebook page.

"Do you have time for a couple beers, Charlie?"

No one had ever called Charlotte by that nickname before Trevor, primarily because she didn't like it. When she was young, she hated how it sounded like a boy's name. However, the moment Trevor said it, the nickname sounded endearing—bonding them together and his voice made the name sound sexy and not at all masculine. A couple of boyfriends had used the nickname since, but it never rang as sexy to her as it did coming out of Trevor's mouth.

"Of course," she said feeling her face blush as she looked at him. His voice still sounded so deep and sexy. "I think I can spare an hour or two for an old friend."

"We can walk up the street to North Beach and hit Vesuvio."

Walking side by side, they started a conversation as if they had remained friends for the past decade. The sun was just starting to set and the San Francisco sky was turning a deep purple with no fog on the horizon. Charlotte loved this time of night—the air was still on the warm side since it was mid-August but it felt balmy as the lights of the city turned on. In about an hour, those lucky enough to get off work for happy hour would be crowding the bars and restaurants along Columbus and Broadway Streets.

"This is surreal," he said as they dodged in an out of pedestrian traffic.

"I know."

"So you've been in the city a few years? Where were you before?"

"I moved to Washington after graduation but moved back after about four years because I missed the sun."

"Still scheduling life around prime tanning hours, I see. How's your family?"

"Good," she replied not feeling very confident in the conversation. Normally, Charlotte hated small talk and this was exactly why—she couldn't get to that extra layer and it bored her. She endured it now primarily because she was still a bit tongue tied. The irony, she thought, was how Trevor hated small talk just as much as she did and this conversation was probably driving him just as crazy.

"What have you been up to?" she asked.

"Well, I moved to San Diego after graduation. Remember Tom from KCPR? He helped me get a job there. After a couple years, I moved to LA and hated it, so I decided to try San Francisco."

"You hated the sun and the beach in LA?" Charlotte asked surprised. "Who'd hate that?"

"Well, I lived near West Hollywood and it just got old. The traffic and the smog were one thing, but the pretentiousness was another."

"I've always had a great time when I visited. Remember Sarah Davenport? She lives in Manhattan Beach and works for Hollywood Tonight."

"Yes, I remember her. Are you still friends? She was cool."

Charlotte met Sarah in line for the bathroom at SLO Brew. It was an all ages show meaning it was extra crowded with an extra-long wait. When Sarah casually mentioned how good the music was that night, Charlotte explained the origins of the band and how she found out about them at KCPR. Turned out Sarah was graduating Journalism with a public relations major and had classes with Trevor. From there, a friendship was born and Charlotte always looked up to her beautiful and sophisticated friend who was now a television reporter.

As they crossed the busy intersection, Charlotte wanted to ask Trevor if he was seeing anyone. The question was sitting on the tip of her tongue just hanging there waiting for her to ask it. *Not yet*, she thought, hoping to avoid the disappointment of finding out her first love was dating someone else or, worse, engaged.

Entering Vesuvio, Charlotte found a table while Trevor went to the bar to order beers. Watching him, she remembered the first day she saw him, a month into her first year at Cal Poly. She had made it into the Fall KCPR training class and was assigned to shadow him during his show for the quarter. When she arrived in the studio for her first training session her whole world changed. It was like everything went into slow motion except him. She watched as he moved effortlessly between the control board and the CD players, cueing up songs before he went live on the air. She completely fell for him when she heard his voice speak smoothly to his unseen audience.

Shaking herself out of a minor paralysis, Charlotte noticed the stacks and stacks of CDs lining the walls. There was so much new music in front of her and it was overwhelming. All these bands she'd never heard of were now at her fingertips. She knew KCPR was an alternative radio station and played the bands the mainstream hadn't heard yet except for a few settled bands like U2, REM and the Talking Heads, but she never realized so many independent bands existed. Although very nervous at the thought of running her own show, she was also extremely excited. She would just have to trust this Trevor guy and hope he was a good teacher.

Charlotte's attention turned back to her mentor as he took off his headphones. "Hi, you must be Charlotte," he said with a huge smile. His hazel eyes bored into hers and Charlotte felt her heart skip a beat.

"I am. Nice to meet you," she replied shaking his hand.

"So, you're a new DJ. Welcome. I'm sure you'll have lots of fun. It's a great gig. What's your major?"

"Journalism."

"Oh, cool—me too. I guess we both belong here. Are you concentrating on broadcast?"

"Yes. " Charlotte wished she sounded more articulate, but the words just wouldn't form.

"This will become your second home as will the TV station. It's fun. I did my internship last summer in San Diego that made this all look like a cake walk. Hard work, but a great learning experience. Where are you from?"

Since most Cal Poly students were from the Bay Area, LA or San Diego, he didn't seem surprised when she said Livermore—a small suburb of San Francisco.

"I know Livermore. I drove through there a couple times on my way to Tahoe," he said as he picked out a couple CDs from the stacks. "What kind of music are you into?"

Music had always been a hobby for Charlotte. She loved discovering new bands with new sounds. She always had her iPod in her ears or her iTunes playing on her computer when she studied. Her parents had constantly given her grief for listening to music when she was supposed to be doing homework. "I'm all over the place," she said finally forming words. "My absolute favorite band is Collective Soul. But I love Died Pretty, Ivy, Kitchens of Distinction, Social Distortion, Suicidal Tendencies, and the 80s new wave."

"Impressive. Kitchens of Distinction are in the stacks somewhere. I haven't played them in ages. Let's pull it. What song?"

Charlotte giggled. "That's like asking me favorite episode of Friends. It's too hard to pick just one."

"Ok, I'll pick for you," Trevor replied as he closed his eyes and pretended to randomly select a song with his index finger.

"Don't tell me. Surprise me," Charlotte said finally relaxing into a pleasant banter with her new friend. The song *He Holds Her, He Needs Her* started and Charlotte automatically smiled because it would have been the song she selected.

Elizabeth Aloe

"Charlotte, you have a lost look on your face," Trevor said setting down two pints of beers on the table and bringing Charlotte back to the present.

"I was just thinking about those old days in the studio and how much fun we had together. I still play Kitchens of Distinction all the time."

"I remember playing that band on your first day. I still dig them, too bad they broke up. Man, we did have fun together."

He sure knew how to say just the right words. "Do you ever miss those days?" Charlotte asked taking a sip of her beer.

"All the time. Cal Poly was so fun and living in San Luis Obispo—it was like living in utopia. I miss surfing at Shell Beach and going to McCarthy's downtown."

McCarthy's.

Everyone had their favorite college bar and McCarthy's was the KCPR favorite. It held so many memories for Charlotte that didn't even include Trevor. "It's still there and they still have the shamrocks on the wall although they did move locations."

"There's no place like McCarthy's. I need to get back SLO soon and have a Higuera Street extravaganza. I drove through on my way up here, but didn't stay."

"I haven't been back in a while, either. I miss it so much. I love San Francisco, but I felt at home in SLO."

The conversation quieted for a couple seconds while Charlotte watched Trevor look around the room.

What was he thinking? Was he remembering what happened between them and how it got all screwed up? Did he even remember it or even care, really? *Say it, Trevor!* Say it, she wanted to scream but held herself in check. Maybe it didn't matter anymore. Maybe he was in a relationship and didn't even want to think about that night. Honestly, she didn't even want to think about that night and how it destroyed her budding relationship with him.

Breaking the silence, Charlotte started a new topic. "I hope I get the job. I really liked Michelle. We seemed to click."

Trevor eyes squinted a bit before he answered. "Yes, she's great. I hope you get it, too. It will be fun to be working with you again."

After another two beers, it was time to go.

"I have to get going, Charlotte. What's your phone number?" he asked as he pulled out his beat up and completely outdated flip phone. They exchanged numbers and hugs and Charlotte felt he was genuine when he said they needed to get together again soon. Feeling her heart skip a beat, she wanted nothing more than to have Trevor kiss her again just like he did that first time back in college. Watching him as he walked down the hill to catch the bus back to Potrero Hill, Charlotte felt like she had woken up after a very long nap. She hadn't realized how much her memories had haunted her, both the good and the bad. That door with Trevor was still open and now it was open even wider. Did she want to step through it? She had no idea where it would take her and she wasn't even sure Trevor knew it was still open. Did he even still have feelings for her after she broke his heart? Something in her gut told her she would find out because she'd be working near him and the thought thrilled her.

Her boyfriend Ben, on the other hand, might have something to say about it, she thought, beginning her walk home as The Kitchens of Distinction played through her headphones.

Two

Charlotte loved walking the city.

Her commute for the past four years was a mile and a half by foot--downhill on the way to work and uphill on the way home. It didn't matter the weather, she always tucked her hair inside a baseball cap and threw her dress shoes in a backpack before hoofing it down Polk and Bay Streets to the wharf where the office was located. It was the healthiest of commutes as she admired the million dollar view of the bay bridge framed by the Berkeley and Oakland hills. Passing different brightly colored Victorian homes and listening to her favorite music, Charlotte never took for granted how lucky she was to be living in one of the most beautiful cities in the world. One plus about landing the new position—she could walk to work again since the station was only a few blocks further than her previous job. *Maybe I'll burn off more calories.*

Making her way along Polk Street in Russian Hill, she noticed Green's Bar was packed with teams from the sport and social club reminding her about her

softball game later that night. Picking up her pace, she
turned the corner on Vallejo Street and crossed Van
Ness and Franklin to her apartment. She loved this
neighborhood. Pacific Heights and cow hollow were
considered very affluent areas of the city. She often
wondered how anyone made enough money to afford
some of the Victorians that were worth millions. Were
they movie stars? Lawyers? Old Money? Danielle
Steel owned the house about three blocks up the hill and
there was a rumor that Chris Isaak owned a house down
the street so obviously celebrities were in the mix.

It was peaceful and not terribly noisy like some
parts of the city, yet still bustling. Equidistant between
the neighborhoods of Russian Hill and Cow Hollow, Pac
Heights, as it more commonly called, was an easy area
to window shop the boutiques or find a restaurant.
Luckily for Charlotte, the apartment came with a
parking space allowing her to do errands at her leisure
and not have to worry about finding the elusive parking
spot on the street.

Finally at the entrance to her apartment building,
she checked the mail box and found it empty. Typical
Edwardian on the outside and very sixties on the inside,
the building wasn't very fashionable for the area, but she
loved it. Three units had been added in the early 80s,
which included hers, so she took the back stairs instead
of the original stairs in the front. Climbing, she passed
the first unit shared by her neighbors Paulette and
Dayna. Both girls were her age and she and Ali had
established good friendships with them. Climbing
another flight, Charlotte smiled at the memories
foursome had shared throughout the years. Unlike
Melrose Place, there was never any animosity or
drama—just gossip, boys and parties. Entering her

apartment above, Charlotte knew instantly Ali was home because Buffy the Vampire Slayer was on TV.

"Haven't you seen this a kajillion times?" Charlotte asked as she hung up her coat in the closet.

"Yes, but it's like background noise to me now. It gets lonely around here sometimes."

Ali's point made a lot of sense. There were a few shows of her own that she liked to play in the background just to hear familiar voices when she felt a bit lonely—Veronica Mars, My Boys, and Supernatural being a few of them.

"So tell me about Trevor," Ali said pausing her cooking. "I can't believe you ran into him!"

"I know. It was a shock," Charlotte said as she hung her coat up in the front closet.

"So what happened?"

"Believe it or not, he is the morning news producer at the station. I just interviewed with a colleague of his."

"Oh my god—so you might be working together?"

"If I get the job, I guess. We wouldn't be working totally together since he is the television side and I would be the online side. The interview went well, but I'm not putting the horse before the cart. Trevor and I went out for a couple beers and caught up."

"Any residual feelings?"

Hesitating a moment before answering, Charlotte wanted to pass the whole thing off as if it didn't matter much to her. So Trevor was back in the picture but things were different now—it would be no big deal to see him on a daily basis. However, that just wasn't true and she couldn't lie to Ali. It was a big deal and Charlotte was the worst liar ever when it came to her heart. She was still very much attracted to Trevor and was ecstatic to have him in her life. There was no way she could hide that from her roommate and possibly even Ben. *This is going to get complicated.*

Neither she nor Trevor addressed the night in school that screwed everything up. Even now, she still had a nightmare once in awhile about it. *It happened so long ago and maybe we are both over it and it doesn't matter anymore. Maybe it would be good to just get to know him as an adult.* "Honestly, I don't know. He still makes my heart beat so hard and he is still so good looking and smart. I have to say a lot of feelings came back to the surface both good and bad. I really want him back in my life, but I'm not sure it's a good thing or a mistake."

Ali sighed and spoke a bit more seriously. "I'm sure. You both have a lot of history and I remember everything you went through. What do you think this is going to do to you and Ben?"

"Right now...nothing. I don't have the job yet and I have to get ready for softball. What are you doing tonight?"

"Rob's coming over for dinner."

Charlotte really liked Ali's boyfriend Rob. They had been together since the dorms in college minus a year-long breakup after Rob graduated and moved up to the bay area. That fall quarter during their fourth year was hard on Ali and Charlotte did her best to help her roommate get over the heartbreak. In true Ali fashion, she bounced right back and had a great rest of the year dating and breaking hearts on her own. Charlotte wasn't surprised, however, when Ali got back together with Rob after she moved up to San Francisco. "Is he staying the night?"

"Probably. Is that okay?"

"It's always okay."

Charlotte didn't mind Rob spending the night but sometimes she liked to be notified so she could go over to Ben's for the night. Four is a really big crowd in this small two bedroom apartment. "I'll probably go over to Ben's after the game anyway, so tell Rob I said hi."

After seeing Trevor, Charlotte felt torn about wanting to see Ben. It had been about a year and things were past the stage of casual dating but not yet to the point of being really serious. When Charlotte thought about marrying Ben, it made her smile but at the same time made her feel a panicked. She liked the way things were right now with their separate lives. He had his own place down in the marina and worked a lot, so she only saw him a couple nights a week. When Ben wasn't working, he was playing basketball with the sport and social club or biking the trails of Tennessee Valley, a set of trails in Marin that overlooked the ocean and Mt. Tam. He was active and that was fine, but he did put all that second after his career. Charlotte wondered if Ben even factored her into his future. *I am happy with things the way they are so why rock the boat?*

An hour later, she was up at the Presidio softball field with her team. It was a clear night, but the temperature had cooled down significantly and she was glad she wore her sweatshirt over her t-shirt. Needing girls to play, she was desperately recruited by a friend who played on a local corporate team. Charlotte always loved sports, so it was a no-brainer. It didn't matter the team, The Hawaiian Hooters as they called themselves, could never seem to win a game. They had so much fun playing and being social, it turned into one of Charlotte's favorite nights of the week. Besides, it wasn't the game that was so important, it was the drinking afterwards.

"Strike!" she heard the umpire say. Standing out at second base, it was the last out they needed to end the game for a very rare win.

"Come on Mason, you can do it," shouted first baseman Brad to the pitcher. Looking over at him, Charlotte almost laughed how he stood there with a glove in one hand and a beer in another. He knew his priorities. Charlotte instinctively caught the ball when it was hit softly to her and tossed it to Brad for the out at first. It was a minor miracle Brad wasn't mid sip and could actually catch it. Game over.

The team gathered to shake hands with the opponents who also seemed to have a good amount of booze on the breath. But this is what made it all so much fun. It was a party with a bit of exercise.

"Great catch," said Darren, the newest member, as he patted Charlotte on the shoulder.

"Thanks."

Charlotte really liked Darren. He was a bit younger; maybe twenty-eight, but he had such a nice charming smile. Most of the guys on the team had great careers downtown and Darren was no exception.

Charlotte never understood how they could be out drinking until two every night and still get to work on time in the morning. They all had a stamina she never understood.

The girls on the team were just as fun and Charlotte had developed a couple good friendships with Lisa, Stacey, and Kathy.

"Is Ben coming out tonight?" Stacey asked as they were heading to the car.

"I don't think so. He's probably still at work."

"So what is up with you two?" Kathy asked. "Is there going to be a wedding soon?"

Charlotte was so tired of this question. Obviously if anything had changed, her friends would be the first to know. "Just because you're getting married doesn't mean the rest of us are joining the club."

"You can have my fiancé. He's driving me crazy," Kathy said. "Maybe getting married in Florida wasn't such a good idea. We should have just eloped and gotten it all over with."

"Don't think so, Kath. I'm looking forward to a long weekend in Palm Beach. You better not cancel it," Lisa said before she got into her car. "See you all in a few minutes."

Laughing, Charlotte got into her car and headed through the Presidio to the entrance. The new Lucas campus looked really beautiful lit up against the trees. Late in the 90s, CNET and Lucas Film went up against each other in a bidding war over this land. Lucas won and he built a really beautiful campus that housed part of his company, a museum, and a couple cafes. The look fit in with the rest of the Presidio architecture which was considered historic. The sad part, however, was the tear down of the Letterman Hospital and the officer housing next to it. Charlotte's great grandfather had been hospital's Chief Administrator in the 1930s while he and his wife had lived on the working base. It was always amazing when she drove past the house they lived in—it was like glimpsing a piece of her past she never knew much about. With her youngest brother currently serving overseas in the military, that part of her history seems even more important.

Family history aside, Charlotte's favorite area in San Francisco was the Presidio. It was like a small forest located in the middle of a bustling city. Most people thought of Central Park in New York City as the prettiest city park, but it didn't hold a candle to the peacefulness of the Presidio. Maybe because the military base overlooked the ocean and the Golden Gate Bridge. It was truly spectacular. After exiting the park, she drove to the bar, miraculously finding a parking spot near the front. Normally, she circled for about fifteen minutes before finding a space several blocks away.

Entering the *Final Final*, the most popular sports bar in the area, she prepared for the assault of beer, mixed with popcorn and fried food, to her senses. Social Distortion was playing on jukebox and she could feel it was going to be a fun night. Charlotte had come to really depend on seeing this team weekly. One night a week playing softball and going out with her friends really kept her from losing her mind especially when she was out of work and needed the social interaction.

"Need a beer, Charlotte?" Darren said pointing at her from the bar.

"Yes, please," she said as she walked up next to him. Darren stood very close to her and she could feel his arm pressed against hers. Darren always seemed to invade her personal space in a very flirtatious way. *Does he have a crush on me?* Charlotte wasn't used to the attention and it sometimes turned her into a shy school girl but she loved how he made her feel like the most important person in the world. It was a skill only a lucky few seemed to have and it was the same gift Ben had and it always sucked her in. Darren, however, knew she had a boyfriend although he never asked about Ben and she never volunteered. *Why is that? Why do I like keeping my life with these people separate from Ben?* She didn't mind when Ben came to a game because it happened so seldom, but she really enjoyed this time and these people alone. The girls knew everything about Ben because of the brunches and dinners together where they gossiped, but they didn't see him all that often. *And they don't know everything about him. If they did, he wouldn't be so perfect anymore.*

At that moment, she looked over and saw Stacey sit down on her boyfriend Mike's lap. He had such a look of pleasure on his face as he lifted her hair and kissed the back of her neck. They were a couple in love. Charlotte was fairly certain they would be the next couple to walk down the aisle after Kathy and Ian. Seeing them together and listening to Kathy talk about her wedding plans, Charlotte started to miss Ben. Sometimes it snuck up on her—neediness. It made the independence she normally craved feel completely overrated. She just wanted to have it all together and be in a relationship of codependence. *I want Ben to look at me the way Mike looks at Stacey. I'm so tired of doing it all alone and I'm ready to settle down and have a family.* Then, the thought of being with Ben every second of every day, sharing a small San Francisco apartment, and doing his laundry squashed those thoughts. Something about having her own space and keeping the thrill of going out on dates and staying overnight at his place but still having her own space made Charlotte feel more comfortable. She loved Ben and looked forward to seeing him during the week, but she was okay with the way things were. The neediness feeling went away and Charlotte felt normal again. *No need to rush anything.* The one part of a relationship she wished she could have all the time was the 'lying in bed naked together and having lots of sex' part. Charlotte blushed thinking how much she really liked that.

After two hours of drinking and playing pool, Charlotte was ready to leave. She had been ready awhile ago, but Darren had begged her stay "a few more minutes." She couldn't resist his big blue eyes and a few minutes turned into a couple hours.

Normally, after she was done at the bar, she either walked down the hill and across Lombard to Ben's place or she got a ride with someone. It was just easier to leave her car parked where it was than to search for a spot in the Marina. Pulling out her phone, she texted Ben to see if he was home yet.

I'm heading over to your place, the text read. *You home?*

After three minutes, Ben texted back. *I'll swing by and get you on my way home 5 min.*

Wow, different. Ben was usually late coming back to his place on Thursday nights. He played basketball and went out with the guys afterwards which sometimes went way later than Charlotte's group. After saying goodbye to her friends and confirming brunch for

Sunday with the girls, Charlotte went outside to wait for Ben to pull up. Seeing his brand new Subaru Outback turn the corner, she realized he was exactly right when he said five minutes.

"Hi," she said opening the door and sliding in the front seat.

"Hi back," he replied leaning over for a kiss. "How was the game?"

"We actually won for once."

"Did you change beers in the cooler or something?" Ben laughed.

"I didn't notice. I don't think it was the beer," she giggled back. "Somehow the stars aligned."

Crossing Lombard to Chestnut, Charlotte stared out the window at the restaurants as they drove towards Fillmore. "So good to see the Marina picking up business," she said. Thursday nights were usually busy in the area and tonight was no different. After the tech crash in 2000, San Francisco had struggled to come back and many of the restaurants had changed ownership during the past few years. One minute she had a favorite new restaurant and the next minute it was gone.

Pulling up to Ben's apartment on Francisco and Webster, it was always a relief to Charlotte that he had a garage. Charlotte loved Ben's place. It was a nice bachelor pad without all the bachelor junk. He had very good taste and since he made a lot of money, had it professionally decorated. Even his cleanliness was above standard. Charlotte already knew she would find absolutely nothing out of place, not even a shoe in the wrong spot. She was a very clean and organized person but Ben made her feel like a slob.

Oh, perfect Ben with his perfect good looks, his perfect job and his perfect place. He was definitely a catch and she still wasn't sure how she had caught his attention. Next to all the pretty Marina and Pacific Heights girls, Charlotte often felt like a frumpy, overweight mess.

"I need a shower," Ben said putting his keys in the silver bowl on the entryway table.

"Me, too. Can I join you?" Charlotte said following him into his bedroom.

"Uh, sure. I'm not going to be in there long because I'm really tired and sore," he said stripping off his clothes.

Feeling a bit let down, Charlotte already knew what this meant. No sex tonight. Unbeknownst to all her friends who thought she was in the perfect relationship, she and Ben seldom had sex. Ben had the lowest libido of any guy she had ever dated. Not that she had been with a lot of guys, but she had kissed quite a few and there was always a response to which she usually said no. With Ben it took about four months for her to realize something was abnormal. When he was courting her in the beginning, he did everything right— played it cool and polite on the first date, kissed her over ice cream on the second date, sent her roses after the third date, and spent the night after a long make out session on the fourth date. As the dates accumulated and the passion and need grew more intense, Charlotte was wondering if he would ever make a move towards intercourse. Thinking he was being a gentleman, Charlotte remained patient although her hormones were working overtime and all she wanted to feel was relief. After four months of this, Charlotte finally broached the subject with Ben and what followed was a disaster.

He was staying the night at her place and they were both naked under the sheets. "Ben, maybe it's time we went all the way." Blushing at her adolescent use of the term, she couldn't seem to come up with anything more sophisticated.

"You do?" he replied scooting a bit further under the covers.

"I think it's been long enough and I trust you."

"Are you sure?"

"Yes, I'm sure. I have condoms in my top drawer so we don't have to worry."

"I don't like using condoms, Charlotte, they don't feel good."

Charlotte almost laughed because every guy seemed to think he was too big for condoms and yet when he got around to putting one on, it seemed to fit just fine. "Well, I have regular and magnum."

That comment seemed to catch Ben off guard. She couldn't figure out if he was trying to think of another excuse to getting out of it or if he was wondering who before him was endowed.

"Okay then, I'll take a magnum," he said with a sigh.

"Well, fine, if you don't want to do it, we can wait," Charlotte said trying to hide the disappointment and confusion. Never once did she have to talk a guy into having sex. A sudden thought occurred to her that maybe Ben was gay. *Oh God, I hope not. That is so not fair. But it would be just my luck.*

Just as the thought threw cold water on her hope of having intercourse, Ben suddenly took charge, reached over her, and pulled a condom out of her bedside stand. "Okay, then, you ready to have your world rocked?"

YES, she wanted to scream as she waited for him to get ready. She knew without a doubt the magnum condom was a bit too big, but she didn't say a word because she and Ben were finally going to do it. From his hardness and the way he rolled on top of her and kissed her on the lips, she knew then, without a doubt, Ben wasn't gay. He couldn't be gay. It felt awkward as he tried to find his way in, but eventually they got into a groove. Although she was a bit nervous and expected him to be as well, it was so quiet and not the passionate lovemaking she expected from him. It wasn't like their intimate life prior to having sex was bad. Ben always seemed to like fooling around and being naked and kissing her passionately. Now his technique ended up a huge letdown because he seemed so stiff and quiet. She almost laughed out loud when she remembered the Sex and City Episode where Carrie and Jack Berger first had sex. Despite the passion during the dating, the sex itself just totally sucked. There is chemistry and then there is *sexual* chemistry and this was an example of the former without the latter.

As expected, her world was not rocked. After about fifteen minutes of just thrusting, Ben finally came and dropped all his weight on her practically suffocating the air out of her lungs. There had been no passionate kissing, no exploring, no nothing—just boring missionary sex. Once he rolled off her, Charlotte laid next him trying to catch her breath and trying not to cry from the disappointment.

"That was nice," Ben said. "Did you come?"

Charlotte didn't even know what to say. *Did I come? Did you hear me come? Did you feel me even move underneath you while you just kept moving up and down and didn't even look at me?* "Um, yes, it was nice," she lied.

Then Ben did something unexpected—he rolled her over on her side so they were in a spoon position and started gently rubbing her arm and her back. Chills went up and down her skin relaxing her into the post sexual glow she had been looking forward to during the intercourse. Okay, so she didn't have an orgasm and it wasn't the best sex, but it would get better. It was just the awkward first time. *He's really good with the snuggle part and that's just as important as the sex, right?*

Now, standing with Ben in the shower as he hogged the water while washing his hair, she wondered if the snuggling was worth the lack of sex. Here she was naked in the shower and he barely noticed.

"Here, you want the water? I'm done," he said moving his body behind hers. "I'm getting out so I can catch up on the news."

Great—that meant going to bed with ESPN. Sighing, Charlotte just stood in the water letting it erase the dirt from the game and insecurity about Ben down the drain. Suddenly Trevor popped into her mind and she started thinking about her happy hour with him earlier. Remembering how good he looked in his black leather jacket and green t-shirt, she wondered what sex was like with him. They had almost done it once, but it didn't happen and she was always left imagining. Feeling her heart beat again at the thought of him, she wondered if she could recapture those feelings for Trevor into feelings for Ben. She really loved Ben and wanted to be with him, but seeing Trevor shed some light on what she and Ben were lacking. While Ben made her heart beat when she was with him, she wasn't sure she did the same for him and it stressed her out. Shouldn't a man in love want to be with his woman all the time? Shouldn't they be spending more time together since they only lived five minutes apart? Shouldn't he want to have sex more than she did? It's all so confusing. Then again, maybe Trevor is just as bad in bed. That thought added absolutely no comfort.

What was worse was Ben always shut her down when she tried to discuss her feelings. It's been a year and she should feel comfortable bringing this stuff up with him. Ben made her feel like she was talking at him and not with him causing her to end up frustrated, mad, and accusatory. He would totally clam up and turn completely away from her. He would never discuss why he didn't like sex. After reading several articles and case studies on the subject, Charlotte finally gave up and figured he just had a very low libido.

Pushing her thoughts aside, she turned the water off and got out knowing it wouldn't matter if she set up a stripper pole in front of his bed and threw her panties in his face—he wouldn't notice at all.

Three

Trevor couldn't sleep.

Charlotte's face filled his mind as if she was on a constant loop behind his eyes. Why did he talk so much about himself? He should have asked her more questions. More importantly, he should have asked if she had a boyfriend. He wasn't sure why he withheld the question because he kept thinking about it, but the words just wouldn't leave his lips. It didn't escape him how she evaded that particular subject as well. Tossing and turning, he couldn't get comfortable and his mattress started feeling lumpy.

Even after all these years, Trevor still felt something when he thought about Charlotte Campbell. *Damn, those feelings are still there and she is still so freaking hot.* Finally giving up on falling back to sleep, he got out of bed cursing silently at the cold floor beneath his bare feet. San Francisco is a fine city, but not in the chill of the early morning hours when getting out of bed. He loved the Victorian feel to his place, but it seeped hot air faster than a deflating balloon. People don't realize that San Francisco is normally damp and cold and are often surprised when they visit in their shorts and t-shirts thinking it's like an episode of Baywatch.

Feeling cranky, he prepared coffee and booted up his computer ignoring the sounds as it slowly lit up. Fully awake, he looked at the clock which read a quarter past three and sighed when he realized he would be getting up in an hour anyway. Trevor hated this time of the morning. It was always disturbingly quiet and he often felt lonely—like he was the only one awake in the world. It didn't matter if he played music or turned on the TV, just knowing the rest of the world was still sleeping made it that much more isolating. Trevor was most definitely not a morning person. His perfect schedule would be to stay up till two in the morning and get up at eleven. He must have been a bartender or waiter in another life.

Sipping coffee, he decided to Google Charlotte to see what came up. Links to her Facebook, LinkedIn and Twitter accounts made him feel like a bit of a spy. Not one for social networking sites, he only opened his own Facebook account so he could see pictures of his niece and nephew his sister Carrie posted. Several months had gone by since he logged in so he had a lot of friend requests and a lot of emails. *This is why I don't do this—I would be spending way too much time on this site.* From what he heard, Facebook and social networking in general were horribly addictive. Ignoring the friend requests, he entered Charlotte's name and her picture popped up. Since it was completely protected from the general public, he would have to wait until she accepted his request to see any of her information.

Just before he clicked send, he thought about what it was going to be like having her back in his life. He had fallen hard for her when they first met in college—completely losing his thought process that first day she had walked into the studio. She looked nervous, but she hid it with a big smile and big blue eyes. Her hair fell in gentle waves just below her shoulders which accentuated her boobs. She was the reason he became a boob man.

He felt himself respond physically to the memory and clicked send so he could move on.

"What are you doing up this early?" Michelle asked from behind him.

Startled, he quickly closed his browser so Michelle wouldn't see what he was he was doing. Luckily, she went straight for the coffee and poured herself a cup. "I couldn't sleep."

"I'm surprised at that considering how much sex we had last night," Michelle chuckled as she leaned against the counter.

True, but I wasn't thinking about you.

Looking at Michelle, Trevor laughed feeling somewhat trapped—and a little bit guilty. It hadn't been his intention to get involved with someone from work, but his hours prevented him from going out at night during the week and he had no desire to be out in the bar scene anymore. He wanted quality over quantity and it was just easier to hang out alone or with his guy friends than to try to weed through the barflies. Work was the easiest option if he wanted to get laid. Not that he usually dated anyone from work but loneliness caught up with him. Michelle was the first person he let himself get involved with thinking it wouldn't go very far.

Starting out five months ago with a couple hookups after happy hours, it eventually turned into a casual but very sexual relationship. They were now in that space where they needed to decide to jump in or abandon ship—that place where "the talk" needed to happen. He genuinely liked Michelle and they had good chemistry, but he couldn't figure out why he didn't want to commit completely. Michelle was gorgeous, smart, fun, and great in bed, the whole package. It wasn't until he saw Charlotte yesterday that he figured it out. His feelings for Michelle were nowhere near what he'd felt for Charlotte when they dated—and they hadn't even slept together.

"Are you going to hire Charlotte?" he asked not meeting Michelle's eyes.

"Charlotte? The interview from yesterday? Probably. She seemed like a good fit and I liked her better than the other two," Michelle replied before another sip of coffee. "You said you knew her from college. Do you really think she is a good hire or were you just showing off?"

"Charlotte would be a great fit. She picks things up super fast. She'd be fine."

Deep down, Trevor knew hiring Charlotte would cause all sorts of drama. He wasn't exactly sure what would happen, but by his physical reaction at the mere thought of her, it was sure to be the kind that would cause trouble. *Stop thinking with your penis, man.* But he knew he could never sabotage Charlotte—not in a million years. If she deserved the job, she should get it.

Trevor saw Michelle nod through his peripheral vision as he pretended to get back to the internet. Truth is he really wanted to see Charlotte every day. This was a door he needed to either open again or close for good. Maybe his feelings weren't as strong as he once thought and everything he was feeling was just the rush of memories. Maybe she didn't feel a damn thing for him and was just happy to see an old friend. *You're just being stupid to think Charlotte would even have feelings left for you.* Fifteen years was a long time and he was really surprised at the physical reaction she still caused in him.

Trevor sighed wondering why they had stopped talking at all. Things had been going great between them until that one night. He wasn't sure why she wouldn't speak to him much after that but she had made it very clear they were no longer an item or even friends for the matter. She repeated over and over that it wasn't about him and it was about her, but even now he can see that was a load of crap. He finally just left her alone, slept with a couple other girls and graduated never to see her again. Now she acted as if that night never happened. Does she even remember and still blame him? *This trip down memory lane will only drive you crazy.* Maybe he wanted her near him so he could finally figure out why she blamed him and to finally move on and close that door completely.

Back on his Facebook page, he started accepting the waiting requests. A few from high school and a few from Cal Poly, he actually started smiling as he looked at the profiles. He was tagged in a few pictures he couldn't quite remember. One was of him, Charlotte, Cameron and Jamie on the big brown velvet couch in the studio lobby. *Oh man, I have one helluva happy grin on my face.* Trying to remember when it was taken, it must have been before Charlotte stopped talking to him because Charlotte looked extremely happy as well. *Those were the days.*

Later that morning after the newscast was complete, Trevor was back in his office going through notes on the broadcast and preparing for Monday's show. Relieved it was Friday, he couldn't wait to leave work behind for the week and enjoy the weekend. He loved Saturday mornings because he got to sleep in and catch up on chores he neglected during the week like dirty dishes and laundry.

"Knock knock," Michelle said from the doorway. "I just wanted to let you know the offer is going out to your friend today. Hopefully she'll start Monday. "

Charlotte would be here every day—assuming she accepted the job. Somehow it felt wrong to be excited when it was Michelle giving him the news and he made sure he seemed nonchalant. "Great. Will she be reporting to you?"

"No, she'll be reporting to Jake."

"I'm assuming her desk is upstairs with the rest of the team?"

"You assume right. So anyway, I just wanted to let you know. You owe me one," Michelle said with a wink. "Are we on for dinner tomorrow night? Trattoria Contadina?"

"Sure?" Trevor had thought dinner was canceled because the couple they were planning to meet out had a family emergency. "What time?"

"Seven. So I guess this is our official first date as a couple?"

Trevor knew his answer would be very important. *A couple?* He never thought of her as a girlfriend and never considered them a couple. *Are we?* Thinking back to all the times they went out, they were with friends or coworkers and never alone. They would end up at her place or his alone, but that was to have sex. It never occurred to him to officially ask Michelle out on a date and the thought made him a bit uncomfortable. Now he was stuck. This relationship—and even he wasn't such an ass as to think they didn't have some kind of relationship—suddenly turned very real and "the talk" seemed that much closer. The restaurant was a small, dimly lit and very romantic Italian place in North Beach and of course Michelle would think of it like a romantic date. He probably wouldn't have minded if he hadn't seen Charlotte last week. *Great.*

"I guess so," was the only thing he could think of to say. He didn't want to hurt her feelings. Michelle was a good person and he knew at that moment he needed to break it off. He couldn't continue sleeping with her knowing she expected it to go further and he definitely couldn't continue sleeping with her when he was thinking about someone else. *Fuck, how did this go from fun to complicated?*

It was finally Friday afternoon and he was about to leave the office for the weekend. First, however, he wanted to call Charlotte and congratulate her on her new job.

She picked up after three rings. "Hey Charlie," Trevor said nervously. Why are there butterflies in his stomach? How ridiculous.

"Trevor—hey!"

Elizabeth Aloe

Her voice already made him smile and he could feel himself responding to it. It was low and out of breath like she was working out. "Where are you?"

"I'm down in Chrissy Field for a run. Sorry, just trying to catch my breath."

"I just wanted to say congrats. Are you excited to start your job on Monday?"

"I'm very excited, Trevor. This is a great opportunity for me. Thank you so much for helping me out."

"It was my pleasure. I didn't do much. Michelle really liked you," he replied followed by an awkward second where he had no idea what to say. He wanted to see if she wanted to hang out this weekend, but decided against asking. It was too soon. "Well, I guess I'll see you on Monday?"

"Definitely. I'm looking forward to it. I'll come by your office and say hello."

"That'd be great."

Another weird pause.

"Bye, Trev," she said before hanging up.

Trevor said goodbye and hung up feeling like the stupidest person on earth. *Could that call have been any more embarrassing?* He should have just texted but he had wanted to hear her voice. He had expected the conversation to go way better than that and it didn't help at all that she sounded nonchalant about hearing from him. Of course she was outside running, but still, he wanted her to sound a bit more interested at the thought of him calling. *Shit, she is so over me. What was I even thinking? I need a drink.*

Texting his friend Craig about meeting up for happy hour, Trevor closed up his computer and headed out the door willing his memory to forget the phone call ever happened.

Four

Charlotte hung up her phone totally confused. Looking at it, she wondered if she should call Trevor back because that was the most awkward conversation she ever had with anyone.

She had been so lost in thought thinking about him and Ben during her run, she almost missed the sound of *Lonely is the Night* by Billy Squier, her ringtone. The lack of oxygen in her lungs got worse when his name popped up on the caller ID. It was sort of the same feeling she got when she did her very first solo show on the radio. She couldn't catch her breath and it took so much extra energy to spit out one simple word.

After she finally calmed down enough to really talk, the conversation was over. She wasn't sure if Trevor was calling simply to say congratulations, or if he wanted to talk about something else. Charlotte considered calling him back. Maybe he wanted to talk more about their past now that they'd be seeing each other on a daily basis. They both needed so much closure in order to move forward. Holding her phone as she stared out across the water towards the Golden Gate Bridge, she decided right now was not the proper time to have that sort of conversation. It needed to be done in person—with lots of alcohol.

Returning her phone into the belt case, she placed her earphones back in her ears and turned the music on to continue her run. She was shaky from the adrenaline rush but willed her muscles to move again. After a few steps, she felt the phone vibrate again and smiled thinking it was Trevor calling back. *Maybe he wants to meet for a drink tonight and declare how much he's been in love with me all this time and can't go another second without seeing me.* Charlotte laughed out loud at how ridiculous that sounded.

The name she saw on her ID wasn't Trevor but it didn't disappoint her.

"Hey Sarah," she answered.

"Hi," Sarah Davenport hiccupped. Charlotte's smile faded when she realized her friend was crying.

"What's wrong?"

"I'm just so upset," the sobs continued. "Someone has a sex tape, Charlotte. A sex tape!"

What was she talking about? "What do you mean?" Charlotte turned around away from the beach as if Sarah was waiting for her a few steps away.

"Someone recorded Cooper and me having sex and is going to sell it to the tabloids."

Charlotte then connected what her friend said. Sarah Davenport was dating Cooper Bancroft—the

Elizabeth Aloe

biggest and most popular star in Hollywood. They'd been dating off and on for a few years, but ever since Cooper got famous, they've kept it a secret at the request of his management. "Are you in LA?"

"Actually, I'm in San Luis Obispo. I just had to get away and I started driving north."

"Can you make it up here? You can stay with me in the city."

"Yes," Sarah said her crying subsiding. "I'll be there in three hours."

"Drive safe. If you need me to come get you, call me," Charlotte said, making her friend promise to call her if she needed help.

Charlotte hung up realizing she was looking forward to seeing Sarah. Upset or not, Charlotte didn't get to see her much anymore since Sarah became a reporter for Hollywood Tonight. Cutting her run short, Charlotte turned around and headed back through the Marina and up the hill to her apartment. It must really be a crisis for Sarah to lose composure like that and ask for help.

Three hours later, Sarah was seated on Charlotte's couch spilling everything about her latest drama.

"You two are still together?" Charlotte asked sardonically. "I can never tell because I hear he's dating the latest 'It' girl and I never seem to hear from you much anymore."

Sarah sighed and hugged a sofa pillow tighter to her stomach. "I'm sorry for being a bad friend and not calling you. It's not intentional, I promise. Yes, we're still together and still in love. What you hear is simple PR to keep his fans happy. I want to be with Coop but everything is so complicated."

Complicated was a major understatement. Cooper's face was everywhere—tabloids, billboards, magazines. He had a following that rivaled the guy from the Twilight series. Charlotte had always liked Cooper but hadn't really talked to him since he made it big. He was always busy when she visited Sarah. "What happened that there is a sex tape going around?"

"I have no idea. It was taken at the Chateau Marmont and looks like it was done through a webcam."

"Someone planted a webcam?"

"Apparently so. He wants money or it goes to the tabloids."

"Did you contact the police?"

"Why? It's easier to just pay him off."

"Who would want to do that to you?"

"Just about everyone who needs money. This wouldn't be the first time a celebrity was caught doing something like this. Scandal sells."

Charlotte wondered how Sarah did it. Loving a man who was adored by the world and keeping the relationship a secret. "I'm sorry this happened. I don't know what to do for you."

"There really is nothing to do right now. I'm waiting for Cooper to return my call."

"I can't believe Cooper is the big star now," Charlotte said thinking back to that night she met him for the first time. She and Sarah were at a Hollywood Hills party being hosted by an acquaintance of Sarah's. Cooper was one of the caterers and it was love at first sight for him. He begged Sarah for her number until she relented just to get him to stop following her around the party. Come to find out, he was working not to be an actor, but studying for his MBA.

After letting Sarah vent and cry about her situation, Charlotte decided she needed to tell Sarah about Trevor or she was going to burst. "I have some news of my own and I'm glad you're here so I can tell you. Guess who I bumped into last week at an interview of all places?"

"Hmmm, the famous movie star Cooper Bancroft? Oh my God, I would DIE if I saw him!!"

Both Charlotte and Sarah giggled over the joke. "You are going to flip—Trevor Sheldon."

"Trevor from Cal Poly? The same Trevor you were in love with for so long?"

"The one and same," Charlotte said before filling Sarah in on the details.

"Wow. I can't even believe it. Did you get the job?"

"Yes, I did. Just heard from them a little while ago and I start Monday," Charlotte said. "Part of me is really excited to see Trevor every day again and part of me is scared."

"No shit. I remember how he put you through the ringer."

"It's so weird. I know that was a rough time for me, but it's in the past. Seeing him was like closing a door yet opening a new one. Does that make sense?"

"It makes perfect sense to me. Did you talk about that night at the station?"

"No. I wasn't about to bring it up. I still have no idea what really happened that night and I don't want to talk about it," Charlotte said. And she didn't want to talk about it—ever. But she knew Trevor would bring it up at some point.

Thankfully, Sarah changed the subject. "How's Ben?"

Charlotte was plunked back into reality. "Ben's good. We're supposed to go out tonight, but since you're here, I told him I'm staying in with you. That is what you want to do, right? I didn't make any other plans thinking you wouldn't want to go out."

"Looking like this," Sarah said pointing to her puffy eyes. "Maybe we can just invite the other Ben and his buddy Jerry over instead?"

"Sure," Charlotte said with a small laugh. "Maybe we can talk Ali into hanging with us, too. A Supernatural marathon is just what you need to get your mind off things."

It was Sarah's turn to laugh. "Ah, the Winchester brothers. It's been a long time since I've seen an episode. I got to meet Jensen Ackles last year at upfronts."

"I know. I seethed with jealousy," Charlotte said in her best haughty voice. "Okay, let's go for a short walk to the corner market and get the ice cream."

"I know I've got issues, but we're celebrating your new job, Charlotte. I think two pints of Ben and Jerry's are needed—and some vodka. Are you sure it's okay to stay in? Maybe you want to see Ben?"

"No—it's a girl's night and I'm hanging with you," Charlotte said leading her out the door and down the stairs. Her heart fluttered nervously thinking about the new job and how her life will change. Will it be for the better? Would Trevor be as excited as she to work together again? Was he even thinking about her like she was about him? Maybe he didn't even want her that close again? *Get out of your head—none of this matters. It's a job, nothing more.*

After selecting Cherry Garcia and New York Fudge Chunk, Charlotte and Sarah were back in the apartment discussing how full of drama their lives seemed to be.

"Shouldn't we both be married with a kid by now?" Sarah said with a giggle as she took a spoon to the Cherry Garcia. "I always knew Cooper would be in the industry at some point but I always thought he would work the business side, not become an actor."

"Well, he is gorgeous. Do you realize how beautiful you both look together?" Charlotte said taking a bite from the other pint. "We all need sunglasses to look at you."

"Shut up," Sarah said faking a scowl. "You're just as pretty and I wish you would realize it. You have a gorgeous boyfriend, too."

"Thanks, but I feel like a total blob next to you and you're right about Ben—he is so good looking." She kind of missed Ben now and felt guilty for thinking so much about Trevor. "I'm going to take a shower. Feel free to watch TV or whatever. I have a bunch of InStyle magazines if you want to read."

"Thanks, but I have a subscription already," Sarah said as studied the view from the bay window. "You have such a great view of everything—Russian Hill, Alcatraz, the Golden Gate Bridge. I'm so jealous. Maybe I should move up here."

"And give up that gorgeous house you have in Manhattan Beach? No way. I won't let you. I need a crash pad in LA when I visit," Charlotte giggled.

"San Francisco is just so awesome," Sarah paused. "I've changed my mind; I think we need to get cleaned up so we can go grab a drink. We shouldn't be sitting home because of my pity party. Call Ben and have him meet us out."

"Are you sure? I'd be up for a cocktail," Charlotte said heading into her room.

"Yes. It's too nice of night not to be out enjoying it. Where's Ali? Maybe she'll want to come?"

"She's down in the south bay at Rob's. She texted she'll be back in the morning for brunch and to say hello."

"I'll be glad to see her. I can't believe she and Rob are still together. Do you think they'll get engaged soon?"

"I have no idea. I think he wants it, but I think she likes her independence which I totally understand," Charlotte yelled from her bedroom. Once undressed, she started the shower and climbed in thinking how age and lifestyle made it so hard to bring everyone together.

Unless it was a wedding, she seldom saw anyone from
her past except for Ali, Sarah, Cameron and Jamie. Now
Trevor was back in the mix. She wondered how many
people Trevor still associated with from college.
Thinking of her Facebook page, she made a mental note
to find Trevor's profile so she could see who he was
linked to from the past.

The water felt warm against her skin and her
mind wandered to Sarah's remark about Ali. When are
they getting engaged? They had been together a long
time and while they seemed content with the situation, it
couldn't last this way forever. Rob was pressuring Ali
to move in with him in Palo Alto. Ali kept resisting and
Charlotte couldn't blame her. Moving forty miles south
meant a two hour commute into the city and Ali was
very vocal about not doing it. She wanted Rob to move
to the city, but that would mean he would have to
commute south instead. Selfishly, Charlotte wanted Ali
to continue resisting because she didn't want to lose her
roommate to the suburbs and marriage. Realistically, she
knew it would happen eventually, but can't eventually
be later rather sooner?

A couple hours later, Charlotte was sitting with
Sarah at Rex's Café on Polk Street.

"Ben just texted to say he's on his way,"
Charlotte said laying her phone back on the bar. The
cocktail in front of her tasted better than usual. Her
muscles felt sore from the workout earlier, but the lemon
drop relaxed her and she started feeling giddy. Being
employed now was a weight lifted off her shoulders and
she loved the days between jobs when there was no
stress from the previous job and only excitement and
nervousness about starting the new one. It was a clean
slate.

Rex's Café was one of Charlotte's favorite neighborhood spots. Within walking distance from her apartment, it was an easy place to grab drinks and food without worrying about getting home or spending a fortune. It was cozy, local and she was very familiar with the wait staff.

"I'm excited to see Ben tonight," Sarah said looking at her phone. "Cooper still hasn't called."

"Do you think you should call him again? He must be wondering where you are about now."

"No. I doubt it. He's too busy promoting the movie. I haven't really seen him in a couple days, honestly. I'll bet my life we see pictures of him and his costar Ashley on the cover of US Weekly and People in about a week. They're doing spreads together. It kills me to read anything about him because his fandom wants him with her and they are rabid about it."

"God, Sarah, I didn't realize how hard this could be. Your job means you have to interview them, too, right?"

"Luckily, I've gotten away without interviewing either, but my manager Toby knows about us and he is chomping at the bit to use it."

"I have to say, I feel extremely privileged about sharing this big, worldly secret with you," Charlotte giggled. "Sex tape aside, I'm sure it will all work out."

Right then, Ben walked in and like a beacon of light, he lit up the bar. He was so handsome in his jeans and blue button down that brought out his blue eyes. However, it wasn't his looks that made him handsome—it was his confidence and smile. Charlotte was buzzed enough to feel her heart speed up at the sight of him.

Maybe she didn't give Ben enough credit. He was very good to her and by the way he spotted her at the bar and waved sweetly, she felt guilty for thinking so much about Trevor. "Don't worry; I won't mention Cooper to Ben."

"Thanks," Sarah replied just as Ben walked up.

"Hey ladies, mind if I join you?" he said. Charlotte let him kiss her before reintroducing Sarah.

"Hi Sarah, it's good to see you again," Ben said pulling her into a hug. "What are you both drinking?"

"Cocktails," they said in unison as Charlotte motioned with a wave to the bartender.

After ordering a Pale Ale, Ben pulled up a stool next to Charlotte. Pulling her stool back slightly to make a small triangle, Charlotte realized this was one of her favorite things to do. Sitting at a bar having drinks with close friends. Sometimes it felt good to have a boyfriend because the pressure to meet someone was lifted, but other times she missed being single where she could wonder if the next guy was "the one". She didn't necessarily believe in soul mates, but she liked to believe that couples were brought together for a reason.

The conversation flowed freely between Ben and Sarah as they talked about their jobs in LA and San Francisco. Charlotte felt a little out of the conversation as Ben, being a financial planner and very good one at that, tried to bring Sarah on board with retirement advice. Both Sarah and Ben made good salaries and seemed to have a great handle on money which made Charlotte feel poor and disorganized. *Retirement? What retirement? I'll be working until I'm dead.* How anyone on a basic salary saved for retirement in a city like San

Francisco puzzled Charlotte. Most people she knew
except Ben barely scraped by.

The night went well and Ben ordered another
round when Charlotte brought up the job offer.

"Congratulations again," he said holding up his
drink for a toast. "It's a well-deserved position for a
well-deserving unemployed woman."

Charlotte blushed when he leaned in and kissed
her on the lips. After the kiss broke, she looked over at
Sarah worried she would feel left out or be upset and
missing Cooper. Sarah, true to form, smiled and hugged
her with more congratulations. Trevor's face appeared in
her mind, but she quickly brushed it aside because the
moment felt right with Ben.

"So pretty lady, can I stay with you tonight?"
Ben whispered in Charlotte's ear causing goose bumps
down her arms from the tickle.

"If it's okay with Sarah, sure. She's staying in
Ali's room, but it should be alright," Charlotte
whispered back.

Once they paid the bill—or rather Ben paid the
bill, they walked outside into the night air enjoying the
above average temperature. Charlotte didn't protest
when Ben grabbed her hand. She was buzzed tonight
not only by alcohol but by how fun and intimate the
evening turned out. She was happy to have Sarah in
town even though she couldn't help her with the Cooper
situation. Knowing Sarah, she would land on her feet
and everything would turn out just fine.

Back at the apartment, Sarah finished the pint of
ice cream before retiring to Ali's bedroom for the night.
Expecting to just take her makeup off and go to bed,

Charlotte was taken completely by surprise when Ben pulled her to him and started kissing her neck.

"I'm sorry I haven't been very attentive lately. It's honestly the stress at work," he said quietly. "I've been so worried about the reorganization and layoffs. I can't seem to shake the anxiety."

"Is there anything I can do?" Charlotte asked not really knowing what to say. She had no idea Ben was feeling anxious.

"You're doing it," he said putting his hand on her boob.

"What about the layoffs? Are you going to lose your job?"

"I don't think so—at least I'm safe for the time being. The industry has just been hit so hard with the banks collapsing and the housing market in chaos. People are too scared to invest."

"I know," Charlotte said hugging him.

"I didn't realize you were so stressed out. You should have said something to me."

"I know, but you had just lost your job and I didn't want you to worry about me."

Charlotte had never felt so guilty. Here was her boyfriend finally explaining why he wasn't interested in having sex and it was all due to anxiety. It wasn't her after all. Mixed with guilt there was definitely relief and a bit of her own anxiety because it didn't erase the excitement she had at seeing Trevor. But it was Ben with her now and he was the one she was supposed to be thinking about—not someone from her past.

When Ben kissed her hard and deep like he did at the beginning of their relationship, Charlotte didn't protest. The sex that followed was fast, hot, and sweaty as if they had been separated for a long time. It was so good that if Charlotte had a headboard against the wall, it would have definitely irritated the neighbors with the noise. Charlotte had to gently hush Ben with a few giggles a couple times because she knew Sarah was in the other room probably laughing her head off at what she could hear. This is the Ben Charlotte wanted all along—the one who took some control of their sexual life and seemed like he couldn't get enough of her.

Spooning during the post sexual glow, Charlotte basked in the intimacy and wondered if Ben would continue this way. What would happen the next time he got really stressed out? Charlotte wasn't so self centered as to think a man couldn't lose his libido once in awhile because of stress—but when it stretches into months and possibly even years, it affects her self-esteem and self-worth. The first year of a relationship should fun and new but if it's full of stress for Ben, what would the next year bring when things are settled and they knew each other and having sex wasn't so much the priority anymore? She was proud of him for speaking to her about it and apologizing. At least he knew she was upset by it and finally acknowledged the problem. Typical man, Charlotte thought, any deep conversation was done on their timetable if at all.

Listening to Ben's snoring, Charlotte's mind wandered to Trevor. What was he like sexually? She'd always regretted missing the opportunity with him. The memories of his kisses were somewhat foggy because of the time that had passed and because Ben was lying next to her now. It wasn't hard to remember the feelings, however, the excitement and anticipation of kissing someone she was attracted to. Ben could still make her feel giddy like he did tonight but it didn't replace the loneliness that settled in between the few times he decided he wanted sex.

Boys aside, Charlotte knew her priorities right now were to start the new job and concentrate on saving money in case Ali decided to move in with Rob.

The next morning, Charlotte took Sarah to Sally's Café in Potrero Hill for brunch. Ali was on her way up from the South Bay and would meet them as soon as she could. Charlotte was a little hung over and needed to get some coffee and eggs in her system. Ben had plans to go mountain biking in Marin with his friends that morning, so he left fairly early but not before initiating morning sex which thrilled Charlotte.

Taking a table in the back, Charlotte sat with her back against the wall so she could see when Ali walked in. Sally's was the perfect brunch place—it was on the cheaper side but provided bigger portions.

"I wonder if Sally and Rex are related," Sarah said pulling out a chair and sitting down.

"What do you mean?" Charlotte asked having no clue what she was talking about.

"We went to Rex's Café and now we are at Sally's Café. I was just wondering if they were related."

Giggling, Charlotte finally got the joke. "Maybe they're lovers."

"Maybe," Sarah said opening her menu. "It sounded like you had a great night."

"Sorry," Charlotte replied blushing hard and completely embarrassed. "I guess I was so caught off guard."

"I had no idea Ben was so talented."

"I didn't either," Charlotte laughed. Sarah knew a little bit about her problems with Ben, but Charlotte wasn't one to give her friends complete details out of respect for him.

"He seemed to be having a great time. I don't get why you think he never wants to do it. I've never met a man like that."

"I know, right? I wish last night was how it was all the time. It was perfect. But I'm usually going to bed disappointed he doesn't have interest in being with me. It's really confusing and I keep asking myself if I should be thankful I have Ben because he is a really great guy or if there is someone out there who is the whole package."

"You're asking the wrong person, sweetie," Sarah replied sipping her coffee. "All I know is no one has ever come close to making me feel the way Cooper makes me feel. I can't imagine life without him— Hollywood and all. He is most definitely the right package for me."

"I know. I wonder how I would feel if Ben asked me to marry him."

"Do you think he will? Are you moving in that direction? It's only been a year. Eh, cross that bridge when you get to it."

Right then, Ali walked in and Charlotte stood to wave her over.

"Hi girls, sorry I'm late," Ali said hugging Sarah. "It's been way too long, Sarah. I'm really glad to see you."

"Me, too," replied Sarah returning the hug.

"What's this about you and Cooper? I've been dying for the details."

Looking quickly at Sarah, Charlotte really hoped she wasn't mad that Ali knew. "I'm sorry, Sarah, she lives with me."

"It's fine. It will come out eventually," Sarah said turning to Ali and filling her in.

"Wow. I remember Cooper. Is he still the same sweet guy? He must love being a movie star," Ali said.

"Well, I wouldn't say that. He's very disillusioned with Hollywood. He can't do regular things anymore like run errands, go to the gym, or walk the strand without being mobbed. He can't stand it."

"That must be hard," Ali continued. "From what I read, he's dating Ashley."

"Hmm, don't get me started."

"You mean he's not? O-M-G," Ali said pretending to be disappointed. "But everything I read in Us Weekly is true, isn't it?"

Charlotte giggled when she realized how jaw dropping this conversation would be to anyone eavesdropping. Those sitting at the tables around didn't appear to be listening—they were involved in their own conversations. *Hey people, wake up--the latest Hollywood scandal is sitting right next you!!* It still sounded weird even in her head.

After two hours of discussing Cooper, Rob Ben, and Trevor, Charlotte wasn't surprised when Sarah stood up and said she had to go.

"I'm going to miss you. Call me if you need me and remember you're welcome to come stay with us anytime," Charlotte said as she put her arms around Sarah.

"I know," Sarah replied. Charlotte could tell Sarah didn't really want to go home.

After watching Sarah drive off, Charlotte realized she had the whole afternoon ahead of her. "Ali, you want to go to Room and Board?"

"Oh, I love that place. Just don't let me buy anything"

Charlotte laughed thinking the same thing. She didn't need to spend any money on furniture, but it didn't mean she couldn't look, right?

Five

Later that afternoon, after Sarah left for LA and Ali went out to meet her other city friends, Charlotte was alone in her apartment. The fog had returned and the temperature dropped back to normal creating the usual gray sky Charlotte had memorized. After catching up on her recorded shows for the week, she decided it was time to pay bills and get them out of the way.

Luckily, being out of work had curbed her shopping habit and her visa bill was clean. Unemployment and severance from her previous job kept her afloat, but she was relieved to know she would be getting a steady paycheck again. After transferring a payment to the cable company, her phone rang and she instantly recognized the tune because it was Def Leppard's *Rock of Ages*—Ben's ringtone.

"Hi!" Charlotte answered.

"Hey sexy," he replied sounding out of breath. "How was brunch with the ladies?"

"Excellent. I miss Sarah already."

"Sarah is cool. So, I'm wondering if you wanted to have dinner with me tonight?"

Although he seemed rushed, Charlotte felt like she was being asked out by the star quarterback of her high school. "Why, Mr. Brawley, are you asking me out on a date?" Charlotte accidentally snorted as she tried to come off sounding coy and seductive. *Well, that was embarrassing.*

"I sure am," Ben laughed. "I have reservations in North Beach."

"I would love to go out with you," Charlotte said and smiled to herself. It wasn't often Ben asked her out formally. It felt good. "What time?"

"I'll pick you up at six. Okay, I gotta go. We were on a break. I can see all the way to the city right now and it's foggy."

"Funny to think you are on Mt. Tam and can just call me."

"I know. Modern technology is great," he said over the wind. "Okay, hon, talk to you later."

Charlotte hung up feeling giddy. What was up with Ben? It was like he woke up from a long sleep and was interested in life and having a girlfriend again. Well, whatever it was, Charlotte liked it. Thoughts of Ben naked in her bed entered her mind and she got a little aroused thinking about the great sex they had both shared last night and this morning. She could really fall in love with this Ben if she hadn't already. But even the good thoughts of Ben didn't prevent Trevor from popping into her head.

Remembering she wanted to look up Trevor on Facebook, she opened the website to find a friend request waiting from him already. *Well, well, well. He looked me up.* The thought tickled her as she accepted the request and went into his profile. Charlotte hadn't been that active on the site for a while, but she already could see they had friends in common. Scrolling through his list of friends, she noticed a lot of KCPR people she hadn't seen nor heard from since she graduated--Adam, Sam, Shelli, Chris, Tony, and many others. Sending out friend requests to all of them, she was really excited to be back in touch with everyone.

Trevor's pictures were limited except for a couple profile pictures and tagged photos from his sister with what appeared to be Trevor's niece and nephew. The little boy looked just like him. Charlotte felt somewhat disappointed there wasn't more to explore, but at least his profile opened her up to old friends.

Later that evening, Charlotte stood in front of her closet completely frustrated. Her hair and makeup were done and now she needed to choose an outfit. *Why is it I have all these beautiful clothes but when I actually have somewhere to go, I feel like I have nothing to wear?* Tops and skirts were strewn all over the floor in piles because she couldn't make up her mind. It wasn't that they didn't look right, it was just that most of them she wore to work and they all felt so boring. Finally, she pulled out a dark lavender silk dress Sarah forced her to buy when she was in LA. Normally, she would save a piece like this for a special occasion, but then realized a romantic date with her boyfriend was special. San Francisco is cosmopolitan city and she might as well dress the part. It wasn't that warm, but with a black pashmina wrap, it would be perfect for tonight. Finding her three inch black patent leather heels in the back of her closet, she pulled them out and tried them on with the outfit. While she was finally happy with her reflection, she remembered why she seldom wore heels—her toes felt like they were locked in the jaws of death. Like most females, Charlotte was drawn to pretty shoes, but the practicality didn't work very well in a city where every street was a hill. She finally gave up buying them and settled for shoes she could wear easily and without pain. Those brands weren't the prettiest, but she at least got her money's worth.

The apartment phone rang which meant it was Ben downstairs calling to be let in the building. Although she and Ali both had cell phones, the door system predated wireless and was still set up on the original phone number. If it were up to Charlotte, she would have gotten rid of that number a long time ago because there was no need for it. However, the landlord wasn't about to put the money into upgrading a functioning system, so they were stuck.

She quickly put her clothes away and checked herself one last time in the mirror. Hearing his footsteps coming up the stairs, she knew he would knock to be let in. Sure enough, two seconds later, the knock came and Charlotte yelled for him to enter.

"Well, you look pretty," he said as if she looked completely different. "I haven't seen that dress before."

"Thanks," she replied blushing as she let him kiss her hello. She did look different. Normally, he saw her in her softball clothes or jeans and a cardigan. This dress was definitely sexier than her usual style and she was thankful to Sarah for making her buy it. "Should we get going? Where are we going by the way?"

"It's a surprise. I figured we can call a cab tonight since it's in North Beach and parking there is hell," he said following her to the door. "Besides, as much as I love you in heels, I don't want you to take it out on me when your feet hurt after walking."

Charlotte laughed knowing he was spot on. "Thanks, I appreciate your thoughtfulness."

Once they were downstairs, they walked a half block to Franklin Street to catch a cab. Successful after about five minutes, they were finally on their way to dinner. Snuggling in the back seat, Charlotte was completely happy in this moment. Ben looked extremely good in his dark jeans and black V-neck sweater and he smelled even better. He never wore cologne, but his natural scent was so attractive to Charlotte. He was very present in the moment as if the last few months were all in her imagination. Feeling a little guilty for being selfish, she settled in next to him letting him put his arm around her. This is what she's wanted in a boyfriend. Even as this moment seemed perfect, she still couldn't fully believe it was permanent. She couldn't quite let those feelings of insecurity go.

The cab came to a stop in front of a restaurant Charlotte had seen a million times but never patronized. She heard great things about Trattoria Contadina and was very excited to finally get her chance to find out if it stood up to its reputation. A small and intimate restaurant, it definitely had the Italian cozy feeling going for it. A teeny bar in the front and several tables in the window, it was the kind of place locals bragged about and tourists would never think to try.

Ben had obviously made reservations because they were seated at a coveted table next to the big glass windows overlooking Mason Street. Settling in, the server handed them each a menu and wine list.

"Are you up for a bottle of wine?" Ben asked.

"Sure. What kind?" Charlotte knew Ben wasn't into wine and neither was she, meaning it was the blind leading the blind in selection.

Once Ben ordered a bottle they both agreed upon and the server poured it, Charlotte took a sip feeling her insides warm up. The weather was cool and foggy outside, but inside the atmosphere was warm, romantic and cozy. Charlotte now understood why this restaurant was reviewed well.

Twenty minutes later, they ordered dinner and had just handed the menus back to the waiter when Charlotte felt the door open and the energy surrounding her change. She didn't even have to look to know Trevor just walked in the door—with a date. Her instincts wanted to fix her hair and put on her lipstick, but she was trapped because he was going to notice her any second. When she looked up and saw Trevor with Michelle, her heart sank and she was surprised at the negative reaction she felt towards seeing them together. She was even more surprised when she realized it was jealousy.

Shaking, she waited for Trevor to see her but he and Michelle were quickly led to a table in the far back and they walked right by her.

"You look like you've seen a ghost," Ben said concerned. "Do you know them?"

"Actually, yes. The guy is Trevor Sheldon and I went to college with him and the woman he's with is the woman I just interviewed with last week."

Charlotte followed Ben's gaze and they both watched Trevor and Michelle sit down at their table. "Stop staring," she said not wanting Trevor to know they were being watched.

"Wow. That's a huge coincidence. Small world, huh? Do you want to go say hi?"

Charlotte didn't want Ben to feel her escalating panic. "No. Not now. Maybe I'll say hi later."

Without further explanation, Charlotte turned the subject back to Ben's job hoping it would distract him—and prevent her from looking at the other couple. Unfortunately, Charlotte couldn't concentrate on a word Ben was saying as she watched Trevor out of her peripheral vision. *So he is dating Michelle. Maybe they were just out as friends? Doubt it.* Friends don't make Saturday night reservations as a romantic restaurant. Sneaking a glance at them, Michelle was laughing at something Trevor said and Charlotte could tell she was very comfortable in his company. Watching her as she reached across the table and grabbed his hand, the friend theory went out the window. Why did it bother her? It was like she caught him cheating on her and yet she knew these feelings were inappropriate. Why wouldn't he have a girlfriend? Trevor was a total catch and she had been so naïve to think he would still be single. Turning her thoughts and focus back to Ben, she knew she was a very lucky girl and she felt extremely guilty for even thinking about Trevor.

She noticed immediately when Ben got quiet and stared past her outside the window. She didn't want to turn around for fear there was someone standing there but then she realized he was trying to gather his thoughts.

As if he read her mind, Ben reached over and grabbed Charlotte's hand. Noticing the nervousness on his face and his heavy breathing, Charlotte's heart dropped like it always did right before bad news. He looked genuinely uncomfortable. *Oh no, is he going to break up with me? No, No, No—not here, Ben. Not in front of Trevor and Michelle.* Embarrassed, she pulled her hand back and poured more wine hoping for the distraction. A thought occurred to her as she waited for Ben to drop the bomb—although it would be embarrassing; she was almost relieved he was breaking up with her. The luxury of being single flashed through her mind and the constant worry about Ben and his stress went away. She forced herself to focus on Ben and the moment and not let her mind move to Trevor.

"Ben..."

"Shh, Charlotte, please. I have something I want to ask you," he said as he pulled what looked like a ring box from his jacket pocket that was hanging on back of the chair. *Oh no.* "I've been through a lot over the past year, and with you in my life, I got through it. You're the kindest and prettiest person I know and I just can't picture life without you," he paused. *OH MY GOD, he's proposing—not breaking up. What do I do? I can't say no in such a public place.* Stunned, Charlotte held her breath hoping Ben wouldn't say it. "Will you marry me?"

It was like slow motion as Ben opened the ring box and out came a sparkly solitaire diamond in what she guessed was a platinum or white gold setting. It was very plain and not what she expected Ben to pick out. "Please don't worry about this ring. It's a plain setting on purpose because I know you and you would want to be with me when we picked the setting. The diamond is very real, however."

Charlotte was speechless and her mind went completely blank. Looking at Ben and then the ring, she knew deep down she should be ecstatic. It was the one moment most women dreamed of from birth. But for her, despite the perfect guy and the perfect romantic restaurant setting, it felt more like a noose wrapping around her neck. Her world shifted and she no longer felt like a thirty-something girl, but a thirty-something woman facing a major decision that would become permanent. *What should I do?* She didn't really want to say yes—actually, she didn't want to say yes at all, but she didn't want to say no. She couldn't hurt Ben after what he just said to her. Watching him as he waited for her answer, she knew she had another split second to decide. *Say yes, Charlotte, just say yes. You can deal with it all later.*

"Yes," she said with what she hoped was the perfect smile. "Yes, I'll marry you."

The table to her left clapped catching the attention of the table to the right and the wait staff. As the applause grew louder, she could feel Trevor staring at her as if they were connected by some magic force. Ben stood up halfway and leaned over to kiss her on the mouth. "Now we need to celebrate. How about some dessert?"

"Sounds great," Charlotte said thinking something chocolate and fattening was just what she needed. Looking down at the ring, she used all her mental strength to avoid looking at Trevor and pretending she didn't know he was there. Through her peripheral vision, she saw him get up and make his way over to her table. *Oh, please no.*

"What a small world," Trevor said when he approached.

"Trevor!" Charlotte said a little too loudly as she tried to act surprised. "What are you doing here?"

"Apparently nothing as exciting as you," he replied nodding at her ring. "I guess congratulations are in order?"

"Yes, they are," Charlotte replied introducing him to Ben.

"Congrats," Trevor said to Ben shaking his hand. "You're a lucky man."

"Thank you very much. So you went to college with Charlotte?" Ben asked

"Yes. We worked for the radio station, KCPR," Charlotte interrupted.

"I trained her," Trevor said winking at Charlotte.

"Trained by the best," Charlotte giggled. *Is he at all upset I'm engaged?* Charlotte couldn't tell if he was hiding it or genuinely happy for her. Why wouldn't he be happy for her? It wasn't like he was in love with her. The thought sounded ridiculous to Charlotte.

"Well, I should get back to my table," Trevor said.

"Is that Michelle with you?" Charlotte asked looking over at Trevor's table.

"Yes, it is."

"Are you and your date close to being finished? Charlotte and I were going to head up to Moose's after we pay the bill. You should join us," Ben suggested.

We are? That was news to Charlotte, but she
just nodded along. Seeing the hesitation in Trevor's
eyes, she expected him to say no, but her heart skipped
hoping he might just say yes. Everything felt surreal
and confusing. She was engaged to Ben yet she wanted
to be in the company of Trevor. The world she knew
last week just turned upside down and backwards.
Maybe she was just shocked at the proposal and seeing
Trevor tonight, forcing her status quo out of balance.
Someday she will look back on this day and laugh—
maybe telling the story to her grandchildren. Looking
over at Ben, she noticed just how blue his eyes actually
were reminding her of a Hawaiian lagoon in the bright
sunshine. His skin glowed as if he had just run a mile
and his smile was deep and sincere. Ben made friends
so easily with his genuine nature and it never failed to
surprise her when he mentioned meeting new people.
The ring on her finger started feeling heavy as she
glanced down at it. *What is wrong with me? Why am I
questioning my love for this man?* They may have had
some rough months sexually, but he was good to her and
she was proud to be with him. *Charlotte, get your
priorities straight. Stop thinking about the man from
your past and start thinking about the man of your
future.* Her heart shifted and it finally let Ben
completely take over. She was engaged to Ben and he
was the one for her because she loved him and he loved
her.

Then the unexpected happened—Trevor
accepted the invite for a drink as long as Michelle
agreed. Quickly snapping out of her own head,
Charlotte looked up at Trevor. *What? He was actually
going to meet us out?* Her gut flip flopped at the
thought of Ben and Trevor becoming friends. What if
they hit it off and became best friends and Trevor was
the best man at her wedding? What if Trevor and

Michelle get engaged and she and Ben end up in the wedding party? What if she and Ben don't make it to the altar and Trevor and Ben stay friends? *Good lord, Ben puts a ring on my finger and suddenly I'm a puddle of neurotic instability. Carrie Bradshaw would be proud.*

The biggest *what if* worried Charlotte the most. What if Trevor tells Ben about what happened to her in college and how she and Trevor ended their relationship because of it? That particular thought turned her stomach as she watched Trevor walk back to his table.

Six

Waiting for the check to arrive, Trevor finished his wine as he glanced over the table Charlotte and Ben were seated at just minutes earlier.

"Are we really going out with them for another drink?" Michelle asked bringing Trevor back to attention.

"Do you mind? I just thought it would be nice to hang out with another couple."

"I don't mind but I was really hoping to get you home and naked as soon as possible," Michelle said with a grin.

Trevor didn't mind the idea of just going to bed and he now wondered if agreeing to meet Charlotte and Ben was a mistake. He wasn't even sure why he said yes to the invitation. His instinct was to say no thank you, but somehow seeing Charlotte in the purple dress with her hair loose down her back changed his mind. Maybe it was a bit masochistic, but he wanted to know more about Ben and why Charlotte was with him. It wasn't that he disliked Ben—it was just the opposite. Ben came across as very genuine and cool and Trevor had no problem thinking he could easily hang with him for a few beers if they met randomly in another situation.

Charlotte's engagement came out of left field. He had prepared himself for finding out she was dating someone, but she didn't give off the impression she was close to being married. *Why didn't you mention Ben last week? Wouldn't that be something you would be very excited to tell me?* Trevor was really confused at Charlotte's calm exterior when he congratulated her. It was as if she'd been caught in an awkward situation and she couldn't excuse herself. Something seemed *off* and Trevor would bet his life she wasn't in love with Ben. She might think she is, but her reaction wasn't the normal reaction of a woman who'd just received a proposal from the man she loved. His sister wouldn't shut up about it for weeks when her boyfriend proposed and yet Charlotte seemed almost catatonic as if the whole idea of marriage rocked her world and not in a good way.

Once the bill came and he paid it, Trevor escorted Michelle out to the street and let her grab his hand as they walked down the street to Washington Square Park. North Beach was his favorite part of the city for dining. The energy from the Italian restaurants and coffee shops that lined Columbus Avenue was relaxed, yet vibrant, as everyone enjoyed wine, pasta, and cappuccinos.

After cutting through the park, they arrived at
Moose's. It was busy tonight with one group standing
outside smoking and another waiting in the bar for their
turn at a table in the dining room. Finding Charlotte and
Ben at a tall table in the center, he walked up practically
shouting over the noise to say hello.

Trevor didn't miss how close Ben was standing
next to Charlotte with his arm around her lower back.
Possessive much, Ben?

"Hey, you both made it," Ben shouted as he
introduced himself to Michelle. Trevor watched as
Charlotte said hello to Michelle and mentioned how she
couldn't wait to start her new job.

"What do you want to drink?" Ben asked the
table. "I'll get this round."

Trevor followed Ben to the bar so he could help
carry back the drinks. The bartenders were working hard
and that meant it was going to be awhile.

Trevor listened while Ben small talked. First it
was about the weather, then it was about baseball, and
then Ben finally asked about Charlotte.

"I'm sorry I was a little caught off guard back at
the restaurant. Charlotte never mentioned you, but it
sounds like you both worked at the radio station? I
guess that makes sense since she was journalism major."

"Yes, but she was also a DJ. That's actually how
we met—I was her mentor," Trevor answered hoping he
didn't dig any further.

"That must have been fun—to be on the radio.
Charlotte didn't tell me she'd been a DJ. I think I love
her just a little more, now."

That surprised Trevor, but then again, after what happened to Charlotte during college, he wouldn't be surprised if she didn't talk about it much. "She was really good. We were both journalism majors so we had a lot in common," Trevor said knowing Ben wanted that one particular question answered—had they dated.

"I'll have to ask her about it," Ben laughed. "I guess since we're officially engaged, we need to start getting to really know everything about each other, right?"

"I think that is probably a good idea. She can be a bit of a loner sometimes, keeping her thoughts to herself. I do remember that about her."

"So true," Ben said waving his credit card for attention and getting none. "It's going to take forever to get our drinks."

Trevor noticed Ben wave over to Charlotte who was staring at both of them with a funny look on her face. What was she worried about—he would spill all her secrets to Ben? Apparently Ben didn't know anything about and Trevor was somewhat disappointed by it. He wanted to have been important in Charlotte's life. For all he knew, she didn't even consider him an ex-boyfriend. Looking at Charlotte, he smiled as he watched her pull out her lipstick and nervously re-apply it. That one particular movement made him think back to the first night they kissed.

There were two nights from college permanently branded into his memory and that night was the first. The night of the KCPR party he hosted at his condo. The smell of alcohol and a vision of Charlotte putting on her lipstick pulled that particular memory out of a lock box in his mind.

He flashed back to his crowded condo where a keg flowed filling red plastic cups with cheap beer, loud music thumped above the voices, and he saw Charlotte from his upstairs porch as she approached the front door with Jamie and Cameron.

"Who's that?" Trevor's roommate Evan asked as he nudged Trevor in the arm. "The tall blond is a hottie."

"That's Charlotte, Jamie and Cameron." Trevor said now flying high as a kite from the sight of Charlotte below him. "I think Jamie has a boyfriend. Too bad for you, loser."

"So that's the Charlotte you keep talking about," Evan said. "You're really into her."

Trevor was surprised Evan even knew about Charlotte. "How would you know? And I'm not that into her."

"Bull. Practically every sentence out of your mouth mentions her name. 'Oh, Charlotte and I played this on the air today' or 'Charlotte and I hung out at the station doing this and that.' It's so obvious because you talk about her all the time."

"I had no idea," Trevor said, fully catching the change in his roommate's vocal inflection when he repeated Trevor's words. *Am I that pathetic?*

"Well, why are you standing here with me, dumbass. Go talk to her."

Laughing, Trevor walked away to greet the new guests as they walked up the stairs to the living room. The party was full of KCPR people and a few of Evan's fraternity buddies who showed up for the free beer. His third roommate Ethan was out of town for the weekend which Trevor didn't mind considering they didn't have much in common. KCPR parties were always fun and brought such an eclectic crowd especially with Evan's friends mixed in the group. Although KCPR and the Greek system didn't mesh, Trevor and Evan got along very well and were close friends. They always joked how opposite the KCPR crowd was to the Greek crowd. The radio crowd, with its alternative college lifestyle, often meant lots of tattoos, piercings, concerts and a general "non-conformist" attitude. Trevor always laughed at that thought because weren't they actually conforming to being different? The Greeks, on the other hand, spent a lot of time blending together over traditional activities that involved dressing up, playing sports, and singing weird songs in the university union. As different as they were, both crowds had a couple things in common—studying and partying. Trevor met Evan his second year of school when they were partnered up in physics lab. One night after studying late, they went out for beers, got completely wasted, but bonded and remained friends ever since.

Seeing Jamie first, followed by Cameron and then Charlotte, Trevor's heart did a flip when his eyes met Charlotte's. The light blue t-shirt she wore brought out her eyes and her blond hair. Apparently, she had been to the beach earlier because she had that glow she always got when she spent time in the sun.

"Hi ladies—welcome. I'm so glad made it," Trevor said hugging Jamie and Cameron first and saving Charlotte for last so he could hug her a little longer. "I'm really glad you came," he whispered in her ear.

"It was between you and my sociology paper and I decided I shouldn't have to torture myself on a Saturday night," Charlotte said. They were standing alone now because Cameron and Jamie found their friends at the keg.

"Can I get you a beer?" he asked.

"Sure," Charlotte said looking around and waving to her other friends at the party.

Trevor had hosted a few of these parties in the past which lasted well into the early morning and he always got laid. Tonight was going to be different, but he was okay with that.

Handing Charlotte a beer, he walked her to the empty porch where they could talk quietly.

"Cool condo, Trev," she said as she sipped her beer.

"Thanks. I like it."

"Which bedroom is yours?"

"The one downstairs. I love it because I have my own bathroom," he said.

Charlotte nodded. "I love these condos. I wouldn't mind moving here next year. They seem so fun and they are really close to campus."

"The grocery store is right down the street and so is the liquor store."

"That's really good to know," she laughed and paused. "I bet you're going to really miss living here when you graduate."

"No doubt about that."

The conversation continued on a surface level for the next fifteen minutes which sort of bugged Trevor. Things were never this awkward at the station when they were together. *Is she nervous because she's at my place? What if she isn't into me? Why is she so quiet right now?*

After awhile, Charlotte decided to go inside to mingle with her friends. Hesitant to let her go, he tried to think of ways to keep her out on the porch, but realized he needed to be the host and not ignore his guests.

The party continued inside with everyone's conversation mingling over the music blaring in the background. Trevor was definitely feeling the alcohol as his buzz grew deeper. He couldn't stop staring at Charlotte as she laughed with Jamie and Cameron.

"Are you going for it tonight?" Evan said as he stood next to Trevor. "You're not going to be around forever."

"I know," Trevor sighed. "I'm not sure if she is that into me."

"Are you kidding? I've seen her watching you when you haven't been looking."

"You're lying."

"Why would I lie about that, dude? You've never had problems with the ladies before so this one must be special. Get over yourself and go for it."

Evan was right; Trevor was wasting time pining for her instead of making moves. He didn't have much longer in school and once he graduated he would be leaving San Luis Obispo. She was almost done with her weekly training and just had to do a final show on her own after Thanksgiving and he would officially be done as her mentor. For the first time, he was actually scared of rejection. He was only rejected once in his life and that was in high school when he asked Amy Halleck to Homecoming. He was crushed when she denied his invitation, but it was nothing compared to what it would feel like if Charlotte rejected him now.

Okay, its time. Just do it, Trevor. Make a move. He was just drunk enough to make a move but not too drunk where he would make a fool out of himself. He could see Charlotte was buzzing because she was giggling uncontrollably with everyone.

Making his way over to her, he stood next to her for a few seconds until she noticed him.

"Hi!" she said.

"Hey," he replied gathering up his courage. "I was wondering if you wanted to see the downstairs."

"Oh," she said surprised. "Sure."

Leading her down the stairs, Trevor was already nervous. *What am I possibly going to say to her? Should I just kiss her? Would she get mad at me?* He could feel the courage he had a few moments ago start slipping away as he walked into his bedroom. Thank goodness no one was in there using it as couples often do at parties.

"So this is the famous Trevor Sheldon man cave," Charlotte said with a giggle.

"What do you think?" he replied as he turned to look at her. Any awkwardness he'd felt upstairs had disappeared. He smiled at Charlotte's interest in his pictures especially when she pointed out a couple with her in them.

"I can't believe you have pictures of me up in your bedroom," she said looking at him now. The air got still and he could feel the electricity coursing between them.

Okay, this is it. "Why can't you believe it?" he asked in his most serious voice as he moved closer to her.

"I don't know," Charlotte said looking back at the pictures again. "I just wouldn't think you would put up pictures like these."

She did have a point. He had three pictures of just him and her in the studio and at a KCPR event. The rest were of family and group shots. If she didn't get that he had a thing for her now, she would never get it unless he out right just told her or kissed her on the mouth. Either way, this was his chance. He had to make a move now or it would never happen. The liquid courage certainly helped his confidence and he didn't fight it as it as he waited for her to turn around and face him. *Turn around, Charlotte. Come on.*

"Charlie," he whispered taking another step towards her. She turned around to face him but stood completely still as if she was debating to run. "You're so pretty."

He couldn't help but put a strand of hair behind her ear as he stood as close to her as he could possibly get. The look of surprise on her face was priceless. *Hadn't he been obvious with his feelings all this time? How could she not know he wanted her so badly? Even his friends knew apparently.* His body started responding as he stood in front of her. They were so close he could feel her breath. The electricity continued to flow between them and it was like a magnetic pull that forced his feet to stay planted where they were. Finally, he made the move by cupping her face in his hands. *God, she's beautiful.* He could smell her scent through the beer—the same scent that turned him on so much in the studio. It was flowery, but clean. *Ok, big guy...now or never.* Bending his head down, he finally just went for it and kissed her. It was a peck at first—he didn't want to overwhelm her by forcing his tongue down her throat. He wanted to do it right. Never had he put so much pressure on himself for a silly kiss. Normally this part was the easiest but this kiss was anything but silly.

He found out her feelings about being kissed as soon as he pulled away. Charlotte hadn't backed away nor did she run screaming from the room. She was the one that went in for the next kiss with more intensity than the first.

And that's when the fireworks went off. Skyrocketing all around him, he never in his life felt a kiss like this one. The blood rushed to his groin and all he wanted to do was pull her body against him hard and get her clothes off. *Oh my God.*

He wasn't sure how much time passed, but when their lips parted, he noticed how plump and swollen Charlotte's were and it made her look so innocent and intoxicating. "I've wanted to do that for a very long time."

"Me, too," Charlotte said, her mouth curving into a huge smile. "But I don't want to go any further right now."

At first he thought she meant she didn't want to go any further dating him after tonight, but then he realized she didn't want to go any further physically— meaning kissing was all that was going to happen. "That's okay, we can take our time. I'm not going to rush you."

"I don't want this to hurt our friendship," she said earnestly.

Trevor kissed her again gently and then paused. "I don't know what will happen, but I want to try."

He remembered not returning to the party as he spent the rest of the night with Charlotte in his bed talking and kissing. No one got naked and he didn't get laid, but he was happier than he ever imagined just waking up with her next to him in the morning.

Now, as he watched Ben order the drinks, this girl was back in his life and it was like she never left. Even though their relationship ended about as quickly as it started, it was still more memorable to him than his other long term girlfriends. One of his biggest regrets in life was leaving San Luis Obispo without truly telling her how he felt. Now he had the chance to find out exactly what happened from her perspective and it made him anxious. *Well, Charlotte, now that we work together and you're in my life again, you're going to tell me exactly what happened and why you shut me out of your life.*

Seven

A month had passed since Charlotte went from single girl with a boyfriend to engaged woman with a fiancé. Girlfriends got engaged every minute of every day and it never occurred to her the heaviness of the decision. The pictures of brides in magazines made it look so carefree and happy as if this was the best decision in the world. Why was she feeling so different? Why wasn't she happy and elated and full of picture perfect smiles? Along with starting a new job, Charlotte felt as if a stranger took over her body and was making decisions for her. Everything was the same and yet everything was different.

Sitting at her computer with a glass of wine, she toggled between Facebook and bridal sites while listening to her iPod. Researching wedding information completely overwhelmed her. So many details and lists to make, she couldn't keep them straight—the wedding location, number of guests, flowers, gifts, catering, alcohol, invitations, band tryouts, accommodations, and that was just the tip of the iceberg. It was no wonder brides turned into bridezillas.

Charlotte did take pleasure in one part of the process. Secretly addicted to the TV show *Say Yes to the Dress*—she couldn't wait to try on wedding dresses. She and Ali obsessed over the show primarily because of the drama that surrounded picking the perfect dress. Charlotte often shook her head at the price people paid to wear a dress for a few hours. She often calculated the hourly rate of the dress only to realize it was more than she paid for a month's rent.

As she sipped her wine, Sweet Caroline by Neil Diamond started and she smiled thinking about how she and Ben had met. It was at the Final Final after her softball game and he was there with his buddies watching the college basketball games. The bar was crowded and crazy but they found each other at the jukebox choosing songs together. She had picked Sweet Caroline and when it played, the whole bar started singing including Ben who was a few beers into the night. She admired his taste in music after he picked some tunes by Social Distortion and The Ramones and when he invited her back to his table, she accepted. Once Ben and his friends discovered she knew her way around sports, they started calling her the perfect woman and teased her about marrying her. Charlotte spent most of the time blushing and giggling because she could feel the chemistry between her and Ben. It didn't hurt he was good looking and funny, too. After the games ended and the bar cleared, Charlotte was even more impressed when Ben stayed to talk one on one with her. After a while, her girlfriends interrupted, bursting the tiny little bubble she and Ben shared for the last hour. Charlotte felt relieved when Ben's charm won them over instantly.

Her friends were right, Ben was the perfect boyfriend. He was easy going, attentive and he courted her perfectly—flowers after the second date, taking it slow physically, and calling her when he said he would. Charlotte had never been out with someone who treated her so well. With her past boyfriends, except for Trevor, she was never completely comfortable. They made her over analytical with each phone call or lack thereof. Ben was the complete opposite and she never had to wonder if he was really into her—she just knew it.

But after that awkward first time they had sex, things changed. The honeymoon was over and the sheen of the perfect boyfriend faded. He still called when he said he would and never made her feel like he didn't want to be with her except when it came to sex. He just never seemed interested.

Ever since the proposal, Ben was back to being disinterested in sex. Things were great for about a week afterwards and Charlotte thought maybe the problem resolved itself, but that wasn't the case. She couldn't remember the last time he leaned in for a random kiss or just hugged her.

What should she do? Ben was such a good person and she loved him but did she really want to marry him? The ring still felt heavy on her left hand and she felt uncomfortable when people made a big deal about it. When other people brought up her engagement, it meant it was really happening. Her emotions were so conflicted and she couldn't figure them out. Some of it was general anxiety because it was a big decision and a lifetime commitment. She was sure everyone experienced those feelings at some point during an engagement, but some of it she knew was more than just cold feet. Ali told her she was just overthinking it and to relax. Then Charlotte reminded Ali she wouldn't take the plunge and move in with Rob.

Then there was Trevor. When she started her job, he poked around a few times to say hi. It was like any other coworker relationship but there was that cloud hanging overhead reminding them they had a past together they weren't talking about. She found it weird that Trevor and Ben had become friends since meeting that night at the restaurant. There had been a few more double dates and in all honesty, Charlotte enjoyed them. She and Michelle were getting closer which both excited and scared Charlotte. She liked Michelle a lot, but she was afraid her past feelings for Trevor would eventually come out and jeopardize everything—her relationship with Ben, her friendship with Trevor and most importantly her job. Sometimes she felt she was caught in a spider web where the more she tried to sort things out, the more she got stuck.

But what exactly where her feelings for Trevor?

She wasn't sure as she softly sang the words to *Edge of the Ocean* by Ivy, a song she put back in her rotation when Trevor came back into her life. She often thought of Trevor when this song came on—it had been their song in college and he played it on his show dedicating it to her even after she stopped talking to him. Unfortunately, it always brought back the guilty feelings of how she had treated him. Her behavior back then had surprised even herself, but it was never about Trevor but rather about that night and how traumatizing it was to be around Trevor afterwards. The memories flooded back as if it all happened yesterday.

It was a Saturday night and she was about to start what was the final test to becoming a DJ—completing a full show on her own without the help of Trevor. Since it started after midnight, she would be the only person at the station after the DJ before her left her to take over.

Since it was a party night, she was receiving quite a few calls from drunken partiers who had returned home from the bars after closing. It was fun and kept her awake and her adrenaline kicking. Of course she played all her favorite songs feeling proud when she got to announce them over the air and chat with her "audience". She even dedicated Edge of the Ocean to her mentor and "friend" Trevor who she knew was staying awake listening and would probably be waiting for her in his car downstairs in the parking lot when she was done. He couldn't stand her walking back to the dorm alone and since she didn't have a car, he insisted he drive her. Ever since that night they kissed at his party, they'd been inseparable and Charlotte was giddy about it. She was definitely falling in love with him if she hadn't already.

Everything seemed to go smoothly until about three in the morning when she started receiving one ring phone calls. The same one ring phone calls she received for the past month in her dorm room. Someone would call and hang up after just one ring and Charlotte couldn't figure out who was doing it since there was no caller ID on her dorm phone. Star sixty-nine didn't work either. When it went on into the early hours of the morning, she forced Ali to go with her to the university phone company to find out if there was a paper trail. Unfortunately, the numbers were all from pay phones around the campus. Who would do that and why?

It continued for weeks to the point where Charlotte felt threatened and couldn't sleep at night. Finally, she and Ali got permission to switch dorm rooms, but even that didn't stop the calls from coming. Charlotte wanted to crawl out of her skin at the sound of a phone ringing—even when it wasn't hers.

Trevor was attuned to her anxiety and Charlotte could tell he felt helpless. He begged her to stay with him at his place, but she didn't feel it was necessary. She finally just turned the ringer off and let it go to voicemail picking up messages when she felt like it. Ali wasn't too cool with that idea, but knew it was the only way they both could keep their sanity. In the end, it was probably just someone playing a cruel prank. It was also a good excuse to ask her parents for a cell phone.

She should have listened to Trevor that night at dinner when he suggested he be at the station with her.

"I'm worried about you being alone," he had said as he picked up his cheeseburger.

"Thank you for your concern, but I'll be fine. You can come pick me up afterwards if you want to," she replied thinking it was almost cute how concerned he was. "I have to grow up sometime, Trevor, and you can't be everywhere with me."

"I know, but I would feel a lot better if you had someone there with you. I don't like how they let girls run shows overnight alone."

"I'll make sure to lock the door to the station. Does that make you feel better?"

"A little. But I'll be there when you're done to take you back to my place."

"Just make sure you don't fall asleep and forget," Charlotte laughed picturing Trevor drinking several cups of coffee and cokes just to stay awake.

Charlotte had locked the door. She remembered that much. She also remembered pulling the music for the night and filling her water bottle at the drinking fountain. After that—the next thing she remembered was seeing Trevor sleeping in a chair next to her bed in the hospital.

"Charlotte," he whispered when her eyes opened. It took a long few seconds to understand what she was looking at, but it was Trevor's face framed by an overhead light that made him look almost angelic. Nothing felt familiar and her head throbbed. Was she dreaming? Was she at Trevor's house? Trying to move, her body completely resisted and that's when she realized she had something attached to the back of her hand—the needle to an IV. *I'm in the hospital? What, Why?* Everything seemed so loud and confusing and she felt so weak—as if she had been run over by a car.

"Trevor, what happened?' she whispered, alarmed at how much strength it took just to say those words.

"You're in the hospital, hon."

"Why?"

"Someone hurt you."

Even through the pain and the haze, she could see his expression—guilt mixed with sadness. Trying to recall what happened, her memory couldn't come up with anything after filling up her water bottle as if it was trying to protect her from the truth. The clearest memory she had was the walk from her dorm to the station. The walk to the station had been memorable because the Santa Ana winds were blowing, highly unusual for that time of the year, and she had felt like a complete mess as her hair blew all over the place and the dust stuck to her lips and teeth.

Someone hurt me? Hurt me how? Why? Who?

For a moment she wasn't sure she even believed him. San Luis Obispo, let alone the Cal Poly campus, was fairly safe. She never felt threatened as she walked around campus at night alone. She had a bit of street smarts considering her dad had been a cop when she was growing up, so she knew her boundaries and trusted her gut. She hadn't felt anything out of the ordinary that night as she entered the station.

"Oh wait, I think I do remember something," she said closing her eyes and willing her brain to let it loose. Something *was* off about that night.

Phone calls popped into her mind and then she remembered all the crank calls she and Ali had been receiving the weeks prior. They must be related. Visualizing the station empty late at night as it would have been, she could hear a song playing in the background. Suddenly, a memory burst through like a lightning bolt.

"I remember calling you to come to the station," she said as he nodded a confirmation.

"Yes you did call me. You said you felt spooked and needed me to come early while you finished up your show."

Spooked was a complete understatement. She was feeling okay until about two hours in when she started to feel like she was being watched. Her mind started playing tricks on her and she couldn't help but think about every horror movie she'd ever seen.

"I had to go to the bathroom."

"So you left the station for a few minutes?" Trevor asked.

"I didn't want to because I knew I couldn't shut the door behind me or I'd be locked out. I put on the song *Sound* by James because it was really long." It was the same song she could hear in her head now. "I remember thinking the hallway was very quiet and everyone I knew was probably sleeping."

"The smart people were," Trevor said softly and Charlotte knew it was his attempt to make her smile. "So you went to the bathroom. What happened?"

"I was washing my hands and I heard the volume of the music turned up super high as if someone was in the station playing with the dial."

That moment she heard the volume increase made her jump out of her skin. It was so unexpected and random.

"As I walked back to the studio, I half expected to see you there with a beer or something. But the station was completely empty. No one was there and yet the dial was physically turned up all the way."

Charlotte remembered moving past the feeling of being spooked to genuinely scared, and once that feeling settled in, there was nothing she could tell herself to make it go away.

"That's when I wondered where you were and what was taking you so long."

"I'm so sorry. I stopped by the 7-11 to get a soda. I was really tired and needed something. Now I feel so guilty."

"Don't. I probably should have called the police."

She had thought about calling campus police, but decided against it. What would she say? *Please check out the building because the volume turned up high on its own and I have a bad gut feeling?*

"But that's all I remember. Nothing else after that," she said feeling strange. A block of her memory was hiding and it was incredibly unsettling. It was there, she just couldn't recall it. Whoever hit her over the head and bruised her face was never found and that was worse than anything. When the news broke about her assault, she was interviewed by the campus police. She told them everything she could remember but when the word got out around the station and the Mustang Daily newspaper, she refused to talk about the details. She was embarrassed and humiliated and seeing people read about her on the way to class wasn't going to help her move forward. She just wanted it to all go away.

Thank god the news was cyclical because people lost interest in her story once a lesbian volleyball sex scandal broke a couple weeks later.

Her parents, of course, came down to school and wanted to pull her out, but she convinced them she could get through finals and they would discuss it over the holiday break.

The physical bruises faded by Christmas, but the emotional bruises remained and she honestly wasn't excited to return back to school after New Year's. The week after the attack, she tried to reconcile why Trevor had taken the time to make a stop before coming to the station. Part of her was upset he hadn't hurried, but the other part knew she was being hard on him. In the following days and weeks, however, she sometimes wondered if Trevor was behind the attack. *Could he have done this to me?*

It was a week after returning from the break when Charlotte decided she needed distance from Trevor. He was suffocating her with worry when she just needed space to get back to normal.

"I just need to be alone for a while, Trevor," she said when he was visiting her in her dorm room.

"But why? Did I do something to upset you?" Trevor asked sounding sad and very confused. Charlotte felt very guilty considering he just wanted her to be happy again like she was before the attack. She'd come to terms he was not the one who hurt her because she'd always knew in her gut Trevor could never do something so cruel. She couldn't even believe she'd considered the idea. Charlotte felt so bad for doing this to him, but she really did need the time to separate herself from what happened. She didn't want to give KCPR up completely because she loved being there, but she needed to kind of start over.

"No, you didn't do anything. Honestly, I just need some space to figure my head out. I'm overwhelmed being back and need to focus on classes and getting through my graveyard shift this quarter."

Trevor looked like he was about to cry and she'd never seen him so withdrawn and sad—it broke her heart. But she couldn't lie to him. She wanted to be honest. He deserved that.

"I understand," he said as he hugged her. "I'm so sorry, Charlotte. I love you, you know."

Charlotte tensed in his hug. That was the first time he told her he loved her. That was the first time anyone other than her family said the L word. It felt strange and very intimidating. She tried to say it back, but it felt alien and weird. She didn't know how she felt at all. She really liked Trevor and loved the relationship, but saying "I love you" was that next step she was scared to take.

"I wish I could say the same, but…"

"I know—you don't have to say anything," Trevor said as he stroked her hair. "It's just when I found you on the ground so hurt, I knew right then and there how I felt."

The hug continued in silence for a few more seconds before Charlotte felt she needed to end it. "Trevor, I wish I could say it back to you. God, I wish I could. Honestly, though, I'm so confused about everything right now. I'm starting to feel like I need you too much because I'm scared about being alone at the station and scared to walk around campus at night. I need to get over this fear or I'm going to lose my mind."

"It's okay to need me. I want you need me and I want to help you."

"But I don't want to be with you because I'm scared to be alone. It's not fair to you or to us. I need to feel safe again but that will only happen on my own."

"You will feel safe again. This, too, shall pass. It was just a random thing that happened to you. Even the police said that."

Charlotte sighed still feeling it was not random, but rather a calculated act and done on purpose. The trust in her friends was hanging by a thread. Except for Ali, who she knew was not a part of it because she was out of town that night; she felt she couldn't trust anyone. They were all suspects. Even people she didn't know were suspects and it could have been a stalker for all she knew. But she had no idea why she would even have a stalker. She hadn't been on the air long enough for it to be a listener. The police didn't seem too concerned about the crank calls, either, so Charlotte put the stalker angle to the back of her mind. It didn't escape her, however, how the crank calls stopped after that night. She and Ali never received another hang up ever again.

It took all her strength after the breakup not to call Trevor. She missed him so much and not having him in her life was misery. Every week she did her shift on the air, she wondered if he was listening and if he missed her as much as she missed him. Part of her felt sad he hadn't fought harder for her. Apparently, Trevor got over loving her quickly because he moved on to dating Katie Bishop, another DJ, pretty quickly. He might as well have rubbed salt into her broken heart.

How could he go from loving her to dating someone so fast and someone she knew? Katie was a pudgy goth girl with a weird sense of style who never even acted interested in what was happening at the station, let alone with Trevor. During Charlotte's many jealous internal rages, she envisioned Katie burning cute puppies at an altar to Satan but then would push it all out of her mind knowing she was the one who let Trevor go and Katie wasn't at fault for wanting to date him.

The whole situation broke her heart, but her emotions were too paralyzed to make amends. Sometimes she would let the anger at him flow. *Why did he have to stop for soda when I needed him? Why didn't he fight harder for me? Why did he move on so quickly?* Charlotte was relieved and upset at the same time when Trevor eventually graduated that spring and moved completely out of her life. She regretted not talking to him about her feelings and why she cut off their relationship, but she just wanted to let it all go and move on. By then, she was used to being on her own and single. She hadn't dated anyone, but she wasn't scared to be at the station alone anymore.

Now, on this perfect Fall Sunday afternoon sitting in her apartment overlooking Russian Hill, Fort Mason and The Golden Gate Bridge, and listening to the song *Long Time Coming* by The Delays, she knew she was going to have to face those memories head on again. The irony of the song versus her long overdue conversation with Trevor was not lost on her.

Pouring another glass of wine, she cruised Facebook feeling more excited at the friend requests of people coming in from the Cal Poly days. It was like her past was coming back and it both terrified her and excited her. Glancing at her profile, she realized it still said "in a relationship with Ben Brawley" and she never changed to "engaged to Ben Brawley." Looking at her ring finger resting on the keyboard, she was conscious once again of the heaviness of diamond. It was still the same ring Ben proposed with because they hadn't scheduled a time to go look at settings, but it still sparkled. Soon, she would have to let her Facebook friends know she was getting married.

The song changed to *Homespun* by Grant Lee Buffalo which was a great song with a happy memory. She had met the lead singer Grant Lee Philips when the band played at Bimbo's. It was during the time she was single before she met Ben and she went to the show alone. She never expected to sit at a table with the lead singer's brother in law. When he invited her backstage, she jumped at the invitation knowing this was a once in a lifetime memory in the making.

Elizabeth Aloe

She now recalls that night with fondness because the band couldn't have been nicer and she got to check it off her bucket list. *Those times seem so long ago and care free. I can't believe I actually went to the show alone.*

When Ali burst through the door, it not only scared Charlotte out of her thoughts, she almost spilled her wine. Ali was always at Rob's on the weekends and it was a shock to see her back to so early—and with a box full of her stuff.

"We broke up," Ali said dropping the box before Charlotte could even ask what happened.

"Oh no," Charlotte said gently, noticing Ali's puffy eyes.

The sobs started again and Charlotte got up to give her a hug while piecing together her explanation. *They were drifting apart...he didn't want to move to the city...she didn't want to move to the peninsula. ...she wanted to get married...he wasn't sure.* Charlotte knew it wasn't uncommon for a couple who'd been together for so long and needed to take the next step to have their relationship come to a head like this. Ali herself had just been saying she felt like she was hitting her head against the wall trying to move to the next level and Rob wouldn't talk about it. It was a long time coming, which seemed to be the theme for the day, and it didn't shock Charlotte but it surprised her it happened today.

"I'm so sorry, Ali," Charlotte said as Ali picked up her box and took it to her room.

"I don't know how to feel. On the drive home, I was a little relieved," she said. "Now I'm kind of shocked. How will I get over him? How will I get through this? It's like someone tore me in half and I can't get that other half back."

"I know. Break ups suck hard. It will take some time to get used to it, you'll be mad at him and then you'll finally move on and date someone else. I know it sounds awful right now, but it will happen."

"I've never had to do this before."

"Yes, you did. Remember when you broke up with him when he graduated?"

"Yes, but that was different. I knew we would get back together and I did the breaking up and had one more year in college to party and have fun. Now it's so much different. It feels like a real break up or a divorce. He's been in my life for so long and I don't know how to act without him around."

"Like I said, it will take about three weeks to adjust and then you'll be used to it and you can start being social again. The anger stage will last awhile. Do you want to order in some pizza or get a pint of Ben and Jerry's?" Charlotte hadn't had ice cream since Sarah visited and they ate a pint each individually. "I told Ben I would be over tonight, but I can cancel."

"No, no. Please don't cancel because of me. I'll be alright. I just need to be alone," Ali said with tears in her eyes. "I'll probably just go to bed."

The guilt over leaving Ali to go see Ben consumed Charlotte's thoughts as she watched Ali close her bedroom door. How awful it must be for her friend to know Charlotte was engaged and she was in the midst of a breakup. *If it makes you feel any better Ali, I'm not that happy myself.* Her thoughts felt remarkably real as she considered how it would feel if roles were reversed.

How would she feel if Ali got engaged and she and Ben broke up? Would it devastate her? Would she cry as hard as she heard Ali crying right now? How long would she grieve for the relationship? How would she get back to dating? Her emotions confused her because on one hand, she would miss Ben. He's a really good person, mostly a good boyfriend, and to be honest, she liked having a boyfriend in her life. On the other hand, there was just something missing and she knew she wasn't feeling the way a woman should feel who was engaged to the man of her dreams.

At that moment, she saw the fork in the road. Like a bolt of clarity, she knew she had to make a choice. Go left and continue her engagement into marriage knowing her sex life would be a rollercoaster and that feeling in her gut would stay, or go right and get back to being single and free to date other men— especially if one of those men was named Trevor. Then again, there was no guarantee Trevor had any feelings for her and would want to date her. What if she never dated again? What if she ended up totally alone because Ben was right man after all?

Despite the conflicting emotions, she knew she wasn't ready to get married. Looking at the diamond on her finger and thinking about Ben's proposal, she liked the idea of a wedding and a party, but everything else after that was blurry and uncomfortable. She couldn't picture the house, the kids, and the minivan—with Ben. Did she even know him well enough to call him her husband? She felt she knew Trevor better than she knew Ben and that's when she realized she had to give the ring back.

Crap.

Eight

Later that evening, after a shower and a goodbye to Ali, Charlotte walked down Union Street window shopping as she made her way to Ben's. Being the middle of October, it was the one weekend San Francisco experienced summer. Charlotte could feel a buildup of sweat under her clothes and on the back of her knees as she stopped to study the wedding invitations in the window of the stationary store.

That bolt of clarity she had before her shower dimmed as she realized what would happen if she broke off the engagement. Still conflicted over her feelings, she knew she couldn't just break it off with Ben. She needed more time to sort through exactly what her heart and brain were arguing about. Her heart said she was conflicted because of Trevor and her head said she loved Ben but was conflicted because of her fear of commitment—and his libido. So where did that leave her as a whole?

Her feelings for Ben were very strong and certainly genuine. When she said she loved him, she meant it. Why should she throw away everything with Ben for Trevor when she and Trevor weren't even dating? Now in front of a jewelry store, she stared at the diamond rings in the window wondering when Ben was going to take her shopping. Studying the modern cushion settings, she began listing the pros and cons of marrying Ben. The most obvious pro was the way he treated her—he was a wonderful person and she knew she could trust him to give her the life she wanted. The most obvious con was the loss of intimacy in the bedroom. She wasn't sure she could live in a sexless marriage and she didn't want to be one of those couples to start off a marriage in therapy. While it might work for some, she wanted to know she was marrying the right person before she said yes. *So what if Ben doesn't want to have sex as much as I do. What if our roles were reversed? What if he wanted sex all the time and I didn't? Would it still be an issue?*

Moving on to the stationery store next door, she thought about the actual wedding. Maybe planning it would bring her and Ben closer as they both got used to the idea of being together forever. Something inside of her stirred as she compared the fonts and colors of the invitations. Trevor shouldn't even be an issue with how she felt about Ben. It didn't matter that she still had feelings for him—he was a part of her past and they were never going to be together. She didn't *want* to go back to the past. Ben was her future. She should give this engagement a real chance. Isn't that what engagements are for anyway? Taking the time to get to know one another completely before completely committing? Most people seem to think an engagement is strictly time to plan a big party, but Charlotte looked at it as time to plan a life. *I want to fully know who I'm marrying and if that takes six months, then great. If it takes two years, so be it.* She didn't particularly want it to take that long, but she also didn't want to rush it.

Standing outside of Ben's building; she took a moment to catch her breath. Living in San Francisco, she and the rest of the city dwellers never seemed prepared for temperatures above seventy, let alone ninety-five. Since most apartments had no air conditioning including hers, she never got to cool off from blow drying her hair earlier. Now, it was a hot, sticky mess soaking up the sweat from the back of her neck. Taking a black rubber band out of her purse, she quickly put her hair up in a ponytail providing instant relief to her neck. Checking her reflection in a pocket sized mirror, she fixed her makeup and puckered her lips enough to spread what was left of her lip gloss around. Dialing Ben's door code, she waited patiently for him to answer.

"Hello?"

"It's me," Charlotte yelled into the speaker before hearing the buzz allowing her access. Thirty seconds later, she walked through Ben's door.

"Hey sweetie," Ben said from his desk.

By habit, Charlotte walked over and kissed him on the lips. He was shirtless and smelled like he just got out of the shower. "How was football?"

"Awesome. I got in four games," he said now standing and holding her close.

Unexpectedly, Charlotte heard the toilet flush and out came Trevor from the bathroom. Feeling her heart speed up and the blood drain from her face, she froze not sure what to do or say. It was very awkward and yet she still couldn't move after Trevor said hello and pulled a bottle of water out of the fridge. Charlotte couldn't figure out if she felt awkward because Trevor caught her and Ben in intimate embrace or because she felt guilty at how excited she was to see him.

Looking up at Ben to speak for her, she was completely caught off guard when Ben mistook her look of confusion and kissed her hard on the mouth.

"Get a room, you two," Trevor said from the kitchen.

"I do have a room," Ben laughed. "Charlotte, want to join me?"

Charlotte felt herself blush a million shades of red. What was going on here? She felt as if she had been caught by her boyfriend in the arms of her secret lover. It was the cliché chick flick triangle where the girl was with the wrong guy as she pined for his friend. *Stop it Charlotte. You made the choice to work on the engagement with Ben. Stop thinking about Trevor.*

"What are you doing here?" she asked Trevor trying to hide the annoyance in her voice. By now, she had composed herself enough to comprehend these two boys had spent time together without her. *Is that jealousy or insecurity I'm feeling?* She had to be careful because when it came to her feelings, she was about as transparent as a glass window.

It was odd to feel like the third wheel for once. There were so many secrets between the three of them and the last thing she wanted was for Ben and Trevor to share stuff about her without her knowing it. What if Ben mentioned their sex life or lack thereof? What if Trevor mentioned they were an item and she was the victim of an assault? The last part she knew she would have to tell Ben at some point, but she wanted it to come from her, not Trevor.

"Ben and I played a few games of football and then had some beers. I came over because he wanted to show me some financial software he uses."

"I hope you didn't sit down on Ben's couch, because he'll kill you if you get it dirty," she said to Trevor after noticing the grass stains on his shorts. It came out a little harsher than she intended.

"She's right about that," Ben laughed giving her a funny look as if to say 'what's wrong with you?'

"I know, I know. I can tell Ben is a bit anal retentive."

"You got that right," Charlotte snorted in a softer tone. She still felt somewhat left out as Ben and Trevor started discussing finances. She didn't know what to do with herself as they gathered around the computer and she stood by the couch. In what bizzaro world would her fiancé and ex-boyfriend become buddy-buddy? Ben was her fiancé and Trevor was her ex which, to her, meant they shouldn't want to hang out with each other. But then she remembered Ben didn't know Trevor was an ex. At first, it was a great idea and Charlotte liked it, but lately, they seemed to hang out more together than she did with either of them individually because of sports. *Jealous much, Charlotte? Not everything is about you.*

An hour passed before Trevor decided he needed to be somewhere else. "Okay, I think I gotta run and leave you two lovebirds alone. Thanks for the lead on that software, Ben. Are we still on for Thursday?"

"Absolutely, be there at seven," Ben replied walking him the short distance to the door. "See you later, man."

"What's on Thursday, Ben?" Charlotte asked as Ben closed the door behind Trevor and locked it.

"Remember the local band my buddy Eric from work is in? They're playing a gig at the Hotel Utah and I thought Trevor would want to go."

Charlotte felt her blood pressure rise a little at Ben's last sentence. He and Trevor were going to see a live band and they didn't invite her? What the hell was going on? These jealous feelings reminded her of high school when she was left out by friends she introduced. She was the one who ended up becoming the third wheel. Logically, she knew it wasn't true because neither Ben nor Trevor would consciously make her feel left out, but she was beginning to feel that way. The more she tried to stop the insecurity the worse it got.

"Why didn't you tell me about it?"

"I'm telling you now," Ben said.

Remembering the few live shows she attended with Trevor back in school, it hurt that he asked Ben instead of her to go. Music was the bond she shared with Trevor and she possessively didn't want Ben to be a part of it. She refrained from asking him to cancel because her rationality kicked in and she understood it wasn't Ben's fault. He was just being his normal nice guy self because he genuinely liked Trevor. *Let it go, Charlotte. Just let it go. Stop being a jealous drama queen.* But the hurt she felt over not being invited wouldn't quite go away. "Why didn't you invite me?" she asked softly.

"You have softball that night. I didn't think you would want to miss it," Ben said concerned. "You're always invited, Charlotte, you should know that."

Charlotte was surprised he remembered her softball game. Amazingly, his words were like a bucket of cold water over her jealousy. Just like that, the green eyed monster melted and so did she. "Oh right. I forgot all about that."

"You can join us afterwards, if you want. The show doesn't start until eight."

"I have an eight o'clock game and then we go out, so you guys go ahead and have fun. I'll meet you back here," Charlotte said before changing the subject. "Do you need to get dressed before we go to dinner? I wrote down some ideas for the wedding and thought maybe we could talk about them. "

Ben looked at her blankly. "I don't think I have the energy, Charlotte. I played so much football in the sun and then drank a few beers. I just want to rehydrate, lie down on the couch, and pass out."

This time, it was disappointment Charlotte had a hard time hiding. Not that she was in any hurry, but she thought they could go over a few details—like maybe a date, for starters. If she was to start planning anything, she needed to know what season it would be. The three times she tried to bring up wedding planning, Ben had rolled his eyes and changed the subject. At first it didn't bother her, but now she was seeing a pattern and she started making note of it. It wasn't like she was pressuring him or hounding him to discuss it. In fact, it was the exact opposite—she had delayed any discussion of wedding details with him because she couldn't bring herself to talk about it. Now, however, she was ready.

She wanted the wedding to bring her and Ben closer and to fill in the blanks of his life she didn't know.

Standing near the door as she watched Ben channel surf until he found the 49er game, she suddenly felt trapped. Realizing she knew little about her fiancé, she felt a slight panic coming on. All the questions she knew she needed to ask started going off in her head like firecrackers. Did he want kids? How many? What was his debt like? Did he pay taxes on time? Did he want to stay in the city forever or move to the suburbs? Questions like these made her feel as if she was marrying a stranger. She had no idea what Ben's finances were. Sure, he made good money, but how much? What about his parents? What were they like? She hadn't even met them because they lived in Minnesota.

Watching him, it occurred to her just how private he actually was with his life. He was great on the surface, but try to get information about his past like ex-girlfriends or college buddies, he would reply with minimal details or change the subject. She couldn't remember any of his friends or family ever visiting from the Midwest.

Money was a big issue because she was raised not to discuss it with others. She had no idea how to approach a financial conversation. Charlotte was very independent and had been taking care of her own finances since she went away to college. What if Ben wanted full control of all that considering he was the expert? The only thing they'd ever discussed was their living situation. He'd mentioned casually in the past she should move in with him, but she had kept the topic at arm's length treating it with a laugh as if it was something to be discussed way into the future. However, the future was here and she needed to get serious. It scared her silly to think about giving up her apartment and own space. It was something she cherished. They couldn't be married and live in separate apartments. Maybe she could talk Ben into moving into her place.

But the biggest issue was and always will be sex. Knowing she needed a full discussion before she even considered a trip down the aisle overwhelmed her because she knew Ben hated talking about it. The great sex they had around the engagement was gone and they hadn't done it in three and a half weeks. She was waiting to see if he would come around again, but he hadn't and it was so disappointing. The intimacy they shared the night of the engagement and week after was gone. She missed it very much.

Now feeling somewhat angry, she wanted Ben to feel a bit of her frustration. "Ben, I was hoping we could go have dinner and start talking about stuff."

"What stuff?" he replied before cheering a first down by the 49ers. He wasn't even paying much attention to her. Normally, she wouldn't mind watching the game with him because she likes football and the 49ers, but not tonight. Tonight should be spent outside in the rare warm temperatures having a cocktail at the new Mexican restaurant on Chestnut Street.

"Stuff that includes the wedding and our life."

"We can do that watching the game," he said in that dismissive tone he used when she tried to discuss their sex life. It was so annoying and she could feel her blood start to boil. Deciding she didn't want to get into a fight, she unlocked the door and opened it.

That got his attention. "You're leaving?" he said finally looking genuinely shocked she would even consider abandoning his company.

"Well, yes. I'm hungry and I was looking forward to going out tonight," Charlotte replied pulling out her phone.

"We can order pizza."

"I'm not in the mood for pizza," Charlotte replied sending texts to Cami and Jamie.

When both girls replied right away they could meet up in about thirty minutes, Charlotte couldn't help but feel she won a small, if not super tiny, victory. No way was Ben going to be lazy about the biggest day of their lives. Feeling confident at the moment, she made a pact with herself to start writing down the issues and forcing him to discuss them with her. Engagement was the period to open up and share each other's lives and talk about everything. It really wasn't just about the wedding details and she surely didn't want to be one of those brides who couldn't see past the big party and the honeymoon. *Ben, we are going to have this discussion and many more before I even think about buying an expensive dress.*

Feeling much better, she left Ben's building and started the walk towards Chestnut Street. The sun was going down but the sidewalk was still emitting heat keeping her warm. Still in her head, she wondered what she would feel like if she and Ben broke up. While she was afraid of losing him, part of her kind of wanted him to completely drop the ball and not live up to her demands so she would have an excuse to back out. It would relieve her of all the decisions, all the secrets, and all the worry. Did every newly engaged woman go through these thoughts? What was wrong with her and why did she have such cold feet? One minute she was totally infatuated and in love with Ben and the next, she felt like she was drowning and didn't know how to get that next breath of air. Normally she was a very decisive person, but this engagement made her more fickle than child trying to choose a piece of candy in a candy store.

Her thoughts switched to Trevor and a part of her longed for him to sweep her off her feet so she wouldn't have to deal with these issues. What would she do if Trevor asked her to leave Ben to be with him? Would she do it? Is she committed and in love with Ben enough to say no? It was concerning how much she thought of Trevor when Ben annoyed her. She knew it was wrong, but it was a fantasy she couldn't let go.

Finding a spot outside on the back patio, she waited for Cameron and Jamie to find her as she ordered a lemon drop on the rocks. The alcohol mixed with the lemonade tasted wonderful—especially now after becoming so annoyed at her fiancé. When the waiter brought the drink to the table, she remembered another time when she was annoyed with a guy. She wasn't sure why the memory popped up in her head, but it seemed like yesterday and it also seemed so justified at the time. Now it just seemed silly.

Charlotte and her friends were at SLO Brew for a show by a local band sponsored by the radio station. It was the end of her freshman year and it was the last hurrah before finals. Charlotte had taken a break from studying for her English Lit final to attend the show with Cami and Jamie. As she and the girls ordered burgers and fries, she looked around the crowd hoping to see Trevor. She knew he would be graduating soon and it wore on her they never really closed the door. He was still the only guy she thought about, but she was too embarrassed and insecure to try to talk to him. She heard from a couple other DJs he was seeing Katie Bishop and that confused her. What did he see in her? She wasn't pretty, wore too much makeup and seemed very clingy. But even Charlotte could admit to herself that Katie intimidated her and she was just jealous and petty. Katie was probably a cool person. If she wasn't with Trevor, Charlotte might want to get to know her better.

They were halfway through dinner when she finally spotted Trevor. Putting her hamburger down, she watched him as he made his way to the bar. He was twenty one and could order beers, something she and her friends could not. Her heart started fluttering and the sight of him but when she spotted Katie, she felt the blood drain. It was one thing to hear they were dating— it was another to actually see them together in person. Charlotte hadn't seen Katie in a couple months and she almost fell off her chair at the change in Katie's appearance. Gone was the extra 30 pounds she'd been carrying and all the makeup. Her hair was back to its normal blonde color and she was dressed like a normal college student. Her heart sunk even further realizing she and Trevor made a cute couple. Feeling the tears form, she diverted her gaze hoping Trevor would stay at the bar amongst the crowd and not see her.

Unfortunately, her friends noticed the couple.

"Oh my god—is that Katie Bishop?" Cami asked.

"Wow, I think so. She looks so good now that she took off all that ugly makeup. Did she take out her piercings, too?" Jamie replied.

"Charlotte, what the hell? Why is he here with her?" Cami asked.

"I heard they were dating," Charlotte said trying sound nonchalant.

"I heard that too, but didn't believe it," Jamie said.

Charlotte stared at the couple again. Remembering Trevor's need to constantly touch her and hold her hand when they were together, she was surprised he was standing about a foot away from Katie. *That doesn't mean anything.* What mattered was how they acted alone later that night and the thought depressed Charlotte. She pictured Trevor kissing Katie like he had kissed her that one night at his party. Were they sleeping together? She remembered the quote from Nick Hornby's book *High Fidelity* where the male character Rob Fleming thinks about his ex in bed with her new boyfriend. "No one is having better sex than Laura is having in my head." That's how Charlotte felt now about Trevor.

The sudden urge to pee brought her out of her thoughts. "I have to go to the bathroom and the only way is to walk by them," Charlotte said aloud to no one in particular.

"Sorry, sweetie. Maybe you should go talk to him," Cami said as Charlotte watched her eat a french fry. "I bet he is dying to see you and you look so pretty tonight."

She didn't feel very pretty. She wished she had dressed in something other than shorts and a t-shirt. Working up her courage, Charlotte sat listening to the band as she strategized her route. Maybe she could walk through the crowd on the opposite side but then that would mean walking in front of the stage and Trevor would surely spot her. There was no way around it, he would spot her regardless and since her bladder was about to burst, she couldn't put it off any longer. Maybe Trevor already knew she was there and was purposely ignoring her.

Keeping her head down as she made her way through the crowd, she prayed to remain invisible. Through her peripheral vision, she felt his eyes on her and she quickened her pace towards the ladies room. Maybe if she just ignored him, he would ignore her too. Her heart was thumping so hard, she almost stopped to catch her breath. Once inside the bathroom and on the toilet, she released the energy she had been holding in since she saw him. A big relief passed through her, literally and figuratively, as she wondered about his reaction to seeing her. She couldn't tell if he had been excited or nonchalant. She just felt his eyes on her as she walked by the bar. Now, how was she going to get back to her table? *What would it hurt just to say hi?*

She didn't have to go far because Trevor was waiting for her outside the bathroom. They were totally alone even though the noise from the crowd echoed through the hallway.

"Hi Charlie," he said. *Was he nervous?*

"Hi," she replied back. Why hadn't she thought to comb her hair and reapply her lipstick? *Dummy.*

"How are you?"

"I'm really good, how are you?" This time, the small talk didn't bother her because she was too nervous to care. She was just glad he was standing in front of her right now. Her heart sped up again but her tongue was tied in a knot.

"You look nice."

"Thank you. So do you," she said thinking he was still so handsome when he smiled. *I miss you so much, Trevor! I just want to kiss you right now.*

Charlotte watched him sigh as if to build some courage. "Charlotte...I miss you so damn much. I don't know what I did that pissed you off, but I wish we could fix it."

Fix it? He wanted to get back together? Charlotte's mind went blank. *What do I say? What should I do?*

"I want us to be friends again," Trevor continued. "I feel so bad at what happened and I don't want to graduate thinking you hate me."

Friends? Her heart sank as if it had just hit an iceberg at full speed. *Just friends?* "But I don't want to be just friends, Trevor. I love you and I can't live without you anymore," was what she should have said. Instead she told him she wanted that too.

Letting him reach in for a hug, she fought back the tears that were about to explode. This is the end. The total end of any hope they would get back together. Her mind was now as fuzzy as her eyesight from the tears she was holding back. She barely felt the kiss on her cheek.

"I have to get back to the bar," he said.

And back to Katie.

All Charlotte could do was nod in return. Her bubble popped and completely deflated and she felt even worse than she did when they broke up in January. He was over her and just wanted to be friends. Now the tears completely spilled down her cheeks. There was no way she could return to the table. She texted Jamie and Cami hoping they would pay the bill and meet her outside.

Twenty minutes later, Charlotte was crying on her friends' shoulders as she explained through sobs what happened.

"I can't believe that," Jamie said. "Why would he even bother?"

"I, I, I don't know," Charlotte hiccupped. "Jamie will you take me home?"

"Sure, hon, I can do that."

"I can't believe Trevor had the nerve to say that to you," Cami said as the trio walked towards the car.

"Please don't be mad at him. He isn't the bad guy," Charlotte said quietly and speaking the truth. "I was the one who messed everything up in the first place."

"By getting attacked by your stalker at the station? I don't think so. Trevor should have been more supportive."

Charlotte really didn't want to get into that discussion right now. "Please just take me home and remind me how much I owe for dinner."

That night at the SLO Brew was the last time she saw Trevor until two months ago.

"I think you're being too hard on Ben," Jamie said after Charlotte explained Ben's behavior. "Most guys hate planning weddings."

"But it's not just that," Charlotte said taking eating a bit of the fried calamari. "He doesn't want to talk about anything—and I mean anything."

"Again, most guys are not the most communicative," Jamie repeated. "I've heard many friends say their grooms wanted nothing to do with the wedding planning."

"Ben will come around, Charlotte, don't worry," Cami said. Charlotte couldn't remember the last time Cami had a boyfriend, let alone a date. She was so pretty, but so picky and wouldn't even consider online dating. "He is such a good guy. You're so lucky."

Yes, so lucky. If that were the case, wouldn't our sex drives match? She never mentioned the sexual problems she had with Ben to her friends. It was so embarrassing to bring up and so she led them to believe Ben was a good lover. In the beginning, it wasn't hard because Ben was attentive. She wanted so desperately to talk about it now, but she didn't want to betray him. It just didn't seem right that she should discuss their intimate life with anyone including her best friends. In the past, she and her friends discussed boys and sex over brunch because the relationships were casual and fun. Not until she got serious with Ben did she understand the betrayal of sharing every detail with her friends. Putting herself in Ben's place, she would be devastated if she ever found out he was discussing their sex life with his friends.

The only person who really knew anything was Sarah. Since she was out of town, Charlotte felt there was a small buffer. However, even Sarah didn't know everything. Charlotte made sure she didn't go into full and complete disclosure. Even telling Sarah made

Elizabeth Aloe

Charlotte feel somewhat guilty, but she had to talk to someone and she knew Sarah would keep it to herself.

Deciding to change the subject, Charlotte asked Jamie about her dating life.

"It's going super well," Jamie replied. Charlotte laughed at how red she turned. "Mitch is so awesome. He keeps sending me flowers to work and treats me like a princess."

"I'm so jealous. Have you done it, yet?" Charlotte asked knowing Jamie was purposely waiting to have sex with Matt. She loved seeing Jamie happy. After a bunch of bad relationships, Charlotte knew her friend deserved to meet a good guy.

"Charlotte!" Jamie replied pretending to be offended but then laughed. "No, actually, it's been three months and I'm enjoying the anticipation."

Charlotte remembered meeting Mitch Ridgewood at one of the city council meetings Jamie dragged her to a couple weeks ago. He was currently a council member with aspirations to become the mayor. Ever so charming, Charlotte immediately saw how Jamie fell so hard so fast. He was a catch and so was Jamie and together they made a very stunning pair. "I hope it all works out. He's so good looking."

"I know, right?" Cami said a bit wistfully. "He reminds me of Matthew Perry when he was hot on Friends."

"So true!" Charlotte said as they all laughed. "Jamie's dating Chandler."

"Could I BE any luckier?" Jamie said laughing even harder at her joke about the Friends character.

Soon the girls were cracking jokes and discussing their favorite TV shows. Relaxing, Charlotte finally let the anger at Ben go. Maybe she *was* being too hard on him. It was a stressful time with the holidays approaching. Ben was flying to Minnesota to be with his family for two weeks and Charlotte wanted the distance to make his heart grow fonder—not only for her sexually but for the wedding as well. Hopefully his vacation will loosen him up.

"Oh, speaking of boyfriends, guess who I got a friend request from yesterday?" Cami said rather mysteriously. "Mr. Scott Hendricks."

Charlotte felt herself gasp at the name. Her first boyfriend after Trevor, Scott took her virginity during the fall of her second year. They were a fun couple for a while—he was a true geek but so smart and funny and when he first kissed her after the KCPR staff meeting at the beginning of the fall quarter, she actually felt comfortable with it. He had shown his interest several times before, but she always ignored it because she hadn't been ready to move on from Trevor. He introduced her to sex in a slow but very romantic way and she always held a deep fondness for him because of that. They might not have worked out in the long run, but her healthy view of sex was because he was so gentle, loving, and patient. Smiling, Charlotte realized she wanted to see him again and get reacquainted. They never had a bad breakup primarily because Charlotte never felt the same for him as she did for Trevor. They were more friends than a couple and it had been easy to make the transition back to just friends right before Scott graduated.

"Wow. Scott. I haven't heard that name said out loud for years." Charlotte said.

"He found me on Facebook, of course. We've emailed a couple times," Cami said. It didn't surprise Charlotte that Scott was back in touch with Cami first because they were good friends even before Charlotte met him. "He mentioned a possible reunion for the station alumni during the open house weekend in April."

"Oh, that would be so much fun. It would be a great excuse to go back to SLO," Jamie replied excited.

"Is Scott married?" Charlotte asked.

"I don't think so. I didn't see any evidence of that and he didn't mention a wife or girlfriend," Cami replied questioningly. "Why does that matter, Miss Engaged to the Perfect Guy?"

Charlotte wondered that herself. *Why did it matter?* "I have no idea. I was just asking."

"I've also seen Trevor on there," Jamie said turning her focus on Charlotte. "I see that both of you are friends."

Charlotte wasn't sure what to say. She hadn't told Cami and Jamie anything about Trevor being back in her life. It was so hard, but she wanted to keep it completely separate. Ali and Sarah were the only people besides Ben who knew about Trevor. Her smile felt fake as she tried not to give anything away. She wanted really bad to spill everything, but again, she felt it would betray Ben. "Yes, we are friends on Facebook together. No biggie."

"No biggie?" Jamie continued. "That guy was the love of your life until Ben and that's all you have to say?"

"What do you want me to say?" Charlotte asked. *Do you want me to tell you I'm doubting my love for my fiancé because Trevor stepped back into my life and I still have feelings for him? Or that we are working together now and I see him almost every day and he is dating one of my managers?* "I'm over him and its okay to just be in touch on social media. What does that hurt? I couldn't be friends with everyone else and not him."

Charlotte noticed the look between Jamie and Cami and it made her feel like a full on liar. "Okay fine, I saw Trevor when I interviewed for my job. It was a complete surprise and we now work together."

"Wait, let me get this straight, Trevor lives here in San Francisco and you work together and you didn't think to tell us? Why?" Jamie asked.

"I don't know. I honestly don't know why," Charlotte said sipping her drink. "I wasn't hiding anything, I just wasn't sure if I even wanted to be friends with him."

"This is a big deal, Charlotte." Cami said quietly. "I don't want to push it, but you must still have feelings if you didn't tell us."

"I don't know what I feel, guys. We're both so different and he has a girlfriend and I have a fiancé. I love Ben and Trevor is just someone from my past. It's no big deal." Charlotte wondered if her nose grew from the lies she was telling. "We're just friends now and work at the same place. I hardly see him."

"Just be careful. It took you years to get over him," Jamie said before taking up the menu to order dinner. "Okay, change of subject. I'm ready to order dinner. What looks good?"

Thankful Jamie read the cue to move on, Charlotte hid her fake smile and her fake aloofness about Trevor behind her menu as she pretended to study the entrees. How could she discuss her feelings for Trevor when she didn't even understand them? Aside from the double dates and Trevor becoming friends with Ben, everything she said was true. They were just friends and coworkers.

Nine

The middle of October was Trevor's favorite time of the year.

Standing on the sidelines after his football game, he marveled at how he lived in one of the most beautiful cities in the world. The Marina was crowded with sweaty players both male and female and everyone seemed happy because it finally felt like summer. No fog and hot temperatures brought everyone out to play. The rest of the country was getting ready for snow but Trevor was still wearing shorts.

After chugging the rest of the water from his plastic bottle, he wiped his face with his t-shirt trying to mop up the sweat. He played four games straight and was exhausted but exhilarated. He loved these weekend games.

"Hey, wanna head over to Chestnut and grab a beer at the Grove?" Ben asked. "A few of the others are heading over there."

"Sure."

Trevor hadn't been to the Grove in ages because it was normally a small scene of Marina hipsters on the weekend. However, it was one of the few places to sit outside and he didn't want to waste this gorgeous day inside. A cold beer sounded delicious at the moment.

Waiting for Ben as he spoke to two of the girls on the team, he thought about Charlotte. He understood exactly what Charlotte saw in Ben—his good looks, easy charm, and inclusiveness. People seemed drawn to Ben because he was so genuine. It surprised Trevor how much he actually liked the guy despite his engagement to Charlotte. Ben easily included him on his football team and Trevor was grateful.

"Okay, let's go. Amanda and Sam will be heading there later," he said referring to the girls. "I think you have an admirer in Amanda, dude."

Really? That surprised Trevor because she hardly spoke to him when they were together on the field or afterwards when the team was out for beers. "She's cute."

"So how are things with you and Michelle? Is she pressuring you for the next step yet?" Ben asked.

Trevor wasn't surprised at the question. He and Michelle had gone out with Ben and Charlotte a few times and anyone who spied the foursome would think they were solid couples. "No, it's not like that. We're both so busy and she seems fine with the way things are right now."

"Never believe that for a second. Women always want to take it to the next level. They just pretend they don't care."

Walking side by side, Trevor thought about that as they exited the park onto Chestnut Street. "Are you sure about that because Michelle really does seem to prefer her independence."

"Ask her if she watches those stupid reality shows like Bridezillas or Say Yes to the Dress. If she does, then she thinks about it."

"A wedding? Nah," Trevor laughed. *No way.* Michelle wasn't into that and he couldn't recall if she ever watched those shows. She never mentioned getting married—in fact, she never mentioned going to the next level in the relationship. It's been about five months now and they just sort of fell into something. Neither one had brought up exclusivity although he wasn't seeing anyone else. "I'm not even sure she wants to call me her boyfriend."

"Yeah, right," Ben said with a half chuckle half snort.

Trevor felt very weird having this conversation, but Ben was easy to talk to and he felt himself asking the next question before he even realized what it was he was asking. "Is that how you felt with Charlotte?"

Trevor waited while Ben thought about his answer, noticing the change in Ben's demeanor right away. He went from half joking to serious in a matter of a split second. "No, it wasn't. The minute marriage popped into my head, I knew it was Charlotte I wanted marry."

"You don't sound very confident with that statement," Trevor replied. He didn't know Ben very well, but he could tell by the canned response something was bothering Ben.

"She's perfect for me—she loves sports, she's smart, she likes her alone time and likes it that I have my life, too. I find I want to spend more time with her than she does with me. I'm very happy."

That's interesting, Trevor thought as they passed the shoppers along the crowded street. Arriving at the Grove, Trevor followed Ben to a table being vacated. He frowned thinking he hadn't spoken to Charlotte in over a week. His schedule was so full of meetings and off site issues, he just hadn't had the time to stop by and see her and now that he was hanging out with Ben, he wished she was here as well. *What was with Ben? Did he not want to marry Charlotte or was he just nervous? Could it be he was insecure about the relationship?* When he thought about marriage, he didn't see it with Michelle at all—they didn't have enough in common. She didn't like sports or the same music and she was completely career minded to the point he thought she was a workaholic. It might be an admirable trait in someone, but he knew he didn't want a partner like that. Someday, she would be offered a big position that would probably take her to New York. Maybe it was the same with Ben and Charlotte. They seemed like a perfect couple on the surface, but no one ever really knows the intricacies of a relationship on the inside except for the two people involved.

After settling into the table and taking menus from the server, Trevor waited for Ben to continue his conversation about Charlotte. Ben finally brought her up after they ordered a couple beers and appetizers.

"I need to call Charlotte," Ben said pulling out his phone.

"What is she doing today?" Trevor asked.

"I'm not sure. I think she said she was going to work out and do errands."

"Wedding stuff?" Trevor asked trying to keep it casual as he sipped his beer.

Trevor was surprised when Ben looked up as if he had said Charlotte was out buying a new car on a credit card.

"Uh, no. I don't think so," Ben said putting his phone back.

"What's up?"

"Eh, its nothing."

Trevor noticed Ben wouldn't make eye contact. *What's up with that?* "Is everything okay?"

"Yes," Ben said without elaborating.

Something wasn't right. "You don't seem happy about getting married," Trevor pushed gently

"It's not that. I love Charlotte very much. It's not her at all."

"Then what's the problem?" Trevor asked not sure he wanted to know the answer. If Ben actually opened up and told him something about his relationship, he would feel as if he was betraying Charlotte.

Trevor waited knowing Ben was getting ready to confide. He had that look like someone who needed to spill a dirty little secret. *Oh lord, don't say anything.* But Trevor couldn't bring himself to stop Ben. The masochistic side of him wanted to know what was going on.

"There's something Charlotte doesn't know about me," Ben started. "Before I moved here, I was living in Minneapolis and had a girlfriend, Nora."

So this is about an ex-girlfriend. Ben was having second thoughts about marrying Charlotte because he was still in love with Nora. "Are you still in love with her?"

"No, it's not like that."

"It's okay, I won't tell Charlotte if that's what you're concerned about," Trevor said feeling dirty.

Trevor was shocked when Ben finally spilled what was bothering him.

"I killed a girl, Trevor."

Trevor sat there with the beer in his hand as if Ben had just told him he was an alien. Not knowing what to say, he stayed quiet wanting Ben to go into details. *He killed a girl?*

"It was a really cold night and the roads were slippery," Ben continued. "I didn't see the black ice and my car slid into the center of oncoming traffic."

"Was it Nora?" Trevor asked quietly.

"No, it was her roommate, Carrie. She was in the backseat and didn't have a seatbelt on. She died instantly."

Wow. Trevor had not seen this coming. He was really expecting Ben to confess something silly like Nora wanted him back. This was so much...heavier. "Were you drunk?"

Trevor waited patiently as Ben struggled with the memories. He really hoped Ben hadn't been drinking. That would be unforgivable. "No. We had just gone to the movies."

"Oh god, Ben, I'm so sorry. I can't even imagine how that must have felt. How did you get through it?"

"Lots of therapy, but I'm still messed up about it. I probably always will be. It's not something that just goes away."

"I would never have known unless you told me. I take it you haven't told Charlotte?"

"No, how can I tell her? How do you tell the person you are about to marry that you took someone's life even if it was an accident?"

That's a big secret to keep from her. If it was me, would I tell Charlotte? "It's a tough spot to be in, Ben. I don't envy you. How about Nora? What happened to her?"

"We broke up after that. She broke a couple bones, but healed. I wasn't hurt at all. I was so in love with that girl and she broke my heart, but I understood the reasons. She said it wasn't because she blamed me, but how could she look at me every day and not be reminded? I'm sure that was most of the reason."

"It was an accident, Ben."

"I know, but it still doesn't bring Carrie back. I never spoke to Nora again after I moved to San Francisco. I really don't talk to anyone back there anymore. I had to cut them all off to move on."

This was so heavy. He had no idea Ben had such baggage. The nice buzz Trevor was feeling from the beers suddenly turned to acid in his stomach. He felt hot and tired. "This is something you have to tell Charlotte before you get married."

"I know," Ben said quietly. "I just don't know how to do it."

"I'm sure she'll understand. It was an accident and it's behind you now."

"But that's the problem, it's always behind me, following me everywhere and haunting me. Every time I get into a car or drive someone in the passenger seat, I think about it. I think about how it might not have happened if we had gone to an earlier movie or took another way home."

"I don't know what to tell you, Ben, except you have to tell Charlotte before you get married. You can't keep that kind of secret from her. It'll eat away at you and eventually your relationship," Trevor said looking away from Ben's face. He looked so sad and guilty; Trevor didn't know what to say that would make him feel better. "I think we need something stronger than beer."

"I don't know how to tell her," Ben repeated. "You've known her for a long time, how would you do it?"

"I can't even answer that. Charlotte and I know each other, but we don't know each other that well. I guess you just have to sit her down and tell her the truth. She's been through a lot herself and I'm sure she can handle it."

"What do you mean?"

"Don't you know what happened to her in college?"

"Um, no?" Ben said surprised. "What happened?"

Uh oh. Charlotte must not have mentioned that portion of her life to him. *Wow, they both have big secrets.* He didn't want to be the one to tell him, but Ben is his friend now. Talk about being caught in the middle.

"Someone jumped her at the station when she was there alone doing a midnight shift."

"Oh my god."

"She was in the hospital for a night. You'll have to ask her more about it."

"Yes, I will. I'm surprised she never said anything," Ben said. Trevor could tell he was getting worked up about it. "How close were you as friends?"

Tread carefully. Should he tell Ben they were dating at the time and how much in love he was with her? He didn't want to worry Ben or make things weird so he told a half truth. "We were really good friends, I trained her and we spent a lot of time together, but she just stopped talking to me after that night and I never figured out why. After I graduated, we completely lost touch until recently."

"That's weird. Why would she just stop talking to you? I'm assuming you had nothing to do with it, right?" Ben asked pointedly.

"Of course not. You'll have to ask her. I'm sure she had her reasons."

"Why would anyone do that to her?" Ben said more to himself than to Trevor. "How hurt was she and be honest."

"I think it was a concussion and she had a bad bruise on her forehead and on her arm."

"Was it sexual?"

"No, no, thank god. That was the first thing I asked the doctor."

"So you were there with her? You must have been good friends."

"I was the one who got to her first. I was at home listening when she called me and asked I come be with her because she felt spooked. I stopped to get a coffee at the gas station because I was so tired. I kick myself to this day because had I not stopped, I might have gotten there before it all happened. I think that's why she blames me for some of it."

"Did you just walk into the station and see her laying there?"

"Yes," Trevor responded thinking about the image that will be branded in his memory forever—the one of Charlotte lying on the ground unconscious.

"Who did it, Trevor?" Ben asked roughly. Trevor noticed Ben had lost the guilt and sadness from before and now looked like he wanted to throw a punch.

"I don't think they ever found out. I haven't even spoken to Charlotte about it. I figured she doesn't want to be reminded because she hasn't brought it up." *But I do want to know why she pushed me away.* "You can't keep your past a secret, Ben. If she loves you and I know she does, she'll accept all of your past both good and bad. It was an accident."

It was so hard for Trevor to say those words to Ben, but seeing Ben's face soften at the words *Charlotte* and *love*, he knew it was the right thing to say. "I sure hope you're right."

"Try to let it go. Are you still seeing a therapist?"

"Not as much, but I still have nightmares about it. Carrie was a good person."

"I'm sorry you had to go through all that. Thanks for telling me," Trevor said after noticing the look of relief on Ben's face now that he confided.

"Please don't tell Charlotte. I probably shouldn't have told you."

"I would tell her as soon as possible."

Trevor sat with Ben as he described Nora. The way he spoke about her reminded him of how close he and Charlotte had been. Trevor wasn't the least bit surprised when Ben said Nora wouldn't return his phone calls since he left Minneapolis for San Francisco. "Do you miss the Midwest?"

"Sometimes. Minneapolis is a great city but I like the San Francisco winter much better," Ben said finally smiling. "My family is back there and I miss them, but I only go back on holidays."

No wonder he wants to get married. He has no roots here. "Has Charlotte met your family?"

"No. They haven't visited California and she's never traveled back with me."

It wasn't that odd that Charlotte and Ben's family hadn't met, but he couldn't help but feel Charlotte would eventually be ambushed with Ben's past. "Ben, do you really think you're ready to marry?"

"Is anyone ever really ready?"

Trevor couldn't argue with that.

The next day at work, Trevor decided to stop by Charlotte's desk. It was a feeble attempt to find out if Ben told her anything. He would never give away Ben's secret, but it's a hard one to keep. How would Charlotte feel if she found out he knew? She would be angry. Trevor knew he would be angry if Charlotte kept a secret about a girl he was about to commit his life to in marriage.

His heart sped up as he took the elevator down to her floor. After getting off, he said hi to a couple people as he passed them in the hallway. Finding Charlotte at her desk with her headphones on, he watched her for a bit wondering what she was listening to. It seemed to make her happy as she slightly rocked her head to a beat as she typed.

"Knock knock," he said a bit loudly so she would hear him.

Turning to face him, Trevor noticed her smile lit up at the sight of him. "Trevor! Hi. What brings you down here?"

"I just thought I'd stop in a say hello. I haven't seen you in a while."

"I know. I haven't seen you, either," Charlotte said continuing the small talk.

"So how are things?"

"Good, good."

"You're settling into the job okay?"

"Yes. It's been great. My team is really good and I like Jake."

"Jake is a good guy," Trevor said about Charlotte's manager. "How are the wedding plans coming?"

Charlotte sighed and stood up out of her chair. "Can I ask you something?"

"Um, sure," Trevor said hoping this wasn't about Ben. He kicked himself for even bringing it up.

"I'm not sure I should be bringing this up to you because I know you're friends with Ben now, but I'm feeling really weird about this whole wedding thing."

Trevor knew she needed to spill something about Ben which in turn made him feel even guiltier. "Can you take a break? We can go outside and grab coffee."

"Thanks, that'd be great."

Trevor walked next to Charlotte in silence hoping she would wait until they got outside to say anything. He needed to compose himself in case she brought up Ben. He didn't want to betray Ben but he didn't feel right about keeping it all from Charlotte. *Why is he the one caught in the middle? They should be talking to each other.*

Trevor could feel the chemistry running between him and Charlotte as if they were connected by a wire running electricity. *Did she feel it too?* Part of him hoped she would break off the engagement and the other part wanted her to stay engaged and get married so he could officially move on.

Walking across the street to Levi's plaza, Trevor ordered two coffees and took them out to where Charlotte was sitting in front of the huge water fountain. He loved it here—a little oasis in a big city with the water rushing from the fountain down through the plaza grassy areas. It was a slightly breezy, but the sun kept the chill away.

"Okay, spill," he said sitting down next to her and noticing the frown on her face. "What's going on?"

"I'm not even sure myself," she replied. "I feel all this angst and trepidation inside of me when I think about planning the wedding."

"Ok," Trevor said pushing her to say more.

"I don't know why I'm telling you this, but since you know Ben and me, maybe you'll understand. I can't really talk to Ali about it because of Rob and Sarah has her own problems. Plus, they love Ben and that makes it difficult."

"What's so difficult?" Trevor asked.

"I'm not sure I want to marry him, Trevor. There, I said it out loud."

Trevor tried to hide his response hoping she was saying this before knowing his past. "Why not?"

"I don't know. Ben is incredible. He's sweet, kind, fun, smart, and handsome—everything I could want in a husband."

"But," Trevor said for her.

"But he doesn't like sex."

"Whoa, maybe you shouldn't be telling me this," Trevor said astonished. That was not what he expected her to say. He expected her to say she didn't feel she knew him well enough or she wasn't sure she loved him. Sex was the last thing he expected to come from her lips.

"I'm sorry. I just don't know who to tell. It's a big deal to me, Trevor because telling someone makes me feel like I'm betraying him somehow. I don't want to do that, but I'm seriously desperate."

Trevor hesitated wondering how far he wanted to go with this issue. "What's the problem? Is he to quick or does he not want to do, you know, foreplay?"

"Oh my gosh, it's not like that," Charlotte said blushing. "It's that he isn't interested in the whole thing at all."

"So he'd rather watch Sportscenter than get it on?"

"Yes, exactly."

Trevor wasn't sure what to tell her. Did she really want him to solve this for her? He had no idea what to say. He figured Ben was disconnected because of the accident but he couldn't be sure.

"I don't know what to tell you, Charlie," he said finally.

"I know. I don't expect you do. I just feel like something is missing from the puzzle and I can't complete it until I get that other piece, but I can't find it no matter how hard I try."

"Have you tried talking to him?"

"Yes! Many times, but he shuts me down," Charlotte said. "It's like if he were to acknowledge it, it would be an actual problem. I can't marry someone who can't talk to me."

"Well, a lot of guys are like that. They don't know how to communicate like women do," Trevor said. That much was true.

"I know, but don't you think mismatching libidos are a big deal?"

"I honestly don't know. I haven't been committed to anyone long enough to worry about something like that."

"How is it with you and Michelle? Does she turn you on all the time or just some of the time?"

Trevor laughed. "No, no, I can't go there, but I will tell you that we aren't anywhere near as serious as you and Ben. She has her life and I have mine."

"Oh, okay. Sorry."

"Don't be sorry," Trevor said putting an arm around her shoulders. "I wish I had some answers for you, but what goes on in a guys mind regarding sex is often a symptom of something bigger in his life. Could he be depressed? Maybe you should ask him again."

"I'm going to have to—I can't get married feeling this way. It's as if a shackle is around my neck and I'm being pulled down a path I'm unclear about."

"Marriage is a big deal and it's okay to feel scared. I like Ben and I like you and I think you make a good couple, but if you don't feel it, you need to do some soul searching. Don't get married just because you feel pressured."

Finally, Trevor got Charlotte to smile. "Thanks, Trevor. Sorry to burden you, but I'm so confused. I miss those days in the station when all we had on our mind was discovering new bands, playing them for the people, and getting our studying done."

"I miss them, too," Trevor said. And he did— more than she knew. He also missed being with her. *Why did you end them? Why didn't you ever want to talk to me again?* He wanted to bring up the unsolved question as to why she wouldn't speak to him after the attack, but let it go because she already had a lot on her mind. It still ate at him, but maybe it wasn't worth finding out. This was the deepest conversation they'd had since those days in college and he didn't want to ruin it.

Ten

Digging through Ben's medicine cabinet, Charlotte felt like the biggest jerk ever. Trying to keep quiet, she ran the water loudly and flushed the toilet. Nothing stood out to her as she picked through bottles of Tylenol, Advil and Benadryl. There were no prescription bottles.

When Trevor mentioned depression, a light bulb went off in Charlotte's mind about an article she read on anti-depressants. The article mentioned how certain types can affect a man's libido. If Ben was depressed, maybe he was taking a prescription. What he would be depressed about, she had absolutely no idea. After quickly checking the drawers and under the sink, she felt a mix of relief and dissatisfaction at not finding anything. Maybe Trevor was wrong.

She wasn't sure why she went to Trevor about her problems with Ben, but when Ben pushed her away once again because he "wasn't in the mood", something snapped. She knew if she didn't talk about it to someone, she wouldn't get over feelings of resentment that were building. Ben wouldn't talk about the wedding and he certainly wouldn't discuss their issues.

Sarah hadn't returned her phone call yet and she didn't want to discuss it with Jamie and Cami. What she needed was a man's perspective and the first person to pop into her head was Trevor. She just needed to finally vent it all out. She didn't expect Trevor to fix it, but she just needed him to listen.

A knock at the door startled her.

"Hey sunshine, are you showering because I need to," Ben yelled from outside.

"Um, yes, planning on it. Can I take one first?"

"Sure."

Turning off the sink water, she turned on the shower and got in after it warmed up. She still felt so guilty about going through Ben's things especially since he'd surprised her earlier at her softball game.

Standing at second base, her normal position on the field, she saw him walk up and stand near the cooler of beer. Her heart sped up happily as she waited for the other team to make the third out. When the batter struck out, she ran over to him.

"Hi, what are you doing here?"

"What? A guy can't support his lady and her sports?"

"No, silly, I just thought you had a game."

"I did, but didn't feel like hanging out with the guys afterwards. I missed you," he said before bringing out a single rose from behind his back.

"Wow, Ben, thank you," Charlotte said feeling a little exposed in front of her friends who were all watching even though they were pretending not to. Kissing him quickly on the lips, she gave the rose back to him. "Here, you hold on to this, I need to bat."

Later at the bar, Charlotte stood at the jukebox with Darren as her girlfriends circled Ben trying to get information out of him about the wedding. *Good luck.*

"So, the fiancé actually does exist," Darren said as he scrolled through the music.

"Yes, he does. He is not a figment of my imagination."

"So tell me, where did you hire him?" Darren teased. "Hotguys.com?"

"Ha ha," Charlotte laughed. She loved the easiness between her and Darren. He was always so nice to her. "So what are we playing tonight?"

"I'm in the mood for Bon Jovi and, let's see, Foreigner," he said clicking the numbers.

"Ah, a classic rock night. Good choice." Charlotte loved *Livin' on a Prayer* and everything by Foreigner.

Once the music started, they walked back over to the group where Ben put his arm around Charlotte's waist. Through her peripheral vision, she could see Darren pick up a set of darts and throw one at the board. She then noticed Ben glance over at Darren and stare at him as if sizing up his competition. *He's jealous. That's even weirder. Why would he be jealous of Darren? Darren didn't do anything to make him jealous. He's just a friend.*

After a few beers, she let Ben take her back to his place.

"Darren has a thing for you," he said as they got in the car.

"What? How do you know that?"

"I can tell by the way he looks at you."

"I think you're seeing things. He and I are just friends—he's a really good guy," Charlotte said trying to talk Ben out of his assumptions even though she often wondered it herself.

"No, trust me, he likes you."

"Well, fine—but he's a year too late. I'm a marrying you," Charlotte said leaning over and kissing him on the cheek. She wasn't sure how it made Ben feel, but she certainly felt somewhat unsettled. She knew some girls liked making their boyfriends jealous, but she didn't. She didn't like that kind of drama. Maybe they were both just nervous about the wedding stuff. "I saw the girls talking to you. What did they say?"

"Just how great being married is and how fun the honeymoon will be," he said with a small laugh. "I think you're friends want to attend another wedding."

"That sounds like them," Charlotte laughed as they pulled into his garage. "I haven't really told them much."

Ben remained quiet as he parked and turned off the engine. "Charlotte, I know I've been distant about the wedding stuff and I'm sorry."

Charlotte's heart dropped as her brain went to the 'But I'm not sure I want to get married' break up speech. "It's okay. I understand."

"No you don't," he said hesitating as if he wanted to tell her something. Waiting patiently, Charlotte prepared herself for those words ending their relationship. For a split second, she almost said the words first. Instead, Ben just turned and blurted it out. "Why didn't you tell me someone hurt you in college?"

That was the last thing she expected him to say. That part of her past, coming from Ben, was like a knife through her heart. It cut at the memories she'd buried and now she would have to bring them up all over again. "I don't know. I just never wanted to talk about it again. How did you find out? Ali?"

"Actually, Trevor. He thought I already knew."

Charlotte wasn't sure what made her more uncomfortable—talking about it now to Ben or knowing he and Trevor had a conversation about it and she had no idea. She was always worried Trevor was going to tell Ben but she could only blame herself for not saying anything to Ben about it first. "When?"

"At football last weekend. Look, it doesn't matter that he told me—what matters is it happened and you didn't tell me."

"It's not like I lied to you or anything."

"I know, but it's something I feel I should have known about you. It's not right that Trevor has all these memories with you that I can't access."

He didn't sound mad, but slightly hurt. No wonder he seemed a little jealous earlier. "Do you think I'm hiding stuff from you, because I'm not."

"No, that's not it. I trust you, but I just want to make sure I know the whole you."

"Well, you can't know every little detail about me, Ben. I had a life before you that involved other people."

"I know, I know," he sighed. "Now I'm just feeling stupid. I'm sorry. Let's go inside."

Charlotte opened the car door feeling overwhelmed and anxious. Ben just said he wanted to know the whole her but how can he get to know her when he wasn't letting her get to know him? "What about you, Ben. Have you told me everything?"

The look that crossed Ben's faced made Charlotte feel small. He looked as if she just called him a liar. She knew he was ignoring her as he led her up the stairs to his place. *Dammit, Ben, talk to me.* It was no use as he stopped her short from asking anymore questions. Uneasy, Charlotte just wanted him to get mad at her and demand to know everything. She wanted a deep, drag out fight where they could just get all these issues out in the open and deal with them head on. It would never happen with Ben, though. He was too controlled.

Now, standing in the shower, she knew without a doubt Trevor said something to Ben. Although she didn't think Trevor would betray her, she still regretted telling him about her sex life. *Dummy! Why didn't you just keep your mouth shut?* The uneasiness settled deep into her heart as she thought about Ben knowing her past with Trevor. *Did Trevor say anything about their relationship at Cal Poly?*

Climbing into bed, she waited for Ben to finish his shower. Watching TV, she felt tired and bloated from the beers she drank earlier and she couldn't get comfortable. Turning on her side, she noticed Ben's nightstand. She'd never looked in his top drawer. Listening to make sure the water was still running in the bathroom, she scooted out of bed. Her heart pounding, she opened the drawer.

The first item she noticed was a box of condoms. That didn't surprise her because he always reached over to the drawer the few times they did have sex. Digging underneath, she found a pen and a picture of Ben with another woman. They looked young, but happy. No writing on the back and the picture was worn like it had been around for a while. Puzzled, Charlotte's heart sped up even harder as she reached back further into the drawer.

Bingo.

She knew they were prescription bottles before she even pulled them out. There were two and the first one was Marplan which is prescribed for depression and anxiety. The dates were current. The second was for Ambien which she knew was to induce sleep. Making a mental note to look up Marplan tomorrow, she replaced the bottles and closed the drawer. So Trevor was right after all, Ben was depressed. Why hadn't Ben told her? She felt shut out of his life in a way she wasn't used to previously. She had no problems with the medications; she just wanted to know the reason. *Ben, please talk to me.*

Once Ben was out of the shower and in bed, Charlotte wanted desperately to have a conversation, but they both remained quiet in the dark. Rolling on her side, it was his cue to scoot up behind her and spoon. When he didn't move, Charlotte felt her heart sink.

Something had divided them and she wasn't sure she could remove it.

"I was doing a midnight shift and someone hit me," she whispered in the dark hoping if she told her story, he would tell his. "I didn't see it coming and I still can't really picture the person, but I had just come back from the bathroom and he came out of nowhere."

After telling Ben the details, she felt cleansed. She even mentioned Trevor was the person who found her on the floor. Charlotte felt better once Ben rolled over, put his arm around her waist and pulled her closer to him. "I'm so sorry."

"It's okay. It was a long time ago. I think my parents and the school were more traumatized than I was," she said with a small chuckle.

"They never caught the guy?"

"Nope."

"Why didn't you tell me about it?" Ben asked again.

"Because it is so far in my past and I don't like to remember it. It's not how I want to remember my time at KCPR."

"How much did he hurt you?"

"I wasn't raped or anything if that's what you're thinking. I had a concussion and a few bruises. I was in the hospital overnight and it ended up being a big story on campus." Feeling Ben kiss her on the top of her head, she turned over in his arms hoping he would open up to her. "I feel better having told you."

"Good. I'm glad you did," he replied moving onto his back so Charlotte could lay her head in the crook of his arm. "I hate that something like that happened to you. I can see why you and Trevor are close."

Actually, that's what pulled us apart. She decided against telling him how she ended her relationship with Trevor. That period in her life was a blur and she really didn't want to relive it. Burying those feelings hadn't been easy, but she managed enough to not even care if they found the guy who did it. In a way, it made her stronger and more street smart. She knew how to depend on her instincts—something she was conveniently ignoring lately.

After a long pause, Charlotte felt Ben's breathing deepen and she knew he'd fallen asleep. Moving out of his arm and over to her side of the bed, she felt more puzzled than before. She had nothing left to hide but knew Ben was still keeping something from her. The wall between them suddenly grew higher and thicker.

Eleven

Charlotte felt her legs burn as she climbed the steep hill to the top of the Tennessee Valley trail in the Marin Headlands. It was warm for late November allowing her to hike in short sleeves. Once she got to the top, she stopped to admire the view of the ocean spanning from San Francisco to Point Reyes. Since the air was completely clear, she could see the Transamerica building in the far distance peaking up above the hills. It was stunning and normally one of her most favorite views, yet today she couldn't enjoy it.

Charlotte felt so anxious that even the heavy exercise paired with the upbeat music blaring through her headphones couldn't calm her nerves. Listening to everything from The Cult, to Suicidal Tendencies, Nine Inch Nails, and The Yeah Yeah Yeahs, she let the beat carry her pace.

Ben hadn't called since that horrible Thanksgiving at her parents four days ago.

With her brother Matt back east with his wife's family and her youngest brother Ryan serving overseas and away from home, she'd invited both Ben and Trevor to her parents for dinner. Ben's wasn't going home to Minneapolis to see his family due to work on Friday and Trevor's parents were visiting his sister in Virginia for the holiday. Obviously, Ben attending dinner with her was given, but she invited Trevor last minute because he hadn't made any plans and she didn't want him to be alone.

She had no idea the repercussions that decision would have on her and Ben.

Ben had picked her up before they drove over to Trevor's. He seemed quieter than usual, but maybe because they had finally settled on a date for the wedding—the following October—which Charlotte thought was a huge step. It lifted some of the weight sitting on her shoulders and she was starting to feel better about the engagement now that Ben seemed more interested in it. He still hadn't opened up much about his health and Charlotte decided not to push it. She would ask him after the holidays which were approaching faster than a speeding train. The holidays seemed to be such a stressful time to begin with; she didn't want to cause more by nagging Ben.

Trevor, on the other hand, seemed tired and hung over. *Great, my parents are going to love seeing him.* Actually, her mom was thrilled to know Trevor was back in her life. Janice and Gerald Campbell had met Trevor once long ago when they visited her at college. He had charmed them completely and when Janice found out he was coming to dinner, she wouldn't stop talking about it.

"You look like you went on a bender, Trevor," Ben said pulling away from the curb.

"Please, don't remind me," Trevor said. "The guys and I pulled a late one last night."

"Right, the guys," Ben said laughing as he viewed Trevor in the rearview mirror.

Charlotte remained quiet—playing with the MP3 player on Ben's stereo. Finding Ben's collection of Queen, she purposely turned up Bohemian Rhapsody just to torture Trevor.

"Oh god, Charlie, stop. Please," he groaned as Charlotte giggled. *Serves him right.* Turning around and looking at him, she realized he hadn't shaved and his eyes were puffy. "Did you even get any sleep?"

"A little. Remind me never to do tequila shots again. I'm too old for that," he said leaning his head against the window and closing his eyes.

"This is going to be a long afternoon," Charlotte said to Ben who was maneuvering the car onto the Bay Bridge.

Forty minutes later, they were greeted by Janice and Gerald as they pulled into the driveway. Charlotte admired the new landscaping her mom designed over the summer. The grass looked green and healthy while the Japanese maple had turned a brilliant orange illuminating the light gray porch. Her childhood home was now the best looking on the block and Charlotte knew she could never match her mother's green thumb.

"Hi sweetie," her dad said greeting her with a kiss.

"Hi mom and dad—you know Ben and I'm sure you remember Trevor from college," she replied letting her dad shake the guys' hands.

By now, Trevor had miraculously perked up and seemed his pleasant and charming self. Once inside, Charlotte took their coats and hung them in the front closet taking in the smell of her mom's cooking. The TV blared football which she knew would draw the guys in while she stayed in the kitchen with her mom.

"Well, Trevor sure looks good. He's matured very nicely. Got rid of that nose ring, I see," Janice said as she started peeling potatoes. "Help me out. Can you stir the gravy?"

Charlotte picked up the wooden spoon and started stirring. "I know. He does look good. A little hung over today, so don't plan on too much conversation from him."

"Is he seeing anyone?"

"He's seeing a woman we work with—my manager's manager." Charlotte thought of Michelle and wondered what she was doing today and why she wasn't with Trevor or why she hadn't invited him to her Thanksgiving. Come to think of it, he hadn't mentioned Michelle much at all lately.

"He sure had a thing for you in college."

"Let's not go there right now, please. Ben is here and he doesn't know."

"You haven't told Ben you and Trevor dated?"

"No. I know I should, but what good would it do," Charlotte said as she continued to stir. "They seem to have a good friendship going and who am I to ruin that?"

"Charlotte, men aren't like that. Trevor is friends with Ben because of you," Janice said. "I've raised two boys and I know they don't like being friends with the man who is marrying an ex. They don't work that way."

"Oh come on. Trevor and I were so long ago and we barely made a blip on the relationship radar."

"Whose fault was that?"

"Are you saying I should have continued dating Trevor? I was in no place to do that."

"I'm not saying that at all. You went through trauma and it was bad timing but he was good for you."

"Mom, I don't want to talk about this right now," Charlotte said cutting the conversation off. She really didn't want to talk about it because it made her extremely uncomfortable because the words coming from her mom echoed her own thoughts. It was her fault and she still feels guilty. Hearing Trevor talking football in the other room, she remembered again how much she loved his voice.

"Ben seems distracted," Janice said after throwing the potatoes into a pot and filling it with water. "What's up with him?"

"Distracted? I haven't noticed," Charlotte replied trying to sound surprised. Charlotte hoped she'd been imagining Ben's mood, but when her mom noticed it, she couldn't ignore it anymore. Normally, he warmed up to her dad and vice versa but today, he didn't seem his outgoing and talkative self. Listening to the conversation coming from the family room, she could tell her dad and Trevor were controlling it by bouncing football stats off each other. She could hear Ben speak only when spoken to. *Weird.*

Pouring a glass of wine, she started to relax and figured it was only dinner and it would be over in a couple hours and they could all go back to the city. "Have you heard from Matt or Ryan?"

"Matt is knee deep in children under the age of four in New York with all his wife's nieces and nephews and Ryan should be skyping a little bit later."

Charlotte smiled at the thought of using the video conferencing technology to talk her brother. She missed him so much. She hadn't seen Ryan in six months and knew he was under some heavy fire in Afghanistan. "I hope he's okay."

"Your father and I go to bed every night worried about him. He's lost a lot of friends."

Just thinking about the danger Ryan was in added an extra weight on her shoulders but she was so proud of him. Looking down at the ring on her finger, she decided to change the subject. "Mom, do you think Ben and I are right for each other?"

Charlotte waited as her mom turned on the stove to boil the potatoes. "I like Ben—he seems like a good catch. Is he the right person for you? Only you can answer that. It doesn't matter what I think."

That startled Charlotte. She expected her mom to praise Ben and say she was the perfect man for her. Her mom's tone suggested otherwise. "What do you mean? You don't think we're good for each other?"

"I didn't say that—I meant to say no one but you and Ben knows what goes on behind closed doors. If it's right, you know it. Why? What's going on?"

"Nothing."

Charlotte didn't want to bring anything up with Ben sitting twenty feet away. It was a discussion for another time. She didn't want her mom to know anything about her sex life with Ben, either. How uncomfortable. Thinking about the wedding date and being in her childhood home, Charlotte suddenly felt like a small child making a grown up decision her parents didn't understand. She wanted her mom to be more excited for her and tell her she was making the right decision and she'd be happy with Ben forever.

After dinner and doing dishes, Trevor and Ben decided to throw a football in the park next door to the house.

"Come on Charlotte, I know you have an arm," Trevor said pushing her out the door.

"Okay, fine, but be nice," Charlotte retorted crinkling her nose. About a year ago, she broke it playing football in the same recreational league Ben and Trevor play for now. She can still feel the crack and the blood gush after she got hit with an elbow trying to make an interception. Trevor was right, however, she does have an arm.

Once in the park, Trevor ran deep before Ben threw him the ball which he caught. Standing next to Ben, Charlotte felt something was wrong. His demeanor was off and she wanted to ask him what was wrong but was scared to bring it up. He probably would deny anything was wrong anyway.

Without even a beat, Ben threw the ball back to Trevor and turned to her. "Why didn't you tell me you and Trevor were a couple?"

He said it so matter of factly, Charlotte wasn't sure if he was angry or not. "I—I don't know. How did you find out?"

"I overheard the conversation with your mom."

"Oh. I'm so sorry, Ben. I should have told you but I didn't think it was that big of a deal."

"Well it is. If I had known, he and I wouldn't be friends," Ben said catching the ball Trevor threw back. "If Trevor wasn't a good guy, I'd kick his ass."

"It was really long ago, Ben, seriously." Charlotte couldn't tell if he was genuinely upset or making a joke.

"Maybe for you, but I see the way he looks at you. He still has a thing for you."

What was it with Ben noticing the way other guys look at me? Maybe I should start mentioning how other women look at him. "No he doesn't," Charlotte replied weakly wondering if that was true. Did Trevor still have feelings for her? Looking over at Trevor waiting for the ball to be thrown, she felt a tingle but at the same time felt very guilty for how this was making Ben feel.

"I'm sorry I didn't tell you, but now you know. It was a short time and it all ended when I was assaulted."

"How am I to believe that? How do I know you don't have feelings for him now?"

Ben didn't miss the hesitation in Charlotte's response. "Oh super—you do have feelings for him."

Panic settled in as Trevor approached cutting off the conversation. "Hey, what's going on?"

Throwing the ball at Trevor, Ben finally got angry. "Why don't you ask your ex-girlfriend?"

"What are you talking about?" Trevor said sounding confused.

"He found out we dated in college," Charlotte interjected. She stopped short of telling Trevor that Ben thought there were still unresolved feelings.

"Oh, well, that was a long time ago," Trevor said.

"I'm sure it was, but why don't I feel better about it," Ben said. "I feel very uncomfortable about this whole thing."

"Please don't, Ben. Nothing is going on between us now," Charlotte said telling the truth but feeling like she was hiding something or flat out lying. There was something between her and Trevor but she didn't know what it was. *Unresolved feelings? The past? Close friendship? I honestly don't know.* It's so mixed up.

"I think I'm going to take off," Ben said. "You can both take the train back into the city."

"Wait—you're leaving?" Charlotte said surprised and now feeling angry. She hated this kind of drama—especially in front of her parents. "Please don't go."

"You don't have to leave, Ben," Trevor reiterated.

"Well, I'm suddenly not feeling well."

"Ben, that's kind of immature, don't you think? So you found out Trevor and I dated in college, so what?" Charlotte said.

"I just feel like you both lied to me," Ben said walking back to his car.

"That was a little dramatic," she said trying to make light of the situation. She felt so embarrassed. Ben never acted this way. He never lost his cool especially over something stupid like a long ago relationship. However, she knew he was partially right. She should have told him the truth from the beginning. If the roles were reversed, she would have been mad he hadn't told her or at least trusted her to be a grown up about it.

The tears threatened as she watched Ben drive away. Everything was falling apart and her life felt like sand falling through her fingers. The harder she tried to grasp at it, the faster if slipped through. It was so frustrating when this was the time of her life she should be happy and excited.

"Cut him some slack," Trevor said as they walked back to the house. "He seems like he has a lot on his mind."

"Apparently so," Charlotte said sarcastically. "Maybe if he actually talked to me about it, we could avoid all this."

"Well, if I were him, I guess I'd be a little pissed."

"Should we have told him, Trevor? Seriously, how do you tell your current boyfriend he is now friends with your ex?"

"I wonder if that is actually the problem," Trevor said.

"What do you mean?" Charlotte suddenly felt like Trevor wasn't telling her everything.

"I don't know. Maybe work is stressing him out or something," Trevor said a bit too casually.

"Is there something you're not telling me?" Charlotte's thoughts went to the worst case scenario—Ben cheating or something close to that.

"No, no," Trevor replied. "Relax, Charlie, I'm sure this will blow over. He just needs to be alone for a bit."

Be alone? This isn't how a man who wants to marry her should be acting—especially in front of his future in-laws. What was she going to tell her parents? Ben suddenly took off because he was jealous and insecure? Recalling her conversation with her mom in the kitchen, she knew she never said anything that should have really worried Ben. Maybe he overheard her mom talking about Trevor? Whatever it was, it sent Ben running back to the city and that scared Charlotte.

The trip home on BART wasn't any better. Charlotte felt even more anxious now because she felt her life was spinning out of control. The last time she felt this way was when she found out she was getting laid off from her job and there was nothing she could do about it but get through it.

Realistically, she knew this wasn't what she wanted in a marriage, but the more Ben pulled away, the more she grasped at him and the more her heart wanted to fix it. Everything seemed fine before Trevor walked back into her life and Ben proposed. Since then, it's been up and down, sideways, and upside down. She wants to be with Ben and she doesn't want to be with Ben—it was enough to drive a sane person crazy. *My heart hurts.*

"Hey, looks like Collective Soul is playing in three weeks. You want to go?" Trevor said as he looked up from his phone.

"Maybe," Charlotte replied. Nothing, not even Collective Soul sounded comforting right now. The only thing she wanted to do was get back to the city and see Ben.

"I could ask Michelle and you could ask Ben—it wouldn't be only us," Trevor clarified. Funny, the thought never occurred to her, but now that she thought about it, it would have to be this way. Since Ben found out they dated, it would always hang there when she was alone with Trevor. But what was Ben hiding from her?

Her anxiousness at Ben suddenly grew into anger at Trevor. "What the fuck are you hiding from me?"

She knew her language caught Trevor off guard and the look of pain in his face gave him away. "I'm not hiding anything," he sighed.

"I know you are and it isn't fair. You were my friend first," she hissed quietly so the rest of the train couldn't hear her.

Charlotte scooted closer to the window as Trevor turned to face her. "This isn't some sort of contest about loyalty, Charlotte. You both are my friends now and I hate seeing you both struggle."

"Struggle with what exactly? What do you mean?" Frustrated, Charlotte held back the tears she felt forming again. "I told you about our sex life and I shouldn't have. I feel so guilty about that but I can't undo it. I'm pretty sure you know more than you're telling me and its pissing me off. This is my life, Trevor. I'm engaged to this man."

Suddenly it hit her like a cold bucket of water—maybe Ben was seeing someone else. "Is he cheating on me?"

Trevor looked surprised at that comment. "I swear, it's nothing like that."

"So you do know something!"

Charlotte knew she defeated him when his shoulders slumped. "Okay, fine. I'll tell you. But you can't throw it in his face, Charlie. You have to let him explain it to you."

Listening as Trevor explained the accident, Charlotte's heart sped up as fast the train which was now speeding under the bay into San Francisco. Her heart broke for Ben as Trevor described the anguish Ben was going through. Why hadn't Ben told her? It was a lot to process, but it was an accident.

"What about the ex-girlfriend?" she asked.

"I don't know much. I don't think they speak, but I could tell it bothered him," Trevor said quietly. "I feel so bad about being in the middle of this. Part of me wished he never said anything to me. It was killing me I knew about it and you didn't."

"Is that why you told me about the depression? Did he tell you he was taking medication?"

"In short, yes, but I didn't know about the medication."

Charlotte wasn't sure she felt relieved or betrayed. Ben had told Trevor and not her, the woman he was marrying. Did Ben not love her enough to trust her? Isn't that what being a partner to someone is all about—trust and honesty? Is Ben even considering telling her?

"I'm so mad right now," she said as the train pulled into the Embarcadero station. This was her stop.

"I'm so sorry, Charlie. Is there something I can do for you?"

Looking at Trevor, she channeled her anger at Ben towards him. She just wanted to get away from Trevor. "No. I need to get off here. I'll talk to you later."

"Are you sure you'll be okay? Maybe I should get off here with you and we can cab it together."

"No, that's okay. I'll be fine. I need to be alone."

Once the train stopped, Charlotte jumped up and almost ran through the open doors. She needed to get out of there—she needed fresh air because she could feel a pounding headache coming on. Everything felt so overwhelming—from Ben leaving suddenly to Trevor being the one to tell her about Ben's baggage. She felt alone and confused.

She wanted nothing more than to confront Ben and get him to finally talk to her. After saying a quick and awkward goodbye to Trevor, she caught a cab on Market Street, telling the driver to take her to the Marina. She and Ben needed to clear the air and get everything out in the open. There should be no secrets between them—well, not big ones like this. There were so many questions she needed to ask him.

After paying the driver, she stood in front of Ben's apartment ready to go to battle. The streets were mostly empty due to the holiday and Charlotte felt very alone. Staring at Ben's building, everything suddenly felt foreign to her as if her life shifted one way and she wasn't prepared for it. Staring at his window, she wanted it all to go back to the way it was before he proposed. She was happy then—well mostly happy. Even before she rang the doorbell, she knew he wasn't home. The place was dark and quiet.

Punching in his door code, she knew it would ring his phone so he could press a button and let her in, but she got his voicemail. *Damn.* Trying again, his voicemail picked up. After a third time, she knew his phone was turned off. Where was he? She tried his number again from her phone and it went straight to voicemail again. She felt stupid standing in the doorway, so she sat down on the curb and waited.

She waited for three hours.

By now, it was midnight and apparently he wasn't coming home. She was so angry and thought about throwing a rock through his window but even if she got up the courage to do something like that, she couldn't find a rock big enough. *Where the hell are you? I'm standing underneath your window looking like an idiot and you won't even pick up your phone.*

Another hour passed and Charlotte's emotions moved from anger to panic and worry. She wasn't worried about Ben's safety necessarily, but for their future together. Even through the despair and the tears that started flowing down her cheeks, she knew the relationship was over.

The tears spilled so hard she didn't even remember the walk home.

Now, four days later, Charlotte stared out at the ocean from the mountain top. Charlotte knew what she had to do. It didn't matter that Ben had a past. It didn't matter that he took medication to combat a depression he never told her about and it didn't even matter that he wanted sex a lot less than she did. What mattered was that he didn't trust her or love her enough to tell her the truth. Instead, he told Trevor—a guy he barely knew and who was her friend first.

The most unsettling part of all—he hadn't even bothered to call her to talk about it. That's what she wanted most of all. She left a dozen messages and hadn't heard anything back from Ben. Despite knowing her relationship was over, she still clung to a small ray of hope that it would all work out.

Twelve

Well that was a harsh goodbye, Trevor thought watching Charlotte wave down a cab and get inside.

Standing alone on Market Street, he wanted to take back everything he told her on the train. *Why did I open my big mouth?* He felt as if she punished him for Ben's action, however, logically he understood her behavior. She was hurt and devastated. Trevor wanted to grab a cab and follow her, but decided against it because he was already too much in the middle of this drama and there was nothing he could do right now.

Waiting for the bus, he remembered it was a holiday and the normal lines don't run. Staring at the downtown lights, he put on his headphones wanting the music to take away the disastrous events of the day. Now both Charlotte and Ben were mad at him and he didn't know how to fix it.

He hadn't meant to blurt out Ben's story like he did, but he had to admit there was a small devil sitting on his shoulder eager to stir up trouble. On the other hand, the last thing he wanted was to be responsible for his friends' unhappiness. He would be the first person to honestly admit he had a stake in whether Ben and Charlotte's relationship imploded. Would he benefit if they broke up? Possibly. He might then have another chance with Charlotte. While he knew without a doubt Ben and Charlotte weren't right for each other, he would never want to break them up for his own benefit. No matter how much he loved her, he could never to that to her if it was Ben she was truly in love with. He wanted Charlotte and Ben to realize they needed to call off the engagement on their own. Maybe after today, it would actually happen. Even if Charlotte never forgave him for keeping Ben's secret, he would still be there for her. This time, there was no graduation on the horizon and that meant he wasn't going anywhere. *To be fair, Charlotte, you had secrets of your own you didn't share with him, so you're not all in the clear, either.*

The bus finally pulled up and Trevor got on making his way to the middle. It was empty, so he took a seat next to the window. Staring at the passing buildings while listening to his iPod, he thought about his conversation with Ben the other day. It was clear Ben wasn't over his ex, Nora. That door was still wide open because the issues of the accident were never resolved. *Running away never solves anything.* From Trevor's perspective, it seemed getting engaged and staring down the word *forever* undid the relationship for both of them. Thinking about Charlotte's reaction, it seemed she was more concerned about how the secret was kept from her as opposed to how much pain Ben was experiencing. Trevor chuckled softly at how self-absorbed Charlotte could be sometimes. *She isn't pleased to meet you—you're pleased to meet her.* Luckily, she balanced it out with a kind heart.

Fifteen minutes later, Trevor was home and in bed. Every muscle in his body ached. He was tired, but couldn't fall asleep. Lying in the dark, his mind wandered to some of the women he'd dated in the past. There was Charlotte, of course, but before her was Allison, his high school girlfriend whom he dated into his first year of college. Unfortunately, it was the classic case of being young and going to separate colleges which doomed the relationship. They both moved on after breaking up at Christmas during their freshman year. There wasn't really anyone else for the next couple years although he did some casual dating. He enjoyed being single, going to classes, partying with his buddies, and working at the radio station.

Once he met Charlotte, something awoke inside of him and he realized he was ready to try a relationship again. She was young, but they got along well and had a lot in common. All he wanted to do was run his hands over her body and kiss her lips. The attraction he felt for her was both physical and mental and since she was a virgin, he instinctively took the time to get to know her without pressuring her. She never seemed uncomfortable exploring, but she was shy. The many hours they spent studying together, going to movies, hanging out at the station, walking the beach and hiking Madonna mountain pushed them closer together enough for her overcome that shyness and trust him. He never got tired of her company, either.

Once things with Charlotte crashed and burned, he was lost. He was about to graduate and all he could think about, aside from finishing his senior paper, was Charlotte. Every day he battled himself not to call her and beg her back. It was obvious she didn't want him in her life. Once spring quarter rolled around, he let Charlotte go and started casually dating Katie Bishop.

He'd known Katie through the station, but she hadn't been very active with it during that year. Trevor remembered thinking she was the exact opposite of someone he'd normally be attracted to—she was tall, a little heavy, wore lots of black clothes and heavy goth makeup. He started really getting to know her when she came over to study with his roommate Ethan. That was an interesting combination—the nerdy engineer major and the goth girl. Trevor would laugh at how funny they looked together at the kitchen table. It wasn't long before Trevor found himself alone on the couch with Katie discussing everything from politics, to religion, to how reality television has effectively destroyed the world.

On a particular boring night out at McCarthy's, he ran into Katie and her friends outside on the patio. Trevor hadn't been in the mood for drinking, but he needed to get away from reading headlines and old news articles for his senior paper and he wanted to unwind a bit. Katie had changed a lot—she dropped some weight and toned down the makeup. Two hours later, she was in his bed.

Lying in bed now, Trevor couldn't shut off his thoughts about that time in his life as the memories kept flooding out. Turning over on his side, he stared at the alarm clock remembering one memory in particular.

It was close to the end of the quarter and finals were coming up. He had planned to stay home and study, but one of his favorite local bands was playing downtown and he wanted to see them one last time before he left town for San Diego. It would be bittersweet for him since he wasn't all that happy about leaving SLO. He had a job lined up with the local news station as an assistant producer, but even that didn't excite him. It was leaving KCPR, his friends, and most of all Charlotte. Despite dating Katie, he still couldn't get Charlotte out of his head. He listened to her show every week and spent a lot of time at the station hoping to run into her. It was masochistic, but he couldn't help it.

His casual fling with Katie backfired on him and she was now pressing for a relationship. She called and texted more than he liked and every time he made plans to go out with his friends, she would somehow show up to the same place. He tried numerous times to break it off, but she wouldn't give up. If he wasn't moving away in a few weeks, he would have changed his number although that wouldn't help because she would probably just find a way to get it through mutual friends. Unfortunately, she was a good person and he just couldn't be mean.

When he walked up to SLO Brew, Katie was somehow there waiting for him. At first, Trevor was puzzled at how she knew he'd be there, but then he remembered mentioning the show when they were together in bed—weeks ago. He'd stopped sleeping with her awhile back feeling too guilty and not wanting to use her that way.

"Hi," she said as he approached. "I tried calling you, but you didn't pick up."

"Hey," Trevor said flatly. "What are you doing here?"

"I like the band, too," Katie said defensively.

Trevor didn't want to get into another fight at the moment and conceded to Katie. He paid the cover for her and they walked up the stairs together. He knew before he even spotted Charlotte that she was there, too. Somehow he just felt it.

He stood at the entrance and spotted her instantly with Jamie and Cameron eating at a table near the window. The place was crowded as the opening band played loudly on the small stage at the back of the restaurant. Making his way over to the bar, he could feel Charlotte's eyes on him without even turning around. It never astonished him the power of electricity that ran between them even when they weren't speaking.

"I'll have a pale ale," Katie said behind him and bringing him back to the present. He was now regretting letting her come in with him. Charlotte would probably think they were still together if she even knew they'd been dating. The way gossip went around the station, he was pretty sure she knew. He could feel her looking over at him but when he turned to glance back at her; she was happily talking to Jamie.

"Who are you looking at?" Katie asked when he handed her the pint of beer.

"No one," he said. Katie knew about Charlotte and had tried to get him to talk about what happened between the two of them, but he wouldn't budge. It was between him and Charlotte and to be honest, he wouldn't even know how to explain it if he could. Right now, he was so uncomfortable he was drinking his beer much faster than normal. He felt a slight buzz coming on.

"It's Charlotte, isn't it? Is there something still going on between the two of you?"

"No."

"She keeps looking over here."

"Okay."

Trevor knew Katie was frustrated as she turned her back to him to watch the band. He also knew he should pay more attention to her, but right now all he could think about was Charlotte sitting on the other side of the room. When he looked over, she was gone from the table, but he quickly caught sight of her walking to the bathroom. Gulping down his beer, he followed her and stood just inside the small dark hallway and waited for her to come out. He was just buzzed enough to feel it was the right move.

As the door opened and she came out, he lost all ability to speak. He knew she'd been avoiding him for months and it hurt. He just wanted to know she still had some feelings left for him.

"Hi Charlie," he said as he watched her eyes go wide. *Surprise, you have to talk to me now.*

"Hi," she replied back quietly.

"How are you?" he asked worried she wanted to get by him and run back to her table. She seemed uncomfortable and wouldn't look him in the eye.

"I'm really good, how are you?"

"You look nice." *You look nice??!!* Trevor wanted to kick himself for saying something so lame. What he really wanted to do was grab her and kiss her and make the last few months go away.

"Thank you. So do you."

Okay, this is it, Trevor. Tell her. Just tell her. "Charlotte…I miss you so damn much. I don't know what I did that pissed you off, but I wish I could fix it."

The look of astonishment and then disappointment on Charlotte's face deflated Trevor. He felt his buzz disappear as his heart sank. Her silence said it all—she didn't want him back in her life.

"I want us to be friends again," Trevor continued anyway. What the hell—being friends was still better than nothing. "I feel so bad about what happened and I don't want to graduate thinking you hate me."

"I don't hate you, Trevor. I want to be friends, too."

Why couldn't she have said she wanted something more than just friends? That's what he wanted so desperately to hear. He'd have to settle for friends and maybe that is what it was meant to be. Something inside him shut off. He was so exhausted from thinking about her and he was ready to move on. Why pine over someone who's made it clear she doesn't want you? Charlotte had three more years of school and he was about to move south—the deck was stacked against them anyway. At that moment, he picked his heart back up and he resolved to enjoy the last couple weeks of school free from thoughts of Charlotte. "I have to get back to the bar," he said finally and that was the last time he saw Charlotte—standing there in the hallway at SLO Brew.

"Katie, I'm leaving," he said as he walked by the bar.

"Okay, let me just finish this beer."

"I'm leaving now," he said wishing he could just leave her there and go home alone. Looking over at Charlotte's table, he saw Jamie and Cameron staring at him. *They must know something.* Diverting his eyes, he took the stairs down to the street and felt instant relief after taking a breath of fresh air. Garden Street, with its trees lit with white lights, was one of his favorite streets downtown. Normally, it made him happy to be there, but tonight, he just wanted a black hole to swallow him up.

"What's the matter?" Katie caught up to him out of breath.

"Nothing," Trevor said picking up his pace.

"Trevor, you need to talk to me," Katie said pulling at his arm.

Stopping, Trevor had had enough. He wanted to be alone and that meant alone without Katie. "Look Katie, this isn't working. Seriously, we can't see each other anymore." It sounded harsh even to his ears and the look on her face was a double blow. "I'm sorry, I don't mean to hurt your feelings, but I'm trying to get over someone else and graduate at the same time."

"Is that person Charlotte? I saw you talking to her," Katie said through her tears. "What is it about her you can't get over? She's so plain."

"I don't know why, but it's none of your business."

"It is my business, Trevor. We've been sleeping together."

"No, we *were* sleeping together and I enjoyed our time but it was over weeks ago. I said I didn't want a relationship and I meant it. I'm sorry if you felt otherwise." Everything was coming out wrong—so wrong.

"I don't know what you want," she said moving closer to him. Trevor gently removed her arms when she tried to put them around his neck.

"I don't want anything," he continued. "Actually, no, that's not true—what I do want is to be alone right now." They walked a little further in silence. "I'll put you in a cab."

The problem with San Luis Obispo—there were no cabs waiting. Trevor rolled his eyes wondering how he could get Katie home.

"Trevor, you're pissing me off."

"Well, you wouldn't be the first person."

"Stop and talk to me!"

Trevor stopped, surprised at the tone of her voice. A caution flag went up in his mind.

"You've been using me, you asshole," she started—rather loudly. "That is so unfair to me. I've been in love with you for so long and all you can do is think about Charlotte. Were you thinking about her all those times you fucked me?"

This was Trevor's complete nightmare—a loud confrontation in the middle of Higuera Street where everyone was bar hopping. "Katie, lower your voice."

"Fuck you, asshole," she repeated even louder. "You're an abusive son of a bitch and I can't believe I even once thought you cared about me. I fell for it all."

"I do care about you," he said quietly trying to subdue her. "But you knew I didn't want anything serious. I tried not to lead you on."

Trevor could see the look in Katie's eyes and he actually feared for his safety. Had there been something close for her to grab, she probably would have hit him over the head with it. She looked as if she was going to explode and he'd never seen this side of her. He remembered his buddy and fellow DJ Dean telling him Katie did some hard drugs but he'd never seen her do anything around him and she didn't seem high now. She approached him and slapped him and then started punching him in the shoulder. He was caught so by surprise, he didn't have any time to react except to push her away from him. The next thing he knew, he was being thrown to ground to two men.

"Hey buddy, leave her alone," one of them said.

This was so stupid, Trevor thought as he tried to pull away. "Let go of me."

Both guys clamped down on him even harder forcing him to lay still. What the hell was going on? In the meantime, Katie started crying hysterically and several girls huddled around her telling her she was okay. As if things couldn't get any worse, a police car rolled up stopping traffic and gaining even more attention. *Fucking great*, Trevor thought clenching his teeth.

"What's going on here," the officer said as he walked up and shined a flashlight in Trevor's face.

"Just a misunderstanding, sir," Trevor said.

Katie's hysterical wailing suddenly turned into screaming, "You asshole, how dare you hit me?"

"Can you tell me what happened, ma'am?" the officer asked. Trevor was relieved when the officer stepped in front of Katie preventing her from getting closer to him.

"He hit me. We were walking and he got all mad at me and hit me," she said pointing at Trevor.

"No, I didn't," Trevor said trying to remain calm. This was completely absurd. Of all the worst case scenarios, this was it—being accused of abusing a woman. Why was she doing this? He knew he hadn't treated her right, but he didn't deserve this. "I was walking home and trying to call her a cab when she slapped me and punched me in the shoulder."

Trevor waited as the officer took notes. "So you didn't hit her?"

"Hell, no. I would never hit a woman." He felt silly even saying that out loud. His face throbbed from the slap Katie gave him. If anything, that should prove he was the one being abused.

"Have you been drinking tonight?"

"Yes, I had one beer at SLO Brew but then decided to walk home. I was trying to get her home, too."

"I see," the officer said looking at him. "Get up and stand over here."

Cautiously standing up, he averted his eyes away from Katie knowing she wanted him to look at her. A crowd had gathered and everyone was staring and whispering—some actually laughing and betting on his arrest. Trevor tuned all the voices out and concentrated on the problem before him. He did not want to spend the night in jail.

"Okay, I need you to follow this line, please," the officer said pointing to the crack in the sidewalk.

After Trevor completed and apparently passed the tests, the officer let him and Katie off with a ticket for disturbing the peace.

"You go your own way, I'll make sure she gets a cab ride home," the officer said dismissing Trevor.

Never so happy to leave downtown, he almost jogged home to his apartment. His adrenaline was still coursing through his blood as his brain tried to register what exactly happened. Is this what happens when you break up with a woman? She goes crazy? Katie literally went berserk. Then he started flashing back on episodes such as the time he was at her place and she was screaming at her mom over the phone and the time she yelled at her friend Stacey over something small like stepping on her backpack by accident. Red flags for sure—the woman has definite anger issues.

It's no surprise to him how that night and the breakup with Charlotte impacted his relationships since. His heart was broken and his trust in women was tarnished that year and he never bothered to work out those issues. Now in his mid-thirties, he's established a track record of casual relationships but nothing serious. There were a couple long term relationships which lasted a year or so, but he always felt pressured to take them to the next level which was moving in together or marriage. He never pulled trigger because there was always something missing and that something was being in love—the real, mature, adult love. He was attracted to his girlfriends and liked having them in his life, but he enjoyed his alone time and his own space more.

The lack of intimacy and being in love never really bothered him until now. He wasn't sure what it was about today that brought about these emotions. It must be Charlotte—it had to be her. But could he trust his longing for her as legitimate and not just because they never resolved their issues? What if she did break it off with Ben and wanted to start something? Would he want it? Would he want her?

Suddenly, Michelle popped into his head and he realized he was lonely. For the first time in his life, he was lonely and craved true intimacy. He wanted to feel his world included someone other than just himself—to be in love. He thought Charlotte was self-absorbed, but he was just the same. He was so concerned about his own feelings and he never really took the time to consider the women. What did they want? What did Michelle want? He just assumed she wanted to keep it casual as he's assumed with his previous girlfriends, but what if he was wrong. What if they wanted more and never told him?

Sitting up in bed, he knew sleep wasn't coming anytime soon. He wanted Charlotte out of his brain and the best thing he could think was to call Michelle.

Thirteen

The call finally came Monday morning when Charlotte was at work.

Listening to Dave Matthews as she posted the mornings stories, the beat wasn't enough to keep her distracted. Throwing her headphones off, she felt like a caged animal—trapped and anxious. She still hadn't heard from Ben and was now officially worried. She wasn't sure if she should call the police or just continue to wait. Why hadn't he called? Didn't he know what he was putting her through? Her eyes were still swollen from the crying she'd done last night. She felt so lonely and depressed and knew she couldn't be fixed until she resolved everything with Ben.

Her friends were all out of town, including Ali, so no one except for Trevor knew she was upset. She had thought about calling Trevor yesterday after her hike, but couldn't bring herself to do it. What good would that do? He hadn't called to check on her, so she wasn't on his mind anyway. She was still a little mad at him for knowing what he knew. How embarrassing.

When her desk phone rang, she was deep in thought about what she would say to Ben when she finally got a hold of him.

"Charlotte Campbell," she said bringing her focus back to the present.

"Hi," Ben said.

"Ben?" Charlotte said now completely focused. "What the hell? Where are you? Where have you been? I've been so worried."

"I'm sorry, Charlotte," he replied distantly. This wasn't the normal Ben. Something was really wrong. "I need to talk to you."

"Okay, I can take the afternoon off and meet you at my place," she said. "Or we can meet on the Embarcadero and walk."

Charlotte didn't like the pause Ben took before answering her.

"I can't do that. I'm in Minneapolis."

Minneapolis? That wasn't what she expected to hear.

"Why are you there?"

"There are so many reasons and I feel bad telling you over the phone."

"You don't have to—Trevor told me about Nora and the accident. I'm so sorry, Ben. I don't understand why you couldn't tell me about it."

"Trevor told you?"

"Don't be mad at him. I'm mad for the both of us," Charlotte said with a small laugh. She wanted desperately to lighten the conversation. "When you left us at Thanksgiving, I was upset and he told me thinking it would help me understand. I had no idea you'd been dealing with all that."

"Well, that's a conversation for another time. Charlotte," he said before pausing and Charlotte knew by the way he said it something bad was coming. "I hate doing this over the phone but I need a break. I'm staying in Minneapolis through the holidays because I need to be here and fix things."

"Okay," Charlotte said as her heart sank. "Are you breaking up with me?"

"I don't know. I love you and wish I was there to hold you, but I can't get married with this hanging over my head."

"But that's what a spouse and a partner is supposed to help with—the better and the worse," Charlotte said feeling the tears well up. She wasn't sure why she was trying to talk Ben into not breaking it off—and she knew that's what he was doing—because part of her felt relieved to be let out of the engagement. Somehow through the pain, she felt lighter.

"This isn't about us."

"But it is about us. We were engaged and now we're not and I'm not sure how to process it all."

She couldn't help the tears now. They were flowing down her cheeks as she tried to keep her voice down so her cube mates wouldn't hear.

"It's not the end, I swear, Charlotte. I'll be back after New Years and we can figure it all out then."

Charlotte wasn't sure about that but didn't know what to say. "Okay. I miss you."

"I miss you, too, and I'm sorry about the way I acted over Thanksgiving. Please give my apologies to your parents."

"It's okay. At least I know why," she said with a small chuckle. "So what do we do now? Just say goodbye and happy holidays?"

"I think its best. I need to figure things out here."

"Okay, well, good luck," she said. It sounded stupid even to her ears. "I hope you find what you need."

"I hope so, too."

"Well, I gotta get back to work. Bye."

"Bye, Charlotte."

Charlotte hung up wondering how her life had changed so much in just a few days. She stared at her computer but it was like all the words were jumbling together. Her emotions felt the same, but mostly she felt shock and paralysis. She wanted to get up and just go home, but her body wouldn't let her and so she sat there, staring at her screen until Jake walked up and asked her if she was okay.

Wiping her tears, she figured she'd just be honest. "Not really, my fiancé just broke off our engagement."

"Over the phone?"

"Yes."

"What a douche. I'm so sorry, Charlotte. Why don't you go home?"

Charlotte wasn't going to protest and just nodded. Putting her iPod in her bag, she got up to leave and before she knew it, she was back in her apartment. She didn't even remember the walk home. Not sure what to do with herself, she took a shower and crashed on the couch staring a television that wasn't turned on. The conversation ran over and over in her head and she wanted to go back and say things differently or at least fight for the relationship.

Hoping Sarah was available, she dialed her number.

"Hi there!" Sarah answered.

"Hey Sarah, how are things?"

"Same. How are things up in SF?"

Charlotte decided to just spit it out. "Ben broke up with me."

"Wait, what? Why? What happened?"

Charlotte spent the next twenty minutes filling Sarah in on her problems with Ben including the sex. "I miss him, Sarah. I can't believe what happened."

"Well, it doesn't sound like he completely broke up with you," Sarah said. "But honestly, Charlotte, you weren't happy being engaged to him anyway. I'm giving you some tough love here, but Ben was not the right guy for you."

Charlotte thought about those words for a moment. "But what if he was?"

"But what if he wasn't? For one thing, your libidos didn't match. That's a bad matchup right there."

"But it's not a deal breaker."

"Not now, but when you're married, it will be."

Charlotte knew Sarah was right. Everything she said made perfect sense, but her loyalty to Ben still held strong. Looking down at the ring on her finger, she took it off and set it on the coffee table. If what Sarah said was true, then why was she shocked and hurt? "I'm so sad, Sarah."

"It's going to be a tough couple of weeks, but you'll get through them and you'll see that while Ben made a good boyfriend, he wasn't a good boyfriend for you."

"I wonder if he'll ever work through his problems," Charlotte said more to herself than Sarah.

"I don't know, but you can't wait for him."

Charlotte was done talking about Ben. "How are things in LA?"

Later that evening, Ali came home and knew right away what happened. "I can't believe it."

"Neither can I," Charlotte said distractedly as she flipped channels to a repeat of *How I Met Your Mother*. She was all talked out, all cried out and all theoried out. Even now, she still couldn't figure out why Ben suddenly ran off to Minnesota. Was it the engagement that forced him to face his past? Was it because he still had feelings for his ex, Nora?

"I think Sarah was right, Charlotte. Ben wasn't the guy for you."

"How is it that everyone knows that but me?"

"Because you need someone who has more in common with you and wants to be in your life and get you out of your comfort zone. Someone you can talk to—and from what you've said about Ben, your sex life and wedding plans, he isn't that guy. I loved Ben, but he was so vanilla. You'd be bored with him in a year. "

"Vanilla? How come you never said anything before?"

"Because I never thought Ben would propose. Again, I liked him—he was a good guy, but not good husband material for you and you knew that but just wouldn't admit it to yourself."

"But what if I never meet anyone else? What if Ben was the one for me?"

"Oh, please. I never want to hear those words out of your mouth again. You're a beautiful, smart, independent woman who doesn't need a man to make her life full and interesting."

"I think I said those words to you after you and Rob broke up."

"Exactly. Now it's time to take your own advice. Now let's order some pizza—we're officially single girls again."

The next three weeks dragged for Charlotte. She took a few days off from work after the breakup simply because she couldn't concentrate. She wallowed, listened to sad music and generally did everything cliché a person does right after a breakup. After her appetite returned, she ate a few pints of Ben and Jerry's noting she would have to burn the calories off with a few long runs in the Marina. What she didn't want to do, however, was go out. She wasn't ready to face a social life without Ben yet. She missed him and it was still hard to picture another relationship with someone else—even Trevor.

It was a week before Christmas when Trevor showed up at her place with his Collective Soul tickets.

"Come on, you need to get out," he said.

"I love them, but I'm not sure I feel like being at a concert," Charlotte said not moving from the couch.

"Are you serious? It's been three weeks. Get over it, already."

Charlotte was taken aback at his cavalier attitude towards her pain. "Get over it? You try breaking up with the love of your life and tell me how you feel."

"I have been there and Ben was not the love of your life. You need to start somewhere so why not go to a show where you know you'll love the music? We'll have a good time, I promise. You need to stop moping around. I haven't seen you at work in weeks."

"That's because I've been busy," she said with a snort. Part of that was true. There were a ton of protests lately regarding Wall Street which meant longer hours at work posting the updates. Mostly, however, she was avoiding Trevor because she didn't want to hear about Ben or start venting about Ben to him.

Truth be told, she was bored. One more rerun of *House Hunters* and she was going to go crazy. Trevor was right—she needed to face her fear of being out in public again. She needed to finally get used to being single, a status she used to enjoy before dating Ben. She loved Collective Soul and had seen them live before and knew she would have a good time. "Fine, you win. I have to get dressed."

An hour later, they were in a cab on the way to the Fillmore. Charlotte would have liked to walk, but it was up over the pacific heights hill and she was wearing boots with heels. Since the weather was cool, she had on a black leather jacket and thought it was funny Trevor was wearing his as well. He still had the same jacket from college whereas she was about five versions and designs later. She thought Trevor still looked handsome in his jacket and she had the sudden urge to sniff it to see if it had the same cologne smell as it did in college.

Once they arrived, they headed to the bar to grab a couple beers. The show hadn't started yet and Charlotte didn't know the opening band. She loved The Fillmore for live music because it was big enough to hold a good sized crowd, but still intimate enough to feel close to the band. Several groups from the sixties made The Fillmore famous such as Jefferson Airplane, The Doors, and The Grateful Dead.

Trevor handed her a bottle of Budweiser before they stepped away from the bar to mix in with the crowd. Standing together, it reminded her of the time in college they went to see a show in Santa Barbara together. Technically, it was their first date because it

was the night after they first kissed at his party. Like
now, they had awkwardly stood in silence taking in the
surroundings and people watching. Charlotte smiled
remembering how he finally took her hand, pulled her
close and kept her that way for most of the show.

Things were different now. They were much
older and had more experience under their belts. Was
that a good thing? Sometimes she missed being young
and innocent with only grades and beer money to worry
about. Now it was broken engagements, rent and
retirement savings. The stab of pain at missing Ben
went through her for a second as she remembered why
he wasn't the one standing next to her. While it was hard
being out, the pain was slowly turning to anger and she
realized she was glad she was here with Trevor instead.
He was like a warm blanket protecting her from the cold
although she had to keep herself from asking if he had
heard from Ben. *He would tell me, right?*

"So what do you think of this band?" Trevor
shouted over the music. "They look like an eighties hair
band."

"I know, right?!" Charlotte shouted back. "But
they're really good."

Listening to the music, Charlotte started feeling
better. It did feel good to be out again listening to live
music. Ben never wanted to go to concerts with her so
she usually went with Jamie, Cami, or Ali. If the band
was important to her, she had no problems going alone.
Music was therapeutic for her and something about
seeing the music she listened to through her earphones
live and in person helped her feel more in touch with her
past as a DJ.

After the band finished, the crowd started gathering closer to the front in anticipation of Collective Soul. Charlotte was always amazed at how mainstream Collective Soul was and yet very few people could name their hit songs but could recognize them in a second. Seeing the crowd thicken, she realized there were a lot of passionate fans.

"I'm going to get us a couple more beers. Can you stay here and hold our spot?" Trevor asked. He was standing so close to her now she almost said she didn't want him to leave. "Sure. I'll be right here."

Watching him make his way through the crowd, she thought more about that show they saw in Santa Barbara together. It was at the Anaconda—the music venue of the UC Santa Barbara community and it was one of the best nights of her life. There was something in the air that night and not just the warm breeze blowing up the coast, making Charlotte feel exhilarated. It was the first night she felt like an adult—no curfews and no adult supervision. It was a taste of freedom she never knew existed—and she liked it.

Charlotte was so nervous being that far from Cal Poly with Trevor. They had a great conversation on the drive down, discussing music, family, and what they would do if they won the lottery. Trevor did most of the talking as he drove and Charlotte listened, grateful she didn't have to talk much. When they got to the Anaconda, they caught up with a few others from the station standing in a big group during the show. Charlotte relaxed when Trevor put his arm around her and pulled her close to his body.

After the show ended, she and Trevor followed the KCPR crew across the street to Woodstock's Pizza where it was custom to share slices and rehydrate with caffeine before the hour and half drive back to SLO.

"Charlotte, would you like a beer?" Pete asked, pointing to her.

"Oh, no thank you—I'm not twenty-one and I'm driving Trevor back."

"You're kidding? Robbing the cradle aren't you, Trev?" Pete teased.

"Hmmm," Trevor said winking at Charlotte.

Charlotte couldn't help but blush a thousand shades of red. She wasn't used to this kind of attention but since they were practically glued together during the show, she had to assume everyone knew. Did that bother her? No. She really liked Trevor and trusted him. However, she was on the younger side and felt very inexperienced next to everyone else. The night before was the first time she was ever alone the whole night with a guy. He never pressured her for sex, but she knew it would eventually come up.

"Well, Charlotte, you got a good guy here," Pete said slapping Trevor on the shoulder.

"Okay," Charlotte said giggling. She really didn't know how to handle this.

"Aren't you graduating soon, Trevor," said a girl on the other side of the table. Charlotte hadn't seen her before but she noticed right away by the tone in her voice that she was not happy with the conversation.

"In June, yes," Trevor replied. Charlotte was relieved when he finally introduced her. "Charlotte, meet Katie—Katie meet Charlotte."

"Hi," Katie said without even looking Charlotte in the eye.

She's kind of a bitch. Charlotte didn't take an instant dislike to many people but she did to Katie. All the black makeup, black clothes, and jet black hair made her look mean. She had really pretty blue eyes, but Charlotte had to look hard to find them. "Hi."

After an hour, Charlotte was glad to get on the road. It was already midnight and she didn't want to be sleepy on the drive back. Once they said goodbye to everyone, she followed Trevor out of the restaurant and back to the car. It was then Trevor pulled her against him as he backed up to the car.

"You make me happy, Charlotte Campbell," he said before kissing her.

Surprised, Charlotte didn't have time to respond as she let him kiss her. It was deep and intense but different from last night. There was no inhibition, just simple attraction and enjoyment. Charlotte kissed him back just as hard. The wind was blowing around them adding a degree of intensity and mystery.

Once the kiss ended, she pulled back and said she was happy too. "I feel safe with you."

"Good," he said placing gentle kisses on both her cheeks. "Let's get going. Are you staying the night with me?"

"I guess so," Charlotte said smiling as she opened the door and climbed behind the wheel.

Making their way up the 101 back to San Luis Obispo, Charlotte started thinking about Katie. It dawned on her that Katie was looking at Trevor the way a girl looks at a crush. She wondered if they had a thing in the past.

"How well do you know Katie?" she asked.

Trevor didn't stop flipping through the CD case of music. "I don't know her that well. She's a DJ at the station and we've hung out on the couch a few times, but that's about it. She runs in a different circle than I do."

"She likes you," Charlotte teased. Maybe he already knows.

"What are you talking about?" he said dismissively. "I doubt that."

"No, seriously, she likes you."

"Whatever."

Well, that ended that. He didn't seem interested in pursuing the conversation. It was apparent to Charlotte that Trevor had no interest in Katie at all and she felt relieved.

Now, as Trevor walked up behind her and handed her a bottle of beer, she focused on the present. That was a long time ago and she was such a different person then—innocent, naïve, and trusting.

"I think they're about to come on," Trevor said. "Are you excited?"

"Absolutely," Charlotte replied feeling buzzed now from the beer and the crowd. Once the lights dimmed and the music started, she felt genuine excitement. *So this is what being happy feels like.* Although, it had only been a few weeks since her world came crashing down, it felt more like a decade.

"Oh, they're starting with *Welcome All Again*," Trevor said. "Great opener."

She instinctively moved closer to him as the band continued through their set. Now she remembered why she enjoyed them so much—lead singer Ed Roland loves playing for the fans. The crowd was enjoying the show and she was having such a good time, she didn't even notice when Trevor moved behind her and put his arms around her waist. It took a few seconds for it to click that he was making a move on her.

Turning to face him, she could see it in his face and didn't stop him when he kissed her. It was like Santa Barbara all over again. Ben flashed through her mind but she quickly pushed his image away. *Not now.*

"I've wanted to do that ever since you walked back into my life," he shouted over the music.

Charlotte knew what he was saying was the truth and while it warmed her, it scared her too. This was Trevor—the guy who brought all those old memories back—good and bad. She still felt guilty about how she dumped him after that bad night at the station and she remembered how he moved on to Katie without even blinking. But she also remembered how he made her feel when they were alone. The chemistry between them still existed and as he kissed her again, it was like no time had passed. She forgot everything—Ben included—and just let the good feelings of having Trevor back in her life surround her. It helped the band was playing *You,* one of their great romantic ballads, because it put the stamp on her feelings for Trevor.

You, it's always been you... The words circled her brain as if the band was playing the song just for her and Trevor. Pulling away, Trevor smiled at her and he suddenly looked more relaxed. She didn't move away when he placed his hands behind her neck pulling her head against his so their foreheads touched.

"I've missed you so much," he whispered although Charlotte heard him clearly.

"I've missed you, too."

They enjoyed the rest of the show holding hands. She was back in the bubble—a big, giant bubble where she felt safe and happy in the moment. She didn't think about what would come later—if Trevor would be coming back to her place or going home. All different kinds of scenarios crossed her mind—Trevor getting her home and kissing her goodnight at the door, Trevor kissing her and then asking to come upstairs or possibly Trevor just assuming he was coming home with her and following her inside. *Would it be wrong if I wanted him to just come home with me?*

Once the final encore finished with the classic song *Shine*, Charlotte was ready to go. Walking hand in hand, they grabbed the traditional Fillmore poster that is handed out after every concert and made their way out to the street. A case of chills crawled up her arms as she felt the cool air collide with her sweaty skin. Her hair felt frizzy and wet and her ears rang, but she had never felt better.

"I'll walk you home," Trevor said as they strolled up Fillmore to catch a cab. Her feet hurt from standing for hours, but she didn't care. As Trevor took her hand, all the pain went away.

Once they got back to her place, she lit some candles and started some music. "I really need to take a shower. Do you mind?" She asked.

"No, go right ahead. I'm just going to check your place out."

"That's right, you've never been here."

"Where's Ali?"

"I don't know. She's probably out with friends. I thought she'd be home."

"Well, good thing she isn't," he said as he kissed her again before she went into her bedroom.

She took the quickest shower she could, washing her hair and makeup off her face and letting the warm water erase any last doubt about being with Trevor. Somehow it all just seemed natural. She's known him for almost fifteen years and even though they've been apart for most of it, it seems like they've been together all that time.

"Ok, I'm done," she said after shutting off the blow dryer. A sudden feeling of insecurity overcame her as she realized she wasn't wearing makeup. He'd seen her without makeup before, but she wanted to look her best for him. Turns out it didn't matter because he was at the bathroom door before she could even say the word lipstick.

"You smell good," he said as he pulled her into her arms. She was naked under her robe and one pull of the tie around her waist and she would be exposed. In a way, that thrilled her. While everything with Trevor felt similar, it felt completely different. She wasn't the naïve virgin she was back in college. She had experience on her side now.

He took her into her room and for once she was glad she was a neat freak. Her bed, with a white duvet and dark lavender pillows, was perfectly made and stood out in the center of the room. The candles burned, emitting a soft glow and tuberose scent.

She felt like stalling just a little bit in order to process what was going to happen. "Wait, let me grab my iPod and bring it in here." She left his arms and got her music, plugging it in next to her bed.

It was then Trevor kissed her again. "As much as I love The Ramones," he said between kisses. "It's not the best music to kiss you to."

Charlotte giggled. He was right. She switched her playlist to the softer music—the playlist she listened to when she needed music to block out noise as she tried to sleep, like on an airplane. Lately, she'd been listening to it a lot because her heart craved the sad songs. The first song in rotation was *No More I Love You*s by Annie Lennox.

"Much better," he said. "I didn't realize you had such a great view."

Charlotte looked over at her window and realized the blinds were still open. Cow Hollow and the Marina were lit in all their glory and the lights twinkled as if they knew what was going on in her bedroom. "I do. I love my view."

After she closed the blinds, Trevor pulled the pillows off and the duvet down and they both climbed on the bed. The music had switched to *Look at You* by The Screaming Trees. Charlotte floated away as she lay down next to Trevor. It didn't even bother her when his hand slid under her robe. It felt so natural as his warm hand explored her stomach.

She couldn't help but press her body as close to
him as possible. Everything about Trevor felt familiar
and new at the same time. His scent, although masked
by a night of dancing at a concert, smelled just like it did
the first time she kissed him. His lips still felt soft and fit
hers perfectly.

Charlotte let him explore further as the songs
continued to set the mood—*Goodnight John Dee* by
Grant Lee Buffalo, *Dream About Me* by Moby, and
Damn I Wish I Was Your Lover by Sophie B. Hawkins.
She knew he was turned on and she took pride in that
considering how Ben had sexually shut her down. Then
it occurred to her what had been missing all this time
with Ben.

Passion.

She hadn't felt this much passion ever for a man.
Everything she'd been holding back came rushing
forward and she knew instantly she wanted Trevor to
make love to her. Make love. That sounded funny to
her and she couldn't help but giggle.

"What's so funny?" Trevor asked suddenly
stopping.

"Nothing. Absolutely nothing."

"I don't believe you," he said kissing her again.
Edge of the Ocean by Ivy was now playing and she
couldn't help but think it was the most romantic song
she'd ever heard—especially in this moment.

"I love this song," he said. Trevor was now
completely undressed and Charlotte knew the decision
was hers to move forward. "What do you want,
Charlotte?"

He said it so softly, yet she could hear the rawness in his voice. "I want to be with you."

The next few minutes were like fifteen years of catching up and that hole she didn't even know existed in her heart disappeared. She never knew until now how much she regretted the way she and Trevor ended things—or rather the way she ended things with Trevor. She knew by the way he was making love to her that he still had deep feelings. The intimacy she felt when she looked at his face and into his eyes made her feel safe, protected and *loved.* Ben's face appeared to her, but she quickly pushed it away. It was only Trevor right now.

Fourteen

Trevor awoke the next morning to his phone alarm.

It was so early and for a second he thought he'd dreamt everything about being with Charlotte. It only took a split second to realize he was actually lying next to her in bed. The music was playing softly and the candles were still burning. The room was dark because the sun hadn't come up yet and the last thing he wanted to do was get up and go to work.

Turning over, he faced Charlotte who was still asleep. He watched her breathing and smiled at how peaceful she looked. Her face looked the same except for a bit of age which he thought made her look so much prettier. He could hear *Weighty Ghost* by Wintersleep playing and decided he wanted to remain right here forever. It was as if everything had finally fell into place.

He got up to take a shower, careful not to wake her. Opening the bedroom door slowly, he prayed it wouldn't squeak. Suddenly the other bedroom door across the hall opened.

"Ali!" he whispered startled. "Hey."

He could tell Ali was processing his presence in her apartment so he waited patiently while it registered.

Shaking her head she finally spoke. "Hi, Trevor. I'm not even going to ask what you're doing here."

Smiling, Trevor was genuinely happy to see her even at the darkest hour of the morning. "I'm so glad to see you. Charlotte and I went to Collective Soul last night and it was just easier for me to stay here then to go all the way back to my place." He had no idea why he felt he needed to explain it all to her.

"I see. Well, it's good to see you, too. It's been a long time," she said reaching out to hug him. "We need to catch up, but right now I need to go to the bathroom."

"Okay. I was just going to shower but I'll wait."

Trevor smiled at how Charlotte was going to be confronted by Ali when she awoke. He assumed Charlotte would probably tell Ali everything. *Well hopefully not everything*, he thought, feeling his groin respond to the idea of Charlotte naked.

"I put a towel out for you, big guy," Ali whispered, patting him on the chest as she passed him to her bedroom. "Let's catch up soon."

"You bet," he whispered back mortified that she might be referring to his physical response about seeing Charlotte naked.

Turning on the water, he let the warmth wake him up. This was shittiest part of his job—getting up at three in the morning. Today, however, he already had more energy than usual and looked forward to the day. He was going on about three hours sleep and his eyes burned and felt bloodshot, but he didn't care.

Once he dried off, he quietly went through the drawers hoping there would be a new toothbrush. Bingo, he thought as he found one. He wasn't sure the Walgreens by the bus stop would be open at this hour.

Back in the bedroom, he found his clothes in the candlelight realizing they had a bit of an odor to them. Oh well, nothing he could do about it now. After he dressed, he leaned down to kiss Charlotte goodbye. He didn't want to wake her, but he also didn't want her to think he disappeared.

Gently rubbing her arms so he wouldn't startle her, he smiled when she awoke. "Hi," she said sleepily. "What time is it?"

"Really early but I have to go. Some of us work before the sun rises."

Charlotte frowned. "Can't you come back to bed for a little longer."

"I really wish I could, but I'm running late as it is. I'll see you at work later, okay?"

"Okay."

He leaned down to kiss her forehead and watched her go back to sleep. He turned off the music and blew out the candles before he left. Making sure to lock the front door behind him, he ran downstairs wondering if he was going to be able to find a cab at this hour.

It was eerily quiet as he walked across Franklin Street to Van Ness. He was desperate for a cup of coffee, but even Starbucks didn't open for another hour. He was stuck and knew he'd have to walk to work. The air was cold and he wished he had a scarf and gloves just to make it more comfortable but after about fifteen minutes, his blood was circulating and he felt warm.

He thought about the night before as he picked up his pace. After all these years of wondering, being with Charlotte was everything he expected. He was still madly in love with her and all his ex-girlfriends, including Michelle, didn't compare.

Michelle.

Now that was going to be sticky. Not only was she Charlotte's boss, she wanted Trevor to move to New York with her. The conversation they'd had late on Thanksgiving night over the phone had gone very unexpectedly. He knew she was being courted by Fox News, but he didn't expect her to actually consider taking the position. She seemed more about network news rather than cable news. However, they offered her the VP of programming position and he wasn't surprised when she accepted it. He was floored, however, when she offered him the producer position for a new program Fox was airing in the winter.

"You want me to move to New York?" he asked.

"Why not? It's a great opportunity for you," she said.

"I don't know, Michelle. I like my job and San Francisco just fine."

"I know, but moving to cable news will mean a huge pay raise and it's a resume builder. Think of all the contacts you'll make. Plus, I'll miss you if you don't."

"I'm not sure what to say."

"It's a big decision. Think about it. I'll be back during the week and we can talk about it then. I'm very excited about this and I can't wait to see you. I've missed you."

"I miss you, too," he said truthfully. He was missing her at this particular moment.

Now, as Trevor passed the Fog City Diner on Battery Street, he knew he had no intention of going to New York. It wasn't so much about Charlotte but more about his life in San Francisco. He was a true Californian and a little too laid back for New York. He loved visiting, but moving there would make him uncomfortable. *But, yes, a lot of it was Charlotte and after last night, there is no way I'm moving.*

Trevor smiled as he picked up his pace. The thought of her body still thrilled him and she felt the same although she had rounded out a bit in all the right places. Flashes of her underneath him kept coming at him until he had to force himself to think about something else—like how he was going to break it off with Michelle.

Later that morning, after three cups of coffee, Trevor was in the studio preparing to go live for the morning newscast. *Why is the news so boring lately?* Now that the financial crisis was second page news, he needed other stories to lead. *I need an earthquake or flood or something big.* No one really cared about the gas company's latest strategies or the newest coffee shop at the Farmer's Market.

Standing at his computer, he was going over the stories for the newscast when his production assistant Tony entered. "Trevor—bad news, buddy. Supervisor Cummings just canceled."

"Great," Trevor said with a sigh. "What do we have from last night to run?"

"Alicia did a story on the SPCA. It's a four minute piece. We can easily reuse it."

"Good. Everyone loves adoptable puppies and kittens. Run it," Trevor said before getting back to his tasks. Normally, a cancellation made his blood boil, but today he took it in stride. It didn't bother him because he was in a good mood. He really wanted to talk to Charlotte again, but it was too early and she'd still be asleep.

His mind wandered again to being next to her in bed. The part he couldn't stop thinking about was right when he was about to have sex with her. He seemed more apprehensive than she did. This was the love of his life and he wanted to make sure it was perfect.

"Are you sure you're ready, Charlotte," he whispered for the third time.

"Yes," she whispered as she kissed his neck.

"If we do this, there is no going back and I want to make sure it's right," he said again. Trevor kicked himself for making such a big deal about it. But it was a big deal—this was Charlotte. Maybe he was just asking her because he wanted to make sure it was right for him. He didn't want to ruin the relationship they had now and he didn't want to scare her away. He knew she wasn't over Ben yet and maybe he was pushing her into something she wasn't ready for just yet. This moment was more important to him than any other moment before—except maybe the first time they kissed.

"I'm ready," she said again. "I trust you, Trevor. I trust you to take care of me."

Trevor understood that to mean she trusted him to do right by her and not take advantage of the situation. He'd been in love with her for so long and he now understood what it was like to want to protect someone and take of her and ensure her happiness.

"I've wanted you for so long, Charlotte," he whispered as he finally made love to her. *Edge of the Ocean*, playing softly in the background, will always remind him of the moment he truly loved someone both physically and emotionally for the first time in his life.

The next step was going to be harder, he thought as he emailed copy down to the studio and to the online team. *Will she want to be in a committed relationship with me? Will I live up to Ben?* Not much time had passed since her breakup and he knew she still had unresolved feelings for Ben. *Does she still love him?*

After the show, he got an email from Michelle asking him to come by her office. That's when it hit him he had no emails, calls, or texts from Charlotte. She would definitely be in the building by now. Is it tacky to have "the breakup talk" with someone at work? Maybe he should wait until later, but Michelle always worked late into the evening and he didn't want to wait around. He would prefer to get his slate cleaned right away.

Michelle's office was on the opposite end of the floor from Charlotte so he figured he would stop by and see her on his way to Michelle. Maybe Charlotte would agree to a cup of coffee after his meeting. The thought of seeing Charlotte this morning thrilled him but he was disappointed to find she wasn't at her desk when he walked by. As he got closer to Michelle's office, his heart started pounding, both in excitement and dread.

"Hey," he said as he knocked on her door. "What's up?"

"Hi," she said standing up and giving him a kiss on the lips. "I feel like I haven't seen you in ages. I tried calling you last night, but you didn't pick up."

Trevor turned his phone off when he got to Charlotte's last night otherwise it would have beeped and buzzed all night long with updates and emails. "Sorry, I was out later than expected."

"Yes, you look like it and you're clothes reek of sweat. Where were you?"

"I went to a concert," he said smelling his sleeve. "I ended up staying the night at a friend's place." He should probably tell her the truth, but what good would it to telling her he stayed at Charlotte's?

"So why don't we get lunch today and discuss New York."

"Yes, we should," he said instinctively. He wanted to talk about New York and how he wasn't planning to move there.

"I have it all worked out and I've been looking for apartments on the Upper West side. You'll love it there, I swear."

Trevor remained silent as he digested what she said. She had it all planned out and he hadn't even said yes or no. They'd barely seen each other the past couple of weeks because she was going back and forth to east coast. She had given official notice right after Thanksgiving and was just coming in to help find her replacement and tie up loose ends. "I've been there—I like it."

"New York is wonderful. I love San Francisco, but New York is ten times the energy."

"I know. It's a great city."

"What do you think about the job? Have you gotten your resume and reel up to date? They're waiting for it."

Rip off the band aid and just break it off already. He wanted to do right by Charlotte just like he said he would. Sitting down in a chair, he knew he had to just get it all over with. "Michelle, I'm sorry, but I don't think I'm going to New York."

This was the first time he'd seen Michelle look vulnerable. She was always strong and confident and Trevor was very attracted to that. He knew part of her success was because she treated people as equals yet commanded the room when she entered. Right now, however, her normal composure and confidence had disappeared and she looked like she was in shock. "You're not?"

"No, I'm not," he said quietly and as gently as he could. "I appreciate how you want me there and how you want to help my career, but San Francisco is my home."

"But you haven't even interviewed. I know you'll love—"

"I'm sure I would," Trevor interrupted. "I'm so sorry, Michelle. I think you're going to do really well there but there is no future for me in New York."

The silence was deafening because he knew Michelle got his double meaning. "So we're done, too?"

"Well, I don't think a long distance relationship would work, do you?"

"I don't know. I've never done it before but we could work something out," she said as her eyes welled up with tears.

"I feel really bad, I'm sorry," he said.

"I'm fine," she said as she wiped her eyes.

I feel like such a jerk.

Standing up, he pulled her in his arms and hugged her hard. "I know you're going to do well there and San Francisco will be an afterthought before you know it."

"I'm going to miss you a lot," she said as she hugged him back.

"I'll miss you, too," he said kissing her on the forehead. "I have to get back to work so I can go home and sleep. Are you okay?"

"Yes. For some reason, I had a feeling this was going to happen."

After they said their breakup goodbyes, Trevor smiled at her as he left her office feeling horrible and relieved at the same time. He did what he had to do. It was over and now he could move forward with Charlotte. The thought took the edge off of how he broke Michelle's heart although she was a strong woman and would get over him quickly. Trevor always knew they weren't in love with each other. She probably knew it, too.

He was really excited to see Charlotte and tell her he ended it completely with Michelle. Charlotte would probably want to keep their dating a secret until Michelle moved and he agreed with that idea—it was only fair.

She was at her desk when he walked up. She had her earphones on so he gently tapped her on the shoulder.

"Hi there," he said after she took off the headphones and put them on her desk.

"Hi."

"How's your morning been?"

"Good."

Wow, this was way more uncomfortable than he imagined. She was very standoffish and almost cold. He knew instantly something was wrong because she wouldn't look him in the eye. Was she regretting last night? That thought never even occurred to him but seeing her now, he knew she was having second thoughts. To say he was devastated would be a huge understatement.

Waiting for her to continue, Trevor finally got the broke the silence. "Do you want to get some lunch today?"

"Um, okay," she said.

"Is there something wrong? You seem upset with me?"

"No, I'm not upset. I'm just super busy right now. You caught me proofing copy that's going live in a few minutes."

Trevor wasn't completely assured that was the reason. "So, meet me downstairs at eleven?"

"Sure."

"Bye."

As he walked away, he could feel her eyes on him. Her reaction towards him was so unexpected, he wondered if maybe she was still in love with Ben and felt guilty. His heart sunk at the thought, but he wasn't about to give up on her.

Fifteen

Charlotte was so glad to be back on the softball field.

It was mid January and she needed a distraction after the horrible holiday season that came and went. Between Ben and Trevor, she felt like she had her heart broken twice—at the same time.

"Good to see you back, Charlotte," Darren said handing her a beer. "How are things?"

"Eh, could be better," Charlotte said. "Am I on second base again?"

"You're the queen of second base," he said smiling before realizing what he said.

Charlotte laughed. "I know what you meant, don't worry about it."

Standing with her team as they started the first inning at bat, she sipped her beer hoping it would help push the feelings of anger and loneliness to the back of her mind. It seemed that every second of every day, she thought about Trevor. How had she managed to mess everything up with him? When she wasn't thinking about Trevor, she was mad at Ben. It was a rollercoaster of emotion and it was taking its toll.

Trevor had taken the sting out of Ben leaving, but she still felt guilty about being with him so soon after Ben left. Charlotte hadn't heard from Ben in about two months and had finally gotten used to knowing her phone wouldn't ring with him on the other end. He wasn't coming back and she knew that. Yet, still, she wasn't completely over him or the relationship.

In her mind, however, Trevor wasn't a rebound. Everything about that night after the concert felt right and, in fact, felt perfect. When he kissed her goodbye and left, she knew he wouldn't run away or treat her as if she was another notch on his bedpost. Every woman has that fear when they have sex with a man for the first time—will he bail? That's why she usually liked to wait a few months and get to know the guy before consummating the relationship. Trevor felt different because she knew him and they already had a good foundation. Granted, they weren't in each other's lives for over a decade, but being with him felt like they'd been together that long.

Charlotte had walked to work on a cloud that morning after Trevor left. Maybe it was her post sexual glow, but she was floating. Her music sounded positive again instead of sad and she felt a part of her heart heal itself after being broken by Ben. Ali had cornered her that morning wanting details and Charlotte gladly told her what happened, but kept a few of the details to herself—like how his skin felt against hers or how his body had developed in areas she adored. He still had the same tattoos which she remembered from college but he was now a man and not a twenty- two year old boy. She didn't think she could be more attracted to him now, but she was.

"So what are you going to do, Charlotte?" Ali had asked. "Trevor has been so in love with you."

"I know. I have strong feelings for him, but I just got out of a relationship. I'm not one to drag a dead horse into a new relationship and I don't even know if Ben is coming back. I thought he would come back after New Year's like he said, but I haven't heard a word from him."

"Have you tried calling him?"

"Every time I pick up the phone, I get pissed and talk myself out of it."

"You need closure."

"I know. Believe me, I know. I had such a good time last night but was it because of Trevor or because Trevor took Ben out of my mind for a while?"

"I don't think you're the type to use a guy like that—especially Trevor."

"I hope I'm not. I loved being with him and he makes me feel so good about myself. I can talk to him about everything and he won't judge or pull away," Charlotte said. "But at the same time, it kind of scares me."

"Why would it scare you?"

Why does it scare me? Trevor was a great man with a good soul and somehow that intimidated her. Deep down, she knew she wouldn't end up with Ben forever but Trevor had that potential. He didn't have the baggage Ben did and was ready to be in love. *Maybe I'm the one that is not ready to be in love?*

"Oh get over it, Charlotte," Ali said reading her mind. "Don't let your issues mess this up with Trevor. So what if you still have some feelings for Ben? Lots of people break up because they fall in love with someone else. Just be thankful you didn't go through with the marriage to Ben. At least it all happened now so you can make a clean break."

Charlotte knew instantly that Ali was right. She'd failed at so many relationships in the past and she automatically assumed her future relationships wouldn't work out as well. Is that a self fulfilling prophecy? Did she go for the men she knew she wouldn't ever fall in love with? Trevor was so different because her feelings and history with him ran so much deeper. Her heart told her he was the right one for her, but her head just wasn't ready to accept it. If she started something with Trevor, it would have to be a real commitment. *What if he breaks up with me and it doesn't work out?* Now that he was in her life, she didn't want to lose him.

As she walked to work that morning, she realized she was being foolish. Trevor made her feel good and there was nothing wrong with that. She shouldn't be scared or feel guilty about it. Loyalty only went so far. Ben obviously had no loyalty to her, so why should she feel guilty about being with Trevor? The dark clouds in her mind cleared and she allowed herself to be completely excited about seeing Trevor at work that day. Edge of the Ocean played through her headphones and she smiled remembering the last time she heard the song and what it now meant to her—and hopefully Trevor.

The morning continued as usual—posting stories and video from the morning show. She smiled thinking Trevor was downstairs going through the post mortem with his team, probably on his fifth cup of coffee. He would be preparing for the midday newscast in a few minutes which meant more work for her later that afternoon. She didn't mind. She liked the work—it was autonomous and on a day like today where she needed a distraction, it was the perfect match.

She was on her way back from the bathroom when she heard Trevor's voice in Michelle's office. It took a second for her to register what was being said, but through the pounding of her heart she heard Trevor mention he was thinking about moving to New York. *What?* Then she heard Michelle laugh and everything fell into place. He was still with Michelle. In her haze of issues, she completely forgot about her boss. She assumed Trevor had broken it off—at least that was the impression he gave her in bed last night. They were still together? He wanted to move to New York? Why hadn't he said anything? It was as if someone took a baseball bat and hit her in the stomach. It was all she could take when she heard them kiss. *Why is this happening?* She was just letting herself feel happy again and her life came crashing back down. *Why would he do this to me? I'm not going to let him break my heart. I thought you really wanted to be with me, Trevor.*

The fragile bubble she'd built around her heart completely burst and the anger at Ben came rushing out again combining with the hurt about Trevor. For a split second, she once again considered Trevor being the one that hurt her in college. But even through the pain, she knew without a doubt it wasn't him. Trevor might break her heart, but he would never break anything on her body.

Back at her desk, she put on her headphones and pretended to be working. The tears were threatening but she was in shock over going from such a high to such a low. What was she going to say to him?

She was so lost in thought, the tap to her shoulder made her jump.

"Hi there," Trevor said standing in front of her as if he didn't just kiss current his girlfriend after making love to his ex-girlfriend. Surprised, she wasn't sure what to say or how to act. What she wanted to do was yell at him for betraying her. "Hi."

"How's your morning been?"

How could he look so happy knowing he was breaking her heart? Was he just planning to sleep with her until he left for New York? Was he even going to tell her? *Fuck you, Trevor.* "Good."

"Do you want to get some lunch today?"

She was so amazed at how nonchalant he acted. It was like he was waiting for her to say something. *I'm not the one who has something to say.* "Um, okay." She needed to tell him how she felt and she couldn't wait until later, so lunch it was.

"Is there something wrong? You seem almost upset with me?"

"No, I'm not upset," she lied. "I'm just super busy right now. You caught me proofing some copy going live in a few minutes."

"Meet me downstairs at eleven?"

"Sure."

"Bye," he said before turning to leave. He seemed puzzled at her reaction, like he wanted to say something else. *Good.*

When lunchtime rolled around after the midday show, she met him down in the lobby. Her heart was racing and she wasn't sure how she was going to make it through a meal when everything inside of her was jumbled. When he smiled at her, she almost forgot about what happened upstairs. *Trevor, with your charming smile and deep voice. Why did you have to go and do what you did? Am I just a conquest to you— something you've wanted since college?*

"So where do you want to go?" he asked.

Charlotte knew she couldn't sit with him in a crowd and pretend to eat a meal. "Honestly, I'm not that hungry. Can we just go for a walk?"

Trevor seemed surprised. "Um, sure."

They walked in silence down the hill to the Embarcadero. The sun was out and a slight breeze blew her hair in her face, but Charlotte didn't even notice. All she could think about was the man next to her and how he will probably be out of her life in a few minutes.

She was surprised when he tried to grab her hand to hold it. Pulling away, she wanted to make a point and apparently it worked.

"Okay, Charlie, what's wrong?" he said pulling her onto the grass of the building next to them.

Debating whether to pour it all out or just deny everything, she knew she needed to be honest. She hated confrontation, but after Ben's secrets, she couldn't keep her thoughts to herself.

"New York?" she spit out. "Were you ever going to tell me you were moving to New York with your girlfriend?"

Charlotte noticed Trevor looked stunned. He was probably wondering how she found out. "What? No," he said. "How did you even know about that?"

"I was walking by Michelle's office when you were in there. I heard everything."

"Everything?" he said shaking his head. "No you didn't. You missed the part where I told her I wasn't moving and broke up with her."

Charlotte wasn't going to let this go. "How come you didn't tell me you were considering it?"

"Well, mostly because I wasn't really considering it myself and it's not something you bring up in bed with another woman."

Charlotte didn't miss the rise in his voice. "But why did you hide it from me?"

"I didn't hide it from you. You need to remember that you were the one dodging my calls the last couple of weeks. I wanted to give you space because of Ben. I was going to tell you, just not when were naked together."

Charlotte wasn't sure how to react. She felt so silly but her pride kept her from admitting it. Now she was just plain confused. It was like she wanted to catch Trevor doing something wrong and felt a slight disappointment when she was wrong. *What is wrong with me?*

"What is going on with you?" he asked concerned. "Please don't think you have to worry about Michelle. I ended it because I want to be with you."

Tears were now blurring her vision. So all this was for nothing. She believed him when he said that, but something inside her shut down. She was exhausted from being heartbroken, then angry, then happy, then angry again. She felt poisoned and toxic.

She knew she wasn't ready to be with anyone—even Trevor.

"I can't do this," she said after a few seconds of silence. Sitting down on the stone bench, she knew she wasn't ready to give Trevor what he wanted. Even though Ali said she needed to get over it and be with Trevor, it wasn't fair to him. Her residual anger towards Ben and her fear of Trevor letting her down overwhelmed her. She hated thinking this, but she was too fragile right now and if she started a relationship with Trevor in this state it wouldn't work and she would lose him permanently.

She could see the crestfallen look through her peripheral vision. "I'm so sorry, Trevor," she continued. "I want to be happy with you and I want nothing more than to be with you, but I can't be that person right now. I need to be alone for awhile."

"Is this because of me or Ben," he asked. His voice was taut and she knew he was holding back his own anger.

"Mostly Ben."

"Dammit, Charlotte—he left you and he's not coming back. I hate to be harsh, but you need to accept it and move on."

His tone angered her. "Just move on? It's only been three weeks! I was going to marry him. How do you get over that in three weeks?"

"I don't think you should be over him, but you sure as hell shouldn't feel guilty about being with me."

"I'm not," she lied. "It's just that I need to be single for a while. I can't go from one relationship to the next. I need to breathe." It was all true, but it didn't mean she didn't want to be with him. She just couldn't say that to him right now.

Trevor crossed his arms. "So were back in college. It's the same thing all over again. We get close and you run away."

"I didn't run away back then—I fucking got beat up. How would you deal with that?"

"Well I wouldn't have pushed you away—that's for sure. I would have leaned on you and needed you in my life. You shut me out, Charlotte. You completely shut me out and that crushed me."

So they were finally having the conversation that was fifteen years overdue. Trevor was bringing up the past and with it a bunch of his feelings. She had no idea he had been so hurt.

"But you moved on right away with Katie," she threw back at him hoping to deflect the spotlight off her.

"No, I didn't. If I recall, it was a couple months after you stopped talking to me and we dated for a blink of an eye before she went crazy—and don't make this about me. It was you who decided to end it."

He was right. He was totally right. It was her choice. "I just thought you would wait a little longer. I was so new to college and you were my first real boyfriend. I'm sorry, but I handled it all wrong." She felt Trevor sit down next to her. Tears spilled down her cheeks remembering the pain from that time. "I'm so sorry, Trevor. I wish I could go back in time and change it all."

She felt his arm around her and it comforted her. "Not a day goes by where I don't wish I had been a few minutes earlier so that wouldn't have happened to you."

"I know," Charlotte sniffed. "I don't know why I took it all out on you. I guess they say you take your frustration out on those closest to you."

"Remember that night we ran into each other at SLO Brew right before the end of the year?"

"Yes, you were with Katie. I do remember that."

"I wanted so desperately to tell you how much I missed you and how miserable I was that year without you."

"Sorry for ruining your senior year."

"Yes, well, I recovered," he said smiling. "Charlotte, you and I belong together but I can't do the rollercoaster again."

"I want to, but I just can't right now. I wish Ben didn't have a part in this, but he does, Trevor. I don't want to get back together with him, but I need closure of some kind before I can date again. I loved our night last night, but it's not fair to you that I'm sad and depressed Charlotte instead of happy and independent Charlotte. I just feel I would suffocate you with neediness or something. You don't deserve that."

"You let me be the judge of that. Please don't push me away," he said.

"I don't want to, but I need to. Plus, you just got out of a relationship with Michelle.

"Shit," he said under his breath. "She and I were not in a relationship."

"Yes you were. You might not have seen it turning into anything, but you were in a relationship and it was enough for her to want you to move to New York."

"It wasn't like that," he said. "Honestly, I never, ever thought it would get to that. She caught me totally off guard by asking me to go with her."

"She doesn't know about us, does she?" That would make things very awkward.

"No, of course not—she gave notice today and will be in New York after the New Year."

"Good," Charlotte said with another sniff. She kept wiping the snot running from her nose on her sleeve. She made a mental note to start carrying Kleenex in her purse.

"So what are we going to do, Charlie? I can't go back to being just friends. I feel like you're breaking my heart again."

It pained Charlotte to hear him say that, but she needed to remain strong. It was so hard because part of her wanted to just give in and let him take care of her. The other part of her felt relief at knowing she could be on her own for a while with none of these issues. She could deal with a broken heart over Ben more than she could deal with losing Trevor forever. *Are you insane, Charlotte? You're throwing Trevor away.* Those words were on repeat in her head, but she couldn't bring herself to change her mind. If she and Trevor were meant to be together, they would find their way back to each other.

"I don't know what to do. The last thing I want to do is hurt you but I'm doing this so I don't hurt you later down the road. Maybe somehow we can stay friends this way. Ben ran away so I didn't have to deal with it. You and I see each other every day."

"So, you're decision is final? I have no say in this? I can't wait again for you, Charlotte."

Charlotte knew he meant it. She wanted to scream at him to fight harder but even she knew that wasn't fair. She knew his feelings and she knew she was making the right decision. "I don't expect you to."

She felt his arm go around her shoulders and she rested her head on his shoulder. Why must this hurt so bad? Even knowing she was right, it was still so incredibly painful. When he brushed her hair back with his fingers, it was almost her undoing as was the gentle kiss he gave her. "I guess we're saying goodbye? I can't have you in my life right now. I need to get over you—again."

She hadn't expected that—life without Ben *and* Trevor? The thought depressed her immensely because this was exactly what she was trying to avoid. "I understand," she hiccupped.

For a second, she panicked not wanting Trevor to leave. She wanted him to call her, text her and email her. She wanted to sit at the bar and drink beers with him or listen to music reminiscing about the old days at KCPR. She wanted him next to her in bed where she felt safe and loved. Before she could speak, he said it was time for her to get back to the office.

"I think its best you go on your own. I'm going to walk a little more in the sunshine. I'm done for the day."

His statement made it so permanent. "Okay," she said softly.

She pulled away and watched as he started walking away from her. "I love you, Charlotte."

Watching him continue down the street, Charlotte felt numb. Did she do the right thing? Did she let the only guy who loved her walk out of her life? He said he loved her—just like he did fifteen years ago. Would she ever be ready to fall in love? Would she ever even meet another man? So many thoughts bombarded her as she walked back to the office. The biggest question was if she would ever be happy again. She was fine before she met Ben and wanted so desperately to be that strong woman again—it just seemed like climbing a mountain and she was stuck at the bottom trying to put one foot forward. *Will this pain ever go away?*

"You silly girl," Ali said later that evening when Charlotte told her what happened. "What were you thinking?"

"Come on, Ali, what would you have done?" Charlotte replied frustrated at Ali's tone.

"If it was the love of my life, I would have jumped all over it. How can you not see you both belong together?"

"But that's not the issue. The issue is my mental health. How can I possibly be with Trevor when I feel so bad about Ben?"

Ali grimaced. "I don't know, but the sooner you just move on from Ben, the better."

"I have finally gotten used to him not being in my everyday life, but I'm not completely over how it all went down. He broke my heart."

"I get that, but really, you were not in love with him."

"Maybe not—but I loved him. He hurt me pretty bad the way he just left and I can't get over it in a day or even a month."

"But its Trevor you've been thinking about so I just don't get why your past with Ben would be such an issue. Trevor is a good guy—he'd understand."

"He does understand, but ultimately, I'm not over Ben. What if he comes back and finds out I slept with Trevor? What would he think?"

"Who cares? You don't owe him any loyalty, Charlotte."

"What about you and Rob? When he broke it off with you, didn't you feel like you couldn't even kiss another man in your life? That feeling eventually goes away but it still takes time to get used to being solo again."

"I see your point, Charlotte. Well played. It did take me some time and I'm still dealing with it, but Rob and I were together a lot longer than you and Ben," Ali said with a soft smile. "Regardless, I'm beginning to think you have commitment issues."

That surprised Charlotte. "You do? Why?"

"Look at your track record. In college, you bailed on Trevor when he wanted to get close. After Trevor, it was Shawn, who you knew was a partier and wouldn't want to get serious. Then there was Steve, who had a girlfriend the whole time, and even though you complained about it, I think you thrived on the drama and you liked not having to worry about moving to the next level. You might as well have been dating a married man. There were a couple others who didn't pan out and I can't remember their names but I think you pick these men because you don't want to commit nor do you want to show vulnerability. Finding the right love means you have to let that wall down and *be* vulnerable."

Charlotte was stunned at Ali's quick analysis. Was it true? Did she have a pattern of picking unavailable men? It occurred to her that Ali was once again right. Feeling angsty about who she was dating was so much easier than being vulnerable and falling in love only to get her heart broken. When did she start doing this to herself? Was it after she broke up with Trevor? *Why do I feel like I don't deserve love?* It was such a glass half empty way to go through life. "I loved Ben. He asked me to marry him," she said more to herself than to Ali.

"Yes, I was surprised by it, but from what you told me, you weren't happy. You might not see it yet, but you both were more friends than lovers. He was a great guy and hopefully he will figure his issues out, but there is no way you would have ended up happy with him."

"Am I that closed off, Ali? I thought I opened up to Ben but he was the one who shut me down."

"That's because you weren't right for each other. Get over Ben, he's gone," Ali said before changing her tone and smiling. "It's Trevor you want to have that mature relationship with. Let him in, Charlotte."

"What do I do?"

"I don't know. Lick your wounds and then start dating men, meaning Trevor, who want to be with you and only you and not the manboys who either have too much baggage or don't want to grow up."

By now, tears were spilling down Charlotte's cheeks. She and Ali hadn't had a heart to heart like this in a long time. "I forgot how well you know me."

"I know," Ali said. "I know this is probably bad timing and I wish it could wait, but I've decided to move down to the peninsula."

Crap. Charlotte had been dreading this talk. It wasn't that she expected it right now, but they couldn't be roommates forever. Charlotte expected she would have been the first to move out and she always dreaded telling Ali. "When are you leaving? I'm going to miss you."

"Not until the end of February, but I wanted to let you know now. I'm just really tired of the city. It's getting too expensive and I just think it's time. I want some space."

"Do you really think I am commitment-phobic?" Charlotte asked wanting to change the subject. She couldn't deal with Ali's move just yet.

"Well, I don't think you're phobic about it as you are serious. When you commit, you commit with your whole heart and you see your decision to the end. You don't quit or back out. I think when it comes to men, you want to date those who you know won't force you to the next level. Ben was an anomaly and he caught you off guard with a proposal. Think about it, you never fully expected him to propose nor did you expect to make it down the aisle, did you? You were overwhelmed and suffocating but you were committed because you said yes."

Suffocated. That's exactly how Charlotte felt about planning the wedding. It wasn't even the wedding itself that bothered her so much as being with Ben long term. "I know. Ben is such a good guy. I wonder why I couldn't fall in love with him."

"He just wasn't the one. How much different do you feel about Trevor?"

Charlotte remembered last night. "It was perfect. He and I have a lot of history and I guess it makes a good foundation. It didn't feel weird at all until this afternoon at work. Even then, we were able to talk about it."

"Well, give it some time. If it's meant to be— you'll end up together. If he isn't the one, you'll meet someone else. It's that simple."

Now, standing out in the damp cold at second base, Charlotte wondered if she'd made the right decision. She missed Trevor so much, she couldn't stand it. She battled everyday not to call him or text him and it was driving her insane that he was actually leaving her alone.

She sometimes stalked his Facebook page just to see if he'd been on it lately. It was probably good for her mental health that he didn't do much with his account because it was seldom updated.

As the days passed, she settled back into her routine of being single which, after the shock of it all, wasn't so bad. The holidays were rough, but she spent extra time at work filling in for co-workers who went out of town. Keeping busy at work not only kept her mind distracted, but it also kept her from spending too much money shopping in Union Square. Her bank account needed some help since Ali would be moving out and she would be taking over the rent. No retail therapy this time.

Her mind wasn't too busy where she didn't look for Trevor when she walked around the office or went on coffee breaks. When she heard he took two weeks off and wouldn't be back until after the New Year, she felt crushed. Her emotions were on a rollercoaster— mad at Ben, mad at Trevor, missing Ben, missing Trevor, glad she was done with both of them, hating being single but disgusted at the thought of dating anyone else. Why hadn't Trevor fought harder? Why did he take her seriously and not see that he needed to just be patient? Why didn't he just show up at her door with flowers and tell her she was being stupid and he didn't care that she was still getting over Ben? *Because he's better than that.* He didn't fight for her because he fought for her last time and she ignored him. *Gah, stop thinking about him!*

Suddenly, the ball was hit straight to her and Charlotte had only a second to react. She fielded the ball but as she went to throw, she slipped on the wet grass and felt a crunch as she broke her fall with her right hand. Trying to throw the ball to the pitcher, her hand just sort of flopped down and the ball dropped to the ground. It took a second for the pain to reach her hand, but as she shook it, she knew it wasn't going to go away.

Running off the field, she knew without a doubt she broke it. *Damn, damn, damn!* "I hurt my hand," she said to Stacey and Kelly as she looked for some ice in the cooler.

"What happened? Are you okay?" Stacey asked concerned.

"I don't know, it's starting to swell," Charlotte said looking at it realizing it was her writing hand.

"Do you want me to take you to the hospital?" asked Kelly.

"Not yet," Charlotte said still in denial. Maybe she just sprained it. As the throbbing and swelling grew more intense, she couldn't deny she needed to get it x-rayed. She didn't want to go to the hospital—not when she depended on being out with her friends right now. The softball games followed with the time at the bar were a lifeline for her socially. None of it was tied to Ben or Trevor—although she did mourn how Ben would pick her up and she would go to his place afterwards.

"What happened out there," Darren asked when the team returned from the field.

"I slipped and fell on my hand," she replied as he took her hand gently in his.

"Yup, that looks broken. You should go to emergency and get it x-rayed."

"Sure thing, Doctor Darren."

"Hey, at least you'll get some good drugs. Do you want me to take you?"

"I don't want you to miss the pitchers of Budweiser at the Final Final."

"I think you need someone to get you to the ER and I prefer Sierra Nevada anyway."

Charlotte was starting to feel a little woozy from the pain. "Okay, thanks."

Once they said goodbye to the rest of the team, Charlotte let Darren lead her across the field to the parking lot. Since they were in the far field, they had to go around the other softball diamond and she could have sworn she saw Ben walking towards her. Why would Ben be here? The pain must be getting to her.

As she and Darren continued to walk towards the cars, the Ben look alike got closer and when she finally realized her mind wasn't playing tricks on her, the rest of the blood left in her brain drained and her heart started pounding.

Ben was back and he was here.

Not only was she in her sweats, but she was getting nauseous from the pain. This is perfect timing. Her mind stayed blank as she tried desperately to remember the words she had practiced to say to him when she saw him again. He looked the same although he hadn't shaved in a couple days and his hair was longer.

"Ben," she said as he approached.

"Ben your ex?" Darren asked.

"Yep."

"Hi, Charlotte," Ben said standing in front of her.

"What are you doing here? How did you know I'd be here?"

"I remember you have softball on Thursday nights. Plus, I stopped by your place and Ali told me you were here. Can we talk?"

This was all so surreal. "Well, I'm off to the hospital. Apparently, I broke my hand."

"Oh wow," Ben said urgently reaching for her hand.

Pulling it away quickly was more of a knee jerk reaction to the pain than it was to Ben. "It hurts."

"Well, let me take you, Charlotte," Ben said before re-introducing himself to Darren. "I can take her."

Charlotte was torn. It would be nice to sit with Darren, but she couldn't wait to hear what Ben had to say. "It's okay, Darren. Ben can take me. I'll try and make it to the bar if I get out of the ER fast enough."

"Are you sure?" Darren said looking from Ben to her.

"I'm sure."

She and Ben stood there as Darren walked back to the team. She knew he was waiting for the right time to start talking but she didn't want to get into it here on the field. She was getting cold and the pain wasn't helping her clarity.

Walking together, but never feeling more apart, Charlotte was relieved when Ben finally broke the silence. "Should we take my car or yours?"

"Let's take yours. I'm not sure I can drive," she said.

She let him help her into the car and she felt better once they were on the way to the hospital. He was listening to Brazilian music which he turned down low. Normally, Charlotte loved this music, but right now it seemed annoying.

"Where am I taking you?" he asked.

That was a good question. Charlotte hadn't been to the emergency room since she broke her nose playing football but she was on a different health plan then. Reaching for her bag, she winced at the pain as she brought her wallet out. "I think I can go anywhere. It's a PPO," she said trying to pull the card out of its place in the sleeve. She knew without a doubt something was broken by the sheer pain she felt as she tried to close her fingers around the card. Since she was right handed, she automatically tried to use it, but it was useless right now.

Ben pulled up to the hospital located at the top of Pacific Heights. Walking in, Charlotte was relieved there was no one in the waiting room. "Looks like it might go quickly."

"Famous last words," Ben laughed. "Everyone waits hours in the ER."

Charlotte appreciated his attempt to lighten the mood between them. Again, this was surreal to Charlotte as she checked in with the nurse. Thank goodness someone was here with her, because she couldn't write and if she had to use her left hand, she would still be filling out the forms hours from now. Ben did it all for her and it felt like they were a couple again. He'd never been so sweet and attentive and she was thankful he was there instead of Darren. She needed someone familiar.

It didn't take the x-rays to tell her she'd broken a bone, but the doctor said it was a small break and would heal well with rest and stability.

"I'm going to give you the name of a doctor where you can get a cast put on," he said as he bandaged her hand tightly.

"I have to get a cast?"

"Trust me after a day or two in this thing, a cast will make your hand feel like it moved into a spacious condo."

Once she was done, she returned to the waiting room to find Ben. She must have been in a little bit of shock, because her body was starting to relax and she was feeling really sleepy. Overall, it took two hours and while she could have returned to the bar to meet her team, she was too wiped out.

"You ready?" Ben asked concerned. "What did the doctor say?"

"I definitely broke it and I have to get a cast. We need to stop by Walgreen's and get a prescription for Vicodin."

"I think a pain killer will help you immensely right now."

"My hand is bandaged so tightly it hurts and I think the circulation is slowing down," she said as they walked to the car.

"Well, be thankful it isn't your leg."

It was midnight before Ben pulled into his garage. "I think you should sleep here tonight."

Charlotte could feel the pain killer kicking in and she felt so much better and lighter. "Okay."

Following Ben up the stairs, she knew she wanted to take a shower. "Do you have a plastic bag I can put over my hand so I can shower?"

"Yes," he said going into the kitchen.

Charlotte wasn't sure what to do now. They hadn't even broached the subject of their breakup and it was like he was back in her life and nothing happened. Charlotte was high, so she didn't really care right now and tried hard to be mad at him but just giggled to herself. Her life had so much drama in it sometimes.

"I hope my car is okay up at the field overnight."

"I'm sure it will be," he said leading her to the bathroom.

Suddenly Charlotte realized she couldn't undress herself all the way. She could get her shoes and pants off, but her shirt and bra were another deal. "Um, Ben, I need some help."

"Here, let me help you," he said pulling her shirt over her head and then unhooking her bra. She was naked in front of him and should have been self conscious but she wasn't. Again, it was the drugs.

"How am I going to get dressed by myself?" she said looking at her hand. Everything was bandaged except her thumb. How would she blow dry her hair? Brush her teeth? Complete her work at the station? She was going to be left handed for a while. *This sucks.*

"I'm sure you'll get used to it," Ben said starting the water for her. "I broke my arm when I was young and I adapted. I'll get in and help you."

Charlotte should have said no but she was relieved to let Ben take care of her. She waited patiently as he covered her hand and arm in a plastic bag and tied it off with one of his dress ties. Charlotte didn't argue with him but thought a rubber band would have done just as well. Once the water was warm, she stepped and Ben soon followed.

It felt comfortable and nice primarily because the sexual pressure was gone. Actually, it was never really there. As Ben focused on washing her back and carefully scrubbing her arm, Charlotte could see how she had been trying to force something that was never going to happen naturally. They never should have been lovers and maybe it was for the best the way things unfolded. Ali had been right that they were probably better off just friends. She wasn't mad at him anymore, but sad that they'd failed at their relationship.

"I think our door closed, Ben," she said after she was dried off and lying in bed.

"What do you mean?" he asked as he got under the covers.

"I was so mad and hurt when you left, but now I just feel sad and that means I'm moving on." Ben remained silent so Charlotte continued. "I loved being with you, but everything changed when we got engaged and it just wasn't right after that."

"I know," he said quietly. "I'm sorry, Charlotte."

"I know you are, Ben. I know you have issues to work out and I just don't think you are ready for marriage and even if you were, I don't think I'm the right person for you."

Wow. Charlotte finally got it all off her chest. As she was saying the words, she didn't even need to convince herself they were true. All the wondering over the past two months about Ben finally concluded and she was done. She loved him, but she was not in love with him and she never was.

"I wanted so badly for it to work out," Ben said sadly. "There was a time I thought you were the perfect woman."

"Well, I am—just not for you."

She liked seeing Ben laugh again. "What did you tell Trevor?"

Charlotte froze wondering if he was trapping her. Did he know? "Have you spoken to Trevor?"

"Not yet."

It wasn't that she wanted to tell him about Trevor but something told her that if she didn't, Ben would find out somehow and be upset. He would probably be upset anyway, but she would rather him hear it from her than from Trevor.

"Ben, there's something about Trevor I need to tell you." Feeling him stiffen, she didn't need to go any further before he interrupted her.

"I know. You don't have to tell me. I could see it all over your face when he was near you."

Was she that obvious?

"I'm sorry. It happened after you left. We're not dating right now, but I do have strong feelings for him."

"He is in love with you. If I didn't like him as a person, I'd punch him in the face."

She was still surprised how Ben could read people so easily. Not sure what to say, she turned the conversation to his life.

"What about you? Did you fix things with your ex?"

"Not completely, but she's the one for me, Charlotte. I'm moving back to Minneapolis permanently. That's one reason I came back—to get my stuff and to see you. I felt so guilty about how I treated you and I needed to make sure you were okay."

"I appreciate that."

"I love San Francisco, but I'm ready to get back to my family and my hometown."

"And the heavy winters? I know you can't wait for that," Charlotte laughed. Somehow it didn't surprise her he was moving back. Then she realized what she said. "Oh my gosh, I hope that didn't hit a bad nerve."

"No, I'm still sensitive about the accident, but at least I can talk about it."

"I'm glad to hear that," she said and meant it. He needed to be able to talk about the tragedy and needed those closest around him to be supportive.

"I ran away and now I need to face it."

"Well, maybe Nora can help you this time."

"I hope so," he said.

"Who would have thought that our breakup would lead us to find out we're in love with other people?"

Ben sighed and shook his head gently. "No kidding."

Charlotte was never more relieved as she was at that moment. She finally got her say with Ben and it didn't even bother her when he said he was in love with someone else. Okay, she was a little bothered, but more because she knew Ben was leaving. It did surprise her she admitted out loud she was in love with Trevor. Feeling Ben's body now pressed up behind hers as he spooned her, she smiled at the familiarity. It was probably the drugs in her system, but she never expected her faceoff with Ben to go this well or this easy, but she was happy it did. Maybe someday they really could be friends again. It would take awhile, but it could happen. In the meantime, she let her mind drift to Trevor. What was he doing right now?

Sixteen

Back at work after a two week vacation, Trevor felt much better than he did prior to the holidays. He needed the time away from the city, work, and Charlotte just to recharge his batteries and clear his head.

After a week with his parents in San Diego, he spent New Year's with his buddies Tom and Sam in Manhattan Beach. The weather was warm as it always seemed to be for the holidays in LA and the beach was the perfect escape. He spent the days running along the strand and playing volleyball with strangers who were on vacation as well.

He would have been happy staying in on New Year's Eve, but Tom dragged him out to a party a few blocks away. The hostess was a friend of Tom's girlfriend, Sabrina, and Trevor felt obligated to go with Tom since he was crashing at his place. It had been Trevor's norm to stay home the past couple of years because it finally dawned on him how overpriced the night actually was. Why pay an extra hundred dollars to get into a bar he could hang out at for free every other night of the year? *New Year's is so overrated.* Plus, if truth be told, he hated the coupled feeling of the night. If he didn't have a date to kiss at midnight, he was made to feel inadequate.

"Come on, Trev, it'll be fun. There is going to be a few single women to talk to," Tom said as they left the house and walked up the hill. "Plus, I hear Sabrina's friend is loaded and the house is gorgeous. You need to pick your mopey ass up off the floor and have some fun."

"I've been having fun this week."

"Well, you know what I mean."

Trevor didn't really care what the house looked like or who was there, he just wanted to get it over with. It had been a nice few days and he admitted to himself he felt much better than he did before he left San Francisco. Spending time with his family, including his sister and his niece and nephew, had been long overdue. The kids were growing so fast and at the ages of three and nineteen months, they were so much fun. He was tired of feeling depressed and wanted to feel like himself again.

Once they reached the house, Trevor followed Tom inside and realized Tom was right—the house was amazing. It was one of the few that faced the ocean and the view was spectacular despite the darkness. He could see twinkling lights leading down the hill to the black of the water. Guests were already mingling in the kitchen and Trevor realized they were all his age. He wasn't sure what he expected, but this wasn't it. The atmosphere was friendly and casual and Trevor waited as Tom said hello to Sabrina and her friends. The hostess, Roxie, was quick to introduce herself to Trevor easing that awkwardness. He immediately felt like he knew these people for ages and relaxed as Roxie handed him a beer.

"How do you know Tom and Sabrina?" Roxie asked him.

"Tom and I went to high school together. I'm staying with him for a few days."

"Oh, right, you're the reporter friend from San Francisco," she said as she cut up vegetables.

"Well, I'm not a reporter but rather a producer," he said.

"You should meet my friend—she's on her way over. She's a reporter here in LA. She'll be here in a few minutes."

Time passed quickly as Trevor drank his beers and snacked on the food that seemed to never run out. He was feeling more like his social self when he felt Roxie tap him on the shoulder interrupting a conversation he was having with her husband Rob. Turning around, Trevor almost choked on the prawn he just put in his mouth.

"Trevor, I'd like you to meet my friend Sarah Davenport," Roxie said.

He obviously didn't need an introduction—he already knew Charlotte's friend.

"Wait, we know each other already," Trevor said pleasantly surprised. "Sarah, it's been too long. How are you?"

"Trevor, wow, I didn't expect to see you here," Sarah replied excitedly as they hugged. "What a small world."

"This is crazy. I haven't seen you since our advertising class together."

"I know. I'm afraid to even consider how long ago that was because I'll feel old."

Once the pleasantries were out of the way, Trevor wasn't sure what to talk about. He knew she was still friends with Charlotte but he felt awkward acknowledging it. Knowing women, he was fairly certain Sarah knew about what went on between him and Charlotte. Pushing her out of his thoughts, he realized he just wanted to know what Sarah had been up to during the past decade.

"So tell me, how is life, really?" he asked.

"Did Charlotte say anything? I know you were back to being friends in the city," Sarah said just as awkwardly as Trevor felt a few seconds ago. Even now, he resisted asking her about Charlotte. "Not really. She said you were busy with your career and enjoying LA."

An uneasy couple of seconds passed until Trevor understood Sarah wasn't sure how much to say about Charlotte. "I'm not sure how much I should say," she said echoing his thoughts.

"I know. I'm sure she told you we got together before Christmas," he said knowing he might not hear what he wanted her to say. Feeling guilty about trapping her into the conversation, he wanted Sarah to know he didn't need her to tattle. "It's okay if you don't want to talk about her, Sarah. I know she's your friend."

Sarah smiled before she answered. "I wish you two would just get over your issues and finally get together. "

Trevor didn't know to respond but he felt flushed and hot. The breeze coming off the ocean felt good against his face as he waited for Sarah to continue.

"You both are the king and queen of bad timing," she said and Trevor was worried she was going to finish her thoughts by saying they could never work. "But you have to understand her. She has never been good at letting someone in especially when she's trying to get over someone else. I think she has an extra loyalty gene or something."

Trevor chuckled, relieved. "You can say that again. I know she needs time to get over Ben but I hate that I'm left on the back burner again."

"You can't think about it like that. You are really important to her. I know that for sure. You were also important to her back in college and it took her a long time to get over you. Do you realize she didn't even really date again until a year later?"

"It didn't feel like that to me then and it doesn't now."

"That's just it, though. She's in love with you but just needs lick her wounds before she comes to the full realization of it all. She never wanted to marry Ben but she just didn't know how to end it because she liked him as a person. You coming back into her life just confused her."

"She never said anything," Trevor said trying to remember exactly what Charlotte had said.

"Well, of course not. Ending a relationship is one thing but ending an engagement is another. Even though she never wanted it, it still takes some time to get over it. I liked Ben—I met him a couple times but he never made her sparkle like a woman in love."

Trevor chuckled at her analogy. "So you think she's in love with me?"

"I'm almost a hundred percent sure," Sarah laughed. "You're not graduating this time and moving away and she isn't going anywhere, so this time you can give her the space she needs."

"True," he said feeling even better than he did earlier. He felt almost giddy now. "How long should I wait?"

"I have no idea but I wouldn't wait too long," she answered and then started to say something else before cutting herself off.

"What?" he asked wanting her to continue.

"She has been talking about the KCPR reunion in April. Are you planning to go?"

"Sure, I think so."

"Well, that might be the best place to approach her. Leave her alone until then and let her really miss you, Trevor. I mean no contact—no phone calls, emails, texts. I know you work at the same place so if you see her at work, be casual. Let her really miss you because I know she will. Women like attention and when you pull it away even if they ask you to, they miss it."

"I'm not really into game playing, Sarah."

"It's not really game playing. It's all about living your own life."

Trevor wasn't sure he could totally ignore Charlotte, but Sarah knew her well, so maybe it was the way to go. "Wait until the reunion?"

"Yes. I can almost guarantee it. How can you not get back together in the town where it all started?"

The more Trevor thought about it, the more it made sense. The reunion wasn't that far away—only a few months and he knew San Luis Obispo was very special to Charlotte. Maybe being around all their KCPR friends would be a good influence. But did he have enough discipline not to contact her until then? Especially knowing she worked so close to him? "Okay, Sarah, I'm going with this. You better be right and not say anything to her. I wouldn't even tell her we ran into each other."

"I won't say a thing," she said pretending to zip her lips. "My lips are sealed."

Trevor was ready to change subject. His brain needed a rest. It was New Year's Eve and there was nothing he could do about Charlotte now so he might as well enjoy the night. "Now that we have that out of the way, what's up with you?"

Sarah laughed. "That's a whole other drama. I'll tell you later. Let's go get drunk," she said leading him back into the crowd.

The rest of night flew by until the countdown started. As predicted, people coupled up but many were there single and when midnight struck, it was more about clinking glasses than kissing lips. Sarah reached out and hugged Trevor giving him a kiss on the cheek.

"My guess is next year will be very different for you and Charlotte will be by your side."

"Thanks," he whispered in her ear. "Happy New Year."

The party ended two hours later and Trevor decided to walk Sarah home. She lived in the area and it wasn't out of his way.

"Are you sure?" she asked.

"Yes. I want to make sure you get home safe."

As they walked along Manhattan Avenue, Trevor listened as Sarah filled him in on her drama with Cooper Bancroft. "It's been tough. Everyone dreams of dating a celebrity, but it's not that easy. Every day I wish he just had a normal job."

"I don't envy you. How long have you been dating?"

"Four years but that doesn't matter since he is apparently dating Ashley McGregor," she said sarcastically.

"That's his costar, right? I never saw his movie."

"You're about the only person on earth who hasn't seen it."

"What are you going to do? Just wait? Do you love him?"

"I love him very much. I can't imagine life without him."

"Where is he right now?"

"He had a party to host in Vegas. I wasn't invited," Sarah sneered. "I decided to stay low key here at the beach."

"Understood. Partying in Vegas is not my idea of fun," Trevor said. "So I guess you and I both have to be patient."

"I think you're right. Okay, this is my place."

"Nice house," he said admiring the small bungalow exterior. He couldn't really see too many details in the dark, but he could tell Sarah took good care of it.

As they were about to say goodbye, Trevor heard Sarah's name called softly from the front porch. "I think someone is here," he said walking slowly up to the front door. "Who's there?"

Trevor felt Sarah grab his arm. "It's okay. It's just Cooper."

Startled, Trevor waited for Sarah to take the lead before he moved any closer.

"Cooper, what are you doing here?" she asked.

"I missed you. I left Vegas as soon as the countdown finished," Cooper said appearing from the shadows of the porch and walking towards them.

Trevor stood back as they hugged. "Did anyone follow you?"

"No way," Cooper said before looking at Trevor. "Who's your friend?"

"This is Trevor—he's a friend of Charlotte's."

"Oh right, I've heard about you. Nice to meet you," Cooper said extending his hand.

Trevor was surprised Cooper knew his name. "Nice to meet you. I just walked Sarah home to make sure she was safe."

"It's cool, man. I get it," Cooper said before turning to kiss Sarah on the lips. "That's about two hours overdue."

"Why don't you both come in for a bit," Sarah said but Trevor could tell she wanted to be alone with Cooper. They looked so happy to see each other and that stabbed at Trevor's heart. He would give anything to have Charlotte look at him like Sarah was looking at Cooper.

"Thanks, but I think I'll head back and get some sleep. Good to meet you, Cooper, and great to see you again, Sarah. Hopefully, we'll see each other again soon," Trevor said hoping she would get his double meaning. The only real way they would see each other again was if Charlotte was back in his life.

"I'm sure we will, Trevor," she said breaking away from Cooper to give him a hug. "Please take care and remember to just give her time. I'll be very excited to hear how the reunion goes. Oh, and if you would please not tell anyone you saw Cooper? I'd appreciate it."

"Don't worry. Although I think I might just take a pic with my camera phone and email it anonymously to the tabloids and see how much I can get," he said jokingly as he started walking down the hill.

"Ha ha, jokester!" Sarah yelled after him before giggling.

Trevor left the couple alone and decided to walk back to Tom's place along the strand. It was fairly quiet except for the waves and a few people here and there returning from parties. The moon was bright in the sky so he could easily see the path in front of him.

Maybe it was divine intervention, but Trevor felt like he was supposed to run into Sarah tonight—as if someone was giving him a message. It was silly, he knew, but it made the waiting a little bit easier. Hearing Charlotte was in love with him from her friend was like balm to the cracks in his heart, but he still needed to see it to believe it. Looking up at the moon and the stars, he wondered what she was doing at that exact moment and if she was thinking about him like he was thinking about her.

Seventeen

San Luis Obispo hadn't changed much.

On his way up from LA back to San Francisco, Trevor decided he was long overdue for a stop in the town he once called home. It had grown somewhat—a new Starbucks, Barnes and Nobles, but it was still the same small college town he remembered.

Walking Higuera Street, the memories of college rushed back. How many nights had he spent walking this street between the bars and restaurants or at Linnea's cafe studying and listening to music? Then there was the Thursday night Farmers Market which was like a weekly party of good food and fresh produce. Returning to SLO was like opening the vault to his past.

After spending some time in the Cal Poly store where he replenished his wardrobe with a hoodie, t-shirt and basketball shorts, he made his way over to Boo Boo Records. The record store was like a second home to him in college. Not only did he work behind the register for extra cash, he spent hours going through the CD bins for music discarded by customers. Seeing it today, he felt very nostalgic to think how much influence it had on his life. Even though it was slightly different and had adapted to the new world of downloads, Trevor was proud to see it still standing and noted as one of the best small town record stores in the nation. Apparently, diehards still made and effort to find rare vinyl issued albums.

After buying another t-shirt, he walked back out into the warm air. He had just put on his sunglasses when he heard his name called from behind. Turning around, he was stunned by the person standing in front of him. "Katie!"

"Hi there," she said walking up to him and giving him a hug. "It's been so long. How are you, Trevor?"

It wasn't that he was shocked to see her, necessarily; it was just the surrealism of it all. First he ran into Sarah in LA and now Katie in SLO. *What is it with running into my past, lately?*

Katie looked completely different. She was still tall but her hair was long, wavy and blonde. Trevor noticed her makeup looked soft and subtle unlike college where it was hard and dark. But the one thing he noticed most was how she seemed happy and gone was the scowl and the invisible wall she carried around with her. She had a glow about her.

Katie was stunning.

"I'm very well, Katie. Wow. This is really surreal. You look great, by the way."

"Thank you. I appreciate you noticing. So what are you doing here?"

"I'm just passing through on my way back up to San Francisco. I'm a morning producer."

"That's great. You always were good with the broadcasting thing," she said.

"So what are you doing here?"

"I live here now. I'm a fourth grade teacher. I'm on my way to grab a coffee. Want to join me?"

The invitation startled Trevor and he wasn't sure how to say no. After thinking about it for a couple seconds, he didn't want to say no. He wanted to find out how the Katie he knew in college turned out to be a beautiful fourth grade teacher Katie standing in front of him. "Sure, that sounds nice."

Once they found a spot on the patio at his old haunt Linnea's, they started to really catch up. Trevor filled her in on his life all the way up to Charlotte. He wasn't sure it was necessary to mention Charlotte to Katie who once had a meltdown over her.

"Wow, you've been busy. Sounds like you love living in the city," she said wrapping both her hands around a cup of coffee.

"I do. It's a great city. So tell me about you. How did you get to be a teacher?"

"It's such a long story—you sure you want to hear it?"

"Of course I do," he replied thinking he was having a really nice time with her. She seemed so relaxed that it was hard to remember the old Katie.

"So, gosh, where do I start?" she said looking up as if to find that place in her past to start. "Well, I don't need to tell you that I wasn't the nicest person in college."

Trevor smiled at her as if to agree.

"College was so hard for me. My parents went through a nasty divorce just as I graduated high school and I know now that's where a lot of my anger came from. Luckily, I was over eighteen so they didn't fight over me, but my little sister and brother got caught in a really bad custody battle. It was so hard to see the two people you counted on your whole life suddenly hate each other."

"That must have been so hard. I'm sorry," Trevor said.

"Yes, it was. I found out my dad had an affair and that basically ruined any hopes for the sanctity of marriage," she said with a small sarcastic laugh. "It took a long time for me to trust a man and I'm so sorry with the way I acted towards you. I'm still embarrassed."

"Don't be—it was a long time ago. We've all changed."

"I know, but I was so clingy and jealous. I realize now I just didn't have the trust to be in a relationship. Plus, I had a major drug addiction."

"You did?" Trevor remembered Dean saying she was into drugs but never fully believed it.

"Oh yes. I put what little I made working part time up my nose," she said shaking her head. "I made a lot of bad decisions during that time."

Trevor didn't press her but let her continue. He figured she'd tell him as much as she was comfortable with.

"I can't believe I actually graduated. It took a little longer, but the one thing about being on coke, it was easy to stay up late to study. After college, I moved to LA, but fell in with an even worse crowd. I couldn't keep a job and when I woke up in some strange bed because I had nowhere else to go, I knew I needed to get my shit together."

"Wow, I had no idea."

"No one did. I didn't really talk to anyone from school—I purposely fell off the map. I have to say, however, my problems helped my parents stop fighting and call a truce. Once they realized they had to actually co-parent instead of fight each other, they got over their issues."

"Well I guess that's a bright spot," Trevor said with a tight laugh.

"I went back to live with my mom in Paso Robles and got clean. The next step was figuring out what to do with the rest of my life. Since I studied English, the next logical step was a teaching credential which I finished. I've been teaching for about nine years now."

"That's great," he said and meant it. He was very proud of her.

"I got married and now have two boys."

That statement surprised him since he didn't see a ring on her finger.

"Oh, the marriage lasted four years but we're on good terms. He's a great dad."

"What happened between the two of you?" Trevor asked hoping he wasn't crossing a line.

He watched as Katie sighed. "I'm not sure. I don't think I was ever in love with him. He was just the first relationship I had that lasted more than a couple months. Marriage and children were the next step, but after a couple years, it just wasn't what we both wanted anymore."

"So, I take it you're friends?"

"We're friends which is good for the boys. I would never put them through what my brother and sister went through. He's remarried now and very happy and I just want the best for our kids. I like his wife and she's good to them."

"I guess that's a positive?"

"I suppose so," she replied. "What about you?"

"Me? Well, I've been the happy bachelor. No special someone at the moment," he said with a pang.

"I can't believe that. Whatever happened to the girl you were so in love with in school?"

"Charlotte?" Trevor said not surprised that Katie brought her name up. Stalling a bit, he wasn't sure how much to tell her. Should he tell her the truth or make something up? Somehow, this time, he didn't want to talk about Charlotte. She seemed far away and he'd thought so much about her lately, he was actually sick of it all. "I'm not sure. We never got back together," he lied.

"Oh, that's too bad. Despite my jealousy, you both made a cute couple."

After discussing their jobs and lack of love life, they never even noticed the sun had set until the patio lights turned on. It was such a surprise to Trevor how much this person in front of him had changed for the better. Listening to her stories, he felt almost proud of her for overcoming the obstacles she faced in college.

"Wow, it got dark all of the sudden. I didn't think I'd be out this late. Normally, I'm home in my pajamas doing homework with Jack," Katie said. "I don't know how long you're planning to stay, but if you want, we can go back to my place and open some wine."

Trevor knew if that happened, he wouldn't be able to drive home. He'd have to stay the night. He wasn't sure what she was hinting at or if she was hinting at all, but he didn't want to get back in his car and drive for another four hours. He wanted to hang out and enjoy her company. "A glass of wine sounds wonderful but that would mean crashing at your house. Is that okay?"

"The boys are with their dad and I have an extra bedroom so that'd be fine."

"In that case, would you mind if we made a stop at McCarthy's? It's been so long since I've been there."

"Sure. You do know it moved, right. It's no longer the shoebox it once was."

"I noticed. Apparently Banana Republic and Pottery Barn took over the block. Leave it to the women to replace the only good bar in town," Trevor said laughing as they walked out of the café.

Elizabeth Aloe

"Oh come on, this town needs a few good stores. Even a man needs Pottery Barn once in awhile."

"Proud to say I've never set foot in one," Trevor said.

"You don't know what you're missing," she replied with a small punch to his arm.

Trevor let Katie lead him down the street to the new location of McCarthy's. It was definitely different with the patio outside and the new jukebox, but the actual bar was the same as were the shamrocks on the wall. He knew it was better business for the bar with the space, but he sure missed the old location. Katie was right—it had been a shoebox with the small cocktail tables, red vinyl chairs, and an old school jukebox that played Patsy Cline. There was nothing like sitting at the bar on a cold night sipping Irish coffees. "Wow, this place is huge compared to the old one."

Ordering a couple beers, in cans no less, Trevor pulled a stool out for Katie before settling on one himself. Since it was a Thursday evening, the atmosphere was casual and excited because of the Farmers Market starting in an hour and the true beginning of the weekend. Thursday had always been his favorite night to go out.

"So here we are," Katie said raising her can of Coors.

"Here we are—cheers," he replied. It was almost surreal to be sitting her once again at the place that held so many good memories for him. He was even starting to forget the old Katie and replacing the memory of her with the woman sitting next to him.

"I want to apologize to you for the way I treated you in college, Katie," he said after taking a few sips of his beer. He was already feeling a small buzz from the beer despite the coffee earlier. Not only was his stomach, but his gut was telling him drinking before a meal was going to come back to haunt him tomorrow. Ignoring it, he continued to sip mostly out of nervousness but a little bit out of excitement.

"No need for an apology, Trevor. I was a mess."

"I know, but I felt like I led you on and I shouldn't have done that."

"I guess I always knew you had a major crush on Charlotte. I was hoping you'd get over it."

Trevor wasn't sure how to reply. He realized he had gone a few hours without thinking about her and it was actually a relief. For the first time since Charlotte came back into his life, he was spending time with another woman and not thinking about her.

"Yes, she did a number on me," Trevor said. "She went through a lot her first year."

"That must have been hard. I heard what happened."

Trevor really didn't want to talk about it nor did he want to think about Charlotte. "That's in the past. Speaking of KCPR, are you going to attend the reunion in the spring?"

"I didn't know there was a reunion, but I guess so. I was never a KCPR junkie like the rest of you."

For the next two hours, Trevor enjoyed getting to know Katie again. Laughing over cans of Coors Light at

McCarthy's was unexpected and for the first time, he felt light and refreshed. He didn't even mind listening to the stories of her boys and how much energy they had in school and sports. He couldn't help but compare the Katie he knew now to the Katie he knew then and it was like light and day. He still wasn't sure they had the right chemistry, but they had enough to enjoy the evening together.

"Should we think about heading back to my place?" Katie said averting her eyes from him.

"I think so. Thanks for coming here with me," he said thinking he had no memories of McCarthy's with Charlotte at all because she hadn't been twenty- one when he knew her then.

"It was fun. I never seem to get out much anymore so this was a very pleasant surprise."

Walking back to her place, Trevor reveled in the quiet. Once they made their way off Higuera and away from the Farmers Market, he could almost hear crickets. He forgot how quiet the streets of SLO were after dark. The temperature had dropped significantly enough for him to wish he had brought a coat. "Wow, I forgot how much the temp drops at night. Are you cold?"

"I'm getting there, but we're almost to my place."

Once they approached her small house, Trevor entered behind her nervously. He knew what was going to happen if he spent the night, but did Katie know? He felt the vibes from her—she wouldn't mind sharing her bed with him but he wasn't absolutely positive. Did he even want to go there? What if some of her anger issues from the past came back? There couldn't be any future for them because she lived here and he lived in San Francisco. Keeping emotional distance usually wasn't difficult, but he knew Katie. Was he opening a bad can of worms by going home with her? Since she wasn't a stranger he picked up in the bar and they'd been intimate before, it wouldn't really be considered a one night stand, would it? *Shut your conscience up and just have good time.*

Pushing these thoughts away, he followed her into the house instantly surprised by the décor. He wasn't sure what he expected, but seeing children's drawings and pictures on the refrigerator wasn't it. He knew she had kids, but he hadn't let it sink in until he could see their presence.

"Your boys are really cute," he said studying the pictures she had framed hanging on the wall.

"Thanks," she said pulling out a bottle of vodka and two glasses. "They are the loves of my life."

"I'm sure you must feel proud."

"The only perfection in my life," she said handing him a vodka spritzer. "I try to be a good mom, but its way harder than I ever expected."

"I can only imagine," Trevor replied feeling uncomfortable as he sat down on the couch. "You have a nice place."

"I rent it, but its home and I like it," she said sitting down next to him.

As she talked about her life in SLO with her boys, all he could think about was kissing her. He tried to remain interested, but the alcohol had really taken its affect and he just wanted to get past the uncomfortable bullshit that seemed mandatory before things got heated. What would she do if he kissed her right now? Would she kiss him back or rebuff him?

When she finally paused to take a sip of her drink, he decided he didn't want to wait any longer. He finally just kissed her and was relieved when she responded.

"Wow, wasn't expecting that," she said smiling. "You still kiss just as well as I remember."

"Thanks," he said absently as he kissed her again. He could feel his whole body responding and wanted desperately to just get to the next level. Suddenly Charlotte popped in his head and he remembered kissing her but she was far away now and he didn't want her to ruin this. Pushing the image of her face from his mind, he asked Katie if they could go to her bedroom. When she said yes and led him in there, he knew she wanted the same thing he did.

Yet while his body responded positively to the idea, his gut was telling him to stop now because somehow he would pay for this later. It couldn't be this easy and smooth, could it?

Eighteen

"Well, Charlotte, the x-rays look good. Time to get that cast off," the doctor said when he walked into the room. "Just remember, while the bone is healed, the ligaments in your hand are tight, so take it easy."

Charlotte felt so relieved. She was miserable writing with her left hand and taking showers with a bag over her arm. The biggest luxury she missed—at least she now considered it a luxury—was blow drying her hair. Unable to bend her wrist, she was unable to use a blow dryer therefore leaving the house everyday with a wet head after a shower. Ali had taken pity on her a few times and blew it dry for her but life would be so normal again once she could do it herself.

"Can I get back to playing softball?" she asked as he started cutting the cast off.

"Yes, but again, take it easy. I want you wearing an ace bandage for awhile just as extra support while your hand and fingers get used to moving again."

As she watched the doctor cut away the cast, she couldn't help but feel like he was cutting away part of her life along with it. The last six weeks had been almost as confining as her cast, but when it completely fell away from her hand, not only did her hand feel back to normal, but her mind and heart felt back to normal, too.

And it was time to get back to *normal*.

Walking home, she realized she hadn't thought about Ben or Trevor for the past day. Mostly, she had been excited to get her cast off and play softball later that evening. Work had gone well because of a meeting with her manager Jake who assigned her more responsibilities. No raise, of course, but she knew Jake only assigned the extra work to people he was looking to promote at a later date—at least that's what her coworker Shanna told her.

She was truly back on her own again. Ali had moved to Palo Alto the week before and at first Charlotte felt really out of sorts coming home to an empty apartment, but once she bought a futon to replace Ali's bed, she understood why people liked living alone. She no longer had to cajole someone into cleaning the bathroom or doing the dishes before they piled up in the sink.

It wasn't until she heard Collective Soul through her headphones as she walked home from the doctor that she thought about Trevor. The memories of that night at the concert came flooding back and she smiled remembering how he kissed her amidst the crowd and how they spent the night with each other. Bits and pieces flashed in her mind like a strobe light but what she remembered most was seeing him bend down to kiss her goodbye the next morning. It was the tenderness in his eyes coupled with the intimacy she just couldn't shake and she wanted it back. She never had that with any other boyfriend and that is what separated them from Trevor.

Suddenly the Go-Go's interrupted Collective Soul which meant Stacey was calling.

"Hey love, how are you? You going to the game tonight," she asked after Charlotte answered.

"Yes, I am. Can't wait. I got my cast off, finally."

"Woo hoo," Stacey practically screamed. "I was beginning to wonder if that thing was ever coming off."

Charlotte looked down at her hand, opening and closing her fingers, and laughed. "It's gone, so yes, I'll be there and hopefully I can play."

"What happened with you and Darren last week after the game?"

Charlotte sighed as she remembered about how she and Darren kissed. "Um, it was fun, I guess."

"You sound disappointed. What happened?"

Charlotte really didn't want to get into it while she was standing on the corner of California and Van Ness. "Can I tell you later? I'm walking home."

"Sure. I'll see you tonight."

Continuing with her walk, Charlotte smiled to herself remembering how her night with Darren went and how she now understood that episode of Sex and the City when the character Charlotte complained about one of her dates being a really bad kisser.

She hadn't been sure Darren actually was flirting with her until she was up to bat and hit a single to get on first base. Never a fast runner, if she had to run around the bases, the person behind her usually caught up to her by the time she was passing home base. Tonight, it was Darren behind her and he made no attempt to slow down as they both rounded second on the way to third.

"Hurry, Charlotte," he yelled as he caught up to her.

Oh shit, she thought feeling embarrassed. She wasn't wearing cleats, so she couldn't really pick up her pace and the next thing she knew, Darren's arms picked her up and carried her around the bases and across home plate.

Stunned, she didn't really even notice when he put her down yet kept his arm around her waist. Both teams were laughing and cheering and Charlotte couldn't help but blush and laugh along with them. It wasn't until his arm went up to her shoulders pulling her back to the bench did she realize he had a crush on her. Then she remembered all their conversations, how he followed her around the bar, and how seemed incredibly disappointed when Ben had shown up a few weeks before after she broke her hand.

"Good job, missy," he said pulling her close.

"Good job?" she said with a nervous laugh. "You carried me from second base to home."

"You still made it around the bases, right?"

"I sure did," she laughed, high fiving Darren when he raised his hand.

It wasn't until after everyone left the bar a few hours later when she and Darren shared the kiss. Never one to judge quickly, especially after a couple beers, but Darren was the worst she'd ever kissed. Not that she'd kissed many men nor she was an expert, but she was fairly certain if she was wiping her chin because of his drool, something wasn't right. It was so disappointing because he was good looking and truly a sweet guy. She couldn't see him being inexperienced at his age, so someone must have mentioned it to him. Or worse, maybe she was the bad kisser. Groaning, Charlotte thought back to all the men she had kissed over the years and no seemed upset about her technique.

Later that night after she got her cast removed, Charlotte and the team were at the Final Final as usual. She and Darren flipped through the songs in the jukebox—a weekly ritual they shared before they joined the rest of the team at pool and darts.

"I'm in the mood for something smooth tonight," Darren said pushing the buttons.

"Is that so? What do you consider smooth?" Charlotte replied.

"Well, that depends—it could be smooth jazz, R&B, or something more popular like Johnny Cash," he said as he picked Cash's song *Girl from North County*. "What will you be picking tonight?"

Charlotte could feel the electricity between them and it made her blush but it wasn't because she had any attraction towards him. She liked him as a friend, but any attraction she felt before diminished with the awful kiss from last week. There was no real comparison, but he didn't come close to making her feel the same way Trevor did or even Ben. She thought about Trevor for a second as she pretended to study the song catalogue. She kept picturing him as he was when he was in bed with her. No shirt, his head perched on his hand as he leaned in to kiss her on the lips. Then she thought about him walking next to her and realized she missed his company more than she wanted to admit.

She finally got over the engagement debacle with Ben and didn't feel the pain from it anymore. If anything, she felt like she dodged a bullet. She was never comfortable with the idea of getting married and could see that clearly now. Sometimes, she missed Ben like she missed any of her close friends after they moved away, but she didn't feel the need to the contact him. She wanted to get to the point where she never thought about him at all and if she did, it would be with mere indifference or as an acquaintance. While she was doing very well on her own, she just wasn't quite there yet.

Trevor, on the other hand, was still in town and working near her, she had to control herself from calling him or "accidentally" bumping into him. It had been about eight weeks since they parted on the street at lunch. He'd probably gotten over her by now because he made it clear he wasn't going to wait for her. She kept analyzing his words over and over, remembering how he told her he loved her. Was she being stupid? *Maybe I'm not as strong as I think I am and should just call him.* However, the longer she went without speaking to him, the more in control she felt and she certainly didn't want to hear he'd moved on and met someone else.

"So what song are you picking tonight?" Darren said, interrupting her thoughts.

"I'm in the mood for something slow," she replied landing on Ivy. Picking *Edge of the Ocean*, she looked forward to hearing the song later. Charlotte wasn't sure why the impact of her favorite songs seemed so much greater on the radio or on the jukebox, but it somehow did. She could hear them over and over on her iPod, but when they came on the radio, she turned them up and listened as if she hadn't heard them in a very long time. Not wanting to bring the bar down, she also picked a song by The Ramones.

"What's going on with you and Darren," Stacey asked when they were alone at the popcorn machine in the back of the bar. One great bonus about the Final Final was the free movie popcorn. It always tasted so good, especially washed down with beer, but she always regretted it when she was home in bed unable to sleep because of heartburn.

"I'm not sure," Charlotte replied scooping the popcorn into the plastic bowl. "We kissed last week."

"I knew it!"

Charlotte smiled. "Well, don't get ahead of yourself, Stacey. It wasn't that great."

After Charlotte filled her in on the details as nicely as possible—she really liked Darren, so she didn't want to make him seem like a dufus—she said it most likely won't go any further.

"But he seems to really like you," Stacey said. "Can't you get past the kissing part?"

"I would like to, but it's not just that. I like him a lot personally, but as a friend. I just don't think the rest is there for me."

"Oh, I get it. Do you still have feelings for Ben?"

"No, I'm over Ben," Charlotte replied glad she didn't tell Stacey and her softball crew about Trevor. "I'm just not ready to date anyone."

Charlotte laughed at the look on Stacey's face— as if not being with a good looking guy is the worst possible decision she could ever make. "Yes, I know— Darren's hot, but I'm just not that sexually attracted to him. I don't know what it is or why, but it's something I can't get past."

"Wow, girl, if I weren't getting married, I'd be all over him."

Laughing, Charlotte followed Stacey back to the table where the guys were sitting with the pitchers of beer. It wasn't planned, but Charlotte ended up in the chair next to Darren. Keeping it light, she tried not to give him any vibes that would let him think she wanted to be alone with him after the evening was over. Looking at him as he told the group a story about how he called 911 on his loud neighbors having what he thought was a domestic dispute but turned out to be rough sex, she laughed at his amusing personality. He always kept the group entertained with his intelligence and witty banter. She wished he hadn't kissed her last week so she could continue to enjoy the flirtation. When she mentioned to Stacey she felt a lack of sexual chemistry when he kissed her, she wasn't exaggerating and it disappointed her because she liked the giddiness that comes with a fun flirtation. However, it just wasn't there and she couldn't fake it. Darren came in a very, very distant second to how she felt for Trevor—make that third, because even with his lack of libido, she felt more attracted to Ben. Darren hadn't given her any signals he wanted something more than just some fun. As a matter of fact, he never even called her after they kissed last week when he said he would. *I just don't want to give my energy to those manboys anymore.* If she was going to even consider dating someone, he had to be someone like Trevor who calls when says he will call, communicates, and wants to be with her.

However, Charlotte really didn't want to date anyone new right now at all. She just didn't want to deal with the 'will he call or won't he call' analysis. The thought of getting to know someone intimately still exhausted her which meant she knew she just wasn't ready. Maybe that's why she was so turned off by Darren; she just wasn't ready to open up to him or anyone. *How do people have rebounds so quickly after breaking off a serious relationship?* Some people needed the validation to move on, she guessed. She just wasn't one of them.

The real problem, however, was moving on when she was thinking about someone else. Dating was a real conundrum in Charlotte's mind. How would she ever really meet anyone if she didn't put herself out there? How was she ever going to get over Trevor and Ben if she wasn't willing to give anyone else a chance? If it was only Ben she was getting over, she might be more inclined to date someone new, but it was Trevor who was holding her back. She wasn't sure she could move past her feelings for him and so meeting someone new had no interest for her.

"Earth to Charlotte," she heard Darren say snapping her out of her head. "How did your trip to the beach feel?"

Rolling with it, Charlotte bantered back. "Wonderful. Thanks for taking me away from a beautiful sandy beach and the huge umbrella drink in my hand."

Feigning an injury when she gently hit him on his arm, Darren laughed. "You don't need to feel that warm sand underneath your toes when you can feel the cold fog of San Francisco from underneath a duvet."

Charlotte wasn't sure what the part about a duvet implied, but she wanted to change the subject. "Is everyone leaving?"

"Looks like it. They're going to another bar in the Marina. Man, they can party. I don't know how they do it. Personally, I need eight hours of sleep."

"I'm with you. I think that means we're getting old?" Charlotte said following the group out the door.

"I guess so."

Once the goodbyes were said, Charlotte was left awkwardly standing next to Darren outside.

"Let me walk you to your car," he said.

Not wanting to add to the awkwardness, she agreed knowing she had parked fairly close anyway.

"Thanks for walking me," Charlotte said reaching for her keys in her purse out of nervousness. Darren was standing about two inches from her and she knew he wanted to kiss her again. *What do I do?* Should she just let him kiss her so she could end it and make a getaway? When he finally leaned in, she panicked and leaned away, turning her cheek to his lips.

"I'm sorry," he said rebuffed. "I just thought…"

"No, I'm sorry," she interrupted preparing to give him the 'it's not you, it's me speech.' She really didn't want to go into the details and just prayed he would get the message sooner rather than later.

"What's wrong? I thought we had something here," he asked.

Looking down at her hands, she didn't know where to start. "I'm sorry, Darren. I really like you, but there's sort of someone else in my life." It wasn't a total lie.

"Oh, I thought you and Ben broke up?"

"We did. It's not him."

She looked up at him as he stared at her waiting for her to tell him who it was. "I have to go," she said quickly.

"But wait, Charlotte," he said stopping her. "Can we go grab another beer or something?"

The first thought aside from how she didn't like kissing him was how he never even called her. "I didn't even get a phone call from you."

Charlotte was surprised when he didn't even seem bothered by what she said. "I was busy last week with work."

"I'm sure you were, but it doesn't take more than a few minutes to call someone and say hello."

"I was going to call, I was just seriously busy," he repeated. Why did men think this excuse actually worked? *I'm busy, too, you ass, but I still make time to call people.* Heck, she even found time to make two or three calls.

"Sure, I get it. No worries," she said turning away from him to get open the car door.

"So, that's it?" he said.

Elizabeth Aloe

Shrugging, Charlotte opened the door and climbed in. "Thank you for walking me to my car."

"Okay," he said sounding disappointed.

Finally pulling away, she was relieved she didn't have to kiss him again. Although she knew it wasn't right to lead him on but rather set a boundary, she still felt guilty. Was he going to hate her now? From the signals she got from him—he'd been happy to just have a fling with no strings attached and while she would have been up for that a couple years ago, it just wasn't who she was anymore. She'd rather be single than get involved with someone she didn't wholeheartedly have feelings towards and she hoped she told him early enough that this won't upset the chemistry of the softball team.

"Are you sure I'm making the right decision?" Charlotte said to Ali two weeks later as they stood in the lobby of the Humane Society.

"Absolutely," she replied practically pushing Charlotte into the area with the adoptable cats. "I think this is a good thing for you."

Charlotte looked around knowing she wouldn't be able to resist if she really fell in love with a cat. *This place is seriously heartbreak hotel*, she thought as she started making her way through the rooms. She wanted to pet and adopt all of them and give each cat a home. "I'm not that desperate for company."

"Oh, come on. I'm getting one, too, so it's a good thing. Plus, you're giving a kitty a home," Ali said picking up a black cat. "Look, see, Oliver here would love nothing more than to sit on my bed and get his belly rubbed."

Smiling, Charlotte had to agree with Ali. Maybe adopting a cat would be good for her. Being single was great—at least that's what she told herself, but it would be nice to have another heartbeat living with her now that Ali moved out. A little furry friend snuggling with her as she watched Castle might just be perfect. Now that she was home most nights and not staying at Ben's she could take care of a pet and not worry about leaving it alone.

Charlotte honestly didn't expect to find a cat today. She prepared herself to be patient and keep an eye out for the perfect companion and not a cat that needed too much attention or hid under the bed all the time. While she loved kittens, and there were plenty to adopt, she preferred an adult cat. It just seemed most people would adopt the kittens first and leave the older cats which broke her heart.

Stopping to pet a few, most seemed friendly and healthy, but there wasn't anything outstanding about them she could identify with. Not quite sure what she was looking for, she continued walking past the cages hoping one would just stop her in her tracks leaving her unable to walk away. She seemed to be looking for the three legged kitty missing an eye that would just grab at her heartstrings and not let her go.

"What do you think?" Ali said holding up an orange male tabby. He was large and in charge as she tried to keep him in her arms. When he jumped down and ran to his food, Charlotte laughed. "Looks like you'll be buying lots of cat food. He might just eat you."

"Ha ha," she said moving on to the next one—a black and white female with gold eyes. "Well, aren't you pretty?"

Watching Ali, Charlotte felt a pang at how quickly their lives had changed. No longer were they the young twenty-somethings sharing an apartment in an expensive city, but real adults now hitting the next level in life. It couldn't be stopped, but Charlotte really wanted to slow it down. She would be thirty-three this summer and sometimes she had to convince herself she wasn't falling behind everyone else who was getting promoted in their careers, getting married, buying houses, and having babies. There was nothing wrong with where she was in life, was there? She was content with her job and wasn't in any hurry to be married or have kids. She liked her freedom and her choice to live alone. No, there is absolutely nothing wrong with that.

Getting a cat seemed like the wrong choice—as if she was taking on a responsibility she didn't want. Maybe it was just the stigma that comes with a single woman and a cat—it's looked upon as pathetic. She did not want anyone to take pity on her.

"Ali, I'm not finding any particular cats I think I want," Charlotte said truthfully. She and Ali had walked through all the rooms and Charlotte hadn't bonded with any of them. Part of her was disappointed, but part of her was relieved.

"I'm not, either. Let's go check out the dogs."

Making their way across the building to the dog runs, Charlotte thought about adopting a puppy. She loved dogs and had them during her childhood years, but there was no way she could keep one in her small apartment. She would want a dog similar to a yellow lab, her favorite breed, and she absolutely could not take on that responsibility. At least cats were independent and didn't have to be let out every day or exercised. Dogs were like children that never grew up. Even if she had a backyard, she probably wouldn't consider it because she was still somewhat selfish and loved going to happy hour or to the gym after work and not straight home to let a dog out.

The dogs were adorable as expected and Charlotte felt her heart lift as they all wagged their tails at the attention. "Hey there, puppy, aren't you just the cutest," Charlotte baby talked as she pet a black lab mix. "Oh, you're so cute."

"Look at this one," Ali said playing with a border collie. "Isn't she the sweetest? Her name is Talia."

Somehow, looking at Ali petting Talia, she knew it was a perfect match. It was like Talia chose Ali and not the other way around. "Uh-oh, Ali, looks like you might be taking home a dog instead of a cat."

"I know," Ali said laughing. "Do you think I should?"

"Well, it's up to you. Can you take care of her?"

Bouncing pros and cons off each other, the pros won because not only did Ali have a yard, she had a neighbor with two dogs who could let Talia out if Ali couldn't get home in time. "Seems like it's meant to be, doesn't it?"

"I think so," Charlotte said. "Better go reserve her before someone else finds her."

"I think you better go check out the cats one more time while I get the paperwork on Talia. I just have a feeling you overlooked them all too quickly."

"Fine, but I'm not adopting," Charlotte said as if to convince herself more than Ali.

She slowed her pace as she browsed through the cats again. One after another, she didn't really see a cat she wanted to take home.

"It's just not my day, guys," she whispered. "I love you all, but I'm looking for that perfect match."

Knowing they understood, she was about to leave when she walked past a room and saw a little gray and white kitten sitting up next to the scratcher as if she just woke up from a long nap. She yawned and it was so big for such a little body, it sucked Charlotte right in.

"Where did you come from," she said picking the cat up. When it just melted into her shoulder, she knew she found her match. "Oh my, I think you belong with me."

Finding an employee, she was told the cat was female, about five months old, and given up for adoption because the owner was moving to a new apartment that didn't allow pets. "How could anyone possibly give you up?"

After paying the adoption fees and signing the papers, she patiently listened as the employee explained the right way to introduce a cat to a new environment.

"Make sure to keep her in a small space for awhile so she'll adapt correctly. She'll probably be overwhelmed at first and hide, but she will eventually come around."

"Okay," Charlotte said hearing her new cat yelling from the cage behind the counter. "Wow, she sure does have a set of pipes on her."

"I know. She's loud for such a petite girl."

Looking at her, Charlotte couldn't help but laugh at how much noise her new friend was making. Light gray with white paws and face, she looked so feminine. Her jaw was gray which made her white cheeks look like they were puffed out. *Can you be any cuter?*

"Can you keep her here for a few minutes until I find my friend who is adopting a dog?"

"Sure, we have to take her downstairs to deflea her and give her shots. She'll be ready in thirty minutes."

Walking away, she let the meows follow her thinking she was right when she said Talia found Ali. The kitty with the big pipes found her and there was no way she was leaving without her. Thinking of names, she wanted something unique and feminine yet a name that fit the personality. Since she didn't really know the cat yet, she thought she would wait until it came to her.

Later, she met Ali out in the parking lot. Her cat was in a cardboard box screaming her head off while Talia was dancing around happy to be out in the sunshine and with her new owner.

"Wow, can you believe this?" Ali said, petting Talia. "What's your cat's name?"

"Well, they said it was Miss Kitty, but come on—no way is she keeping that."

"She sure is loud. I hope she stops crying."

"She will. She was fine until they put her in the cage. Then she started up as if the world was going to end."

"She's so cute. I'm sure you'll both be happy."

"I think so," Charlotte said putting the box in the front seat. "It's okay, little piper."

Then, as if a bolt of lightning hit her, she knew what she was going to name her cat.

Piper.

"Cute name," Ali said when Charlotte said it. "I think it fits her. Hey Pipes, enjoy your new home."

Laughing Charlotte hugged Ali goodbye and wished her luck with her new buddy. "Well, not bad replacements for men, right?" Ali said before waving and driving off.

Charlotte thought about Ali's statement as she drove back to her apartment. With Piper screaming next to her, she realized she hadn't thought about Trevor, Ben, or even Darren for the past day or two. She was excited to start caring for something other than herself. Having a pet, even if is a cat, pushed her that much closer to feeling more like an adult—as if she was taking that next step. It was a small one, but she felt content about it.

"Okay, Piper," she said touching the small white paw poking through the hole. "It's you and me, now, but if it's still just you and me when I turn sixty, we need to talk."

Nineteen

"I just haven't had the chance yet," Charlotte said to Cami when pressed about buying a ticket to the reunion. "I paid rent and have to wait for my next paycheck."

"I get it, but only five people have bought tickets and I'm really stressed out about making the budget."

"How many people do you need to buy a ticket to break even?"

"Forty."

"Give it time, you still have six weeks. You know KCPR peeps, they're slackers when it comes to making a commitment. A lot of people are from out of town and are probably just waiting to see if they can plan it."

"I know, but it sure would help if my friends would step up," Cami hinted.

"Okay, fine, I'll do it right now," Charlotte said closing out her current window on her computer. "Never mind that I was just going through my emails from Lovematch.com."

"No way! You finally bit the bullet and started online dating?"

"Well, yes."

"Any potential?"

"I went on two dates."

After being out on those two dates, Charlotte quickly concluded she had no desire to date, let alone online date. She had nothing against it—as a matter of fact she thought it was a brilliant tool for single people. It was getting harder for her to meet people outside of her social circle the older she got and being able to meet someone she would never have met otherwise, seemed the way of the future. It was just all about timing for her right now.

When she first launched her profile and picture, she instantly received fifteen emails by the next morning. Hopeful, but not expecting much, she found only one of those emails interesting. Soon, other emails filled her inbox and Charlotte quickly felt overwhelmed. There was no way she was going to answer them all, let alone make dates with all of them. She learned to delete emails with pictures of men shirtless (too tacky and narcissistic), emails that only said, 'I liked your profile. Email me back if you like mine' and emails of men who had no picture at all (she assumed they were married and didn't want to be seen online). Sadly, that was the bulk of them. There were a couple profiles that eventually caught her interest because the men actually spent a little time personalizing the email to her and seemed to have genuinely found interest in her profile.

"There just wasn't any spark at all," Charlotte continued as she got her credit card out to buy her reunion ticket.

"Were they cute? Why don't you think you sparked?"

"I went out with Eric last weekend and he was nice, but I think I was just too nervous. That was the first blind date I've ever been on. I couldn't tell if he was happy to meet me or disappointed. We only had a drink at happy hour, but it was just so awkward. I didn't feel any chemistry."

"I get that. Chemistry is a big deal," Cami said. "What about the other guy."

"I really liked him, but he just got out of a six year relationship and I could tell he wasn't ready to move on."

"Did he talk a lot about his ex?"

"So much so, I finally told him, point blank, I didn't think he was ready."

"Ouch. So how did you leave it?"

"We just finished our beers and left. No biggie," Charlotte said remembering how relieved she was to get home and be done with it. Dating made her so nervous and blind dating amplified it. The guys seemed nice enough, but she just wasn't having fun. She also couldn't help but compare them to Trevor. She really missed the chemistry and easiness she had with him so she wasn't upset not to hear from any of the Lovematch guys again.

Cami was the one who talked her into joining the online dating site. She really didn't want to do it, but after listening to Cami begging her to give it a try, Charlotte threw her hands up and said what the hell. She didn't want to date anyone right now, but it might get her out of the house. As she expected, after the first two dates, she just wasn't in the proper mindset.

"Can I ask the biggest favor from you?" Cami asked.

"What?" Charlotte asked cautiously. Something in Cami's voice made her think this favor wasn't going to be too *favorable*. "Will you ask Trevor if he plans to attend the reunion? I see he's looked at the website, but hasn't RSVP'd."

That was a big favor and Charlotte felt herself flush at the thought of having an excuse to talk to Trevor. She actively avoided him—well, she avoided him by not letting him see her. She had no problem sneaking down to his floor to spy on him in the studio towards the end of the show when she knew he would be too busy to see her in the background. She'd also seen him a few times outside from a distance waiting for the bus or standing near the elevators laughing with co-workers. Every time she wanted so badly just to say hi but she kept her distance. She knew the day would come when she would have a good excuse to place herself in his path. It did, however, still hurt how he hadn't really reached out to talk to her. He seemed just fine without her like he did back in college.

"Yes, Cami, I'll do that for you," Charlotte said with a loud joking sigh as if Cami was asking her for the world. Charlotte had finally confided in her friends how she and Trevor got together before Christmas and then parted ways the day after. Cami seemed genuinely hurt Charlotte hadn't said anything to her earlier and Jamie was too busy dating Mitch to even act concerned which hurt Charlotte.

"But you owe me big time."

"You know it," Cami laughed. "I'm sure it's a huge sacrifice for you to talk to Trevor."

"Actually, it does make me nervous. What if he doesn't want to talk to me?"

"Only one way to find out," Cami said before changing the subject. "Hey, how's Piper?"

Later that evening, Charlotte went back to the Lovematch.com site to hide her profile. Why did the idea of dating turn her stomach? What was so bad about just meeting someone out for drinks or dinner? Despite all the bad apples in the bunch, there seemed to be a lot of men trying to meet the woman of their dreams, too. She really admired and was somewhat envious of those men and women who actually made a connection with a date and formed a relationship.

Right now, she enjoyed being single. Despite her feelings for Trevor, she enjoyed focusing on herself and not a boyfriend. Did she miss the physical intimacy? Absolutely, but she was getting used to it. She was busy with softball, working out, and walking the city again. She joined a book club hoping to meet new women and she was teaching herself how to make jewelry. Surprisingly, she had a small talent and now she spent not only her time but her extra money at the bead shops buying supplies.

The most important thing was her well-being. Charlotte was on her way back to happiness and it was like a weight lifted off her shoulders. The sky was brighter and the grass was greener and she got through most days without thinking about Trevor and Ben.

"Well, my little friend," she said petting Piper's ears. "You're all the snuggling I need right now and that's just fine with me."

A few minutes later, she had just sat down to watch a movie when she heard a knock at the door. Since she didn't let anyone in the building, it was either her nasty landlord who didn't know she had a cat and was here to make trouble or her neighbors. Opening the door, she was relieved to see her neighbor Paulette with a glass of wine in her hand.

"Hey neighbor," she said. "Come down for a glass. I haven't seen you in ages."

Put on the spot, Charlotte had been looking forward to getting in her pajamas and watching Modern Family, but as she was about to say it, she stopped herself. How lame to pass up an invite to spend time with friends for a TV show. "Sure, I'll be right down."

Five minutes later, she was sitting on the floor downstairs giggling with Dayna, Paulette, and Paulette's friend, Tom, who she'd met a couple times before. It really had been a long time since she spent time with her neighbors.

"I love those earrings, Charlotte. Are they one of your creations?" Dayna asked.

Charlotte instinctively reached up to her ears trying to remember which ones she put on. "Oh yes, I just made them the other day."

"Very nice. I want to see what else you have."

"I've been making a lot of earrings and some necklaces. Just come on up when you want to be blinded by sparkle," Charlotte giggled. She was still getting used to the idea of being an *artist*. She loved showing off her creations, but at the same time, she felt somewhat of a fraud. It seemed so easy for her to design and throw together a pair of earrings and she couldn't understand why others thought it was so difficult. Ali mentioned, rather sarcastically, the phenomenon was called 'talent.'

"Anyone want to go out for sushi?" Paulette asked after pouring herself a glass of wine. "I'm craving a spicy tuna roll."

"Oh, that sounds great. Let's go to Wasabi and Ginger," Dayna said standing up. "Are you coming, Charlotte?"

Again, Charlotte's first impulse was to say no and go back up to her apartment. Why couldn't she just get excited and say yes? If she didn't already have it on her calendar, she had a problem committing. Spontaneity was definitely not one of her strong points. She had tried sushi once and didn't like it and she was hesitant to try it again. "I don't know."

"Come on, Char," Paulette said putting on her jacket. "It's just down the block."

Finally, after practically being pushed out the door and down the stairs, Charlotte agreed to go. What the hell, it would get her out of the house and she could at least say she went out this weekend. Feeling uplifted as soon as she breathed in the night air, Charlotte knew she needed to add more spontaneity in her life. She needed to watch less television and go out more often. Softball was great and lots of fun, but that was only once a week and she needed to keep from becoming a hermit. Making jewelry was another hobby she now loved, but it was also very isolating. There was something great about being single, but she didn't want the pendulum to swing so far in that direction, she chose not to be social at all.

When the sushi was brought to the table, Charlotte's first thought was blech. *How could anyone enjoy eating raw fish?*

"Do you want to try something?" Dayna asked. Charlotte watched as she used her chopsticks to eat one of the rolls. Sushi meals seem so intimate and fresh, she almost wished she liked it. "Come on, this is tuna and its really good."

The one time Charlotte tried sushi was so long ago, she couldn't remember the taste. *Spontaneity, Charlotte. Try it.* "Okay, I'll try it." When she put it in her mouth, the texture was soft, yet almost spongy and it tasted really…*good*. She wasn't sure if it was the fish, the rice or the spicy sauce on top, but the combination was so tasty. "Oh, that is good."

"Watch, you'll now become a sushi addict," Paulette said mixing her soy sauce with some kind of green stuff. "We should do this once a month."

"What's that?" Dayna said.

"A dinner club. We can check out the restaurants in the city."

"Can boys attend or is it girls only?" Tom interjected. He'd been quiet so far, Charlotte almost forgot he was sitting across from her.

"Definitely boys," Paulette laughed. "What do you think? If I set up a monthly event on Facebook, do you think people would be up for it?"

"I do," Charlotte said. It was funny how dining out with friends made her feel more mature and grown up. San Francisco was such a great place for food and she often felt she wasn't taking advantage of something people paid thousands of dollars to experience. *Note to self, make sure Paulette schedules something soon.*

When dinner finished, Charlotte was a now a sushi convert and looked forward to more meals with chopsticks. After the bill was paid, Paulette announced she wanted to go dancing. No amount of cajoling would ever get Charlotte out on a dance floor at a club—it just wasn't enjoyable for her and she didn't feel guilty or lazy for declining this invitation. After saying goodbye, she practically skipped across the street back to her apartment, enjoying the cool air against her skin. San Francisco was a magical city and for the first time in a long time, she felt like a huge cloud had lifted and she was genuinely happy.

Twenty

Trevor made a big mistake.

After turning his phone back on and seeing three voicemails and six text messages from Katie, he shook his head wishing he had some kind of time machine allowing him to go back to the moment he ran into Katie on the street.

It wasn't that he hadn't enjoyed the time he spent with her when he was in SLO, it was how she took it as a sign they were officially dating now. When she called him the first few times after he returned to the bay area, he obliged her and had pleasant conversations. However, she now called every night and texted him at least four times a day. He didn't mind texting, but if he didn't get back to her right away, she got the impression he was avoiding her and she would leave paranoid messages on his voicemail. Trevor wasn't sure what to do because he'd explained several times he couldn't reply to her every text and voicemail right away. Now, he just wanted to do exactly what she was so paranoid about— avoid her. Sometimes he wished he didn't have a conscience so he could cut her out of his life and leave it at that. But since he does have a conscience, it means he needs to do it the right way.

He decided to call her back and let her know, once and for all, they couldn't see each other let alone be friends—and that actually worried him considering how she took it the last time. Dreading the conversation, he was actually surprised when his call went to voicemail. *Is it wrong to tell a girl you never want to talk to her again in a message?* He already knew the answer and knowing his luck; she would delete it by accident and claim she never got it. Why didn't she pick up the one time he actually wanted to talk to her?

After hanging up without leaving a message, he decided to call it a day and head home. Work had been crazy lately with the mayoral sex and drug scandal taking up the headlines. Trevor never liked these kinds of stories—they detracted from the real issues, but he understood the ramifications. The current mayor will most likely resign and leave his seat open. Right now, the rumor mill had Councilman Mitch Ridgeway as the favorite. Super rich and very good looking, Ridgeway oozed charisma, automatically attracting the single female vote. Trevor was fairly certain if the councilman was put in charge of world peace, it would happen.

Lucky for Trevor, Mitch was dating Jamie White, Charlotte's friend from college. He had no problem begging Jamie to get Mitch on the show and if it happened the way it was supposed to, it would be a nice career coup on Trevor's resume. When he received a call from Mitch's 'people' to schedule a date, Trevor felt like he'd parted the Red Sea.

By now, the city was well aware of the scandal, but Ridgway hadn't confirmed he would run. With what was called an 'exclusive' in journalistic terms, he knew he be on top if he could get the councilman to make it official on live TV.

"Hi Jamie," Trevor said when he ran into her in the kitchen. "I didn't expect to see you here."

"I know. This hour is absurd," she laughed as she gave him a hug. "It's so good to see you in person."

"Are you really dating the next mayor?" he asked filling his mug with coffee. He didn't really need it this morning because he was super jazzed up over the interview but his coffee ritual was a habit.

"Maybe. I never expected to date a politician, but we can't help who we fall in love with, right?"

"I guess you're right. You think he's a good guy? I only get to see him in politician mode."

"Yes. I wouldn't be dating him if I didn't think he was a good guy," Jamie laughed. *Touché,* Trevor thought feeling a little embarrassed.

He remembered how stunning Jamie was in college, but she was even better looking now. Her long legs and large chest couldn't be more perfect, but it was always her personality he liked. She was a warm person—someone you instantly felt you could trust to be your confidant. She was the perfect partner for a politician because the people would love her. "I'm happy for you, then."

"And how are you, Trevor? I'm sorry we couldn't really talk after you and Charlotte broke up, but she was my friend first."

Trevor both appreciated and regretted Charlotte's name coming up in the conversation. "Oh, that was so long ago. No worries, I get it."

After an awkward pause, Trevor was relieved when Mitch walked in and immediately took over the conversation. "Hey honey, here you are," he said giving her a kiss on the cheek before giving Trevor the once over.

Trevor thought they made an absolutely stunning couple, like JFK, Jr. and Carolyn Bessette, although Jamie seemed way more approachable. Trevor wondered if he was looking at a future "It" couple. Mitch was from an old money San Francisco family and would definitely go places—he could have his pick of any woman. Trevor had read how he dated a few Hollywood celebrities, but he seemed very smitten with Jamie.

After introducing himself and explaining his past with Jamie, Trevor left the couple alone in the kitchen as he took his place in the control room. Despite his fancy appearance, Trevor was actually disappointed with his impression of Mitch Ridgeway. Like a deflated balloon, Trevor felt his excitement disappear. It wasn't anything Mitch said, but rather the way he looked at Trevor as if Trevor was being dismissed for more important things. Maybe he imagined it, but something about Mitch didn't sit right with Trevor. He couldn't quite put his finger on it, but he developed an unusual dislike for the man on the spot. Wanting it to be a simple bad first impression, Trevor let it go, trusting it might be different the next time they met.

Trevor didn't really even notice nor did he care when the interview ended without Ridgeway confirming he was running.

Now, outside waiting for the bus to take him home, he wondered how many more times Ridgeway would be in the studio prior to the election. He wasn't thrilled at the idea, but that was the nature of the beast. He was the young candidate who usually won based on marketing and charisma. It didn't matter what he said or how he said it, the votes would roll in because he had money to spend on a campaign and the good looks to be on the posters.

Trevor loved journalism, but elections tested his passion. The media should always remain objective to the news, but somehow it's considered acceptable for outlets to publicly back a candidate. He knew without a doubt, he'd be told to put Ridgeway on the show as much as possible. There is such thing as equal time, but Trevor knew it didn't exist much anymore. If it was up to him, he would have all candidates on for the same amount of time and possibly together for a debate about the issues.

Aside from elections, Trevor never got tired of his career. As a producer, he thrived on the adrenaline rush that kicked in right before the show went live. It was his job to make sure all the preparations pulled together, including double checking the order of the stories, making sure the feed worked, the teleprompter was set, and most importantly, making sure the talent and the guests were settled in. There were good days and bad, but his crew seemed to work well together and they trusted each other which made Trevor's job a little bit easier.

The bus was late today and Trevor finally gave up waiting. That was a huge problem in San Francisco—the bus system was often unreliable. He would wait for an hour before a bus showed up. When it finally did, there would be four of the same line right behind it. He never could figure why that happened. *Maybe I should do a feature a story on it,* he joked to himself.

Walking the block back to the station, he decided to catch a cab. While he expected to see coworkers coming and going, he didn't expect to see Charlotte as she walked out the front door practically knocking him over. He was caught off guard but not shocked to see her. The real shocker was how they'd successfully avoided each other the past couple of months. He knew she sometimes walked his floor and was in the studio during some of the shows, but he she never approached him and he was too busy to stop and chat with her. He wouldn't even know what to say—like now. His mind drew a blank. Should he pretend to ignore her or just say hi? Luckily, she made the decision for him.

"Hi," she said quietly.

"Hi," he mirrored back.

So awkward. Maybe she didn't want to see him and would continue on to her destination. But she didn't move out of his way which was a sign to him to start talking.

"How've you been?" he asked.

"Good," she said before another awkward pause. "I adopted a cat."

"You did?" he said genuinely happy for her. He was more of a dog person, but he grew up with a cat or two in his life and felt some affection towards them. "That's great."

"Her name is Piper and she's really cute," Charlotte continued. "You'd like her. She's sweet. We're very compatible."

"I bet you are," he said seeing how nervous she was talking to him. "Maybe I can meet her someday," he continued wanting to put her at ease. Her smile indicated he said the right thing.

"So what have you been up to?"

"Nothing much," he replied thinking that was true. Except for work, going out with his buddies, football, and dodging Katie's calls, there wasn't much new in his life. "The usual."

After another long pause, Charlotte broke the silence this time. "Cami wanted me to ask you if you are going to the reunion in a few weeks."

"I am. I assume you're going?"

"Of course. She said for me to tell you and I quote, 'buy your f-ing ticket.'"

Laughing, Trevor relaxed. "Will she come after me if I don't?" If teasing her kept her here in front of him longer, he would continue it.

"Trust me, I'm starting to question her sanity," Charlotte giggled. "She even threatened me."

"I am excited about it. It will be a nice weekend seeing everyone."

"I'm looking forward to it, too. I hope everyone shows."

Looking at her, Trevor could see she was happy. It seemed the stress that was on her shoulders before was gone. Her eyes glowed and her skin looked refreshed. "You look really good, Charlotte. I see life has been treating you well."

"I feel good. The last few months have been really great and I've gotten back into my running and I'm still playing softball."

"I'm happy to hear it. Any word from Ben?" he asked cautiously. He didn't want to open old wounds, but he hadn't heard a thing from Ben since he moved.

"No, not since he returned in January. I'm okay with it. We worked it out and he moved back to Minnesota. It was the right decision."

"That's good to hear. He didn't call me, so I had no idea what happened to him," he replied. It didn't surprise him Ben moved back and from the sound of Charlotte's voice, she wasn't upset by his decision.

He wanted to keep talking, but since they were standing in front of the doorway, they kept getting bumped around by people coming and going.

"Where are you going now," he asked, gently nudging her three steps away from the door.

"I'm just out for a break. I'm working late tonight."

"I see."

"What are you doing?"

"Heading home. The bus never showed, so I'm stuck taking a cab."

Elizabeth Aloe

The small talk was very annoying. What he really wanted to do was lean in and kiss her. She'd just put on lip gloss and her lips looked very soft and inviting. He could practically taste the flavor, watermelon, because she wore it all the time. What if he took the chance and asked her out? Had enough time passed and she would be ready to date again? He'd stuck with Sarah's advice and not contacted her and he prayed it worked to his advantage. Maybe she'd moved on and was dating someone else. There was only one way to find out. "I was wondering if you wanted to grab dinner with me tomorrow night."

At first, the look of surprise on her face worried him. What if it was too soon to ask her out or too late? But he was the one who ended up surprised when she agreed without hesitation. "Sure. I can do Friday."

Relieved she actually said yes, he tried to think of a place quickly in his head. Where was a good place? *Come on, Trevor. Think.* "How about the Limba Room on Potrero?"

"I love that place. I could use a good umbrella drink," she said sounding genuinely excited.

"How about seven o'clock? I would come get you, but since it's my neighborhood, we can either meet there or you can come to my house and we can walk."

"No worries. I can come pick you up. I'll just park near your house. I've never seen where you live—not here in San Francisco, anyway."

"I'll text you the address," he said smiling at her reference to the past. They were reconnecting—again, and this time there were no obstacles preventing them from dating. If she was looking forward to it as much as he was, it would be a really good night. "Oh, by the way, I saw Jamie and her boyfriend slash future mayor, Mitch."

"That's right! Jamie said she was here this morning and saw you. I hardly see her now that she seems to be with Mitch most of the time."

Deciding to keep his thoughts to himself, Trevor just shrugged. "That's what happens, I guess. I take it Jamie and Cami both know about us?"

"Yes. Sorry, I'm a girl and need to talk about boys," she said. Trevor liked the teasing smile she gave him. "Well, if I don't get going now, I'll never get my coffee."

"Okay. See you tomorrow."

"See you then. Don't forget your lei," she said with a wink and a small wave before she turned and walked away.

Trevor felt lighter, as if the cloud lingering over his head finally dissipated. Suddenly, he noticed what a bright, beautiful day it was in the city. The skies were perfectly clear and the breeze was minimal. The cherry blossom trees he usually walked by without noticing seemed so bold and fragrant. It would be a waste to jump in a cab and pass up such a rare day in the city so he decided to walk. Heading towards Union Square, it occurred to him he should buy a new shirt and a pair of jeans for Friday night. Not that Charlotte would care what he wore, but he felt inspired enough to wear something other than his large variety of logo covered t-shirts. Normally, the thought of shopping stopped him cold—there was nothing he found more boring except maybe yoga—but today he really wanted to find something to impress Charlotte.

After a nice leisurely walk to Union Square listening to everything from Bad Religion to Foreigner, he was pumped up enough to enter Banana Republic. Standing inside the door, he stared at the button down shirts and the fifty different kinds of trouser pants knowing he had no clue where to start.

"Can I help you," asked a petite saleswoman as she approached him.

Feeling relieved, he decided to take her up on her offer to help. "Um, yes, maybe you can. I'm looking for a new shirt and jeans."

After looking him up and down, the saleswomen nodded. "I have something perfect for you. We just got in these dark washed jeans that look amazing on a guy with your height. Since you have green eyes, I think that button down shirt over there would be perfect. By the way, my name is Sonia."

After allowing Sonia to size him for fit, Trevor let her pick out several shirts and jeans for him. When she brought a couple pair of khakis and a cashmere sweater, he tried them on knowing it would be a long time before he went clothes shopping again. He hadn't worn khakis since his buddy George's wedding five years ago.

"You look great in those," Sonia said studying him. She'd put him in the cashmere sweater over a white button down and dark jeans. "That color green looks wonderful with your eyes."

Trevor seldom dressed up, but looking at his reflection, he rather liked this look. It was definitely more grown up than his old t-shirt and jeans. "Could I wear a leather jacket with this look?"

"Absolutely," Sonia said nodding.

Going with three new button down shirts, two t-shirts in army green and brown, the jeans and the sweater, he was set. He decided against the khakis because he would probably never wear them unless he had an interview. He cringed at the total price wondering how women afforded to shop as much as they did.

"Thank you, Sonia," he said taking his bag.

"You're welcome. I hope you have a wonderful time on your date," Sonia smiled flashing a very white smile. "She's a lucky lady."

"Thanks," Trevor said with a grin wondering how she knew he was going on a date. Maybe she was just fishing to see if he was available.

With his new purchases, he felt excited to show them off to Charlotte. *What is going on with me? Did I just turn into a girl? Shoot me if I decide to buy a new pair of shoes.*

Laughing to himself, he put on his headphones as he walked out of the store. Walking a few more blocks through Union Square, he continued to enjoy the afternoon and his good mood.

He walked all the way down to AT&T ballpark where he would have to wait for a bus to take him the rest of the way home. Standing outside the Willie Mays entrance, he couldn't wait for opening day in two weeks. One of his other obsessions, aside from music, was Giants baseball. He loved attending games with his buddies, drinking ballpark beers, and eating ballpark hot dogs. The year they were in the World Series and won was so magical and fun, he wasn't sure it could ever be topped. Maybe Charlotte would want to go to the games with him. They had watched a few games together in college and since he knew she loved playing softball, she would probably love to go.

When the bus arrived, it was fairly empty— unusual for this time of day—and he took a seat towards the back. It felt good to sit down after the long walk and trying on clothes. *How do women make a full day of shopping? What is it that attracts them to it?* It was one of those mysteries about women men never understood. His ex-girlfriend once told him she likes to shop because it's a creative outlet. It's not about buying clothes for practical reasons but rather about the process of searching for new ideas. Each time she tried on a new outfit or a new pair of shoes, she looked at herself differently as if she'd took a blank canvas and painted a beautiful picture on it. He still didn't quite get it but thank goodness for salespeople. If it hadn't been for Sonia and her patience, he would have walked right out before trying on anything.

Once the bus dropped him off at the stop three blocks up the hill from his apartment, he quickened his step to get home. Feeling hungry, he couldn't wait to heat up the lasagna he bought at Trader Joe's last week. Thoughts of dinner were suddenly interrupted as he glimpsed the front of his house. Even from a distance, he could see someone sitting on the steps in front of the door. He came to a stop when he realized who it was— Katie.

Crap.

His first instinct was to turn and head in the opposite direction but he couldn't leave her sitting there alone. Feeling trapped, he slowly walked the rest of the way biding time to figure out what to say. *Sorry I haven't called, work has been super busy, or maybe, I wanted to call but I've reconnected with Charlotte and there's just no chance in hell.* The thought of confrontation burst Trevor's wonderful bubble and the black cloud that disappeared when Charlotte agreed to go to dinner with him returned.

"Katie," he said walking up to her almost startling her. She had seemed very lost in her head as she listened to her iPod. "What are you doing here?"

Pulling out the ear buds, she stood up quickly brushing off her pants. "Hi, Trevor. I'm so glad you're finally here."

"How long have you been waiting?"

"About two hours," she said averting her gaze and staring at the ground at some imaginary spot. "You haven't returned my calls so I thought I'd make the trip up here to see you."

She seemed sweet, sad, and almost pathetic, completely catching Trevor off guard. He'd been prepared for some kind of verbal assault, but not this person in front of him. He felt sorry for her. "Well, come in and have some coffee. You must be cold sitting out here."

"Thanks," she said following him in. "So this is your place. It's bigger and older than I imagined but it's got character."

"I like it. It feels very San Francisco."

Setting his bag of clothes down, he asked for her coat so he could hang it in the front closet. "You drove all the way up here? What about work and the kids?"

"I have the day off and my ex has the kids this week so it was no problem."

Leading her into the kitchen, he motioned for her to sit at the table as he made coffee. The silence was deafening as he went through the excuses in his head. "I did call you, but it went to voicemail. I just didn't leave a message."

"I saw that. I tried you back, but I got voicemail, too."

Trevor felt like such a schmuck. He should never have slept with Katie again. She was a woman who'd been through a lot and made so many positive changes in her life and yet he'd treated her poorly not once, but twice. He wondered how many other girls he'd hurt by not calling them back. It wasn't like he had one night stands a lot, but there were some fun times when he simply kissed a woman at a party or after a night out of drinking with his buddies. They always gave him their phone numbers, but he seldom called them after that night. He wasn't avoiding them, he just felt they had a good time in the moment and that was it. Seeing Katie and her sadness reminded him how selfish he'd been to her and to those other women. What if he'd genuinely hurt their feelings and had no idea? Then he remembered how Charlotte avoided him in college and how it crushed him. All this time, he'd thought of himself as a good guy but maybe he was just one of those douches he heard women complain about.

The small talk was painful and after twenty minutes he couldn't stand it any longer. "Look, Katie, we can talk about the weather in San Luis Obispo forever, but I don't think that's why you're here."

"No, it's not," she said slowly sipping her coffee.

Taking a deep breath, he knew he was just going to have to be honest with her. "I'm sorry I haven't called you back. Truth is, I'm not sure I should call anymore," he said wondering what kind of reaction she will have to his words. "Honestly, that night we shared in SLO shouldn't have happened. I had a really great catching up and getting to know you again, but my life is up here and I thought you understood that."

"I know," she said quietly. He could see the tears welling up and if she started to cry, he wouldn't be able to handle it.

Pulling up a chair next to her, he really wanted to make sure she knew he did enjoy the night. "That night was awesome, Katie. You've come a long way and deserve to find someone perfect. I live up here and have no plans to move to SLO."

"But I was thinking about moving up here to San Francisco," she said interrupting him and letting the tears flow. "I even have interviews for a couple teaching positions."

Oh no. He'd been prepared for her to get mad and upset at him, but he hadn't expected this. "You want to move up here? What about your boys? You don't want to leave them, do you?"

"My ex and I will work it out. I was thinking about giving him full custody anyway. They love their dad and seem so happy with him and his wife. I almost feel guilty about taking them out of that family environment."

"But you're their mother," he said confused. *Why would she want to abandon her children?* "I'm sure they need you, too."

"Oh, they do, but they have a half brother and sister and seem so much better with them. It doesn't hurt my feelings at all. I want what's best for them."

Trevor didn't feel like it was his place to discuss her children. As their mother, she knew best but it seemed she wanted what was best for her, not for them. If it were his kids, he would never in a million years move away from them and give up custody.

"Look, Katie, I don't want you to move up here for me or anything like that."

Lifting her head up to look at him, he finally caught a glimpse of the fire in her eyes he'd seen back in college. But as soon as it appeared, it disappeared. "It's not for you, Trevor. I've always wanted to live up here and I just thought it would be nice to know someone who could show me around."

"Okay," he said slowly putting his hands up as if to show her he didn't want to start anything. "I love San Francisco, but it's really expensive. It might be hard on a teacher's salary."

"I've already thought of that. I'll probably look for a roommate situation," she said looking around his place. "That's where I thought maybe you could help me out."

Trevor instantly knew what was coming next and waited for her to vocalize it in case he was wrong. "How's that?"

"I see you have a second bedroom and I thought maybe I could stay here until I find a place."

Well, it was almost what he'd expected her to say. He had been bracing for her to ask to move in permanently as his roommate. Thinking of the most tactful way to tell her no, he stood up to pour more coffee. He was stalling hoping maybe she would continue the thought and say she didn't expect him to agree and it was a crazy thought. Unfortunately, the silence grew thicker and more awkward.

"I don't know, Katie. I've lived alone for a long time and I'm done living with roommates, even temporarily. It would be even harder since we've been, um, intimate. Don't you think so?"

"Are you seeing anyone?"

"No." It popped out before he could even think about fibbing. He really wished he'd said yes. He wished he'd gone out with Charlotte last night so he could say yes and not be lying.

"Well, then it shouldn't be awkward," she said sounding almost hopeful. "Please just consider it. You are really the only person I know up here and I desperately need someone to help me out."

"You don't even have a job yet, so don't get ahead of yourself. It could be a very long time before you get a job in teaching. I know those positions are scarce now with the layoffs and the budget crisis."

"Well, we can talk about it later," Katie said standing up and suddenly perkier. "I hope you don't mind if I spend the night tonight. I don't think I can make the drive back."

There was no way out of this one. Putting her on the road for a three hour drive back to San Luis Obispo would be selfish and he couldn't in good conscience do that to her. Trapped, he had no choice and was thankful he had the extra bedroom. "You can sleep in the guest room. The bed is a futon, but I'll fix it up for you."

"Great. Now let's go get drunk. Is there a cool bar around here?" she asked.

That's exactly what he needed to get through the night—a few shots of tequila. Hopefully, it would ease the guilt he felt knowing he would never consider letting her crash with him while she looked for a job.

Twenty-One

"How does this look?" Charlotte asked Jamie as she came out of the Nordstrom dressing room.

Charlotte almost laughed at how Jamie gave her the once over before giving an approval. "I love the color on you and the cut is flattering."

"Gee, thanks," Charlotte replied twirling right to left in front of the three way mirror. "I think I'll get a lot of wear out of this dress."

"You can dress it up or go casual with a jean jacket and flats."

Staring at herself, Charlotte liked the look. After trying on several black dresses, she had to admit, this fuchsia A-line sleeveless dress was definitely something out of her comfort zone. She would never have considered it except Jamie pushed it into her arms saying the color would go perfect with her skin. She realized Jamie was a good shopping buddy by forcing her to try on dresses she would have overlooked. "Do you think Trevor will like it?"

"How could he not?" Jamie replied. "I don't think it really matters what you wear."

After taking the dress off and putting on her own clothes, she took the dress up to the register and winced when the saleswoman rung it up. This was definitely going to cut into her monthly budget.

"Don't worry, I've got it," Jamie said handing over a credit card. "Or rather Mitch has it."

Stunned, Charlotte protested. "Jamie, no way I can let you do that."

"Sure you can. He gave me his credit card today specifically for this kind of thing. He won't even notice, trust me. If he does, I'll tell him your date with Trevor is a worthy cause."

Knowing there was no way she could convince Jamie otherwise, she let her friend buy the dress. "I take it things are going well with Mitch?"

"They are," Jamie said as her smile brightened. Charlotte liked how genuinely happy her friend seemed. "He's really good to me."

"How do you feel being on the campaign trail with him? Think about it, you could possibly be the first lady of San Francisco."

"I know!" she said as if the shocked her. "He is ahead in the polls. You wouldn't believe the parties and fundraising he has to do. I get tired just thinking about it."

Charlotte giggled. "But you're in your element schmoozing and attending glitzy parties."

"I like it, but it does get old after a while. You don't know how many nights I've come home from work and just want to crash only to realize I need to be somewhere in an hour all dressed up and on my best behavior."

Charlotte couldn't imagine being so tied down like that. She liked using her free time after work to go running, play softball or just watch her shows. "I don't envy you, my dear, but I'm glad you're happy."

"I am, Charlotte. For the first time, I'm in love," Jamie gushed as she led Charlotte into the lingerie department.

"Do you think you'll attend the KCPR reunion in a few weeks?" Charlotte asked as she admired the lingerie. Thinking about her date with Trevor, she considered buying frilly undergarments that she knew she'd only wear for a special occasion. *Does he even care about this stuff?*

"I don't know," Jamie said as she fingered some lacy camisoles. "I'm pretty sure Mitch will have something scheduled."

"Cami is going to be pissed, Jamie."

"I know. I feel bad, but I doubt I'll be able to get away and I really want to go. Remember the show we did between quarters? What was it called? Lovelines or Lovein or something like that?"

"How could I forget? Those shows were hilarious. I can't remember what we called it and I certainly can't believe we got people to call in with their love problems."

Reminiscing with Jamie about their time at KCPR made Charlotte more excited for the upcoming reunion. Cami called her every day with updates about who was attending and Charlotte couldn't help but look forward to seeing everyone. She also couldn't wait to get on the air and play music again. She'd started making a playlist and burning her downloaded music to disc.

"I really miss those days," Jamie said wistfully. "We were so young and stupid."

"We're still young and stupid," Charlotte said with a giggle.

"I can't be young and stupid anymore. I'm in the public eye now and can't screw up," Jamie said and Charlotte thought she heard some sadness in her voice.

"Well, not yet. You aren't married to him and he isn't the mayor. You still have time."

Charlotte thought she saw Jamie's eyes well up slightly, but couldn't be sure. Jamie turned away pretending to look at the bras hanging on the wall. "Now, tell me about your date tonight."

"I'm excited," Charlotte said surprised at the quick change of subject. Obviously, Jamie didn't want to talk about her love life anymore and Charlotte let it drop. "I can't believe I'm going out on a date with Trevor."

Honestly, she was excited *and* incredibly nervous. She had no idea what to expect tonight. She didn't want to get her hopes up, but she couldn't help it. Would he want to have sex like last time? She felt her flutter and her groin area grow warm at the thought.

There's chemistry between us even when we're not around each other.

Later that night, after getting ready while sipping on a cosmopolitan to soothe her nerves, she parked near his house and walked a half block to his door. Almost hyperventilating, she had to pause a few seconds to catch her breath. She was about to knock when the door opened.

"Hi," Trevor said. Charlotte relaxed at the sight of his smile. Then she noticed what he was wearing. Gone were the normal t-shirt and jeans replaced with a soft cashmere sweater and dark washed jeans. He looked so handsome, it took her breath away.

"Hi."

"Come on in," he said opening the door wider and motioning for her to walk in. "Did you find parking okay?"

"Yes, I did," she said looking around as she took how close he stood behind her. She could feel the current flowing between them. "You have a nice place."

"You sound surprised. What did you expect?"

"I don't know—maybe a place similar to college?"

Trevor laughed. "I think I've grown up a little since then. I've developed some form of good taste by now."

Charlotte was very surprised, actually. She wasn't sure what she'd expected—maybe a true bachelor pad with IKEA furniture? What she saw was something akin to Restoration Hardware. Dark furniture and a leather couch. "It's really nice."

"Thanks," he said. "Do you want to hang out here or go for drinks now?"

Oh, the pressure. Why did she have to make the decision? What she really wanted to do was stay here and kiss him until her lips swelled. Instead, she chose drinks—in her mind the more mature decision.

As they walked to the restaurant, Charlotte let Trevor hold the conversation. She giggled as he explained his venture to Banana Republic. "Are these the new duds?" she asked.

"Yes, they are," he said looking down at his sweater. "What do you think?"

"I think you look smashing. I've never seen you dress up like this."

"I don't think I'm dressed up, do you?"

"Well, compared to Fugazi and Pearl Jam t-shirts, I'd say you're dressed up and I like it."

Charlotte smiled when Trevor pretended to slightly push her. "Well, don't be expecting this all the time."

All the time? Did that mean he planned to keep seeing her? She was out on a date with Trevor and it finally felt so right and comfortable. There was no engagement, no breakup, and no feeling guilty about Ben hanging over her head. Seeing her relationship with Ben through hindsight enabled her to see what she already felt for Trevor. Gone was the heavy chain around her neck and the worry she wasn't with the right person. She finally felt free to express herself knowing Trevor would always listen.

Her feelings for him ran deep. She didn't believe in soul mates or "The One" but she knew she didn't want to live her life without him. Trevor was one of a kind. His heart was good and honest and she was always attracted to his integrity and kindness.

Entering the restaurant, Trevor led her to the small bistro table at the window. Instead of chairs, they sat next to each other on the velvet bench that ran along the wall under the window. The ambiance was tropically romantic with palm trees providing just enough privacy and candles providing just enough romance.

"Makes me wish I had a beach vacation coming up," he said handing her the menu. "You don't mind if I'm sitting next to you, do you? I just don't feel like talking across a table."

"It's totally okay," she replied feeling his thigh against hers. His face was inches away and she wanted so bad to kiss him on the lips. The thought thrilled her.

After ordering drinks and appetizers, Charlotte let Trevor small talk about work. It didn't matter what he was talking about, she just loved listening to his voice. He then asked her about Jamie, Cami, and her softball games. She was reminded about the game last night and chuckled at how Darren sort of ignored her now as he turned his focus to the new girl on the team. It had bothered her at first, but she got over it quickly. It wasn't because she missed Darren; it was because she missed the attention he gave her. Just because she was in love with Trevor didn't mean she didn't like attention from the opposite sex. *Plus, Trevor isn't my boyfriend so it's still innocent, right?* Charlotte was extremely relieved her dalliance with Darren hadn't hurt the chemistry of the team in any way. The last thing she wanted was to be ostracized by half the team for turning Darren down, but she doubted the guys even knew she and Darren kissed.

Once the drinks arrived, Charlotte admired the tall, pink creation. With the pineapple wedge attached to the side and the cherries sticking out from the top, it was almost too pretty to drink. After a few sips, the rum kicked in. Charlotte started feeling relaxed and warm. She was completely aware of the heat emanating from Trevor's body as she watched him drink his beer.

"Are we on a date?" she asked suggestively before realizing what she said.

She felt him cock his head towards her but kept his gaze forward. "I would say so." She could tell he was grinning.

Giggling, she liked flirting with him because he always understood where to take it. "I think I like being on a date with you."

"I like being on a date with you, too," He replied.

By now, she could feel the alcohol buzzing through her blood. She wasn't drunk, but she was so content and happy, she didn't want the night to end. She liked being here, in this dark place on this soft, pillow covered bench with him. They were alone—or at least it felt that way—and time really had just stopped.

"How do you feel about this?" he asked quietly.

"I don't know. How should I feel? What do people do on first dates? I can't remember," she said, masking how flustered she felt at the question.

"I don't know, either. I don't go on too many first dates."

"You? No, I bet you go on at least four a week," Charlotte teased. "And I bet you take half of those ladies home."

"How did you figure me out?" he said with a laugh. "Honestly, though, I'm not much of dater, Charlotte. If I'm single, I prefer doing my own thing. I've played a lot of football and have run a lot of miles over the past couple months."

The mood suddenly shifted from flirty to serious. On their second round of drinks, Charlotte wasn't sure if he wanted to engage in a heavy conversation here in the restaurant or wait until they were back at his place. Did he even want to talk about the elephant in the room which was whether they could bury the past in order to start something new?

"Me too," Charlotte said. "Except if you substitute football for softball."

There was a long pause before Trevor leaned in closer. Setting the beer he'd been holding in his left hand down, Charlotte willed him to start the conversation that would spur them forward. Feeling the wheels turn in his head, she thought he was about to say something, but he just sighed and smiled. "This beer tastes good," he said.

Trying to hide her disappointment, Charlotte kept a smile on her face not wanting him to think she expected him to say something else. She knew it was a lot to expect of him right now and he wasn't going to spill his guts. Men don't work that way.

"My drink is so yummy. I need another one," she replied knowing they were going to go back to small talk. That's okay, she would still enjoy it. She was with him on a date, after all, and she was happy.

After another hour and two rounds of drinks consumed, Charlotte felt antsy. The romantic restaurant was starting to feel confining and her buzz was taking over. She hadn't eaten much that afternoon and now regretted that decision. She knew she couldn't order another drink or it would put her over the edge. She wasn't even sure how she was getting home tonight—if she didn't stay at Trevor's.

"Do you want to order food?"

"I think so. What about you?"

"An appetizer sounds good," he said picking up the menu.

Trevor ordered spring rolls and when they arrived, Charlotte gladly ate her portion. The food in her stomach instantly made her feel better enabling her to keep the conversation flowing. They had moved past small talk, but not to anything serious.

"I could use some fresh air," he said looking around. "Plus, it's getting really crowded in here now. Are you ready to go?"

Charlotte was most definitely ready to go. Soon after paying the bill, they were outside and once again alone. The cool air felt refreshing against her flushed cheeks. The fog had rolled in and the lights of the city buildings looked blurry through the haze. "Wow, it got cold," she said folding her arms across her chest.

She didn't pull away when Trevor put his arm around her shoulders and pulled her close to his body. Letting his body heat warm her, she felt protected. Not saying much as they walked, she wondered what was running through his mind. Did he want to kiss her? Was she going to spend the night? Would he even invite her inside? She giggled when they walked up to his building. "I feel funny dropping you off after the first date. Isn't it usually the other way around?"

Smiling, Trevor nodded. "Normally it is," he said before pausing. "But you were never a normal girl."

"Oh?" Charlotte replied thinking that was an odd thing to say.

"I mean that as a compliment. My version of normal is kind of boring and blah and you're anything but."

Charlotte wasn't sure what he was getting at with those comments. They didn't bother her, but she wanted to hear him say how much he missed her. As if reading her mind, he leaned in and kissed her on the lips. "I've missed you so much," he said after he pulled his head away.

Standing on the steps leading up to Trevor's door, she was sure the neighborhood could hear her pounding heart. "I've missed you, too. Why is it we're always saying that to each other?"

"I don't know."

Charlotte let him grab her hand as he led her inside his apartment. She felt cold and she didn't want to take off her coat—but she knew it was because of her nerves and not because of the temperature. Watching him turn on lights, she felt rooted to the spot, not sure what to do. Every experience from their past built up to this moment. It was different than it was back in December when they slept together.

Now, they were both completely single and free to pursue each other.

After he got the lights and the heat turned on, Charlotte let Trevor decide what to do. Following him into the main room with the TV, she realized his place was small, but cozy. It needed a woman's touch since the walls were white and the furniture was dark, but she liked it. She laughed nervously knowing this wasn't the time to be thinking about his decorating skills. Thinking he was going to sit on the couch, she stopped short when he turned and faced her.

"I need to know this is for real, Charlotte," he said softly. "I can't be here with you if you're going to pull away again."

She wanted to reassure him this was completely right, that she wanted him, too, but his intensity flustered her. "I won't."

When he finally kissed her, she didn't pull back. She let his lips find hers and it was worth the wait. She felt no guilt or confusion this time. It was warm, familiar and brand new at the same time. When he pulled her down on the couch, she didn't object and fell on top of his chest. As they continued to kiss, all she could think about was being naked with him again.

It felt like the whole night passed by as they became more intimate. She loved the kisses and her lips were as swollen as she hoped they'd be. What was it about Trevor that fit her so well? They were definitely physically and sexually compatible—there was no doubt about that. But their personalities fit together just as well. Thinking about the times they spent together in college, she remembered how he challenged her, but made her feel intelligent at the same time. He had listened to her patiently when she spoke her feelings, but he could also communicate his own. But the most important of all was how he made her feel beautiful and sexy. Even when she had shown up to his apartment in her Cal Poly sweats and a t-shirt with her hair pulled up in a ponytail and no makeup, he still looked at her like she was the most beautiful girl in the world.

"I'm so happy right now," she whispered.

"Me, too."

"Should we move into your bedroom," she asked. It seemed the natural thing to ask.

Suddenly, Trevor paused and pulled away. It wasn't a lot, but enough to break the spell and enough for her to think she said something wrong.

"Charlotte, I want nothing more than to get in bed naked with you," he said. Hearing the "but" coming, her heart sank. What was he going to say? If there was ever a time they should do it, it would be now. "I just want to do this right. I need to get to know you again before we go further." Watching him scrunch his face and rub his hand through his hair, she knew he was choosing his words carefully. "After last time, and don't get me wrong—it was perfect, I just want to make sure everything goes right afterwards."

It wasn't what he said out loud that registered; it was what he hadn't said. She knew he was implying he didn't want to put himself out there only to be rejected again. She understood his feelings, remembering how she hurt him not once but twice. If she could take it all back, she would—especially in college. In hindsight, she understood now she should have let Trevor help her through the trauma. Instead, she had pushed him away. "I understand."

"We're starting over and I want us to do this right. That means we need to take it slow and enjoy everything and not skip past it."

Charlotte wanted to tell him that fifteen years was slow enough, but she liked that he wanted to date her properly. "Okay, I get it. It doesn't mean I don't want to jump your bones, though."

Trevor laughed. "Oh, you have no idea."

After more kissing and a little groping, Charlotte knew there was no way she could drive home. Was he going to make her leave? She was about to ask when he brought it up. "I don't want you driving or taking a cab, so please stay here. You can sleep in my bed with me as long as you promise not to take advantage of me."

Giggling, Charlotte felt relieved. "I promise."

Once in his room, she wanted to explore and take in his sleeping space, but she was too sleepy now. "Can I borrow a t-shirt?"

When he handed her a forest green Cal Poly shirt, she smiled at the memories of borrowing his college t-shirts back in the day. It still smelled like him and she thought about those days in the studio when they would stand so close to each other she could smell his clothes. She felt she knew him well enough, but also understood there was still so much about him she needed to learn. After changing into the t-shirt while he was in the bathroom, she climbed into bed on the side he obviously didn't sleep on. His bed felt hard and she couldn't wait to close her eyes but was prepared for a night of interrupted sleep. It wasn't because Trevor would keep her up, but because she never slept well in a new bed the first night. Hearing him in the bathroom brushing his teeth, she wished she could brush hers. *Not fair.*

Once he returned, she watched him as he undressed down to his royal blue boxers and climbed in next to her. His body added extra heat and she automatically gravitated toward him, snuggling up to his chest. Always her favorite part, his chest was solid, but not the overly muscular in that photoshopped way that was so intimidating to a regular girl.

Laying her head in the crook of his shoulder, she gently rubbed the small patch of hair on his chest. "I have to say, I'm glad you aren't hairy."

"You're the tenth girl who's said that," he teased. Feeling his voice reverberate next to his heartbeat, Charlotte took a deep breath and thought about where she was at that exact moment. Lying in the arms of the man who is probably the love of her life, she was completely content. She couldn't remember a time when she was with a guy and she was just plain happy. Every other man she'd dated never felt right and until this moment with Trevor, she knew why. She wasn't worried about the sex because that would come and since it was great the first time, she knew it would be just as good the second. She giggled to herself wondering how long they could actually hold out. When he pulled her body on top of his, she felt his hardness and thought maybe they would last for another five seconds.

"Wait a minute, miss 'I'm going to take advantage anyway I can', I'm have a strict three date minimum before I get down and dirty," he said semi joking.

"I know, but I can't help but take advantage of you," she said trying to sound coy. Where did the confidence to seduce this man come from? It was so late and she was really sleepy, but somehow she wanted to keep the night going. Part of her was afraid she'd wake up in the morning to find out this was just a dream.

"As much as I want to oblige you, I really want to do this right, Charlotte," Trevor said kissing her on the top of her head. "I want so badly to move forward, but I want you to trust me this time."

"I do trust you," she said moving back to the nook of his shoulder. Part of her was embarrassed but since she did trust him, she knew he'd do right by her. This wasn't like it was with Ben when he rejected her flat out. This was so different and she understood how Trevor wanted to start from the beginning. "Okay, we'll take it slow, just not too slow."

"Goodnight," he said kissing her on the forehead. "Let's get some sleep before I change my mind."

Giggling, Charlotte slowly moved away from him so she could stretch out and get comfortable letting the sleepiness overcome her. Everything felt just right and she would go with the flow this time—and happily so.

Twenty-Two

Opening the door to the hotel room, Trevor whistled as he entered, throwing his suitcase on the bed. Back in SLO, he was looking forward to the KCPR reunion happening this weekend. He'd been on Facebook a lot during the past few weeks updating his friends list and getting reacquainted with the friends he hadn't seen in years, many of whom were attending.

Most of all, he was looking forward to hanging out with his girlfriend Charlotte.

Girlfriend.

He almost laughed out loud at the word. How long during school had he spent thinking about her and wanting her back in his life, nursing his broken heart with dates and hookups he didn't really want? How long had he spent over the past year thinking about her while she was engaged to another man? He'd spent more time thinking about her than he's actually been with her but now that has changed. She was finally his and he smiled at the thought.

Everything felt right.

They'd spent the last month together and the only nights they'd spent apart were the nights Charlotte played softball. For Trevor it wasn't enough, he wanted to be with her every second of everyday. Charlotte, however, enjoyed her alone time and needed that one night to herself.

He would never in a million years admit this to any of his friends, but he loved her apartment. Charlotte wasn't a flowery girly-girl, but she had decorated in a feminine way that felt incredibly inviting to his masculine side. He loved the candles she lit that reminded him of a trip he once took to Hawaii and he especially loved her bed. It was so plush and soft, he felt like he was sleeping on a cloud. He realized now how much good sleep he had been missing in his own bed—his mattress was like sleeping on concrete. She was also very clean—something he wasn't accustomed to, even living alone. He vacuumed and did the dishes, but his bathroom left a lot to be desired. He could tell Charlotte preferred her place to his and he didn't blame her—he preferred her place to his as well. Her subtle hints to sleep over in pacific heights didn't escape him. Actually, she wasn't even subtle about it—she said a few times, he needed to clean if they were going to stay at his place.

Then there was Piper. Somehow that damn cat had bonded to him and he found himself looking forward to her jumping in his lap when he and Charlotte were on the couch watching TV. Piper always snuggled up to him in bed begging to have her belly and ears rubbed. It was now a nightly ritual and he loved every second of it. Maybe it was because he was so in love with Charlotte and in a good place mentally, but he honestly might consider himself a cat person now.

Staying in another room in the hotel, Charlotte was rooming with Cami. Trevor already missed her. She'd already made the hotel plans with Cami before they got back together, so she didn't want to flake on her friend and he understood. He was surprised Jamie wasn't attending but Charlotte had said it was because of her obligations with Mitch. Something in Charlotte's voice worried Trevor and he knew she was concerned about Jamie. Did she glimpse the same thing he did in Mitch? They hadn't talked about it yet and he didn't want to butt in, but he was sure it would come up in conversation at some point in the future.

Pushing those thoughts from his head, he pulled out his CDs, studying the playlist he'd prepared for his KCPR show. So many songs to choose from and he wasn't sure he'd get to everything in the two hours he was on the air. He knew he was going to start his show off with Social Distortion, Grant Lee Buffalo, and The Eels but he wanted to make sure he saved some room for Ivy because *Edge of the Ocean* always reminded him of Charlotte. Since she was doing her show the two hours prior to his, he made sure he told her not to play it because he wanted to do a dedication. She laughed at him and told him he was being silly, but she agreed. The more he thought about putting on the big headphones and playing his favorite music for the listeners, the more excited he felt. This was going to be a great weekend

Checking his phone, two texts were waiting from his old buddies Glen and John telling him to meet them downtown at the place that used to be called Cisco's when he was in school. He'd taken the day off from work, so he was able to sleep in until seven and now he was ready to officially start the weekend and a beer out on the patio by the creek sounded like the perfect way to kick it off. After taking a quick shower, he decided to walk downtown knowing it was going to be a long night of drinking and he didn't want to be responsible for his car. Putting in his earphones as he left his room, he looked forward to the evening ahead.

Fifteen minutes later, Trevor found his friends outside at a table. Most of the tables were already taken with students and professionals out for Friday happy hour. Noticing a single guitar player in the corner, Trevor realized even with a different name, the place hadn't changed much at all.

"Hey, dude," Glen said standing up from his table to give Trevor a quick hug. "It's been, what, fifteen years?"

"I would say so," Trevor answered shaking John's hand before sitting down. "I can't believe I'm sitting here with you guys."

"I know, it crazy. Here's a beer," Glen said pouring Trevor a glass of whatever was in the pitcher. From the looks, it was probably Bud Light.

"So what's going on with you?" Trevor asked both of them after they got the pleasantries out of the way.

Both John and Glen started in on their careers and how they got there after leaving Cal Poly. John was an engineer at a small firm in Santa Barbara and Glen was now a cameraman for television shows like Sons of Anarchy and White Collar. "Since these shows run only seasonally, it's easy to get on to the production crew of another series afterwards."

"I love Sons of Anarchy. I think that could be my favorite show along with Breaking Bad," John said.

Trevor enjoyed hearing some of the stories Glen picked up from Hollywood. He thought about Sarah and Cooper wondering how they were doing. Charlotte hadn't mentioned Sarah lately, so they must be doing fine.

Noticing the ring on Glen's finger, Trevor asked about his wife. "We're going on six years now," Glen said.

"How did you meet?" Trevor asked genuinely interested. Glen was always the surfer party boy girls flocked to despite his mediocre looks and he had that knack for making them relax and feel like they were the most beautiful girls in the world. Trevor was surprised Glen settled down so quickly.

"I was on a surf trip in Costa Rica and we met one night on the beach. It was love at first sight," Glen said with a big smile. "Luckily, she was from San Diego and we were able to continue the vacation. Isabelle is great. You'd like her."

"I'm sure I would," Trevor said before turning to John. "What about you, John. Is there anyone in your life?" Trevor made his inquiry very generic specifically because he'd always wondered if John was gay. He never dated anyone that Trevor could remember nor did he ever talk about his social life when they were at the station. Trevor never asked, but he was pretty sure John wasn't into girls.

"I do. His name is Evan," John said not even hesitating. Apparently, he'd been out of the closet for a long time. "We just bought a house together."

"Wonderful," Trevor said really meaning it. He'd always liked John and was glad to see him happy.

"And what about you, Trevor?" Glen asked. "Who's the lucky lady in your life? You always did have girls ready to take their panties off for you."

Embarrassed, Trevor wasn't sure what to say. "You're joking. That was not true."

"Oh come on. I can name at least four girls who were into you," John said. "Charlotte, Katie, Jessica and Beth."

Trevor obviously knew about the first two, but couldn't even think of who John was talking about for the second two. Well, it didn't really matter. "Funny you should mention Charlotte," he said as he told them how he and Charlotte were now dating.

"No way," Glen said slapping him on the back. "That's awesome. I can't believe you two are back together. I remember that whole drama and how you got your heart ripped out of your chest."

Trevor shrugged. "Not that I wanted her to get hurt, but I believe things have a way of working out like they're supposed to. She's here this weekend, too, and I'm supposed to meet up with her later."

After a couple more hours and two more pitchers of beer, Trevor decided to text his girlfriend to see that she made it safely to SLO. *Hi babe, where are you? When do you want to meet up?*

Seconds later, his phone buzzed with a reply. *I'm at Novo having cocktails. Feeling very tipsy. Come over here.*

"Do you guys know where Novo is?" Trevor asked as he sent his reply back to her that he'd be there.

"It's down the block. It used to be the Cellar when we were in school," John said. "Remember that frat hangout?"

"Oh yes, I remember it. It always smelled like stale keg beer."

"Now it's a beautiful restaurant that seats primarily on the back patio. Good food, too," Glen said.

"I'm heading over there to meet Charlotte and Cami. You want to come?"

"Sure," they said in unison.

Once the bill was paid, Trevor followed them down the block. It really did feel like old times. It wasn't that he'd hung out with Glen and John all the time in school, but they'd spent many a night partying downtown or at a KCPR party.

Once inside, he realized Glen was right. It was now very upscale and nice. Outside on the back patio, he noticed the twinkling lights hanging from the trees and the candles lit on the tables. On a warm, balmy night like tonight, it was the perfect dining ambience. He instantly spotted Charlotte and Cami sitting in a spot overlooking the creek.

"Hi ladies," he said leading Glen and John up to the table. Leaning down, he kissed Charlotte and then said hello to Cami. Luckily, the whole party knew each other so it was easy to pull up extra chairs and get cozy. "What are you drinking?" Trevor whispered to Charlotte.

"Cosmopolitan," she whispered back. "Wanna sip?"

"Yes," he said simply because she looked so cute when she asked. Although not something he'd order, the drink tasted surprisingly good and he could see why Charlotte ordered it all the time. "I missed you. I assume you got into town with no problems."

"Nope," she said with a giggle. "I mean yes, we got into town okay with no problems. All good. I can't believe we're here in SLO together after all these years. It's like the past never happened."

Smiling, Trevor put his arm around her relieved to hear her say that. On the earlier walk into town, many of the songs rotating through his headphones reminded him of his college years. Except for a few memories gone bad, most of them were pleasant reminders of Cal Poly, KCPR and SLO. He'd be lying if he said he wasn't worried about Charlotte's reaction to being here with him. He didn't want her to feel uncomfortable, but watching her now, his fears went away as she laughed with the group. He also thought about Katie wondering if she would stay away after the fiasco in San Francisco, he figured she wouldn't want anything to do with him now, but he couldn't be sure. Something was just so *off* about her.

After sharing stories and memories, it was Cami who finally brought up the time in college when he and Charlotte broke up.

"I can't believe you both are back together," she said. "I always thought you were both so cute in college. I was sad when you broke up."

He looked at Charlotte knowing what was coming next. Biting his tongue, he wanted someone to change the subject, but Charlotte spoke first.

"I know, but I was such a naïve freshman. I didn't know a good thing when I had it," she said and Trevor felt her squeeze his hand. She was making light of the breakup, but he could tell she didn't want to talk about it.

It was Glen who finally asked the question everyone else was thinking. "What do you remember about that night, Charlotte?"

"I'm not sure she really wants to talk about it," Trevor said deflecting the conversation away from her. Now he was uncomfortable because it reminded him of the time she broke his heart.

"I don't remember much about that night at all. It was always kind of blurry," she said.

"They never did catch the guy, did they?" John asked.

"No," Charlotte said. "Can we not talk about it?"

"Sure, sorry," Glen said.

"That's okay, Glen. I just want this weekend to be fun and not have those reminders."

Silence fell over the group and Trevor wanted nothing more than to hug Charlotte and remind her that she was here to have a good time. Finally someone flagged the server for the check and the group decided it was time get to McCarthy's where the rest of the KCPR alumni would be. Turning to Charlotte, Trevor wanted to make sure she was okay. "You look so cute tonight," he said putting his arm around her shoulders. "Please don't let that night ruin your weekend."

"Thanks," she said. "I spent my paycheck on this dress when I was visiting Sarah in LA and I won't. I got over it a long time ago. Being here doesn't remind me of that night at all. It reminds me of other fantastic times in college."

Good. She seemed just fine and sort of her happy drunk self which always put a smile on his face. It was like their past in SLO had been put to rest this weekend and all that was good in their brief college relationship would return. Once they paid the bill, they filed out of the restaurant onto to the street. The positive energy returned to the group as they continued sharing memories on the walk to McCarthy's. Passing the restaurant McClintocks, Charlotte took his hand as if to say she remembered, too.

It was their fourth date and he met Charlotte downtown at McClintocks after a shift at the station. He had subbed in for the alternative 80's show which was probably the most popular show on the air at the time. "So how'd it go? Did you get any marriage proposals over the phone?" She asked when he walked up to her.

"No marriage proposals, but quite a few requests for The Smiths and The Cure," he replied smiling down at her. "Now I need a beer."

She couldn't help but laugh. "Do you remember the particular Cure request for In Between Days?"

"That was you?" he said incredulously.

"That was me," she confessed speaking in a very bad British accent.

"How did I not know? I just thought she was a really drunk idiot with bad taste in music."

"Never bash The Cure or I will start speaking in an accent all the time," she laughed leaning into him.

"Okay, okay. The Cure is the best band ever," he laughed.

Now, as they approached the new location of McCarthy's, he wanted nothing more than to get her alone. They'd really taken the time over the past four weeks to get to know each other again—staying up late in bed talking or taking walks around the neighborhood at night. They still hadn't had sex and it was killing him. Although he was the one holding back, it was getting harder with each passing day. He had been holding out for this one weekend in SLO where they could mend the fence completely and start completely over, but he just wasn't sure how it was going to work out because of the partying. He didn't want it to be at two in the morning "wham, bam, thank you, ma'am." He wanted it to be special and they both deserved nothing less.

Walking into McCarthy's, the place was packed. Charlotte hadn't seen the new location yet and he laughed at her automatic complaints. "It's too loud", "it's not cozy like the other location," and "too many drunken college kids."

"We were once those drunken college kids, Charlie," he said.

"I know, but I just miss the other place. It had memories," she pouted.

"I know, but give this one a chance. It grows on you."

Making their way through the bar, the music blasted Lou Reed as everyone shouted over each other to hear conversation. The patio had more room, but it was full of smoke from cigarettes. *Why do people still smoke? It's so disgusting.* He once kissed a smoker and it was the worst kiss of his life. It was like kissing an ashtray and he never called her again.

Unfortunately, some of his college friends still smoked because he spotted a few of them standing around a table with ashtrays—Steve, Jack, Pete, Shelly, and Tracy.

He forgot about his dislike of smoking once he greeted his friends. He introduced Charlotte to the group since a few of them had graduated before she had started KCPR. After catching up, Trevor decided he needed a beer.

"Should we go inside and get a beer?" he asked Charlotte.

"Yes, I think Cami is inside."

Trevor led Charlotte inside where they found Cami and Glen sitting at the bar. *How did they score the coveted barstools?*

"I think you have a great turn out, Cami, and to think you had to talk Charlotte into asking me to buy a ticket," he said handing his money to the bartender. He laughed at how three beers cost only $7.50. One beer in San Francisco cost more than that. Of course, the beers came in cans, but that was McCarthy's shtick. There were a couple beers on tap, but it just didn't feel right to be a beer snob here.

"I do feel better," Cami said taking one of the cans. "Thanks. I hope we didn't put Charlotte on the spot about, well, you know."

"She's fine. I think she moved on from it a long time ago."

"I understand. I'm glad you're both back together. It took her a long time to tell us you were back in her life, but she's been in love with you for a very long time."

Normally, he'd cringe hearing those words, but with Charlotte it felt right. He loved her, there was no doubt about it, so he certainly didn't mind hearing Cami say it out loud. They hadn't said it to each other yet, but he wasn't worried. He was enjoying the anticipation and the ride to get there. "I'm very happy."

Their conversation was interrupted by old friends coming up to say hi. The next hour flew by trying to catch up with everyone. Trevor kept an eye on Charlotte who was standing in the corner of the patio with a few people he didn't know. They must have started after he graduated. She seemed blissful—her eyes sparkled and her smile was big and wide. Yes, he was definitely in love with that girl. She must have felt his eyes on her because she turned and smiled at him. Smiling back, he felt content going about his own business while she went about hers. However, looking at her in a jean jacket and fuchsia dress, he knew then and there he wanted to get her alone as soon as he could. Waiting was completely overrated.

Turning back to the bar, he bought another beer and decided to check out the jukebox. From what he'd heard earlier, he knew it included bands like Bon Jovi, Nirvana, Social Distortion and The Cult. Scrolling through the list, he noticed it was a lot more up to date than the vintage jukebox at the old bar that played only Frank Sinatra and Patsy Cline. How many times had he heard *I Fall to Pieces?*

Feeling arms go around his waist, he smiled as he turned around expecting to see Charlotte. Instead, he got a big surprise.

Katie.

His heart sank because he'd almost forgotten about the anxiety he carried about seeing her again. Flashing back to the night she showed up at his place in the city, he almost couldn't breathe.

After they'd gone to dinner a block from his apartment, she came back with him and they watched a movie together. She tried hard to snuggle in next to him, but he told her no and moved to a chair. Once the movie was over, he feigned sleepiness so he could go to his room and be alone. He'd made a point of showing her the guestroom where she would sleep. He thought he'd been so clear about that.

After brushing his teeth, he came out of the bathroom and found her naked in his bed.

"Katie, what the hell are you doing?" he asked trying not to raise his voice.

"I just thought maybe we could do it one last time. I know you don't want to date, but that doesn't mean we can't enjoy each other."

When she moved her body from under the covers to on top of them, he had a brief urge to take her up on the offer. He was single and had a naked woman in his bed. It was like dangling a piece of cake in front of a fat kid. He knew she sensed his conflict because she got up and walked over to him. When she started feeling him through his boxers, he couldn't help but respond.

"Come on Trevor. Quit being such a good guy," she said.

Just as he considered it, he thought about all the phone calls, all the texts and her anger issues. It was like stepping into a cold shower. "No. We can't do this. It wouldn't be right."

"What do you mean?"

"What I mean is that I'd be using you because we are never going to be a couple."

"I'm standing here in front of you naked and you don't want me? Is this seriously happening?"

"You need to get dressed and go into the other room."

"But I want to sleep in here."

Trevor could feel himself getting angry. "If you do that, I'll sleep in the other room."

"Can't we just sleep together? I mean, literally just sleep."

He could now see her desperation. What was so wrong with her that she had to beg to be with someone? She was a beautiful girl. "No, Katie. I told you, it's not going to happen. I'm letting you stay here because I feel too guilty to kick you out and force you to drive back to SLO tonight, or to make you get a hotel room."

Katie turned away and Trevor could see her balling her fists. *Oh no.* He didn't want her to unleash that anger on him like she did before. Wishful thinking because when she turned around, she spewed vile words at him. It was a complete repeat of that night in the street.

"Katie, I'm not going to put up with this," he said calmly. He just wanted to diffuse the situation but she was naked and pacing in a circle talking to herself now. "You need to get dressed and take a cab to a hotel. I'll find you one and make a reservation."

"No," she shouted. "I'm not leaving."

This must be what people referred to as a domestic altercation. He was embarrassed and prayed his neighbors couldn't hear anything. "I can't have you staying here when you are acting like this."

"Like what? Like someone who feels completely used and led on?"

"I didn't lead you on nor did I ever use you. I was always clear about us." Maybe he hadn't been clear enough. Maybe that's why he still holds guilt when it comes to Katie. *Maybe I did lead her on.* He would never have done anything with her this past time had he known she would still feel this way.

"But you were thinking about us in bed a couple minutes ago. I know you were."

"Well, yes, any male would have considered it when a woman willingly puts herself naked in his bed. But I never wanted you to do that."

"Fuck you, Trevor," she said sitting on the bed. Trevor tried to keep her naked body from distracting him. "You wanted me and you know it. You wanted me back then and you still want me."

"What are you talking about?"

"We belonged together in college until Charlotte messed everything up."

Charlotte? What? "I'm still not sure what you're talking about."

"We were just starting to grow closer when she decided to move in and take you away from me."

"I don't understand where this is coming from. You and I never went out until after Charlotte and I broke up and that lasted a split second primarily because of your behavior."

"Oh, my behavior? You were so into me before she came along."

Trevor was seriously confused. Her timeline was all screwed up. He never once showed any interest in her before dating Charlotte. Not once. He couldn't even remember having a full conversation with her. "Where did you get that idea? I barely even knew you."

He was really trying to have a conversation with her so she would calm down, but it didn't seem to be working. She was still pacing and sort of talking to herself saying things like "I can't believe this shit" and "I can't believe he doesn't remember."

"You don't remember that one time at the station when we were sitting on the couch and you and I talked about going to the Tori Amos show in Ventura?"

Tori Amos? He hated Tori Amos and couldn't recall that conversation at all. Maybe she dreamt it. "I don't remember, Katie. Honestly, I don't even like Tori Amos let alone enough to drive 100 miles to a concert. I think you have me confused with someone else."

"Oh, fuck off. It was you. I remember it like it was yesterday. Yet, you totally stood me up."

Trevor knew then Katie was seriously off her rocker. She didn't know what she was talking about. Now he just felt sorry for her because somehow she made this whole thing up in her head. He also felt guilty because he hadn't a clue she had this fantasy about him. "I'm sorry, Katie. I didn't mean to hurt you."

That seemed to calm her slightly. "Well, you did hurt me and I didn't deserve it."

Trevor decided to play along hoping to keep her calm. "I'm sorry. You're right, you didn't deserve it."

When she started crying, he let her put her head on his shoulder. He really didn't know what to do and never did when a girl cried in front of him. Tears were something his masculinity just didn't understand and he had no idea how to handle it. He just remained silent as she sobbed hard and loud. When her tears turned to sniffles, he thought maybe she would finally just go to bed. "Do you feel better now?"

"No," she sniffed. "Can I just sleep in here with you tonight? I don't want to sleep by myself."

Trevor knew it was a bad idea, but he wanted to keep her calm and if that meant giving in to letting her sleep in his bed, so be it. "Fine," he said handing her a t-shirt and boxers. He did not want her naked.

Sliding in next to each other, he made sure he stayed as far to his side as he could. He wished he had a king bed as opposed to a queen, but he couldn't change that at the moment. Finally, he drifted off to sleep glad the saga was over.

Only it wasn't.

Later that night or in the early morning, he woke up with lips on his penis. Bolting awake, he pushed her away feeling violated. How long had she been doing that? "Get out," he said jumping out of bed. "Just get out of my room."

"Don't tell me it didn't feel good," she said.

"Get out!" It was starting all over again and Trevor felt trapped. Maybe he should be the one to leave. He no longer felt sorry for her and wanted her gone. She crossed a line with him and he would never forget it nor would he get over it. He didn't care if she was a woman and he had to throw her out in the middle of the night. It had to be done. "You need to get your stuff and leave my house."

"I'm not leaving."

"Then I'm calling the police," he said hoping she wouldn't call his bluff.

"You wouldn't do that."

Pretending to get his cell phone and dialing, Trevor felt a little relief when Katie finally got the message and got out of bed. "Fine, I'll leave."

"Good." He tried not to think about her driving this late and still felt some responsibility to make sure she remained safe. "I'll call in a reservation at the Holiday Inn by the airport. I hope you head there and don't drive back to SLO."

She didn't answer but went into the other room and changed back into her clothes. Trevor was impatient for her to leave and breathed a sigh of relief when she finally opened the front door and stepped outside. He wasn't prepared for her to turn to him and say the exact words he dreaded. "Trevor, I love you."

Now, she was standing before him at McCarthy's in front of everyone as if nothing happened. He was so incredibly stunned; he didn't have time to react as she put her arms around him and kissed him on the lips. Pulling back, he looked over to see Charlotte staring at them.

Twenty-Three

Charlotte was having the best time of her life.

She thought about pinching herself as she chatted with the small group of people she had trained when she was the air staff instructor her final year at KCPR. It felt surreal to be standing at McCarthy's catching up with the friends she hadn't seen in over a decade. She listened as they explained how they'd moved on to great careers, marriages, babies, or all three. Many had traveled extensively and now lived in places like New York City, Austin, Raleigh, Costa Rica and Australia.

"You must be relieved, Cami," she said to her friend a few minute later as they stood together. "This is a huge success."

"Believe me, my stress level has gone down quite a bit, but I still have so much to do."

"Eh, I think everyone will have a good time. Just remember to enjoy it yourself."

"Oh, I'm enjoying myself—no need to worry. It looks like you and Trevor are doing well. I feel like I haven't seen you in weeks."

"I know. I'm in that honeymoon phase with Trevor. I apologize because I don't want to be that girl who dumps her friends for a boyfriend."

"You didn't do that with Ben, so I wouldn't worry. I figure you both are making up for lost time and things will be back to normal soon."

"No doubt," Charlotte said with smile. Thinking about the past couple of weeks, Charlotte felt like everything finally came together. It wasn't that her life wasn't full already, but being with Trevor was the cherry on top. It was the first relationship she felt balanced and content. She didn't stress about anything because Trevor easily walked the fine line between giving her too much attention and not enough. He was just perfect. Despite working in the same building, they seldom saw each other unless she made a point to stop in the studio. Since she worked later hours, she would walk home after work, go for a run, and Trevor would meet her back at her place in the late evening. She loved how respectful he was of her independence and she meant it when she said to Cami she didn't want to lose herself to her relationship. Her friends were just as important.

"Who is that?" Cami said nodding her head towards Trevor.

Charlotte followed her gaze just as the woman put her arms around his waist and kissed him on the mouth. Charlotte felt the blood drain from her face. The woman Cami referred to was tall, beautiful, and blonde and she seemed to know Trevor very intimately. "I have no idea."

Watching them, Charlotte saw Trevor steal a glance her way as if to say he had no idea what was happening. The woman hugged him so hard that anyone watching would think they were intimate. Feeling jealous and insecure, Charlotte felt her buzz disappear as she stood paralyzed trying to clear her mind.

"Oh, wow, you know who that is?" Cami said. "It's Katie Bishop. Remember her?"

Katie Bishop? The girl Trevor went out with after her? She looked so different. *And by different— she looks stunningly beautiful.* She was definitely not the girl Charlotte remembered in school. Recalling that night at SLO Brew when she saw Trevor and Katie together, Charlotte couldn't believe she was seeing them together again. Unable to pull her gaze away, Charlotte could see Trevor was very uncomfortable.

"I think we should walk over there," Cami said pulling Charlotte by the elbow.

Charlotte felt her body start to shake as she followed Cami. It was the same feeling she got right before she went on the air the very first time—her hands shook and she couldn't breathe. This time, however, it wasn't because she was excited and nervous, it was because she felt her tiny bubble of happiness deflating. She had to come back to earth sometime and it looked like it was happening now. "Cami, I don't know if we should go over there."

"What? Come on. He needs to be rescued."

Rescued? Really? Remembering the jealousy and broken heart she felt knowing Trevor had moved on to Katie after her in college, Charlotte couldn't believe that scene was playing out again. *Trevor needed to rescued, alright. But it isn't from Katie.*

"Hi guys," Cami said walking up to the twosome.

"Hey, Cami," Trevor said a little too excitedly as if he was relieved she was there. "You remember Katie."

"Oh, yes, hi Katie. Nice to see you," Cami said with the biggest fake smile Charlotte has ever seen. Charlotte could tell Cami was enjoying this unfolding drama. "Isn't it so wonderful Trevor and Charlotte are back together again after all these years?"

Charlotte saw the blood drain from Katie's face and she couldn't help but take pleasure in it. "Hi, Katie," she said as pleasantly as possible.

Charlotte felt Katie's gaze look her up and down digesting every inch of her body. *Damn, if looks could kill, I would be so dead right now.* It was a look of pure hatred and Charlotte felt scared. Alarm bells went off in her head telling her not to walk anywhere alone. Looking over at Trevor, Charlotte wanted him to interject, but he seemed just as paralyzed as she was a few minutes ago. *Well, you're no help.*

"Hi Charlotte, I didn't know you and Trevor were together. I was just up in San Francisco with him and he didn't mention it."

That took Charlotte completely by surprise and her mind went blank. If only she was in a sitcom where she had a witty comeback to put Katie in her place, but real life didn't work that way and Charlotte knew this would be a moment she would look back and want to change. Looking at Trevor again, she wanted the explanation from him.

She felt Trevor move closer to her as if to show her he wasn't with Katie. Charlotte still felt paralyzed but knew Trevor would offer an explanation.

"It was right before you and I went out. She surprised me, but nothing happened, Charlotte. I swear."

"That's not true, Trevor," Katie said and then laughed. "We had a great time and I spent the night with you."

"No you didn't. I sent you to a hotel because you kept coming on to me."

Suddenly Charlotte's world went black.

She didn't faint, but it was as if someone knocked the wind right out of her. Everyone around her moved in slow motion and it was all she could do to keep standing upright. It wasn't hearing Katie say she had spent the night with Trevor. That wasn't it at all.

It was her laugh.

Charlotte was suddenly back at KCPR. Back to that infamous night she couldn't remember—the night that changed her path with Trevor and the night she was victimized.

She was in the hallway after going to the bathroom. The music blasted loudly but it wasn't loud enough to hide the laugh. The memory came back as if someone just threw cold water over her memories washing off the dirt and allowing her to see them. As she walked into the station expecting to see Trevor, she felt someone shove her down on the couch. Shocked, she got up just in time to see Katie and another woman laughing at her. Katie said something and then backhanded her knocking her to the ground where she must have hit her head on something.

Katie was the one. She was the one who hurt me.

"Charlotte, are you okay? Honestly, nothing happened and I'll explain everything, I promise," Trevor said sounding panicked. "Katie, go away. I mean it, I don't want you here."

"I have every right to be here as you do," Katie said now ignoring Charlotte and Cami.

"It was you," Charlotte said feeling the anger coming as the shock faded. There was no way she could be discreet about this. It was a confrontation Charlotte fantasized about for the past fifteen years. Never did it include Katie, but it sure did now. "You were the one who hit me, Katie. It was you!"

Silence fell over the group despite the music blasting out of the speaker above them. Charlotte kept her eyes on Katie as everyone turned towards her. She could Trevor and Cami's expressions through her peripheral vision and she knew they were both stunned. Katie, on the other hand, stared Charlotte right in the eyes as if to challenge her claim.

"Charlotte, are you sure?" Trevor asked.

"I'm positive. I remember seeing her with someone and I remember her laugh."

"What the hell?" Cami said turning to Katie. "Why would you do such a despicable thing?"

Charlotte almost felt sorry for Katie as she broke eye contact and looked to Trevor for help. But there was no way Charlotte could feel sorry the person that turned her life upside down. Instead, she let the anger fuel her from head to toe.

"I...I...don't know what you're talking about," Katie said slowly. "You were hit in the head and obviously can't remember clearly."

Charlotte was absolutely sure it was Katie and she was further infuriated by the blatant lie coming out of Katie's mouth.

"Fuck, Katie, admit it. You were there that night. Why?! Why would you do that to me? I never did anything to you," Charlotte yelled trying to hold back the tears forming behind her eyes. She was so mad and so hurt, she didn't even care she dropped the F-bomb in front of everyone.

By now, a small crowd had gathered, watching the drama unfold. Charlotte hated drama like this and she felt the urge to run away. Noticing the bouncer heading toward them, she knew she had to break away now or it would be an ugly scene. Backing away, she turned and ran out, knowing she was leaving Trevor and her friends stunned. She wanted to be anywhere but there.

The tears spilled as she slowed to a walk. She wanted to catch a cab, but the air felt refreshing against her skin so she kept going. What just happened? She was having a wonderful time and it suddenly went so wrong. Remembering Katie's laugh, she turned and vomited into the bushes. She thought she'd buried those feelings and memories for good, but they flowed like a faucet she couldn't turn off.

"Charlotte!" she heard Trevor call behind her. "Wait!"

She wanted to stop for him but her feet just propelled her forward. Feeling embarrassed and foolish, she knew everyone would be talking about her now. How would she face everyone again? She must have looked crazy to the people who didn't know what happened. When Trevor caught up and grabbed her by the arm, she fought against him. She wasn't sure why because she needed him and just wanted him to put his arms around her.

"Charlotte, stop," he said gently. She didn't fight him when he pulled her into his chest and put his arms around her. She was sobbing now, trying to talk, but not getting the words out. After a few attempts at a sentence, she finally just stopped and relaxed into Trevor's arms. Thank god he was being patient and just holding her as the tears continued but less violently. *Why would she do that to me? I didn't deserve that.* Charlotte had absolutely no idea the hate Katie had towards her. The only explanation was Trevor. To think he went out with her after that not knowing she was the reason they broke up. Then she remembered what Katie said at the bar and how guilty Trevor had looked.

"So are you going to tell me what Katie was talking about?" Charlotte said as she wiped her nose with her sleeve. The tears were winding down, but she now hiccupped between words. "Be honest."

Noticing how sad and remorseful he looked, Charlotte prepared herself for the worst.

"It's not what you think."

"What am I thinking?"

"She turned into a hardcore stalker, Charlotte," Trevor sighed. "I honestly thought she'd changed, but I was so wrong."

"What did she mean by what she said?"

"I want to be honest with you, she and I did date briefly in college after I thought I'd moved on from you," he said. "Although I hadn't moved on and when I ran into you at SLO Brew that one night, I realized I was just using Katie. I'm not sure you even remember it."

"Oh, I remember," Charlotte said. "I wanted so badly to tell you I wasn't over you."

Noticing a small smile cross his face, she started feeling better. It was as if he was happy to hear her confess. "We had a huge fight that night in the street and I realized Katie was just crazy. I distanced myself and after I graduated never saw her again until right after New Year's when I was passing through SLO on my way up from LA."

Charlotte could feel the bad part of the story coming. She already knew what he was about to tell her and she braced herself for the words. How was she going to feel, let alone react? Feeling jealousy bubble up, she almost vomited again picturing him in bed with a naked Katie. "You don't need to tell me the rest, I figured it out," she said flatly.

"No, it's not what you think. Well, yes, I did spend the night with her, but it was only once and it was here in town. I had no idea what a mess she was because she hid it really well, but I still had no intention of dating her after that."

"So you used her again?"

"Well, she lives here and I live in SF, so it didn't even cross my mind that we'd date," he said defensively.

Standing there on the sidewalk in front of one of the several craftsman houses that lined the street, Charlotte looked at Trevor—really looked at him trying to figure out if she was upset at Trevor for sleeping with Katie or upset at herself because she felt jealous. She didn't like hearing Trevor say he used Katie, but a part of her was relieved because if he hadn't used her, it would mean he had feelings for her. She should be upset with him in a sisterhood kind of way, but she appreciated his honesty and could tell he regretted it.

"So what happened afterwards? Why did she say she stayed with you in the city?"

"Oh my god, that is where she went all crazy again. I got home from work and she was at my doorstep. This was after ignoring her phone calls and texts."

"Really? She drove all the way up from SLO because you didn't return her calls? I don't believe that."

"Believe it, Charlotte. I didn't know what to do. I set her straight and told her again there was nothing between us, but I couldn't very well put her back on the road that night."

"So she stayed with you?"

"Yes. Well, kind of," Trevor said. Charlotte listened as Trevor told her the rest. She wanted desperately to believe him. All this happened before they got back together so he didn't really do anything wrong but Charlotte wished she could erase it all.

"I just wish you hadn't let her back in. I was so upset when you dated her in college. I never understood it."

"I can't remember why I asked her out, either. I must have been super depressed or desperate to erase you out of my mind."

"I'm sorry, Trevor. I'm not upset about you with her; I'm just shocked she turned out to be the one who basically broke us up."

She let Trevor pull her back against his chest. "I'm so sorry I wasn't there that night. I never felt so guilty in my life."

"It wasn't your fault, although I will confess a small part of me wondered if you were the one. My gut wouldn't believe it, though, but I couldn't help but think it."

"You know I would never do anything like that to you or anyone," he said surprised. "If that night hadn't happened, do you think we would have stayed together?"

"I don't know," she replied thinking about it. "I really believe that things happen for a reason. Not to say I should have been assaulted, but maybe breaking up then allowed us to come together today. We never closed the door completely. Had we dated longer, we might have broken up after you graduated and gotten over each other. Does that make sense?"

"In a way it does. Although I don't think I would have ever broken up with you or gotten over you, but I see what you're saying. I guess we were meant to be together now when we're more settled and mature," he said pulling Charlotte back into a hug. "Now that we know we're mature, can we start walking back to the hotel now?"

Giggling, Charlotte said yes. Walking side by side in silence, Charlotte thought about how they came back together. Was Trevor right? Were they destined to start their life together now as opposed to back in college? Maybe he *was* right—time and maturity had allowed them to work through their past together and be able to communicate about it.

Remembering how naïve and young she was when she met Trevor, she couldn't imagine they would have stayed together after he graduated. She'd gained so much experience in college and in the years afterward. She had no regrets about her choices or her past and couldn't picture changing any of it—even for Trevor. *Yes, we were supposed to break up and meet again when we were both ready. We can appreciate each other now.*

When Trevor reached for her hand, she let him take it and enjoying the warmth of his skin on hers. It felt right to be with him and all of the drama about Katie faded. She was with him now in the present and Katie couldn't take that away again.

Trevor finally broke the silence. "Why *did* you push me away, Charlotte? You never really told me why."

At first she thought he was referring to last December, but then she understood he was asking about college. "I don't know."

"I wanted so badly to be there for you."

"I know, Trevor. I guess I was just so young and confused. I pushed a lot of people away for a long time.

I didn't even realize what I'd done until the new school year started and you weren't there."

"But it sounds like you ended up enjoying the rest of your time at Cal Poly."

"I did," she said as she fondly recalled some of the dates, parties, and KCPR shifts in the years that followed. They helped her plug the hole in her heart where Trevor was concerned. "That summer between my first and second year really helped. I went home and worked and my parents helped me get back to normal. When I returned in the fall, it was like starting over fresh. I even had a few dates."

"Dates, huh? I would never have thought," Trevor chuckled as he put his arm around her shoulders. "I'm sure you had lots of them."

Giggling, she was relieved the conversation was getting away from the drama. "Yep. Tons. I was out every night of the week on dates with different guys."

"I believe it," he said kissing her forehead.

"Trevor," she said feeling serious again. "I'm sorry. I didn't mean to hurt you then or again in December. I have such strong feelings for you and sometimes I just can't process them."

"It's hard to be vulnerable."

"For me it is. I wish I was different."

"I don't. I think you're perfect," he said as they reached the lobby of the hotel. "Come back with me to my room."

Charlotte wanted to be with him, so the decision was easy. Entering his room, she felt as if the bubble of happiness from earlier in the evening returned and she could relax and let him take care of her. Trevor was right again—it was hard for her to be vulnerable and to ask for help. It was almost like the time Ben took care of her when she broke her hand. She had no choice but to ask for help. This time, however, she was in love. She completely trusted Trevor and knew he spoke the truth and that made all the difference.

After lighting a candle—she was surprised he even thought to bring a candle to his room—she let him pull her onto his lap when he sat down on the bed. Her heart sped up when he placed a gentle kiss on her lips. There was something so safe and right about Trevor and she knew she could open up to him whenever she needed to. He didn't run at the first sign of emotional bonding and he didn't shut her down.

"Charlotte, I love you."

The words startled her. She wasn't expecting him to say it so soon. Looking at him, she could see he genuinely meant it. In the past, she'd choked out the words when she said them. This time, however, she meant it wholeheartedly when she said them back. "I love you, too."

After that, the mood shifted and she knew it was time. They'd waited patiently for this moment, getting to know each other as adults and not the college kids they once were. Charlotte was thrilled with the man Trevor had become.

Quickly undressing, they got under the sheets and revisited the one night in December. This time, it all felt so right and perfect. There was no guilt, no baggage—only a clean slate where they both could build a future.

"I love you so much," Trevor said as he got on top of her. "You're so beautiful."

She let him make love to her as if they were going to be together the rest of their lives. It was so worth the wait and after they were done, she silently thanked Trevor for letting the anticipation build.

"You know I would have done it that first night I spent the night a few weeks ago, right?" she said.

"Yes. You're a total horndog. It took all my strength to keep you from seducing me."

"Uh-huh," she giggled as she snuggled up to him. "Can you believe we did it here in SLO? The place we met? I think it feels right to have happened here."

"Yes, this place holds a lot of memories," he said kissing her on the forehead. "It's like coming full circle or something."

The next morning, they skipped breakfast so they could stay in bed together. "I wish I didn't have to get up, but I think I need to shower and get to the station," Charlotte said climbing out from under the covers.

"Hmmm," Trevor said pulling her back down and holding her tight so she couldn't move. "I don't want you to go."

"I know. I don't want to, either, but duty calls— or rather the airwaves call," she said wiggling away and kissing him on the head. "I'll see you up there a little later?"

"Yep," he said before turning serious. "Are you sure you're okay? That was a lot to go through last night."

At first Charlotte thought he was referring to the sex, but then realized it was about Katie. It was still surreal to know she was behind her attack. "I'll be okay. It really helps to have you here with me."

When she walked into her room, Cami was sitting on the bed drinking coffee. Seeing a tray of food from room service, it appeared Cami had someone with her. "Oh wow, that looks like a tray for two. Who spent the night?"

Noticing Cami blush, she waited patiently for an explanation. "I figured you were sleeping in Trevor's room, so a few of us came back here after the bars closed. I hooked up with Shawn."

Laughing as she changed into her robe, Charlotte couldn't help but tease her friend. "You slut."

"Thanks," Cami said laughing back.

"Is it going to turn into something?"

"I have no idea," she said. "How are you? After last night, I figured you would be with Trevor so I didn't want to bother you."

"I'm fine. Just a bit shocked."

"I know. After you left, there was a bit more drama. Katie's ex-husband came and got her after explaining she was bi-polar and apparently off her meds. Did you know she has two kids? Her ex is paying her rent and has full custody of them because she lost her teaching job last year for hitting a student."

"Hitting a student? Wow, I had no idea she was that bad," Charlotte said really feeling sorry for her now. It explained the anger issues and insecurities. "Poor girl. What did everyone say when we left?"

"Not much. They figured out what happened and those who knew the story were surprised and hoped you were okay."

"It didn't stop the fun, did it?"

"I don't think so," Cami laughed. "I'm sorry I didn't call to make sure you were okay, but I figured you and Trevor were fine together."

"We were," Charlotte blushed.

"Oh, sounds like you had a great night after all."

"I did."

After showering and doing her hair and makeup, Charlotte got dressed and headed downstairs to parking lot. It was too late for breakfast at the hotel, so she would have to stop at a coffee shop on her way to campus. After drinking last night, she needed food in her stomach. The only place she had time to stop at was the Starbucks down the street. Once she made her purchase, she drove up to the station getting more nervous by the second. She hadn't worked the controls in over ten years. Would they still be the same? Would she remember how to segue and start the vinyl records?

Walking up the steps of the graphic arts building, she was finally in the hallway and the first thing she noticed was how everything smelled the same. It hadn't changed at all. The floor was still the same turquoise blue and the walls were still a boring ivory color. She even found her name on a couple trophies in the glass case against the wall.

She could hear the music playing before she entered the station. All those days she spent hanging out with her friends here and all the hours she spent spinning discs or producing the news felt like yesterday. Seeing the same brown velvet couch, which actually grossed her out a bit, she remembered that one night when Katie attacked her. It was all so clear now how it happened and why. It was just a love triangle—one she didn't even know existed. The melodrama of it could probably make a TV movie or a book. But despite that, most of her memories were good and she smiled thinking about her friends from the past who changed her life.

Once inside, she noticed everything seemed relatively the same except the control board was new as were the CD players. After a quick tutorial, she felt ready to start. Everything fell right back into place once she slipped on the headphones and cued up the first song which was by The Darling Buds, one of her favorites. She continued her first hour with School of Fish, Kitchens of Distinction, The Cult, The Sammies, Screaming Trees, and even Collective Soul, explaining how they got their start on Atlanta college radio.

She was feeling very energetic thanks to the coffee when Trevor walked in forty-five minutes later carrying his CDs.

"Hey, babe. I didn't realize how dirty this Goldfrapp song is."

"I know. She's a naughty girl," Charlotte said referring to the song *Twist* she was blasting through the speakers. The lyrics were definitely racy, but the beat was so good. Putting on the headphones to go live, she pushed the microphone on and waited as it ended. It was a given that when the music volume turned off in the studio, the DJ was about to go live on the air and everyone else needed to be quiet. Trevor obliged as he quietly sat down in the chair across from her and remained silent.

Being on the air never scared Charlotte and it didn't now. At first she was a little nervous, but that feeling quickly went away as she continued through her playlist and took requests from callers. It was all about having a conversation with the listeners.

"What are you planning to start your show with?" she asked after turning the microphone off and setting the headphones on the table.

"I was thinking about starting off with some classics like The Pixies and Pearl Jam."

"Nice," she said walking over to him and putting her arms around his shoulders. She didn't protest when he pulled her onto his lap. "I can't believe this is where we met."

"So long ago. You were the worst trainee I ever had, but definitely the hottest."

Giggling, Charlotte knew he was teasing her. She was so proud of how they finally made their way back to each other after all this time. She was enjoying the kisses Trevor was placing on her neck when she saw Cami walk in with bags of food.

"Get a room," she said to Charlotte and Trevor. "Seriously, there is just way too much sexual energy in this room. Everything might combust."

"Hey Cami," Trevor said. "Sorry, but I can't seem to dial it down at the moment."

"Hmmm," Cami said pulling the food out of the bags. "You better, because people are going to be showing up soon."

"Wow, looks good. I'm still hungry," Trevor said gently pushing Charlotte off his lap. She didn't mind, she needed to cue up a new song anyway. After another thirty minutes, people started filing in to the station to revisit their past and just hang out. Everyone seemed to agree that the velvet brown couch, as comfortable as it once was, needed to go.

"Maybe we can raise some money and help them buy a new couch," someone said.

Soon, it was like a small party had gathered and Charlotte really wanted to celebrate. Debating her last song, she almost went with Nirvana, but decided on a classic instead. Not that Nirvana isn't now considered classic, but the song she chose fit the moment and atmosphere. When she started *Radio Gaga* by Queen, she turned it up loud to get everyone's attention. Soon, the group was singing the lyrics at the top of their lungs. Oddly, it wasn't a song she, nor the rest of the DJs, would have considered playing back in the day. Now, these old bands that that were nostalgic seemed cool again.

Singing right along with them, Charlotte thought about how this would be the perfect ending to a movie celebrating friends and radio. The medium had changed a lot since the Queen song was popular, but college radio was still a huge influence on the industry exposing new bands and music but keeping its alternative flair. KCPR will always remain dear to her heart to her dying day not only because of its influence on her life both as a DJ and news producer, but because it introduced her to the love of her life.

"Maybe we can make this an annual event," Trevor whispered in her ear as he pulled her close.

"I think that would be a fine idea," she said looking up to him for a kiss. "Maybe someday we can move back here."

"Maybe. I love you."

"I love you, too," Charlotte said as the song wound down. "Now it's your turn, Mr. Mentor. Show us what you got."

Epilogue

Six months passed since the reunion.

Waiting for Trevor at Starbucks on Vallejo and Polk, Charlotte took the seat closest to the window so she could see him as he approached. Everything was still going very well and they had both settled into the relationship as if they'd been together for years. Charlotte was very much in love, a feeling that seemed to grow stronger the more time she spent with Trevor. They were both so compatible, she wondered if they would ever fight over anything. Sure, they had disagreements, but he was very good at communication—something Charlotte still needed to work on. She was getting better at it, learning to be a bit more vulnerable and making sure Trevor knew she needed him. She never took for granted how he accommodated her need to remain independent to some degree. When she'd invited him to play on her softball team, he declined gently saying it was her thing and maybe they could play on a volleyball or football team together instead.

When she spotted him walking across the street, she noticed right away he had a scowl on his face. So unusual and she wondered what happened.

"Hi," she said standing to give him a kiss when he walked up to her table. "I got you a latte."

Trevor didn't even acknowledge what she said. "I was just in the newspaper shop buying a lotto ticket and I saw this."

Charlotte took the tabloid magazine Trevor handed her and glanced at the headline. Her heart sank and she felt like throwing up.

Cooper Bancroft's Sex Scandal Goes Viral.

Underneath the headline was a blurry picture of Cooper and Sarah in bed together. "I think it's time we took a trip to LA."

"Absolutely," Trevor replied. "We'll leave tomorrow."

Acknowledgements

First and foremost, this novel is intended to celebrate San Francisco, San Luis Obispo, Cal Poly and most importantly, KCPR. No character is based on any one person. Except for the places and the cat, this story is complete fiction.

I want to thank my family for supporting me and especially my brothers, Rob and Mike, who kept me confident even when I wasn't sure I could finish. I would also like to thank my mom and dad because they're awesome parents and I know they will buy many copies of this story.

There are so many friends to thank and acknowledge—my KCPR friends past and present who gave me the inspiration behind the story, my San Francisco friends who I miss so much, and those who helped me by reading drafts in the beginning. You all know who you are.

Thank you, Leticia and Monika for editing and designing. It made it all very real.

I couldn't publish this without acknowledging my "wine" club with a "book" problem. You ladies rock.

Last but not least, I want to thank Collective Soul for letting me use their lyrics. Honestly, I didn't get permission, so please don't sue me. I love you guys and just want everyone to love you as much as I do.

17099255R00213